The Legend of Ahya
Target of Interest

Matthew Colvath

This first book is dedicated to
My lovely spouse
For putting up with my passions.

TABLES OF CONTENTS

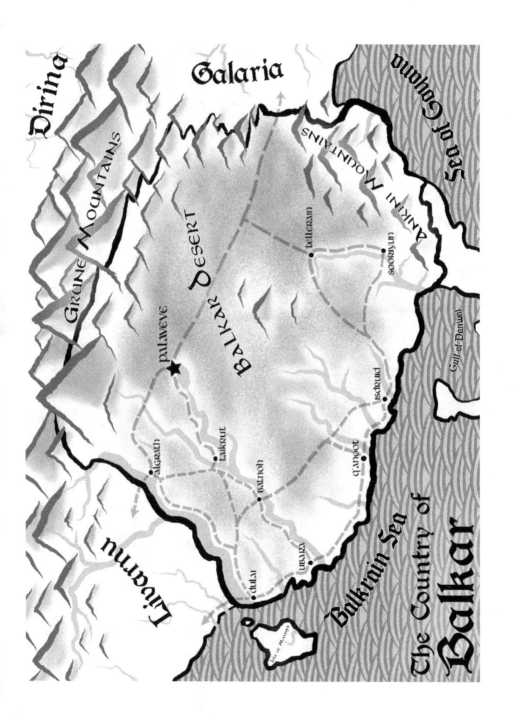

Galaria

Dirina

Grune Mountains

Balkar Desert

Ankini Mountains

Sea of Cohan

palaveve

tellerain

soodaylun

isdruid

Gulf of Danlwil

algrath

talkrut

balnoh

qamoot

Livarun

dulai

ubara

Balkrain Sea

Isle of Malivy

The Country of
Balkar

7

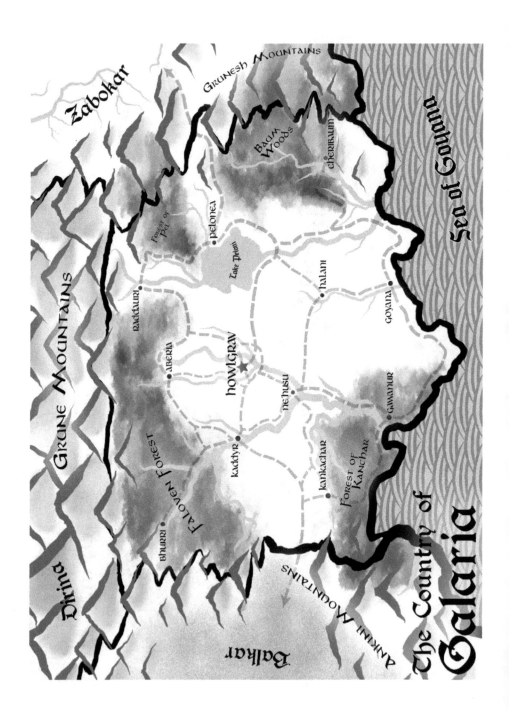

The Country of
Galaria

1
TAYLOR

Drip.

Taylor's eyes opened to the sound. She could tell it was early morning, the sky brightening to just before the point where it would sting. She blinked hard at the light, then sleepily rubbed her eyes. Although she remembered last night's dream being extremely vivid, she couldn't recall anything about it. She felt like she was on the run again, being chased by unknown assailants, just like how it was a few years ago.

Drip.

Another drop of water fell from the sagging blue tarp that hung above her head, its descent landing in a small pot. She glanced up and regarded the loose knots tying them to the jutting wooden rods, protruding at intervals along the upper length of each squat adobe building that sandwiched her little home.

Drip.

Taylor knew she would have to readjust the makeshift roof of her little shanty abode before the next rains; it was the season for them. She groaned as she rolled over and stared up at the sky just beyond the tarp. It was clear blue with nary a wisp of white to be seen. She sniffed the air. She could tell it was going to be a blazing hot day today, most likely humid too after that evening rain.

Drip.

Annoyed now with the sound, Taylor got on her hands and knees and pushed her lower haunches back onto her legs, getting a good stretch in her arms as she pushed them out forward, keeping her head down. Satisfied, she shook herself from head to tail to excavate any droplets that had settled into her fur from the rain.

Drip.

She adjusted her white tank-top then padded over and lifted the pot before vaulting up onto a nearby weathered cargo crate. She stood on her claw tips and reached over to the sunken portion of the tarp,

9

squeezing the edges of it to increase the funnel as she drained the rest of the fresh water into the metal container. Pleased with the haul they got this morning, she hopped back down onto the ground, sand getting between her paws.

Taylor took a slurp from the pot—though made sure she left enough for her companions—then knelt down and placed the liquid next to their separate bed mats. The small, albino skunk and oddly colored raccoon were sleeping soundly away beneath a small piece of sack cloth that she managed to scrounge for them at the market from a discarded, empty rice bag. They were born runts like her, smaller than was common for their species. She petted both their heads, smiling as their tails twitched at her touch, but did not wake.

Dragging down the beige wool cloak from one of the building pegs, Taylor wrapped it around her back. She clasped it at the front, then stopped briefly when a flash of red caught her attention, directing it to the broken mirror she had managed to hang at an awkward angle. She had quite forgotten where she had acquired it. The reflection had fractured into several broken shards, but enough was there to piece together a full image of oneself. She had placed it there to remind herself to cover her red-furred head every time she went out.

Taylor pushed a bang up and around towards the back of her ear before drawing the hood over her hair. Feeling a bit less self-conscious, she walked through the small devices, boxes, and other pieces of scavenged, impromptu furniture that made up their home. Looking at the tall stack of crates blocking the entrance to her small alley between the buildings with a sigh, she began her usual routine of climbing up and over them.

Taylor turned to look back around at her two sleeping charges before whispering, "I'll be back soon guys. Sweet dreams."

She squeezed through between the adobe siding and the uppermost box, its contents having long expired, then surveyed the street before her. A few other canids, suidae, mustelids, equines, and even a lone vulpine wandered the early morning traffic. Deciding that she would be well concealed dropping behind the dilapidated van that was permanently broken down right in front of their home, its wheels long since stolen, she slipped off the wood and onto the ground.

10

Taylor moved to relieve herself from cover when she felt a nudge in the palm of her paw. She turned around to see a smiling mouth of red, complete with a nice row of teeth, opening on the wide tip of her tail. "Hey, Ahya. Are you going to be giving me any trouble today?" She cracked a grin that was shared.

She knew Ahya was a mischievous sort, but she also knew that when things got serious, she would comply with her demands. With a nod from the maw, she patted it lovingly before pushing it down below the level of her eyes. "Then be a good girl and please stay under the cloak this time. I don't want another incident like last week."

Confident that Ahya wouldn't cause any trouble, she readjusted her cloak and stepped out into the broad sun and made her way down the road. Nobody paid her much mind. The scant few that did just nodded their heads in greeting, which she returned before sweeping past. It was still rather early, but the open-air bazaar would be in full swing within the hour. She could hear the rising din of stall vendors pulling into the square with their vans and setting up shop. Her keen wolf nose could smell the delicious foods in the square from here.

Taylor appreciated the small town she temporarily called home. The mix of stucco and adobe lent itself well to the overall sparse look of this remote settlement. The round domes and spiral tusks of some of the more influential homes brought diversity to an otherwise stale skyline. It was not nearly as technologically advanced as other towns or cities she had grown up in, but she could spy the common cellphone in a passerby's hoof or the earbud propped comfortably in an ear.

She had been here for the past year, surviving off the residents where she could. She had picked this place specifically because of its distance away from any big metropolises, yet still in the centralized trading routes so that she wouldn't starve. The lack of technology also assisted in her being able to lie low without too much news of her whereabouts to the outside world. Still, that defining feature was slowly slipping away as the months wore on. More and more people began to purchase and use their social media devices as they became available in the region from foreign traders.

Taylor slipped past a fruit vendor—who was rather overachieving by being fully set up this early—and soon after was flipping an apple into her paw before continuing on into the main square. She ducked under a pub awning to take a bite. It was rather dry and not as juicy, being completely out of season. She wrinkled her snout, but continued to consume it anyway.

Her ears flicked back as the widescreen television perched above the bartender began to blare the morning news jingle. Although not entirely interested in what was going on outside Palaveve, the town she temporarily came to call home, she always left one ear out for any news pertaining to her situation; the last thing she wanted was a broadcast plastering her mug across the screen and identifying her to all around. It didn't seem likely since it had been over a year with no hide or scent of anyone chasing her, but she couldn't be too careful.

"In other news," the elephant anchor continued, using his trunk to flip the page of his script, "residents are asked to please stay inside the city walls if they do not have business traveling to other local villages. The mayor has also asked to keep noise levels down. There is currently what is now referred to as a 'behemoth' wandering around south of Palaveve. Authorities reported seeing it come into the local region five days ago. There is still little information to be had on their origins, but the military has stated that…"

Taylor's attention to the newscast was interrupted as she felt a rising lump slithering up her side. She swiftly pushed it back down her cloak with her free paw. "Ahya, seriously? Not now. I know you are a hungry girl, but you need to wait until we're in a more secluded spot. I'll be sure to get enough food for all of us."

The maw, mollified by her answer, remained still beneath the fabric. Finishing up the rest of her apple, she stepped back deeper into the shade and let the core drop behind her, settling just behind her hind paws. Within seconds, a deeply red, slick appendage slinked down below the hem of her cloak to curl around and snatch up the core before bringing it back up into the darkness. A moment later, Taylor licked her lips as the taste of the apple registered on her tongue again, and a small bead of fullness permeated her belly.

It didn't take long before her target of interest arrived on scene. She observed the old kamori wrapped in faded clothes of refined silk hobbling along, clutching her wheelbarrow of baked goods, her brown and white spots of fur dulled against her pelt of black. Taylor smiled as she observed the old goat clopping around her stall, lifting up the baskets with sluggish precision and placing them in fastidious order on her designated stall counter.

The crowd had just begun to flow into the square in earnest. Taylor wanted to hit up this vendor first since she knew she'd be able to get a free bag from her that she could use to carry the rest of the items she was to bring home. As the kamori waddled around to the business end of her setup, Taylor made a beeline straight for the goat, putting on her best grin as she sidled up to the stall.

"Oh, is that you again, Taylor?" the old goat warbled, a weak, yet intense vibrato to her voice.

"Yes, Mrs. Hircus. How do you always know it's me?" she marveled, shaking her head and resting a paw on her hip.

"It's your eyes, deary." She motioned with a hoof towards Taylor's face. "I can never forget those eyes."

"Oh…" Taylor flushed, looking down from the goat.

It was true, her eyes were rather unique. Taylor's left was as deep as the ocean was blue, yet her right iris was filled with the incandescent glow of a golden sun. She would get odd looks from passersby if anyone stared hard enough to notice her heterochromatic eyes. Only Mrs. Hircus never judged her for it.

Taylor had met the aging kamori on her first week stumbling into town, running from pursuers that had long since lost her trail. She was terrified and suspicious of everyone. To this day, she had never revealed to Mrs. Hircus all that she was. For what the goat knew, she was just another orphaned wolf looking for a place to call home—one that just happened to have a few unusual features.

Ever since then, Taylor would do the odd job for pittance change from her—just enough to be able to buy some sustenance to last at least another few days more. The goat had taken a rather protective stance over the wolf, despite Taylor being a foot taller and not of her species. She could always depend on Mrs. Hircus to provide wonderful treats of baked breads, tarts, and cakes.

Her paw went up to her nose instead. "I thought it'd be more because of my red nose-fur."

13

With a waving hoof, the goat dismissed Taylor's brief concern. "Don't mind this old nag. We all have our birthmarks. You are just blessed with more than one of them, and that makes you special, Taylor. It's not every day I get a wolf of your sweet disposition gracing my stall."

The wolf beamed at the praise, but cleared her throat to remind herself why she was there in the first place. "Thank you, Mrs. Hircus. I'm here actually to get another bag and buy a loaf of bread, please."

"Only one, deary?" she bleated, concern showing on her face. She always seemed to thing Taylor wasn't eating enough.

Taylor dug into the pocket of her cloak and rattled up some coins: a symbol of a tiger emblazoned on one side, a city of spires on the other. "I only worked for you once last week, Mrs. Hircus. Don't you remember? I'm a bit low on funds, so I can only afford one loaf."

The goat's brow furrowed. "That's certainly not enough for your two friends, is it? What are their names?"

"Pine and Mitchell," she responded with a chuckle. "I keep telling you every time."

"Yes, yes…" The kamori rubbed her hoof along the length of one of her broken horns. "I know you've told me so much about them." She clacked the hoof onto the counter. "You know, your friends don't have to be so scared of me all the time. They can come work for me, and all three of you could pool together enough money to provide for the lot of you."

"I know, Mrs. Hircus." Taylor shrugged. "I keep telling them that all the time, but they prefer to avoid other people and just stick with me."

"That's a shame." Her face sagged. "I would have loved to meet them; they sound like nice kits by the stories you tell of them." She began to unfurl and shake out a cloth bag before slipping in a rather long piece of bread, probably her lengthiest one. She held out her hoof for the coins which were deposited promptly.

"I wish you could meet them too. They are such good friends. I'll be sure to send them your regards." She bowed slightly before hooking an arm through the hoops of the bag, the end of the loaf peeking out the top.

14

"Don't be a stranger now, Taylor." The goat smiled. "My door is always open if you need more jobs to earn money. You know you can always find a steady job here in town that'll suit your talents."

"I know. I'm just…not ready to handle that sort of responsibility yet, Mrs. Hircus." She quickly bowed again, feeling rather uncomfortable with the way the conversation was going.

Given what she was, she'd rather not be in a position to be working in front of others for extended periods of time. The last thing she needed was someone to recognize her, and for word get back to whoever it was that had chased her all the way from the capital. She liked it here. She didn't want to have to run again.

A hush descended upon the crowd as an unearthly cry pierced the air. It sounded like a dull, mechanical roar that caused all eyes to look skyward. Each person directed their attention south, to the origin of the sound. Powerful thuds could be heard as blasts of air that sounded like steam bursting forth punctuated each shockwave that trembled through the ground and quivered their hind paws.

All business and din had stopped. Some of the children were just as afraid to move a single muscle as the adults. Taylor could hear a kit crying in a far corner of the market. In time, the sounds and the occasional bellow faded off into the distance. Time seemed to stretch forever until no one could hear any traces of the monstrosity that had appeared just beyond their city border.

"Hope you do good business today. Have a great morning!" Taylor flashed her pearly whites before waving and walking down the row of vendors, using the distraction to escape.

Taylor really didn't like to lie to her like that—a better job would help her take care of the three of them more reliably—but she just couldn't take the chance of being exposed. She had carved out a meager, yet bearable living here, including a small place of her own and two friends to share her days with. It wasn't all bad, yet sometimes it did wear on her.

She could feel Ahya twitching behind her with some agitation. "Yeah, I feel you, Ahya. I'm going to get us some food soon. Just be a gal and stay out of sight this time, please?"

The market square wasn't exactly a sprawling place, but one could get lost there if they weren't careful or didn't have their wits about them. There were clotheslines of banners and flowers strewn across the top between the various stall roofs. Hanging pottery, cured meats, and clove bunches dotted the visual landscape as she traversed the bazaar. Baskets of overflowing produce spilled out onto the sand, and the little children of shopkeepers were shooed out to help pick up the product to be placed back in and look presentable.

Taking a deep breath, Taylor set out through her predetermined path. It had taken months, but she knew just the vendors to hit. She would target the ones that grew flustered when a huge swath of customers assaulted their booth. Their situational awareness would not be very high at that point, and she could easily shuffle her way through the bustling bodies and dart out her paws and grab a few items here and there and stuff them into her bag.

One of her favorite places to go in the market was the "menagerie of carpets". It was a quasi-indoor section with draping fabrics, which were dyed various colors that skewed the sunlight into a myriad array of light that played wonderfully across the shopping landscape. The dirt floor was instead covered with plush, thick carpet that felt good beneath her paws.

After several hours of surreptitiously dropping things into her bag, she was really starting to enjoy herself; in over a year, she had never managed to gather this much food in one day. The bag was near to bursting and it wasn't even midday. The sun overhead was baking, making her thankful for the hood to cover her head. With this much food, she could call it an early day. This would last them for at least a week, maybe two.

However, there was still one stall she had planned on visiting— more of a splurge than anything else. She could have gone home now, but the allure of those sweet-smelling pies from her favorite baker was a bit hard to betray. The sow was busily handing out little samples to the young cubs visiting her booth.

Squeezing the bristles of the carpet between her toes and shifting the bag further up her arm, Taylor pressed herself between two waterbucks, trying to get closer to the counter. Her favorite was within paw's reach, nose twitching at the divine scent of freshly baked apples. She couldn't recall the last time she had a treat like that. After such a glorious haul today, she felt the need to treat herself to at least a little reward. Ensuring that no one was looking her way, she reached out for a wrapped slice when the female waterbuck beside her screamed.

"What? Ahya, no!" Taylor shouted.

She knew what had occurred before she dared to look to confirm it. Taylor cringed as the grinning maw of a tail had revealed itself to the waterbuck beside her. It must have seemed like a scene from a monster movie. Sliding out from her cloak unbidden, it had split open the bulbous tip of her tail to reveal a cavernous opening lined with razor-sharp teeth and a tongue of darkest hue that dripped profusely with thick, viscous saliva.

Taylor's heart sank as her tail began using its long tongue to lap up several plates' worth of pies into its open row of teeth. The multitude of flavors invading Taylor's mouth did little to fix the pit of terror in the base of her stomach as all eyes turned to her. Abject fear was present in all their faces as they beheld the horror that was her tail: a massive, grinning devil of a mouth that could swallow any of the young cubs whole.

"It's her! The murderer of Talvia!" said one fox, pointing at her.

"And of Bree!" said another ocelot.

"And several missing kits!" a parent screamed, desperately hunched over her child in a feeble attempt to protect her.

Taylor began to shake her head, baking up slowly. "No...you got it all wrong! I didn't kill those people!" She frantically began grabbing and shoving Ahya back underneath her cloak, but it was too late.

"She's a monster!" the sow shopkeeper shrieked.

"A demon!" a male lion growled.

"Someone call the police!" a filly neighed, her hooves already in his pockets to draw out his phone.

"No, please! You don't have to do that!" Taylor pleaded. Ahya was rising up against her wishes and will to keep it down, baring its teeth at the crowd and loud noises assaulting it.

A fellow wolf snagged her cub away, picking it up and backpedaling fast as Ahya began to seemingly grow in size. She glared at Taylor. "She can't be allowed to escape! She could kill again!"

A rising chorus echoed for her blood. Taylor immediately turned tail and ran when they surged forward to grab her. She struggled through the crowd, bumping and pushing mammals down around her. The entire market slowly became aware of the situation and her presence, her hood now flapped back and gleaming red hair brilliant in the morning sun. Many stopped to point and stare, some took pictures on their phones for their social media platforms, while others ran off to get the authorities.

"What is wrong with you, Ahya?" Taylor yelled angrily as she banked a corner and exited the square down a side alley. "You couldn't have waited a few minutes more?"

She could already hear the sirens in the distance, their aural position homing in on her location. It seemed there were witnesses everywhere. There were usually at least some empty alleys or backstreets she could duck into and reestablish her disguise, but for some reason the town populace was out in full force. She couldn't hide anywhere.

"There she is!" a coyote officer blared.

The drone of the hovering squad car was fierce as it whined to a stop just feet from her position. Taylor skidded to a halt, scrabbling her hind claws into the sand for purchase as she switched directions, causing several pieces of fruit to topple out of her bag. She leaped over another squad car coming in from the opposing street, thumping the hood before sliding off in a dead sprint. Hurdling a railing to a lower residential area covered by a tawny canvas, she ducked into the first open door she saw.

She glanced up and praised the gods that it had a loft built into the rafters of the living den. Shoving the bag of food under the table before climbing onto it, she launched herself into the air. She twisted her tail upwards, Ahya's mouth chomping down on one of the horizontal support beams. Flexing her muscles and swinging her way up onto the loft floorboards, she crawled her way to the far back and hastily found a stored blanket up there with which to cover herself. No sooner had she stopped moving did she hear voices outside.

"Did anyone see her go this way?" one deep voice bellowed.

"I saw her run down this way, sir!" the meeker voice squeaked.

"This door is open! Check it, Grunier!" the gruff voice ordered.

"Yes, sir!" came the response.

Hooves clapped hard on the dirt flooring below. Taylor could hear the gruff snorts and breathing of the city police. She winced as she heard furniture and articles of the household being roughly moved and tossed around, feeling guilty for using this person's house as a place to hide. She never meant for it to get demolished. The callous cops continued to search the premises for what seemed like hours.

"Hey! I found something," the smaller voice of Grunier called out.

Taylor moaned inwardly as her ears detected the sounds of the bag being dragged out from under the table. She heard its contents being pilfered through. She had to try hard to keep her panting under control; the exertion of running had taken its toll.

"Wow, she really did nick a lot of stuff, didn't she?" Grunier gaped.

"So, a thief on top of being a murderer," the first voice scoffed. "I would love to get my hooves on her neck. Just me and her alone. I'll show her what true justice looks like."

"But Boss, you know that's against the rules!" Grunier quietly reminded.

"Don't tell me what I can't do!" he brayed, causing the other to yelp. "Hmm…" Peeking through the boards, Taylor could see a large horse investigating the bite marks on the ceiling beams.

"Do you think she could still be in the house?" Grunier's voice began to quiver. "I don't really like the look of her tail. I'd rather not be eaten."

There was a faint odor of burnt fur, then a deep grunt from the larger officer as he shifted towards his smaller companion. "Grunier, you're sparking again. Must I remind you to keep that under control? The only reason I brought you under my wing was a promise I made to your father to take care of you. Don't make me regret my decision."

"I'm sorry, Watters." Grunier was hyperventilating, but his commanding officer was doing his best to calm him down. "I just don't think I'm ready to be out on the force yet. What if she's still here?"

19

"Then we'll deal with her." Watters snorted. He regarded the bag for a moment or two before answering, "Besides, I think she just chucked the bag under this table to implicate the citizen living here and ran."

"What are you doing in my house?" a voice rang out.

"Speak of the devil," the angry horse whispered before shifting his bag of evidence, then puffed out his nostrils. "Nothing, ma'am. Perhaps you recognize me? Sheriff Watters? We were tracking down a criminal, and we had cause to believe they entered your home. It seems they are no longer in the vicinity. We will be taking our leave now. Our apologies."

After some more words were exchanged, Watters and Grunier left with the rest of the food Taylor had acquired. She lightly thumped her head onto the board she lay on, frustrated that all her hard work today had gone to waste. Times like this, she wanted nothing more than to rip off her tail for what good it did her. Most of her life was marred by the mere fact she was born with this tail that just happened to have a mouth that was rapacious in its appetite for food.

The rest of the day was an agonizing slog. Whoever lived here hadn't bothered to leave again. Surely she had some errands to go do, but no, the tenant of this den decided it was better to spend the rest of her time at home watching television—nothing but corny soaps and home shopping networks. Every time Ahya bumped her mouth on Taylor's cheek to prompt her to look for food, she pushed her away.

"Sometimes I hate you," she whispered, which seemed to cause Ahya to wilt.

At long last, Taylor heard soft snoring from below. The length of shadows from the filtered light coming through the doorway pegged the time to be late evening. The sun was just starting to set, and she cursed her luck. Pine and Mitchell were probably starving as much as she was now, and she would have nothing to show for it when she got back. She'd let them down.

Deftly dropping from above back onto the table, Taylor spied an older bongo sleeping in a recliner, a plate of food perched on her rather plump belly. The light of the screen was still illuminating her ruddy features. She licked her lips at the collage of greens and cut fruits on that plate. She wanted nothing more than to sneak over there and grab a few morsels to eat, however she'd risked enough already today.

Stomach rumbling, she drew the hood back over her hair and secured Ahya back under her cloak before gliding out into the night. Avoiding the occasional patrol car hovering through the major streets, Taylor took the backways and sidestepped the trash and refuse that abounded in those spaces. Several drunkards tried to make grabs for her, but a quick tongue-lashing from Ahya was all it took for them to frighten off. Hopefully no one would believe their stories later.

She had to take the long way around town to get back to her little cul-de-sac. The heightened level of security did little to ease her anxiety. She finally made it back over the wall of crates blocking the small hideaway she called home. Two pairs of eyes rose up to meet her, each one looking eager for what she had to bring, but their faces sagged at the look she gave them.

The first was an albino skunk, his irises red with the traits of his genetic makeup. The only spot of color on his body was the box-canyon-like black stripe on his tail that had both ends starting at the base of it. The second was a raccoon with a rather dark complexion of brown fur with black splotches that covered a good majority of his face, and marring the perfect stripes of his tail. They were orphaned outcasts like her, and together they had made an unorthodox family.

"Did you get anything today, Taylor?" Pine asked hopefully, his little skunk tail trembling with hopeful excitement.

"I'm afraid not." Taylor unclasped the cloak morosely, setting it upon the wall peg where she usually put it. Now free, Ahya began roaming the place in search of food. "Because of this idiot here—" She gestured to her tail. "—I almost got caught, and I lost everything to the town guard."

21

"No!" Pine wailed.

Although Mitchell's shoulders slumped, he continued to maintain a semblance of a smile on his face. "It's okay, Taylor. There is always tomorrow. You did your best."

"No, it wasn't my best. I shouldn't have gone for that last stall of food. I should have been happy and content with what I had." She plopped down onto her rump in misery.

Mitchell crawled over to her and placed a tiny paw onto her arm. "You can't blame yourself, Taylor. You were doing all of it for us. Every day you sacrifice to come bring us food and water."

She exhaled loudly. "I know, but it is just so frustrating!" Her gaze fell upon the small pot of water. She took the handle and sloshed it around a bit. "Guys, you barely drank any water! You're going to dehydrate if you don't!"

"Don't worry, Taylor. We drank," Mitchell assured.

"I didn't feel like drinking much today," Pine joined in, twiddling his paws.

"If I'm going to be taking care of you two, try to meet me halfway here." Exasperated, she shifted to lean on all fours over her bed mat to where she kept a stash of emergency rations in case of a bad day. Sitting back with legs crossed, she held out a dried, crusty piece of old bread. "I know this isn't much, nor will it be very tasty, but it's all we have."

"Wish we could have had those delicious tarts you brought the other day. Those were amazing," Pine whined.

"It's fine. Thank you for taking care of us," Mitchell said gratefully.

Breaking off stale pieces, she handed each of them a sizeable portion. They all ate in silence, sitting around a lone, rusted lantern that was placed in a crude firepit located equidistant from both their sleeping mats.

Ahya was continuing to root out food other than bread, her maw passing over Pine and Mitchell, ignoring them completely. At length, she grew bored and settled down beside Taylor, withdrawing its tongue back in and closing up the mouth. If one didn't know it was there, they couldn't tell her tail was unique.

"She's getting worse, isn't she?" Pine stared at Ahya.

Taylor followed his line of focus, looking down at her tail. "Yeah, she is. It's getting harder to control her every day."

"But you can control her, right?" Mitchell asked hopefully, taking another nibble.

"I don't know." She placed a paw on the tip of her tail, feeling the wrinkled skin underneath the red fur. "Sometimes I feel like I can. Most times, she has a mind of her own."

"It's still weird," Pine mumbled.

"Pine!" Mitchell chided.

"It's not like I like you any less though, Taylor!" the skunk recovered, stuffing a rather large bite into his mouth to shut himself up.

"It's okay, guys. I'm used to this...I think." She cast one last look at her tail before returning to her living-partners. "Eat up. We got a long day ahead tomorrow. I'm not sure how much more we can stay here in this town."

She had met Mitchell in the first month after arriving in Palaveve. He was digging through trashcans, completely dirty with the filth of others. Sensing a kindred spirit, they became inseparable. A few months later, they both found Pine crying in a dumpster, left abandoned by his family. Taylor felt compassion for his plight and took him under her wing as well. Although both slightly younger—and much smaller—than she, they'd become this family of mutual dependency, each needing the other for different reasons.

Taylor's stomach was still growling after their meager meal. It would not be enough for them, she knew, and she would have to try again tomorrow. She got up and dusted off her fatigue pants before stepping over to her bed space. She settled down onto it. Beside her pillow, made from a rolled-up sweater she had found, was a modest stack of books she had stolen from various residents. They didn't get much in the way of entertainment here in their alley, so they had to make do with what they could find.

"So, what story did you want me to read to you two tonight?" she asked, trying to fake a smile for them. She couldn't let them see her despairing over their food situation.

"How about that one about the fox and the rabbit?" Pine requested, climbing up into her lap and snuggling up onto her chest.

"Really? That one? We've read that one a dozen times! Surely there is another one you'd prefer to read instead?" She laughed. "How about Llydia and the Castle of Sand?"

"I'm not feeling fantasy tonight." Pine yawned.

"That's disappointing." Taylor pouted. "I used to love those books when they were read to me as a child."

"I'd like to hear about your life back in the big city instead, Taylor," Mitchell suggested, taking up the other half of her lap, his eyes turning to her with expectation.

She went silent for a moment, her expression serious. "Is this what you both want?"

"I wouldn't mind, actually," Pine admitted.

Nodding, she leaned her head back against the wall, then looked up at the tarp. She was instantly reminded that it needed fixing tomorrow. She let her thoughts drift as Ahya yawned before curling around the three of them like a warm blanket. What could she tell them that she hadn't before? They already heard about how magical and majestic the capital city of Zabökar was. Reiterating it wasn't really going to be anything exciting.

Finally deciding on a topic she could scarcely remember, she began. "I remember my family. They were my guiding light when I was growing up. I didn't realize it then, but I do now."

"How did they take to you having a mouth for a tail?" Pine asked.

Taylor chuckled. "As well as can be expected. I never truly appreciated all that they went through with me. They tried to give me a normal life. Going to school, attending afterschool sports events... I even became a cheerleader for a season. I didn't really have any need to want for anything else in my life. And then..."

She became lost in her thoughts, her countenance fading as bad memories came back to her once more. The abrupt silence brought Mitchell's attention as he looked up at her and shook her arm. "Taylor? What about your mother?" he probed.

Shaking her head, she looked down and reassured him with a smile. "It's fine. I'm fine," she said, more for her own comfort than for Mitchell's. "My mother… My mother was such a beautiful wolf. Her name was Murana, but she never allowed me to call her that." She chuckled. "I always looked up to her. She always seemed so refined and elegant, yet she never let that define her. She was always willing to let her tail down and hang out with me and my friends, playing our silly games."

"She seems like an awesome mother," Pine commented dreamily, sinking further into Taylor.

"The best." She sighed, reaching up to wipe away a single tear forming. "I wish I could remember more about her. I was too sheltered and carefree then. I didn't really pay much attention to anything until it was too late. Now I wish I had spent more time with her than I did…before all the bad stuff went down."

"What about the rest of your family? I remember you once mentioned you had siblings." Mitchell settled more deeply into her lap, snuggling close enough to hear her heartbeat.

Taylor gripped both of them in her arms, lifting them off of her slightly. "I had two older brothers, almost exactly like you two!" She giggled, rubbing her cheeks up against the both of theirs as they all laughed.

"They can't be like us! We're not wolves!" Pine snickered, making a playful pawing at her face.

Taylor set them back down again, contemplating the two of them. "Actually, they kinda were. My mother was a huge supporter of adoption. She couldn't have any cubs of her own, so she adopted both a skunk and a raccoon as children! They were the best siblings I could ask for. I could have sworn I told this to you two already!"

"Just like us!" Pine cackled, pointing to both Mitchell and himself. "We could be your brothers too!"

"Aren't you already?" Taylor soothed, petting the albino skunk to get him to calm down a bit. "You two are such blessings. I really don't know where I'd be if it weren't for you two."

"Probably just as alone as we were." Mitchell gazed around their small makeshift home, constructed of nothing but refuse and things most

25

other mammals would consider trash. They sat there in silence together. After a few moments, he tugged on her shirt. "Um…Taylor, if your mom couldn't have cubs of her own, how did she have you?"

She blinked, her mind racing hard for an answer. "I really don't know."

She was rather astonished that she had never questioned the manner of her birth; she just took it for granted that Murana had her like normal, not giving it much thought that she wasn't adopted like her two brothers. Her mind was on more immediate things at the time. Why did it matter to her the nature of her birth? The more she thought about how unique she was given her tail, the more that question seemed to scream for a response.

"I'm sorry. I shouldn't have asked," Mitchell apologized.

"You're fine. There are just some things even I don't know." She leaned back against the wall once more. "I may be the oldest of us, but even I don't know everything."

"Oh, Mitchell!" Pine buzzed, his eyes bulging.

"Right!" The raccoon winked as both of them bounced off her lap and skittered towards their shared bed mat, each of them rustling amidst their meager belongings.

"What are you two doing?" Taylor raised a brow, crawling over on all fours to peek.

"Happy birthday, Taylor!" They both squeaked as they turned around and delivered to her a small piece of bread with a single candle sticking out of it.

"Aww, you guys…" She began to tear up, taking the small morsel from them.

"Sorry we couldn't find anything better." Mitchell wrung his paws lightly.

"Or that we could find nothing to light the candle," Pine added.

"I had almost forgotten…" She brought it up to her face, seeing the small green twinges of mold starting to grow. It was the thought that counted.

"You're nineteen now! Go on, blow out the candle!" Pine beamed, urging her on with his paws.

26

Giggling at their mirth, she blew out the invisible flame, congratulated by their small claps. "You guys are too sweet. Thank you." She swooped them up in her arms, giving them both deep hugs. At length, she set them down and began to set their blanket over them.

"No... Not bedtime yet!" Pine complained.

"Yes, bedtime!" Taylor admonished. "We have a long day ahead. We need to be well-rested."

"Can't we sleep with you, Taylor?" Mitchell asked, eyes wide.

"I'm afraid not." She glanced back at Ahya, who seemed bored at the proceedings. "I love you two very much. I don't want to take a chance that something could happen to you while I'm sleeping and I can't stop her."

"I wish she wasn't around," Pine blurted.

Mitchell smacked the skunk's arm. "Pine! That's not cool!"

A pained look etched itself onto Taylor's face as she forced some semblance of happiness back onto her features. "I know he didn't mean it like that, Mitchell." She bent low and kissed each of their foreheads gently. "Good night, you two."

"Good night, Taylor," they piped in unison.

She rolled back onto her mat, watching them rustle and fidget for a few minutes more before seeing them fall still. She had never thought about it before, but she knew this wasn't the life she had expected to lead when she was back in the great metropolis of Zabökar. Where did things go wrong? When she was born? What damage had she caused her family just by her very existence?

Taylor didn't want this life for Pine and Mitchell. She never told them, but instead of a wish, she made a promise on blowing out that candle. She was going to do everything in her power to see that they got a better life than they've known. There was no plan yet. There was no clear goal in mind. There was just the wanting to make sure they experienced what she had when she was younger—what she could remember.

"I'll do right by you. Things will be different tomorrow, just you wait," Taylor whispered. Curling up with Ahya wrapped around her front for warmth, she eyed her companions once more before closing her eyes and drifting off to sleep.

2
AHYA

"She's been here," Trevor said with finality, crumbling the pieces of bread and letting them fall onto the sand. "And she's not alone."

"How do you figure?" his wolf companion asked, tilting his head as he looked around the small hovel of an alleyway home.

Trevor pointed to the two mats opposite each other in the confined space, twisting his lower body to face the entrance of the alley as he knelt on the ground. "Nobody steals two pads for kicks. She's been taking care of someone here. And these." He picked up a few other bread chunks, seemingly left carelessly on the ground. "These have different bite patterns than the other, almost like a tearing sort of bite."

The other wolf sniffed the air. "It's kind of hard to make out any other scent but hers though."

"Probably another mammal that doesn't have nearly as strong a musk." Trevor smiled as he stood up, dusting his pants off with his one good paw.

Trevor was a wolf, like his comrade, however he was so far gone with his injuries that he required cybernetic enhancements to keep moving. His entire left forearm was gone, replaced by a crude iron paw, with braces that extended up to his pauldrons—each covering a shoulder to secure and keep his collarbone from fracturing due to previous injuries. He wore nothing but brown utility pants held up by securely fastened belts, and a brown tail-length scarf for harsher weather.

"Do you think she's still around?" Gregor queried, looking a bit bored now.

Gregor was a bit spindlier for his species, not as fully formed as Trevor. He sported a rustic brown tank-top and a matching pair of utility pants to Trevor, though had far fewer scars and scratches, especially around the face, where no fur grew. The two of them together seemed like they had been through some rough scraps, yet unlike Trevor he was without missing limbs or enhancements.

Trevor rolled his eyes as he slapped on his flat cap, the shades on the bill flipping down to cover his eyes as the early morning sun inched into the sky. "Yes, Gregor. She is." Trevor scuffed the patch of wet ground by his feet onto Gregor, causing him to wildly kick his hind leg to get the sticky sand off. "This is not yet dry. She is close."

"Come on! Did you have to do that?" He whined. "You know I hate it when I get gross stuff like that on me!"

Trevor barked a laugh, "It's sand, Gregor. Seriously, you are positively the worst wolf I have ever met. Why did I bring you along anyway?"

Gregor gave a nice, playful shove back. "Only because I was your best pal in training, carrying your ass through it when no one else would!" He chuckled, shouldering his gun, signaling he was ready to move out.

Trevor returned the smile. "Yeah, all while keeping your tail out of the mud!" His expression grew solemn. "All those years ago. It was definitely a different time back then." Shaking his head, he swung his own gun over his left shoulder.

"Do you feel this payday is still worth it?" Gregor sighed, looking up at the sky to judge the time. "We've been tracking her for over a year now. Most jobs we've had, we would have folded by now."

Trevor watched his friend for a moment. "You're right, but we're so close now we might as well finish it." He gave him a warm smile.

"Think we should call it in now to the Arbiter?" Gregor began scaling the crates leading out, turning around only when Trevor failed to respond.

After a few moments, Trevor shook his head. "Not yet. Come on, let's follow her tracks." He motioned to Gregor before hopping up onto the crates himself to exit back out of the alley. "I have you now," he whispered to himself.

Taylor had arrived to the market area earlier than normal this morning. The church-goers were just now shuffling out of their chapels, some probably having had their Scripts read to them. Taylor sneered at the thought of those supposed prophetic writings, but swiftly ignored the emerging gathering. What did it matter to her what people believed in or were controlled by? She made her own destiny.

Seeing as some were already heading to the bazaar, she moved forward alongside them, cloak hood drawn tight around her head. Just another figure in the crowd.

"Do we have to do this?" Pine snuggled in closer to Taylor's neck.

"Yes, we do, and can you please keep it down?" Taylor shot him a glare, continuing her straight walk through the bustling crowd. Ahya thankfully stayed hidden under the ankle-length fabric.

"I haven't stolen food in such a long time," Mitchell mused, plodding alongside on all fours. "Guess I got so used to you gathering food for us that I didn't really expect to be coming out here again to be taking some for ourselves."

"Remember, we also need to get some canteens of water too. We're almost out, no thanks to little guy here." She jabbed a finger up to the white figure on her shoulders, hogging up the majority of the real estate up there.

"Hey! Not my fault you tipped the pot so far that it spilled over my face!" Pine huffed.

"You got a hole in your lip," Taylor fired back.

Mitchell stopped midstride and placed a reminding paw on Taylor's ankle. "Let's try not to fight. It was an accident. We have enough water for another day or two at most, but yes, we should go get some more to replace it. We have no idea when the next rain will come."

"We'll need more water than just for a day or two." Taylor looked both ways before crossing the street, relieved that no patrolling cops were around, idly fingering the small rope that held her pine tree necklace.

The tone in her voice caught Mitchell's attention. "What do you mean by that?"

Determined, she continued along the street, keeping to the shadows of the awnings along the buildings. "I think I've lingered here too long. With recent run-ins with the police and how many people recognize me now, I don't think it's safe for me to stay. Word might get out that I'm here and they'll find me again."

"We're leaving?!" Pine wailed, squeezing her neck tighter. Taylor tried to shush him to prevent people from staring.

"What do you mean find you? Who will find you?" Mitchell kept close to her hind paws to avoid being trampled on by the growing throng.

Taylor stopped short from leaving the last overhang, choosing to butt up against the final pole holding it up, her gaze surveying the central market square. "Remember when I told you two about some group shadowing me all the way from Zabökar?" They both nodded. "For over a year, I couldn't shake them. It wasn't until I came out to the wasteland here and found Palaveve that I lost them."

"What do they want from you?" Pine was sniffing the air, feeling uncomfortable being back out in the open.

Taylor shook her head. "I don't know, but I think they're after me for what I am." She glanced down at the bulge behind her that was Ahya. "For what I can do."

"Well, last night was just an accident. That doesn't mean we have to leave," Mitchell tried to reason.

"No, it's happening more often lately. I can hardly go out without my cloak to hide my red hair. The people here know me by sight now, and it isn't positive." She fastened the strap for her hood a bit tighter. "And the last thing I want is harm to come to you two because of me."

"So that's why you decided to take out your necklace," Mitchell mused, resting back on his haunches.

She stuffed the exposed pine tree air freshener back into her cloak, its scent long since evaporated. It was a dingy old thing, looped together with a cord of rope that was a far cry from the chain-link that it once sported when she was first given it as a gift from her mother. It was truly the last thing left of her family, and the one heirloom she could claim as a link back to where she had come from. To outsiders it was nothing but trash. To Taylor it was something far more precious.

"Yeah, I'm leaving tonight. I would like it if you were to come with me." She eyed them both, gauging their reactions. She could sense a lot of hesitation from Pine. "I know it's going to be scary. I'm quite terrified, truth be told, of being back out on the road again. Vulnerable."

As Pine was wringing his paws together, Mitchell did a small slap to his chaps and got back up to standing. "Then I guess we better make this shopping trip our best yet."

Taylor beamed as she knelt to hug Mitchell, standing up to nuzzle Pine, who was still on her shoulder. "If it'll make you feel any better, you can stick with me while Mitchell and I do all the work."

"I'd prefer that." Pine shivered, snuggling close to her nape, taking care not to disrupt her hood and reveal her hair.

With renewed purpose, they stepped out from the shadows. She had not taken a single step before bumping into a frightened rabbit, seemingly lost in his own world of business. He stared up at her, nose twitching anxiously. He appeared frightened of her, whether it was because she dwarfed his size, his head only reaching to just above her waist, or the fact she was a predator, she couldn't say.

"Um…" he started haltingly. "Was there something you needed of me, ma'am?" He was gripping the bottom of his shirt oddly.

"No, sorry for bumping into you." She waved him off.

He seemed immediately relieved and gave her a grateful nod, bounding off on whatever errand he was on. She shook her head. Such odd creatures. She saw them every now and then in town, usually in the company of other mammals, trailing them and such. Seeing one brought vague memories of the one she had briefly met back in Zabökar. Her paw went subconsciously back up to her necklace, as if remembering something forgotten.

Shrugging off her reverie, she went back to work. Their first stop was her usual with Mrs. Hircus. The aging kamori was already in full swing with a long line of customers at her stall. The goat's keen eye spotted Taylor from a distance and she gave a slight nod to acknowledge her existence before tending to her current customer.

Not wanting to disrupt the crowd and draw more attention to herself, Taylor dutifully got to the back of the line and patiently waited her turn. She was drumming up all sorts of excuses as to why she would need yet another bag so soon after getting one from her yesterday. She was so intent on reaching the front of the line and figuring out what she would say that she barely noticed the subtle tugging of her cloak hood by Pine.

"I don't like the look of them." The skunk pointed out two wolves off to their left, just entering the open market. The guns affixed to their backs and cybernetic enhancements did little to conceal the fact they did not belong in Palaveve.

Taylor shivered involuntarily. "I don't like the looks of them either."

She gazed around to see if there were open avenues of escape. It became clear she could not stand in line and wait for them to come to her, their eyes and noses already roving the plaza. It seemed irrational to automatically assume they were here searching for her, but deep in her gut she could feel that they were. Flashes of pursuit years ago galvanized her to action.

"We'll have to take what we need on the go. Focus less on stealth and more on getting what's important." She sidestepped the line and skipped to the front, doing her best to put on her best smile as she greeted the old goat. "Morning, Mrs. Hircus! I'm sorry for this interruption." She excused herself towards the irritated customer. "But I really need another bag today."

"Is something the matter, dear?" Hircus's voice was tense; she knew something was up before it needed to be said. She was very astute in that way, swiftly picking up nonverbal cues.

"Just in a bit of a hurry, that's all." Taylor shifted her eyes briefly towards the last location she saw the wolves. Slipping her hand into her cloak to take the proffered coins Ahya had covertly stole with her tongue from a nearby fox, she drew out the silver and placed them on the table between them. "This should be enough to cover the bag."

"You seem to be in an awful hurry. Did something happen?" Hircus had all but shunned her current customer, who was starting to get irate at being ignored. She gripped her cane leaning up on her counter and attempted to hobble around towards Taylor.

Sensing that her approach to the whole situation was wrong, Taylor inwardly chided herself for not being more tactful and just abandoning the bag altogether. She could find some other way of carrying the stolen goods. Her interaction was already drawing the attention of other shoppers nearby, and soon she locked eyes with the taller wolf, his metal arm flexing at the recognition.

Snatching a bag from the stall, Taylor began to step back from the gathering mob, their keen instincts detecting something wrong. "This was not the way I wanted to introduce Pine and Mitchell to you, Mrs. Hircus! I'm very sorry about this." She gave a squeeze to Pine on her shoulder and turned to run.

"Wait, Taylor!" Hircus looked utterly confused, her hoof reaching out futilely to stop her. "Where will you go?"

Taylor chanced a look back, and could see the two wolves pushing and shoving people aside, their dogged sights set firmly on her. She was on the run again—from who or what, it didn't matter; they were all the same. They just wanted to use her for experiments or harm her in some other ungodly way. She remembered the one time she got caught, and the pain she experienced then was unbearable. She would not allow it to happen again.

"We have to hide!" Pine's claws dug into the cloak fabric.

"He's right," Mitchell agreed, keeping pace alongside her on all fours. "If we escape the town, there will be nothing but miles of open desert with nowhere to hide. We need to lie low until nightfall and escape then."

"I know that!" Taylor winced, not wanting to snap at him so harshly. Her rising terror caused her thoughts to leap minutes ahead to what she was going to do next. Looking aside to the nearest barrel of fruit, she grabbed a pawful and kept running. "Just grab what you can and keep going. We just need enough to get to the next town!"

Weaving in and out of the clustered groups of people, they each started nabbing all sorts of pastries and fruits, tossing them into the bag she had hooked around her arm. If there were outcries of protest from onlookers who noticed the outright theft, she did not feel the weight of their consequences. Her mind was focused solely on getting enough for the journey ahead, and finding shelter where she could ditch the two following her.

Several more cries erupted from behind them, causing them to look back. The two wolves were gaining ground fast, and it wouldn't be long before they would overtake her. Panicking, Taylor dropped all pretense of preparing for a trip and began running.

"Forget the food, Mitchell!" She panted, scurrying around a corner and into a tarp-covered alleyway. "We just need to get away!"

Mitchell was already gasping, not used to this amount of exercise after being sedentary for so long. "Taylor… I can't…keep up with…you!" He wheezed as his pace slowed down.

She skidded to a halt, turning back to see the hunched over form of Mitchell, his paw resting on the nearby building for support. She bit her lower lip before setting Pine down beside him amidst his objections.

"Taylor, what are you doing?!" Pine whimpered, trying to clamber back up her leg to be by her side.

Pushing him down off of her, she backed away suddenly. "If they catch me, you'll be caught too. I don't want you two captured on my account." She set down the bag of food beside them. "Take this back to our home here and I'll meet you tonight under the cover of dark. If I don't show by—"

"Can't we come with you?" Pine implored, ignoring the bag, his eyes only for Taylor.

"If I don't show by the morning," Taylor continued, flouting his concerns, "you take what you can and you leave Palaveve without me. Mitchell knows how to leave a scent trail. I'll follow you when I can."

Mitchell understood the keen noses of wolves, and that she could easily track them wherever they went. Putting a tiny paw on Pine's shoulder, Mitchell pulled him back slightly to comfort him. "We understand, Taylor. Do what you have to do to survive. We will too. We'll see you tomorrow."

Pine shoved off Mitchell's paw. "You're just putting on a brave face!"

Mitchell's eyes betrayed his fear. "So what if I am? Taylor doesn't have much time before those two wolves catch up. We're only slowing her down. They're looking for her and not us, so we are safer separating. Let's split up for now and come back together when they've gone."

"Fine." Pine sniffled, wiping his wet nose. "But you better be there tomorrow!"

With a nod, Taylor fought back the tears before turning and bolting down the back alley. She could already hear the sirens of the squad cars howling through the congested streets. Her ears flicked back to the sounds of labored breathing, growls, and claws digging into dirt. She knew they weren't far off.

The next few minutes were a blur. She recalled her hood falling back to her shoulders at one point, drawing pointing stares from those around her. She even remembered sliding underneath a passing police car, its levitation engines whining to a halt as the officer grinded the gears to perform a U-turn. Using Ahya to bite onto and swing from several support beams overlooking a side street bazaar, she deftly landed on the cloth overhangs, casting the road below in varying hues of dyed fabric.

Taylor swiftly descended down the rooftop steps into an unfamiliar home. It looked lived-in, filled with the trappings of an old grandma complete with sewn dolls of grassland mammals lining the shelves along the walls. There was a scent of jasmine hanging in the air, its source from a tea kettle set off to the side after having been removed from the stove probably hours prior.

A jangle of keys at the front door made Taylor's heart skip a beat. She dove for the floor and rolled behind the only sofa in the room. It wasn't much, being meant for a smaller mammal than she was, but it was the best she could do to manage to hide herself from the view of the entryway. The door creaked, the hinges rattling as a small huff was heard from the home's occupant upon closing the heavy wooden contraption.

Taylor chanced a peek over the top of the couch only to recognize the pelt of black, broken by faded spots of brown and white. "Mrs. Hircus?" she breathed.

The old goat let out a shriek before stumbling back and catching her breath, hoof clutching her breast. "Heavens, child! What are you doing in my home?"

All pretense of hiding gone, Taylor rose, continuing to ensure Ahya stayed safely beneath her cloak. "I'm sorry. I wasn't even aware this was your home. I was just trying to find a place to hunker down and avoid being caught again."

"Again?" Mrs. Hircus snorted, her bearings now recovered. "I couldn't possibly imagine why anyone would be wanting to chase after you in the first place." She took her cane and began shuffling over to the couch Taylor was standing behind, pausing briefly when police sirens passed by her home.

"It's…a long story." Taylor's shoulders slumped as tension began to seep out from her body. "What about your stall? I thought you had to be manning it. Don't you need to make a living too?"

With some considerable effort, Mrs. Hircus managed to sit down onto the plush cushions. She patted the one next to her as an invitation for Taylor to come join her. "I got some young, helpful volunteers to do that job for me these days if I'm not feeling well. My shop will do fine without me for a time. I was a bit concerned over what happened with you that I decided to come back and make a care package for you."

Taking the offered space, Taylor stepped around the end rest and sat down next to the goat, their size-difference evident as she seemed to tower over her by almost two head lengths, despite being small by wolf standards. "You don't even know where I live, Mrs. Hircus."

"That's where you are wrong, deary." She cracked a smile. "Don't think for a moment I don't care about my street children in this town. I've followed you a couple times, just to make sure you were safe."

Taylor flushed. She could have sworn she was being careful when entering and exiting their alleyway abode. "I didn't realize you cared that much." This elicited a grunt of affirmation from Mrs. Hircus. After a moment of realization, Taylor's eyes widened. "All your street children? Surely you've met Pine and Mitchell already then?"

The goat's brow furrowed a bit in thought. "I can't say that I have, unfortunately. After all this time of you talking about them, I've

38

been quite eager to meet them." This caused Taylor's ears to droop. Thumping her cane softly on the dirt floor, Mrs. Hircus cleared her throat. "So, what will you do now? From what I'm gathering, you are on the run from the law enforcement here. Did you do something bad?"

Although there was no malice in her voice, Taylor could feel that question pierce her soul. This pure goat, that was almost like a quasi-mother figure, seemed to hold so much weight to Taylor. Telling her that she had stolen food and things from the locals here and even accidently killing a few because of Ahya felt like it would be nothing but a disappointment. The last thing she wanted was the sole bastion of kindness in Palaveve to evaporate into thin air.

Sagging visibly, Taylor sunk into the cushions and sighed. "I wasn't trying to hurt anyone. I just wanted to be left alone and live my life." This answer only drew a pointed, curious look. Realizing the old goat wasn't going to accept just that, Taylor continued. "Yes, I might have accidently killed a few people here. I didn't want to, but it was out of my control."

Mrs. Hircus's pupils grew, but she remained steady. "I see," she answered cryptically. "Accidently killing a few people with it being entirely out of your control is quite a lot of coincidence, even for the most-lucky—or rather, unlucky person."

Taylor couldn't fault Mrs. Hircus's reasoning there. It did seem farfetched that every death was accidental, but she couldn't just blame it all on Ahya, could she? Ahya was part of her, and she could enact some measure of control over her. So would it really be a lie to say her tail went out of control each and every time it ate someone? Would anyone really believe that?

She grimaced at having to reveal to Mrs. Hircus her true nature, worried that she might abandoned her like everyone else, save for Pine and Mitchell. "Yeah, I can see what you mean." Ahya was bobbing slightly under her draped cloak, almost like she was struggling to breath, despite not having any biological need to do so. "It is because of Ahya," she said with shaky resolve.

"Ahya?" Mrs. Hircus seemed baffled. She had never heard the name in all the time she had known Taylor. "Dear, do you have someone

39

here with you right now?" She was pointing with her cane at the rising bulge threatening to expose itself to the goat.

"Not exactly," Taylor sheepishly responded. "I can control her most times, but she's being very obstinate right now. This...is Ahya."

Lifting the lower portion of her cloak up and setting it aside, revealing her hind legs, Taylor's tail slowly poked its head up. The crimson fur was brilliant, even in the muted sunlight from the windows. Her tail seemed to be getting longer as the rounded end of fluff was enlarging to an unnatural degree, becoming larger than Taylor's own head.

What caused Mrs. Hircus's nostrils to flare and her eyes to bulge was when the supposed front of the tail split apart to reveal a gaping maw of jagged, razor-sharp teeth leading back into a yawning, inky abyss. A slithering tongue appeared and continued to grow as it extended out into the open air, dripping saliva hitting the floor like needles on marble tiling. What added to the terror of this monstrosity was the fact it seemed acutely aware of Mrs. Hircus's postion, as if it had a mind of its own and was facing directly towards her.

"Mrs. Hircus...please don't freak out! This is part of me...my tail," Taylor pleaded, seeing the flight or fight response rising critically in the goat.

Her eyes darted back and forth between Taylor and Ahya, unsure of what to make of this new development, and nearly dropped her cane. Quickly fumbling for it drew her back to reality and assisted in calming her nerves just a hair. She scooted a bit further back on the couch away from Taylor, and regarded Ahya with wary eyes like a prey would a predator.

"How... How long have you lived with this...tail?" Mrs. Hircus hesitantly asked.

Taylor glanced at Ahya, the tail's "gaze" looking squarely at Mrs. Hircus. "All my life. I was born with it. I don't know why and I don't know how I have it. I didn't really have much control over it growing up until I had given it a name. Since then, I've been moderately successful in controlling it for the most part, but sometimes she just up and does things without warning."

"Like…kill people?" Mrs. Hircus was both fascinated and horrified.

"Eat them, more like," Taylor confirmed.

"Eat… But then where do they go?" The goat looked Taylor up and down. She was a petite-looking wolf, and the size of some of the potential prey would dwarf the capacity of that tail. It probably boggled her mind where the poor victims went once swallowed by that devilish grin.

Taylor shivered. "I'd rather not get into it. Look, are you going to help me or not? I want to get out of here, out of Palaveve. It's not safe here anymore. Not for me, not for anyone. I feel I've outstayed my welcome."

Shaking brusquely to clear her head, Mrs. Hircus wobbled up to her hooves with the help of her cane. "I think we will need to consult the Script."

Taylor groaned and rolled her eyes. Even Ahya seemed to be visibly irritated with this notion. "The Script? We don't have time to go to the church and have them read it to us. Besides, it's all just bogus superstition anyways!"

"Young lady, I may have a soft spot for you and other lost children in this town, but do not mock what we believe." She thumped the cane once for attention. "If there is a path forward or some sort of guidance they can gleam regarding your future, then that would be the safer road to take instead of running around blindly without direction."

"I just find it hard to believe that the Script can dictate someone's life, and nobody has any issues with the fact they have no control over how to live?" Taylor folded her arms. "Seems more like a cage than something that sets you free."

Mrs. Hircus stared at Taylor a few moments before responding, "There is security in the fact that our lives can be set before us by the Script. Many live happily without knowing theirs, but in these uncertain times, knowing what lies ahead brings a comfort all its own."

"And if the Script ordains someone to die today, what then? Are they going to feel secure knowing that their death is coming?" Taylor fired back.

"We cannot change the Script, child." Mrs. Hircus sighed, resting her hooves on her cane. "That is one of the first things we learn in school, is it not? Knowing one's death could bring about a certain tranquility and inspire them to enjoy what life they have to its fullest before departing. The world is a mysterious place, and the Script helps us navigate through that, for good or for ill."

"It's never helped me in the past, and I've been doing just fine without it," Taylor rebutted.

Mrs. Hircus gave a knowing glace at the two of them. "Running from the law and struggling to make ends meet is working out wonderfully for you then?" She gave a cackling wheeze of a laugh, the air in her lungs rattling. She chuckled before giving Ahya a wide berth, heading to one of the sewn animals on the wall shelves.

Shifting through their multitude of shapes and sizes, she hummed a bit to herself. For someone who has just discovered Ahya, she seemed remarkably okay with it now. Taylor wasn't sure if Mrs. Hircus was just keeping her mind off the fact she had a maw for a tail, or the shock of it had already worn off. If it was the latter, then Taylor was impressed with the old goat. What sort of life had she led to become so casual with something so freakish?

Finally finding the one she wanted, she carefully lifted it off as to not disturb the other dolls around it. She waddled back to Taylor and handed out the diminutive doll. "Would you mind grabbing this from me?"

"Oh, of course." Taylor realized she needed to reach forward to grab it since it was clear Mrs. Hircus would come no closer to Ahya, who was off to the side between them at the moment. "You're still scared of me?" Taylor was hurt, but completely understood the feeling. She was used to it by now.

After handing the doll to Taylor, Mrs. Hircus repeated the wide arc around to her end of the couch to stay out of range of Ahya. "Of you? No, my child. I know you wouldn't hurt a fly, but it is that thing on your tail that I'm unsure of. You saying you can't control it fully does give one cause for worry."

Taylor looked down in shame at the doll in her paws. "I'm sorry I am this way, Mrs. Hircus."

Tears began to well at the corners of her eyes as she regarded the small doll, no bigger than the size of her palm and small enough that it could easily be placed into a pants pocket. It was the shape of a fox, with jet-black thread to resemble its fur. What was unique about the design was that it had six tails, each one with a different colored tip. Its eyes were buttons of a multi-hued dye that changed colors with the refraction of the light as she turned the doll this way and that.

"Don't be sorry for something you cannot control." Mrs. Hircus chanced leaning in and placing a knowing hoof on Taylor's paw. "That there doll is a special one of mine: a mythical creature once said to exist called a kitsune. Many folks nowadays don't believe such nonsense and call these stories about them old wives' tales, and that their magic never existed." She leaned in further and lowered her voice to a whisper and winked. "But between you and me, I believe the old magic still exists. How else can we explain the Script?"

Taylor exhaled, gratefully taking the offered doll with a nod and putting it into a cloak pocket. "I used to believe such things existed. Mythical creatures like dragons and people doing magic feats that could move mountains. My mother used to read stories of them to me in bed when I was young. Then I grew up. I've learned the harsh realities of this world and that it has no place for me."

"Gobbledygook!" Mrs. Hircus blurted, causing Taylor to startle and Ahya to bare teeth at the loudness of it. "There isn't a place yet for you because you've yet to find it! I have faith that you will do great things." She pointed at Ahya with her cane. "As…strange as that tail is, I do believe you were given it for a purpose. Call me a blind devout to the Script, I care not. I simply don't take things for granted, and believe that all things were preordained. And that," she said as she jabbed the cane forward again, "is something you weren't randomly born with."

"If you say so." Taylor slumped back, glancing around the den. "Mrs. Hircus, is it alright if I stay here for a bit before heading out of town tonight?"

The goat pursed her lips, but bowed her head. "Of course. It'll give me time to prepare that care package for you. You've grown on me in the short time you've been here, little one." She hesitated a moment before stretching open her arms. "Come here, Taylor. Embrace me. It's been so long since I had a child of my own, that I wish to feel that warmth of love once again. I'll probably never get this chance again, given how old I am."

"Are you sure?" Taylor gave a sidelong look at Ahya, who seemed eager for the hug.

Mrs. Hircus nodded her head, flexing her hooves to prompt the hug sooner. With timid uncertainty, Taylor scooted in, and for the first time embraced Mrs. Hircus. Their arms interlocked and wrapped around each other. Mrs. Hircus was breathing fast, but did her best to ignore the slinking form of Ahya sidling up beside her, coiling around them both as the tongue casually lapped at the goat's horns. At length, they parted and sat facing each other.

"That…was nice," Taylor admitted, a smile blossoming.

"It sure was. Now let me get—" Mrs. Hircus began.

They both shrieked when the door blew off its hinges with a bang, the explosion hurtling the wooden slab clear across the room. Taylor flopped onto Mrs. Hircus to avoid being decapitated as it sailed over their heads, crashing into the far wall and causing several doll shelves to falter and clatter to the floor, dropping their precious cargo. In stepped the two wolves from earlier. The taller one with the cybernetic arm pointed an iron finger at her.

"There she is. Detain her," he commanded the other.

"Finally, it's over. We can go home, Trevor." The other wolf chuckled, taking aim with a gun with a large barrel opening.

In moments, a net blasted out of the end and spiraled wide, sailing through the air at her position. Taylor leapt from the couch and began to make a dash for the stairs leading back up to the rooftop, but was too late. The rope net made contact with her back, the sudden inertia bringing the ends to loop around to the front and encircle her entire body. She cried out as she tripped over her feet and fell to the ground.

The intertwining metal rivets at each knot intersection came alive, and she shuddered uncontrollably as painful arcs of electricity surged through her body. Trevor came forward and grabbed the end of the net, neatly tied up in a bow. Taking a gruff hold, he began dragging Taylor out the door.

44

Having recovered from the shock, Mrs. Hircus was afire with indignation. "You let her go this instant, you heathens!" She struggled to make her way to the kitchen, where Taylor could see her looking for something— likely a weapon.

"This does not concern you, citizen. Stand down," Trevor growled. Without waiting for her response, he continued to pull Taylor after him until they were outside.

"We caused a bit of a ruckus," the smaller wolf noted, many of the onlookers in the street warily eyeing them from afar. No doubt many had gotten onto their cell phones and called the police.

"If we're quick, we won't have to worry about them, Gregor." Trevor huffed, preparing to drag his prize all the way out of town, since he clearly didn't want to get close to Ahya.

Taylor remained quiet and still. The surge of electricity was still taking a toll on her senses; she felt numb from the elbows and knees out. Being dragged across the dirt was not comfortable in the slightest, but resisting the ropes only instigated more sparks of pain that she wasn't willing to tolerate. She biding her time as she could feel Ahya subtly biting through bits of the rope, avoiding the metal parts.

"So you think he's going to make good on his promise?" Gregor mused, looking way more relaxed than he was a few minutes ago.

"Gregor!" Trevor snapped. "How many times must I tell you that we don't talk business while on the job? Save that for when we're safely away from this hovel." He looked around at the growing crowd while shaking his head. "It's like you still haven't learned those valuable lessons from boot camp!"

Gregor began to snicker at this remark, but was stopped short by the rising tune of sirens. They were always prevalent in the background, but were nowhere near their position. Now that they'd been seen and most likely reported, the tone shifted, and it became clear the police were closing in. Taylor panicked as she willed Ahya to bite through the cords faster.

"Come on, let's pick up the pace!" Trevor barked.

He began sprinting down the roads. Various people quickly moved out of their way, none really stopping them. A few recognized Taylor for who she was and began clapping at what they supposed was the capture of a mass murderer, even whistling and cheering the two wolves on. The faster stride made it difficult for Ahya to continue biting through the ropes.

Trevor and Gregor stopped short when two squad cars screeched to a halt in front of them. Trevor cursed as he looked beyond the vehicles, likely to one of the many exits out of town. With a sigh, he set the net down and faced the primary car directly. A horse and wombat stepped out and put on their official caps before clopping forward to engage the two wolves.

"I am Sheriff Watters," the burly horse introduced himself. "And this is my deputy, Grunier." He indicated the plump wombat beside him, who had probably eaten way too much in recent years to be fitting happily in his uniform. "We will be taking the prisoner now. Hand her over."

Trevor pulled out a writ from his pocket and handed it to the sheriff. "I am a fully authorized contractor legally empowered to apprehend and bring this subject to my employer. You have no right to stop this business transaction."

Watters briefly skimmed the writ and sneered, "Bounty hunters." Crumpling the paper and tossing it callously back at Trevor, he made a motion for Grunier to grab the net with Taylor in it. "The local laws of Palaveve and the greater county of Balkar do not recognize your job status. You are infringing upon the lawful arrest of this criminal. Continue to object further and I will have no choice but to hold you in contempt of the law and arrest you too."

"You can't have her!" Gregor snarled, attempting to make a dive for Taylor.

"Gregor, stay your hand!" Trevor yanked him back, indicating with a motion of his chin to the rest of the cops who had rolled up, the click of dozens of guns aimed at their heads. With gritted teeth, he bent low to pick up his writ and stuff it back into his pants. "You've not heard the end of this."

"If you have a grievance, you are more than free to file it with the mayor. He will see you about it when he is next free." Watters smirked, flashing his faded teeth, then turned back to Grunier. "Fetch our wayward pup and toss her in the back."

"Sure thing, Boss!" The wombat was nervous about the order, but was all too happy to oblige.

Taylor abruptly hopped to her feet, to the stunned silence of all around. Ahya had successfully eaten through enough of the net, and not waiting for anyone to react, she spied an opening between two squad cars and made a run for it.

"Stop her!" Watters brayed, swinging his arm forward as if ordering his troops on a cavalry charge.

Taylor was about to laugh, from out of both exhilaration and terror, when Ahya did the unthinkable. She could feel the need rising in her stomach while she was in the net, but it wasn't until she had just passed Grunier that the pit of hunger bubbling in her belly reached a fever pitch. For days she hadn't eaten a decent meal, and Ahya took the opportunity to grab something for herself.

She tripped over as she seemed to turn in slow motion, watching something transpire like out of a nightmare. Ahya enlarged her frame and stretched her maw wide. In one fell swoop it descended upon the hapless form of Grunier, the tongue curling around the wombat to prevent it from escaping. Within seconds he was gone from view, swallowed into the tail.

"No!" Taylor fumbled, falling hard on her butt as the full weight of Grunier dropped Ahya like a lodestone. "Spit him out! Spit him out!"

She yanked on the base of her tail and raked her claws through the fur. Ahya's maw remained closed. Like something from a horror movie she had watched as a child, except it was happening within her own body. Trevor and Gregor made a move to intercept, but were bullied to the side by several rhino officers, forcing them to back off.

Taylor attempted to drag herself away from the cops, pulling her tail along behind her. The protestations of Grunier continued, his limbs and body writhing from within Ahya, giving everyone a macabre display of bulges through the fur. Everyone shouted at her, Watters threatening with a gun to release his deputy this instant. A bystander fainted at the sight.

Everything was happening so fast that Taylor could hardly comprehend it all. Then a deathly chill settled into her core as she could feel a budding sense of fullness in her belly. She began to beat down on

47

her tail, not caring how it hurt. "Don't do this, Ahya! Spit him out right now!"

Ahya was flooding her maw with her saliva, turning it corrosive to digest the hapless wombat. The thrashing and screaming within her tail became weaker until they stopped altogether. Taylor fought against the process with all her might, but Ahya's will was stronger. With the growing sense of contentment within her stomach, she dreaded what was to come next.

Watters backed up with a snort as Taylor heaved over and vomited what little contents she had left inside. The taste was unbearably disgusting as the flavor of Grunier lingered on her tongue. She knew it wouldn't go away for hours. She could have gone the rest of her life without knowing what he tasted like.

"Release Grunier right now, you evil bitch!" Watters roared, holding the gun barrel to her head. Its cold metal was pressed into her temple.

The diminutive shape of the wombat was getting noticeably smaller inside Ahya. Taylor was wracked with another spasm of bile, this time getting it all over Watters's hooves. Shivering uncontrollably all over, barely keeping herself up on shaky arms, she looked up at the furious horse.

"Please…stop me," Taylor begged.

With a neigh, he pistol-whipped viciously, causing Taylor to hit the ground hard. Blackness consumed her.

3

NONPERSON

The beeping of his alarm clock woke him. His entire body creaked, and he moaned as he shifted in his metal bed, bereft of any cushion or pillows. It would have done him no good anyway, considering he preferred sleeping inside his shell; it was safer that way. Stretching his limbs and peeking them out the holes in his exterior, he rolled over and slapped the top of the alarm to silence its irate blaring.

As if on cue, the intercom near his bed crackled to life and a familiar voice resounded from its speaker. "Good morning, Arbiter. We have received an incoming call from Novak. He is requesting your presence, declaring the matter very urgent. Will you respond?"

The Arbiter grimaced, clapping a leathery palm onto the device and clicking the transmission button. "Keep him on the line. I will be there momentarily." He sighed with the age of centuries.

Taking his time, he used his short limbs to push himself up into a standing position, feet touching the cold concrete flooring as he looked over at the clock. The Arbiter was a tortoise of incalculable age. He never gave his past to anyone and many speculated just how long he had been living, only showing up in Zabökar a mere five decades ago.

He shivered as he wrapped a large shawl over his shell. It was always cold in this city. It was only seven in the evening. What was Novak calling for at this blasted hour? With a groan, he shuffled over to the nightstand set alongside his bed cot, both bolted into the metal paneling. The entire room was makeshift like the rest of their headquarters, but there were few alternatives to a person in his position.

He rummaged around the leafy collard greens and picked out a few grapes and a watermelon slice to munch on as he awkwardly strapped on his vest over his bulky shell. With a little food in his belly, he plodded over to the room entrance and slid the door to the side, deep into the wall recess.

The red lights illuminating the dim corridor did little to liven up the place. It was utilitarian in nature, and he had come to accept his lot in

50

life. The High Council never agreed with his views or methods proposed and he was ostracized, forced to work covertly with his hired men. No matter. He would see his vision complete even if it meant going behind the council's back.

The thudding vibrations of his passage echoed down the hall and alerted his crew of his coming. A figure slipped out from the shadows and fell into step behind him since his bulk was too massive to have them walk side by side together.

"Good morning, Daughter," he intoned without much inflection.

"Evening, Father," she replied similarly.

She was unlike her father in many ways—a product of experimental gene splicing, and the product of his sperm and his wife's egg. His daughter was not exactly the same species, but a mixing of two. He had fallen in love with a crocodile and wanted children with her. Barring the genealogical factors prohibiting this, he turned to other methods for conception and successfully birthed the daughter he saw walking behind him.

An odd amalgamation of the two, she had a shortened snout of crooked teeth ending in a rounded V-point, and a tail with splayed dorsal fins down its spinal length. What was unusual about her stature was the semi-permeable shell that was nowhere the hardness nor heft of her father's. It was quite malleable, and could be easily mistaken for her having a paunch midsection.

"Novak is calling again." He motioned down the hall to the radio room.

She shifted her cybernetic eye up at the back of her father's head, its red iris contracting with consternation. "He hasn't reported in for several months."

"Indeed. I had begun to lose faith that he would ever accomplish the task I hired him for." He shifted to the side, breaching the frame of the door with his massive palm, pushing it in to allow his daughter to go first. He followed and turned to his lieutenant: a sleek-looking cheetah in military garb. "Report."

His daughter melted into the shadows along the wall, her eyes scanning the myriad of screens along the far wall, either depicting various news stations or monitoring security camera footage of key areas in Zabökar. Her red iris roved the massive amounts of incoming data like it was memorizing everything.

The lieutenant stepped up unflustered to the control panel, and handed the phone receiver to the Arbiter. "Novak is on the line, Arbiter. He is in the small town of Palaveve, about nine-hundred leagues to the southwest of us." His voice was curt and respectful.

"Interesting. So she made it that far," he mused, before turning his deep voice to the speaker and clicking the button. "This is the Arbiter."

The road-weary voice of Trevor Novak hummed across the line. "Evening, sir. I have some good news and bad news." The Arbiter grunted, and the wolf continued. "I have found her, Taylor Renee Wolford. She has been hiding in this town of Palaveve for possibly many months now. Unfortunately, the local police have her in custody and will not release her. I do believe they plan to execute her."

The Arbiter did not show how the news affected him, and instead responded in monotone. "You do realize the investment we have in her, do you not? She is one of the few success cases in the defunct project Iapyx, and she wasn't even ours. Get her back by any means necessary. The last thing we need is for her to fall into the hands of the council. Those fools would not know what to do with her."

There was a shuffling on the other end as Novak seemed to weigh his options. "What about your other subject? Wouldn't he be just as good of a specimen as Taylor?"

The Arbiter gripped the receiver tighter. "He is not ready. Proceed forward with your mission and retrieve your objective. Do I make myself clear?"

A low growl. "Yes, sir." Novak clicked off.

The Arbiter handed the radio back down to the cheetah before turning to his daughter who had heard everything. "I think things need to be dealt with a bit more personally."

She stepped forward quickly. "Let me go, Father. I will go track down this Taylor Renee and bring her to you."

"And risk the chance of losing you when we are so close to achieving my goal? I do not believe this is a wise decision, Daughter."

He shook his head and began to lumber out of the room, the rest of its denizens not mattering to the conversation at hand.

She cut him off before he could reach the door, looking up into his face with her one good eye. "Did you not tell me when mother died that life is full of sacrifices? That by accepting the loss for the greater good is how we can achieve greatness?" He stared down at her with no rebuttal. "Then let me go do this for you. Let me make you proud, and when I return, you will have sacrificed nothing at all!"

He beamed with pride at his creation, ruffling her scaly head with his fingers. "Then go, my dear daughter, Ariana, and return with your success."

"And of the two hunters? What should I do with them?" she queried with a curious glint in her eye.

"They are no longer of any use. After a year wasted, they have failed me. Dispose of them as you see fit." He smiled.

"Yes, Father." She bowed before whisking away into the darkness of the hallway.

Taylor yelped in surprise as a bucket of cold water was splashed onto her face. She growled as she shook off the droplets, trying to see through her soaked bangs and focusing on the repugnant face of Sheriff Watters. She flexed her arms and turned her head to see her wrists bound behind her back in knots through the chair's back posts. Ahya was chained by the tail tip to a yoke, studded into the ground to prevent her from moving much or opening her maw.

The horse set the bucket down on the dirt floor unceremoniously before returning to his seat opposite at the table between them. "I hope you'll appreciate the amount of effort that went into your binds. It took some ingenuity to figure out how to secure that abomination behind you."

"Her name is Ahya," Taylor snapped back, licking her lips, feeling the cut on her lower jaw which seemed to ache something fierce. How hard did she hit that ground from that cold cock of his gun?

"It's a monster. Giving it a name does not change what it does." He pointed a hoof at the struggling tail. "I've come to accept the fact that I'll never see my deputy, Grunier, again. He's gone. Lost inside…that thing."

The mere mention of what happened brought a sickening recollection as she finally noticed the disgusting fullness in her belly. The taste of Grunier was gone from her tongue, but the memory remained. Now all that was left was the dread seated in the pit of her stomach. She was no longer hungry and wouldn't be for several days, and the thought of why that was terrified her.

"I want to kill you." Watters grit his teeth, his hoof gripping his holster.

Taylor didn't want to hear anymore. Clearly something was holding him back, but she couldn't put her finger on what. She flipped her bangs back with a swing of her head as she glared at him defiantly, "Then why don't you? You'd be doing us both a favor."

Watters smirked. "Of that, I have no doubt." He leaned back in his chair and placed his hind legs on the table, finding great amusement at the increased thrashing from Ahya behind her. "But certain protocols must be followed first. I have my own integrity and the law to uphold. I couldn't live with myself if I killed a prisoner under my care, in cold blood, without due process."

"I'm sure you pride yourself greatly on that." Taylor rolled her eyes, trying to see if she could slip some fingers in-between the knots of her bindings, the ropes cutting furiously into her fur. "What are you waiting for? I'm right here at your complete mercy." She was pushing the sass, but she didn't care anymore.

Watters tapped a hoof to his gun, considering something, when a click at the door directed his attention. A small dik-dik clopped in with two scrolls with some considerable depth to them. The tawny officer did his best to reach up to the level of the table to set them down, but couldn't quite manage it. At length, Watters reached down and grabbed the two from him and waved him off.

"Was there a third?" Watters scanned the names on the two in his hoof.

The dik-dik shook his tiny head. "No, Sheriff. I even called to the neighboring town's churches to see if they had one for her, but they all returned negative."

"Interesting. Thank you, Officer Minama. I'll handle it from here." He beamed at the diminutive mammal.

Ensuring his colleague left and had shut the door behind him, Watters unfurled the two pieces of long parchment by their glowing handlebars. They seemed ancient, dust flying off their surface as he sifted through their interminable length. They seemed ridiculously long for scrolls of their size, and were filled with foreign text that Taylor could not decipher from her angle.

"You're going to read the letter of the law to me?" Taylor was incredulous. This was rather unexpected. "I know murder is wrong already, but I don't have much control over Ahya and what she does! You can't hold that against—"

"Doesn't matter if you blame your tail or not, it is attached to your body, so you must have some control over it." Watters clucked his tongue. "You don't expect me or anyone else to believe that you just so happen to 'lose' control over your tail when it is most convenient? Whether you like it or not you are the cause of death for over twelve victims in Palaveve alone, and you will be tried for the mass murderer you are."

Taylor scoffed at his upstanding attitude with his position. "Tried... Of course, with what jury?" She looked around the bare room of plaster. "I see no one else here to hear my case."

Watters curled his lip as he continued to scan the documents. "I didn't say it was going to be anything brought to a proper court and judge. As far as you're concerned, I am your judge, jury and executioner."

"Guess you've already got the verdict then. What are you waiting for?" She squirmed some more, drawing her muscles taut to get some play in the ropes around her wrists.

He only looked up briefly to ensure she was still firmly secured in her restraints. He may have been a prideful horse, but he was clearly not an oblivious one. Without giving her much regard, he responded, "I'm assuring my protection."

It was clear that Taylor would be getting nothing further from the Sheriff until he was finished with whatever investigation he was doing. She slumped into the chair and began looking around. There wasn't much of anything to aid in her escape. Beyond the big yoke weighing Ahya to the floor, the only other thing of note was the small, barred window slit allowing the rising moonlight to flow into the room.

She would have gazed back towards Watters if her eye hadn't caught a flicker of movement skittering past the bars outside. Her eyes went razor-focused, narrowing in on the dark silhouettes just outside. Recognition brought a smile to her face as the two shapes resembled her two friends, Pine and Mitchell.

"Pine! Mitchell! What are you doing here?" she hissed as quietly as she could.

"What now?" Watters snorted, irritated that he was interrupted just as he was coming upon an important section of the current scroll.

Taylor flitted back to the horse. "Nothing." She kept her face turned to the ornery sheriff, but kept her attention focused on the exterior beyond the bars.

Pine poked his little snout between the metal, his eyes rapt on Taylor's captor, and whispered, "Are you alright? We tried to come rescue you the moment we found out you were captured, but we couldn't even get close to this place until now!"

Taylor knew she didn't have a lot of time to get what she needed to say out. "I'm fine. I told you two to leave without me if I didn't show. You need to—"

"Who are you talking to?!" Watters slammed his hooves on the table, rattling the ring of keys on the edge a few inches. Pursing his lips, he got up and stormed over to the window slit.

"We'll be outside for you when you get out. There are two wolves here coming for you, can you smell them?" Mitchell shouted out loudly as Pine backed up from the bars.

"Who's out there? Get on, now!" Watters rapped his hoof firmly on the metal, resounding loudly in the bare room. Taylor could hear the yips from her friends, turning tail and scampering off to parts unknown.

"Leave them alone!" she snarled at him, causing Ahya to writhe wildly in her confines.

"Leave who alone? Whatever street rat friends you picked up here? Nobody cares about you. You're alone in Palaveve. Just shut up and let me finish reading this in peace." He brayed, stomping back to his chair, roughly thumping back into it.

Mitchell was right. Taylor sniffed the breeze on the air and detected a small hint of wolf musk. She didn't get a chance to truly memorize their scents, but something about it seemed similar to the two wolves who had attempted her capture earlier that day. Although she didn't trust them one bit for what they did to her, if they at least provided a distraction to escape from this prison, it would be welcome.

"Ha!" Watters's sudden laugh jolted Taylor from her thoughts. The horse tapped the end of the parchment with a bittersweet sigh. "Son of a bitch… Guess it was fated after all." His eyes met hers with renewed purpose. "His Script reads: *The end of days shall come on a day like any other. It will be sudden and you will not see anything further beyond red teeth.*"

"Whose Script?" Taylor leaned forward, trying to see if she could glean anything else.

He held her curious look. "Grunier, of course. I don't think any of us would have recognized what this meant even if he had consulted the priests regarding the day of his death. Now I believe I know exactly what it means now." With a satisfied smile, he reclined back, waving a hoof at Ahya. "The red teeth line is for your tail. He was destined to be killed by you regardless of what he did in his life. Now I don't feel so bad for being unable to save him."

"That's insane." She barked a laugh, stopping at last trying to escape her restraints. "Mrs. Hircus was the same way, believing everything had a purpose and was meant to be a certain way. You live your entire life by some crazy Script that no one knows where it came from, and suddenly you're okay with your friend's death because of it!?"

Watters briefly examined the rest of the blank Script oddly before brushing the scroll of his deputy off the table to the floor with a crunch, drawing the other one to him. "I never said I was okay with it; I just said I don't feel as bad for being unable to stop it. I still firmly hold you at fault for it, regardless of whether you were meant to kill him."

"So what, you're going to check your own Script to see if I kill you too?" She indicated the remaining scroll on the table.

"Well, look at you." Watters mocked, faking a smile. "Figured that out all by yourself? Top of your class, were you?"

"I never believed in that stuff anyway," Taylor remarked, ignoring the blatant sarcasm.

"I've seen enough in my time to put my full trust in its words." Watters actually seemed offended at her dismissal of the Script. He tapped a finger at the tail-end of his Script, having skipped directly to it. *"The end of days shall come like the light of the sun on the hottest day, burning all that you hold dear. A supernova of unbelievable glory."* He chuckled a bit. "That sounds like nothing you are capable of doing to me."

"Unless Ahya has some special superpower that I don't know about yet, that would be quite a stretch." Taylor began to laugh at him.

"And that gives me full clearance and authority to do this." Watters pulled his gun from the holster and pointed it directly at her, cocking the hammer slowly.

Taylor's laugh died in her throat with the barrel pointed at her. "So no due process or anything? Just straight up murder? Seems about right around here."

"This would not be murder; this would be executing righteous judgment." He stood up from his chair and took aim at her head. "With no Script to prove you existed, your death would mean nothing and make any follow-on investigation pointless. You are a non-person, and nobody would mourn your passing. Any last words?"

"Yeah... Fuck you and your Script!" Taylor yelled.

Heaving back, thrusting her legs out in front of her, she kicked the table end hard causing it to flip over. It clipped his arm, jerking it down just enough for the gun to misfire in his hoof. The bullet bore a hole through the wood and disappeared into the dirt, causing him to curse.

Taylor cried out when the chair landed hard with a thud on her tail, scrunching the part where it met back into her spine. Gasping at the shock of it, she rolled her whole body, chair and all, to the side, off of Ahya with relief. To her delighted surprise, there was now enough room within the ropes to slip one paw out then the other.

Not wanting to see what Watters would do next, she kicked the chair away from her and rolled around behind the yoke holding Ahya. Another gunshot clipped the top of wood, sending splinters flying over her head. She frantically scoured the room for something to ward him off with or perhaps kill him, but despaired as she heard another cock of his gun.

She yelped as stabbing pain lanced through her tail, blood spurting out the other end. She collapsed to the floor, reaching around the yoke to grip the part of her tail that Watters had shot clean through. Looking up at him, he had a deadly calm to his demeanor, advancing on her position with the cold calculation of a police officer who'd had to do this many times.

"Why make this harder than it has to be? Just enjoy the fact that your pain and suffering finally has come to an end." Watters stood several paces from her, but took measured aim between her eyes.

"I actually would, if it wasn't for the two wolves behind that door." She grinned at his confusion, having kept quiet on the increasing intensity of their scent.

"What are you..." His ears flicked back to the sound of beeping.

The full midsection of the wall imploded inwards with a cacophonous roar. Chunks of rock and plaster sprayed across the room. The heatwave blasted through them both, singing the hair tips on Watter's tail and mane. The shock concussion knocked him to the floor from the sheer impact. An errant hunk of debris knocked him out cold, his gun clattering to the floor.

In stepped the two wolves she had seen earlier. The taller one with the metal arm locked onto her. She bit her lower lip, trying not to let the pain of her bullet wound show. "Can you hand me that keyring on the floor there?" She pointed to the ring that had fallen when she flipped the table.

Regarding her with interest, he went to a knee to pick it up. "I don't know, little lady. Do you intend to run away from us again?"

"Only if you intend to kill me," she fired back without hesitation.

He shrugged his shoulders, standing up. "Fair enough. We were only sent to bring you back alive, not dead."

A shiver of terror flashed through her body at the memory of being incarcerated before, but she fought hard to repress it. "Deal. Just release my tail from this damned thing!"

Without another word, he quickly swept around to the side of the wooden yoke and fiddled with the different keys until he found the one that matched the lock. Unhinging and flipping the metal flaps up, he tossed the upper part up and backed away. Ahya immediately reared high and opened her maw wide, teeth bared and glistening, tongue slithering out to unnatural lengths.

"Trevor…" The smaller wolf edged back towards the bombed opening at the sight of the malevolent tail.

"It'll be all right, Gregor." He looked firmly at Taylor. "We have your word that you won't resist nor eat us?"

"As long as you keep yours of not killing me," she retorted, Ahya giving a few menacing snaps to emphasis the point.

A low groan emerged from between them as all eyes swiveled to Sheriff Watters struggling to regain consciousness from the bleeding wound to his head. "What is going on here?"

"Relieving you of your charge," Trevor said coolly, taking his own gun out and shooting a bullet into each of Watters's kneecaps. The horse whinnied out an agonized cry, clutching his legs at the crimson soaking through his pants. Trevor smirked as he holstered his gun. "Just to make sure you don't follow us. Taylor, come on."

"How do you know my name?" Taylor struggled to stand up, the pain knifing through the base of her tail.

"We're bounty hunters." He motioned with a metal paw, expecting her to follow and for his response to be sufficient for her question.

She hesitantly took his paw and allowed him to lead her out of the interrogation room. Ahya made sure she lashed her tongue out at the knees of Watters, getting a full taste of iron in the process. He brayed at the sudden smack and pressure of the tail's tongue.

"Ugh, Ahya…" Taylor licked her lips and glowered at her tail. "Did you have to do that? I didn't need that."

60

"You will pay for Grunier!" Watters shouted out after them. "You hear me?!" He swore loudly as they rounded the corner out of sight, not bothering to look back at him. She could hear him grunt and then begin speaking with heated breaths—likely into a radio. "All units, all units! We have a 10-98 at Precinct 2 Jail! Three subjects, wolves, one with red hair and monster tail with a mouth, the other two with cybernetic enhancements. Shoot to kill. I repeat, shoot to kill!"

Trevor's ears flicked back as they bolted around the foyer entrance, having reached the end of the hallway. "It sounds like we're in for a bit of a scrap, Gregor."

Gregor leered, swinging the gun strapped across his chest to the front, locking and loading it quickly. "Good. I was hoping to finally see action on this mission."

Taylor's eyes shifted from the automatic weapon each wolf was sporting. They seemed modified with enhanced laser scopes, and had undercarriages that could potentially hold several different types of ammunition. "You don't intend to harm the civilians here, do you?"

"Only if they get in our way," Trevor responded without humor. He glanced briefly at her oozing wound. "Will you be able to keep up?"

"Don't worry about me." She winced, but stood strong. "I'll make it through." She surveyed the room, pointing to a side alcove with huge piles of junk. "Can we stop quickly to pick up a few of my things they took from me?"

"Are you serious?" Gregor was appalled. He began sniffing, looking down the corridor they had emerged from. "It won't be long before we're overrun. We need to move!"

Trevor could hear the footsteps too. He studied Taylor a moment before nodding. "You got thirty seconds. Make it quick! Gregor, you got the front entrance, I'll check the hall!"

They each split and covered their respective positions. Taylor flew to the pile and began scanning the mess of articles the police had confiscated from prisoners, no doubt never to be returned. She saw her pine tree necklace and snatched it from the pile. Letting out a sigh of relief, she spied her cloak with the kitsune doll placed right on top of it. What luck.

"I'm ready!" She furled the cloak around her, not bothering to fasten it around her neck. She stuffed the plush toy deep into an interior pocket then clasped her necklace, affixing it on her breast.

Trevor eyed the articles she had chosen with interest. "Intriguing. Let's get a move on."

His words were interrupted by a barreling rhinoceros cop pounding towards him. Trevor unleashed an entire clip into the beast, pumping the entire assault to the chest and face. At last, the officer uttered an explicative and collapsed to the ground, bleeding out profusely. His eyes stared blankly up at the bounty hunter.

"Did you have to kill him?" Taylor stared at the riddled body.

"He got in our way," Gregor snarked.

"So it begins," Trevor huffed, shooing both Taylor and Gregor out of the police station and into the streets.

The city was abuzz with activity. Sirens were wailing and police lights were rebounding off the walls in near-seizure-inducing frequency. Using the darkness to their advantage, they slipped between two buildings into a cramped alleyway, sidestepping several carts and bins full of compost or feed.

Trevor shot out an arm, causing both of them to halt suddenly. Two police cars hovered past at breakneck speeds, sirens screeching for bystanders to dive for cover. With a nod that the coast was clear, he signaled them to cross the road and back into the shadows of another side street.

"I hope Pine and Mitchell are okay," Taylor said to herself, her eyes catching the stack of crates that signaled the entrance to their former home.

"Who?" Gregor asked irritated, his senses on full alert.

She shook her head at his question. "Just some friends I had made here."

"Well, hopefully they escape from this scrap pile soon, given what I plan to do next." Trevor looked up to the protruding beams that jutted out from the side of the opposing buildings, forming a sort of bastardized staircase to the rooftops. "We climb." He gestured up them.

"What you intend to do next?" Taylor didn't like the sound of that.

"You'll see." There was no tone in his voice for her to infer what he was planning was either good or bad.

Trevor moved to assist Taylor, but looked mildly surprised as she took point and used Ahya to grip the beams and work her way up the building—her years living on her own and evading the local law enforcement paying off. She stumbled slightly at reaching the top, rolling to break her fall on the rooftop. "We need to stop. I can't go on like this."

"I thought you could keep up?" Gregor ribbed.

"I can, but I need a few moments." Taylor rejoined.

Trevor said nothing, but pulled out a small device from his utility pants as he watched her. She shifted onto her thigh and flipped open her cloak to look back and get a good view of her seeping injury. Stifling a small whimper, she allowed Ahya to curl in on herself so the maw could extend and coil its tongue around the base of her tail where she had been struck.

"What is it doing?" Trevor looked fascinated.

"If you don't want a blood trail to give us away to the police here, let her do her thing!" She panted, the entire process stinging something fierce.

The maw's tongue was pulsating, getting more slick and wet with each constriction around its own base. The ground started to dampen at the sheer amount of saliva that was dripping off the tongue. A look of respite washed over Taylor's face as the tongue loosened and retracted back into the darkness of the tail.

"What in the name of the gods?" Trevor's eyes bulged upon studying her tail. The blotch of deep scarlet was gone, along with the hole that had pierced it clean through. "It's fully healed?"

Taylor nodded wearily, petting her tail softly before flapping the cloak back over her legs. "Yeah, one of the few things she is good for."

Even Gregor seemed awed by this interesting display of power. "Trevor, none of the others we've seen had any sort of healing powers…"

"No, they did not," he responded cryptically.

Feeling much better, Taylor got back up to her feet and looked back and forth between them. "So how do you propose we get out of here?" The revolving lights were practically everywhere in the town now. From their vantage point, they could see no less than twenty sets of car lights illuminating the city like a fireworks show.

Snapped back to reality, he gave her an unsettling smile. "Like this."

He pushed a button, and she crouched to the ground by instinct as shockwave after shockwave slammed into their building. Huge pyres of molten flames billowed skyward into expanding clouds of fiery ash and sand. Multiple buildings went up in explosive pyrotechnics, lighting up the desert all around the town for miles.

"What the hell was that?!" Taylor screamed, her sense of reality coming back after the first blast. She ran over to the edge and looked out over Palaveve, now in flames. "I thought you said you wouldn't hurt any of the citizens?"

"I did, except they are what stand between us and getting out of here." He motioned towards the southern entrance to town a mere six blocks away. "Notice how there are no buildings destroyed that way. I've used the rest of the town as a distraction for our escape. Now follow or get tranquilized and dragged!"

Without waiting for her cry of protest at his methods, he began making the leaps from rooftop to rooftop. She begrudgingly alighted across the gaps behind them. Gregor kept a watchful eye on her from time to time, but she was obedient in tailing them since she had nowhere else to go but with them. They met little resistance all the way to the gate.

"Crap, I was afraid of this." Trevor stopped suddenly, his eyes looking skyward over the town wall.

All their ears flicked to the south as a dull roar lanced the night air. Compressed air shattered the glass of any buildings which had proper windows. The entire earth beneath them trembled with each pound of hydraulic monstrosity. They could hear the rising cries of the townspeople as everyone recognized the sounds and what they heralded.

"Afraid of this?" Taylor slapped Trevor across the arm, eliciting a growl from the hunter. "You lit the entire damn town like a freaking beacon, and you didn't think this would happen?"

"Our rides are just outside. We need to move, now!" Gregor whined, the pounding getting louder.

"I was told to secure you by any means possible." Trevor's voice turned cold for once, forcefully ripping his arm away from her touch. "I intend to do exactly that."

"Hey! You can't be here!" They turned to see two boars in uniform exiting the guard house built into the tower parapets flanking the gate. "We have a level-five emergency in town. You are ordered to return to your—"

Not waiting for them to finish, Gregor raised his gun and put three bullets into both their foreheads. They wilted like flowers. Their lives were snuffed out, their bodies hitting the ground before they realized they were dead.

"You guys are bastards, you know that?" Taylor remarked, cringing at the senseless death of the two boars just doing their duty.

"You can call us plenty of names later. If you don't wish to die, then we move!" Trevor roared, grabbing Taylor by the wrist and yanking her along, causing a near-violent reaction from Ahya.

Tumbling out the archway to the wide-open darkness of the desert beyond, they all stared at the horror approaching the town. It was light enough to make out a huge shape of metallic sheen lumbering toward Palaveve, but any details were shrouded in shadow. Each step of its gargantuan legs was accompanied by an incessant clanking of gears and visible bursts of steam blowing out of its individual joints.

"What the hell is that thing?" Taylor gaped, still being pulled towards the twin motorcycles parked in a small rack for such vehicles.

"You've never seen one of these things before?!" Gregor shouted to be heard over the rising din, kneeling to unchain both their bikes from the rack.

"I've heard them roving outside town once in a while and seen some newscasts on them, but I never went out to see it myself." She marveled in terror at the size of it. It had to be at least five wall-heights taller than the existing border around Palaveve. How could something so massive even exist?

"We can talk about that thing later! Taylor, you'll be getting on behind me. Hold on tight, I will not be slowing down!" he ordered, swinging a leg over and revving up the engine.

Hopping on the seat behind him, she wrapped two arms around his midsection, Ahya curling around them both to stay out of the way. Gregor noted they were ready and rallied them. "We head east. Keep your lights off! The last thing we need is that thing to notice us!"

They gunned their bikes, and in a flash they were kicking up sand as they zipped down the road away from town. Taylor chanced a look back and saw that the colossal beast had reached the city. She could hear the screams of the horrified populace. No doubt all of them were able to see what was hovering about their city.

"It's getting ready!" Trevor yelled into the wind, trying to push as much juice from his motorcycle as he could get.

The creature's head began to split open, revealing an intense corona of light, dazzling the scenery as if it was daytime. Its entire face contorted and elongated into what looked like the barrel of a cannon aimed directly at the center of town. Arcing bolts of flame began swirling around the face, a rising hum filling the air until it thumped their eardrums with the clap of explosive thunder.

"No!" Taylor shrieked.

In a split second, a beam of pure light shot from the creature's maw, hitting the center of Palaveve. There was a flash of darkness and a moment of silence for a mere whisper before the entire town went up in a rising mushroom cloud of morbid glory. The initial shockwave continued to spread, demolishing anything in its path like it was tissue paper.

"Keep going!" Gregor panicked.

They could feel the rumbling beneath their motorcycles, increasing in force the closer the concussive pulse got. Each of them kept an uneasy eye on the chasing storm of hellfire, hoping their bikes would be faster than their impending doom.

At last, the surging destruction ceased just mere meters from their rear tires, but the cloud continued to rise into the air, forming an almost grisly skull in its puffy clouds of ash and flame. They wheeled their vehicles around to a halt, each stopping to gaze upon the sight. The entire town of Palaveve was completely wiped off the face of the planet. Every citizen was dead.

Taylor released Ahya's grip around Trevor and hopped off the bike, take a few running strides back towards the town. "Pine! Mitchell!" she cried out.

"What the hell she doing?" Gregor looked like he was going to use force to bring her back.

Trevor raised a paw to stay his partner's ire. "Let her grieve, Gregor. She needs this moment."

"Mrs. Hircus..." Taylor wept, flopping to the ground in a heap.

Every good soul she'd met since coming here was gone, wiped clean in a single moment of incinerating death. What made it worse was the fact she was the cause of all their deaths. If she hadn't stayed as long as she did in Palaveve, she wouldn't have gotten caught by Watters, Trevor and Gregor wouldn't have had to destroy the town getting her out, and no one would have provoked the beast to nuke them to oblivion. This was on her conscience now.

She wiped her eyes furiously, Ahya doing her best to lick her tears and comfort Taylor. Did Mrs. Hircus know this was going to happen? She was adamant about respecting the Script. Did she consult it, and know her death was today? Was that why Mrs. Hircus helped her out the way she did? Wanting one last hug before accepting her final fate? Was there anything she could have done to change any of it? Were people doomed the moment the Script said so?

Taylor slapped the sand hard, flinging fistfuls of it up into the air. She screamed into the darkness, her rage and anger of what her own life had wrought. Neither bounty hunter stopped her as she continued to unleash her anger into the night, and the monster in the distance paid her no mind as it closed up its face and slowly began its interrupted journey to the south, its sounds fading over time.

"We need to go. I need to take you back." Trevor made a motion to pick her off her feet.

"Take me back to where? To who?" she rounded on him, Ahya enlarging herself and making a lunge for him, intending to swallow him whole.

"Whoa! Easy there!" His quick reflexes saved his life as the maw chomped down just inches from his head. Hopping back several paces, gun out and pointed at her, he ordered, "Stand down, Taylor. My orders were to bring you back alive and unspoiled. My intention is not to hurt you."

"Oh yeah? Then who are you bringing me to? What plans does he have for me, huh?" She was bordering near hysteria. The entire night's events had finally caused her patience to snap. "Was it worth all this death?"

"I will explain on the way, just calm down." Trevor put one paw up to show that he was trying to be reasonable about this.

"The only people left in my life who cared about me died in that explosion! You brought this on Palaveve! Both of you!" She pointed at both of them, advancing on Gregor with a grim determination to have Ahya eat him first.

Trevor sighed. "Tranquilizer it is."

He aimed and fired. Taylor was down before she realized the dart had hit her neck in the jugular. The last thing she remembered before falling asleep was Trevor lifting her up and plopping her limp body over his bike.

4
CAPTORS

Taylor moaned, the jostle of the road bumping her out of her stupor. She was bound to Trevor with her arms around his stomach, her wrists tied yet again in ropes. She looked around, only seeing vast stretches of desert around them. The heat of the afternoon sun had baked the dirt into caked and cracked pieces. The only spot of color was the shimmering mirage of green seemingly miles ahead of them.

Gregor was first of the two to notice Ahya languidly moving behind, the effects of the tranquilizer still coursing through the tail.

Trevor glanced back with a smile. "Good morning, sunshine! Or should I say evening? You've been sleeping almost an entire day!"

"Where are we?" Her voice was groggy.

Trevor shrugged. "Several-hundred miles northeast of what's left of Palaveve. We're heading towards our destination, but we first have to make it through the Falhoven forest between those mountain ranges." He pointed forward, raising his metal arm a bit for her to get a peek.

Taylor turned around as best she could, but she could not see any remains of Palaveve or the cloud that had blossomed from it the previous night. Aggrieved, she faced forward and thumped her head on Trevor's bare back, his scarf blowing in the wind just past her ear. Mixed emotions came flooding back. She didn't know how to feel. It seemed like her entire life was out of her control yet again, and there was nothing she could do about it.

"What do you plan to do with me?" she said lifelessly.

Although she'd said it softly, Trevor's keen ears picked her words up. "Personally? Nothing. I am under contract to bring you back to my employer. We've been tracking you for a very long time, Taylor."

"Are you sure it's wise to be talking to her about our business?"

"It'll be fine, Gregor." He let go of a handle to pat the paws tied around his middle before returning it to the steering. "I wouldn't trust us either. So I feel it best to make clear our intentions and get Taylor's cooperation, because I'd much rather have a willing charge come with us than haul an unconscious body back. Lot less hassle that way."

Taylor looked up at the back of Trevor's head. "Does that mean you'll untie my hands?"

"Only if you are agreeable with our company, otherwise I have no recourse but to pump you with another tranquilizer. Does that sound like a good time to you?"

"No, it doesn't." She slumped her forehead back onto his shoulder blades.

"It won't be much longer before we stop for the night. Just hang on tight and we'll be bedding down soon enough," he reassured.

Taylor's eyes glazed as she numbly watched the passing dullness of the desert, a random cactus or bush breaking the monotony of the scenery. Time seemed to stretch to an infinity while holding onto Trevor, and her own wrists ached something fierce. Every shift to get more comfortable resulted in the tightening of her bonds, so she abandoned the effort.

The flat ground shifted and grew uneven the further they drove. The road began to sink below the level of the rising rock on either side. It was still a good distance off, but it was now clearer that the forest which was their current objective was actually resting on a higher shelf of earth than the route they were traveling on now. She wondered when the road would rise back up, or if there was some cave underneath the forest they might be going to instead.

Taylor considered having Ahya swallow Trevor down to her arms, jerking him off the motorcycle and throwing him far. Though as she thought it through, even if she managed to get rid of him, that wouldn't solve the problem of actually driving the thing—let alone what Gregor would do if she tried. She just sighed.

The sun was setting beyond the elevated horizon when they pulled underneath an overhang that nearly connected the two rock walls together into an arch of eroded majesty. Trevor and Gregor shut the engines off and slapping the kickstands out with their hind paws, then lined their bikes up side by side.

Trevor assisted Taylor in awkwardly maneuvering off the motorcycle with her arms still tied around his waist. Holding her wrist firmly in one paw, he dipped low and beneath them before pivoting on the spot to grip her firmly so she wouldn't escape. Ahya threatened him with her maw, but did not make a lunge for his head.

"Is she going to be nice tonight?" He motioned with his chin towards the tail.

"I'm holding her back right now," Taylor replied swiftly, keeping a straight face.

"You certain didn't hold back with that poor wombat!" Gregor chuckled, unhooking the sleeping bag on the back of his bike and unrolling it with a shake.

"Both Ahya and I were hungry." Taylor glared at him. "We had been for several days. She was starving and she got the better of me then."

"Interesting." Trevor looked at her with curiosity. "So you can't always control it?"

"Not always, no." She avoided his intense gaze. She was not used to being scrutinized this way; it had been a long time since she had been the center of attention. She rather preferred anonymity.

Trevor inspected the surrounding rock formations and pointed at an outcropping projecting out from the base of the arch. "We'll build a fire in the nook between that rock and the wall. It'll hide our light from all but this direction, making it easier for us to keep watch on the road."

He made to move Taylor to where their campsite would be when she stopped him to ask, "Are you going to untie me?" She lifted her paws up to him, giving him a pleading look. "I am being agreeable."

He smirked at her subtle cheek. "Not quite yet, missy. We still need to settle down for the night, and then we can talk more about your living circumstances. I am on business here first and foremost, not to ensure you are comfortable."

She pouted at his refusal of her request as he led her to a place to sit and be quiet. She plopped her back against the rock and stared at the two wolves getting their bed spreads ready. She noted that there wasn't one for her. Probably just as well, since they probably only planned out this journey for the two of them, and her consideration didn't factor into their preparations.

Her line of sight extended down the barren road. She knew there wasn't much back the way they came, and going forward there wasn't much in the way of cover. If she tried to make a run for it, she would not be able to get very far. Trevor would most likely be pumping her with a few darts to the back, and gods knew when she'd wake up then—and where for that matter.

As if on cue, Trevor sauntered over and knelt down to flip out a knife from his side strap sheathe on his leg. With a swift motion, he cut the binds in two, allowing her to move them freely and rub her raw wrists.

"If you haven't figured it out by now, there isn't anywhere you can run. So it would be best if you would just follow my orders, and the trip back will go much smoother." He clapped his knees, satisfied, and slipped the knife back into its holder. Rising up, he lowered a paw to assist her up. "You hungry?"

Waving off his gesture of chivalry, she got up to her hind paws on her own. Now that he mentioned it, she was starting to feel a glimmer of hunger in her belly. She sniffed a few times and scrunched her nose in disgust. "Smells like meat."

Trevor winked at her. "Of course! You can't get stuff this good back in the cities, considering how highly restricted it is for us predators." He turned and walked back to the fire, now lit and gaining intensity, expecting her to follow. "Out here in the middle of nowhere, there is nobody to enforce the rules, so we're taking advantage of it now."

Taylor could sense Ahya's mouth watering, but she could not stand the taste of meat. It reminded her too much of the people she had eaten. She put a paw up to reject his offer. "I can't eat that."

Gregor was already in the throes of bliss as he tore a piece of muscle off the jerky slice he had skewered on the end of a stick. "You what?" he asked with his mouth full. "What you mean you can't eat meat? Of course you can! You're a wolf, aren't you?" He dove in for another bite.

Trevor sat down next to the fire to get his piece, using his small rucksack from his bike as a seat. He stared at her patiently, waiting for her response. Looking back and forth between them, she sighed. "I've just not been very fond of meat. Reminds me too much of how Ahya kills. I much prefer fruit or vegetables. Do you have any of those?" She glanced at their sacks hopefully.

"I might have an apple or two," Trevor said thoughtfully, digging into his bag. "Ah-ha!" he exclaimed happily, taking not just an apple, but a pear as well. "I was saving these for a bit later, but you can have them now."

He tossed both of them her way. Ahya swooshed in from the rear and snatched the pear out of the air. It took fast reflexes on Taylor's part to make a dive for the apple before it was scooped up by the slithering tongue of her tail, already at full length and whipping around to snag the delectable morsels.

Gregor fell back and scooted away from Taylor, the focus on his meal gone. "Gods! That thing actually does grow bigger when it's hungry! Is that normal?!"

Indeed, the tail had nearly doubled in size within seconds when she went for the fruit. To accentuate the point, she had already receded back to a normal size that was only conspicuous due to its red fur. Without missing a beat, Taylor paid her tail no mind and sat down next to the fire, crossing her legs and taking a bite of her apple.

"When she wants to, sure. I haven't tested how big she can get, but she has managed to surprise me before." She happily took another bite of her fruit, enjoying the terrified reactions of Gregor.

"You keep calling it a 'she'." Trevor pointed out. "It's just a tail."

Taylor stopped and rested the apple in her lap as she gave thought to his observation. "I don't know. I've always just felt that's what she was. I don't seem to remember much about my childhood growing up, but I do remember the day I named her."

In response to her story, Ahya poked her head underneath Taylor's arm, putting her maw on her lap. Its tongue snuck out in a coy attempt at snagging what was left of the apple. Seeing through the ruse,

Taylor held it up high, enjoying a third bite. The tail visibly seemed to droop with disappointment, and proceeded to just lie there like a wounded animal hoping for some sympathy that was never to come.

Seemingly unfazed by this interaction with her abnormal tail, Taylor kept going. "She was getting more unruly and harder to control by the day. I think it was my fifth birthday, yet I remember it so clearly. She never had a name before then, it was just my tail. However, for my birthday wish that night, I asked for the power to control her and make her do what I wanted. That's when the name, Ahya, came to me. Ever since naming her, she has been far easier to manage. I think that's all she wanted, was to be recognized as someone different than just my tail."

Trevor smiled at this story. "You are certainly a wolf of many surprises, Taylor." He took another bite of his jerky, making sure to finish it before speaking again. "I won't lie when I said I was more than interested in taking this bounty to come find you. Now that I've met you, I'm glad I accepted the job."

Finishing off her apple, she licked her muzzle. "I can't fathom why. If it isn't you, it's always someone else after me. It has been that way ever since I was a young teen. I…" She hesitated, her mind lost in thought at trying to remember. "I recall my mother trying her best to keep us safe from whoever was chasing us. We moved around a lot, never staying in one place for very long." She sighed. "I guess I haven't changed much since then."

Gregor inched back to the fire, keeping a wide berth from Taylor and her tail. Not surprising, since he had already seen once that it could swallow a mammal whole and digest it within minutes. He picked back up his stick of jerky and fastidiously wiped the sand off of it, frustrated it had gotten dirty.

"Well, to be frank, I was surprised myself when Trevor took the job. We don't really do escort missions." Gregor gave a test lick to his meat to ensure it was still good.

"Yeah, you two seem to be more of the seek and destroy sort of people." Taylor smiled.

"Well, you are not wrong there." Trevor returned the humor.

Taylor let Ahya continue to rest on her legs. Leaning back onto her paws to hold her up, she regarded the iron forearm and pauldrons.

"What about you? What do you call your paw there? Does it have a name?"

"What are you... This?" Trevor was confused at first. His ears turned back in irritation when Gregor caught on first to the joke and began laughing at him. "This is not a living thing. I lost my hand in an accident when going after another bounty." He shifted it away from her view. "Besides, it now has far more utility and use than my previous one did anyway."

Taylor had to giggle at this; she had finally found a crack in this tough wolf's armor. "Fair is fair. You're both talking about how much of a freak my tail can be, yet I can't do the same about your odd attachments?"

"Noted," Trevor conceded. "Good to see you warming up to us at least."

Her expression turned serious. "I wouldn't say that. I'm just accepting my current situation until I find a better one."

"Is that a threat of an escape?" Gregor looked eager for another hunt.

"Not at the moment." Her voice did not betray the concern that her escape may not last long, even if she was brave enough to try it.

"Good. I'd like to keep it that way." Trevor matched her expression. "It has taken a long time to find you, and to be honest, I'm ready to be home and relax with my well-earned money."

"And you don't care what happens to me after you turn me in to your employer?" Being wanted dead was one thing, but to specifically ask to be returned not just alive but unspoiled? That brought all sorts of bad implications.

Trevor scratched his face scars, seeming to ponder how best to answer her question. "Normally, I don't. It is not my concern what my employer wants of my bounties. I do the job I was hired for and I get paid. The rest is on him...or her."

Picking up on what he said earlier, Taylor questioned, "You said before you were interested in taking on this bounty to come find me. So clearly you have some vested purpose in finding me. Why?"

"Trevor?" There was a tone in Gregor's voice that indicated there was more to the answer she was asking for than he wanted to reveal.

Giving his buddy a sidelong look, he focused back on Taylor. "You are a most unique specimen. I can say with certainty that I have not seen another wolf quite like you in all my years. Upon meeting you, I was actually glad for once that my orders were not to harm you."

"Yet you still caught me in a net that electrified me every time I moved," she rebounded, giving him a playful stink-eye.

"Well…" He ruffled the fur on the back of his neck. "I didn't really have time to explain my motives to you, and it was just easier to capture you first and sort things out later. Unfortunately, not everything went to plan."

"An entire town didn't go to plan…" Taylor's mood turned sour. The thought of Mrs. Hircus, Pine, and Mitchell being gone caused her to get angry again.

Both Trevor and Gregor's paws went to their holsters, prepared in case Taylor lashed out at them again. "Are we going to have a problem over this again?" Trevor queried carefully.

She saw their body language and shook her head. "No… I'll be good." Their paws slowly returned to their meals. "I still don't trust either of you though," she added as a bitterly snarky afterthought.

Trevor guffawed at this, causing Taylor to lower her ears. "As I'd expect you not to! I wouldn't trust us either after what we've put you through!" He snickered a bit, wiping a tear from his eye. "It's part of the job, hun. No hard feelings."

"Tell that to the thousands dead in Palaveve." Her eyes bore holes into the two of them.

"It was an unfortunate consequence of securing you, Taylor," Trevor reasoned.

"There was no reason for any of them to die." She fumed, bringing her knees up to her chin and wrapping her arms around them, forcing Ahya off her lap.

"Maybe it was just their time to die," Gregor offered sympathetically.

"What?!" Taylor snarled, getting ready to engage.

"Gregor, stand down." Trevor put out a paw to order his companion to back off. "I think what my friend here meant was that maybe they were fated by the Script to die." He explained.

Taylor clicked her tongue in disgust. "Ugh, that again? That is a bunch of nonsense. Not once in my entire life did that ever dictate anything that happened to me. I can't believe anyone would believe in something they cannot explain."

Gregor seemed ruffled at her blatant dismissal of his belief. "I've always lived by the Script and it has never steered me wrong."

"So if it told you that you were to die today, you would just lie down and accept that?" She fired back.

Gregor took a bite of his meat, thinking. "I've known several buddies who tried to fight their Script, and no matter what they did, it always ended up the same. If the Script told them they would die by a piano dropping on their heads, they would go out of their way to avoid any and all pianos. They still died by one regardless. It's impossible to fight against it."

"And you?" She swiveled to Trevor. "Do you follow your Script?"

He seemed pretty indifferent about it. "I don't even bother paying the church to read mine to me. I'd prefer not to know what is to come next; ruins the entire surprise of life if you ask me."

Pacified by his answer, Taylor relaxed a bit. "I don't even know where they came from. I had never paid much attention to such things growing up. It never really was important until recently."

"I don't either," Trevor admitted. "They are just things that exist. Why should I bother questioning what is? The Script has been part of life since I was a young cub. I knew about it, I was schooled on it, and I even went to weekend chapel with my parents to have their Script read. If nothing I do will change what will happen to me, then why bother to learn about the future at all? I figured it was best just to ignore it and live my life without that deep-seated fear of what was to come."

"Then you are a far braver wolf than others I've seen." Taylor commented.

"Hey, I resent that remark!" Gregor exclaimed with mouth full.

"Thanks for the compliment, Taylor." Trevor chuckled at his friend's displeasure.

"Wasn't meant to be one," she clarified.

"I'll take it nonetheless." He shook his head, smiling as he turned back to finish off the rest of his jerky.

Rolling his eyes, Gregor finished up his meal, smacking his lips. "We should hit the sack if we want to get an early start tomorrow. We have a lot of ground to cover."

Trevor exhaled, exhaustion hitting him suddenly. "Yeah, we probably have many more days yet to ride."

"Where are we going?" Taylor was curious.

"From what I know of…your file, somewhere you've been," he responded without much inflection.

Taylor was confused, but didn't press the issue. She couldn't think of any particular places she had been to where they could be taking her. Was it somewhere she had run away from? If so, then she might be taken back to the very same people who captured her last time and performed so many hurtful experiments on her. Things she could scarcely remember, but were still so vivid on the fringes of her mind.

They had begun to get up and gather their belongings to settle in for the evening when Taylor called out to Trevor. "Hey, that…thing back at Palaveve. What was that thing?"

He started at her for a few moments. "We don't know. They've been appearing more recently in the past decade, and seem to be traveling farther north with each passing year. Gregor and I tend to avoid them when we are doing our job. Seeing what they can do, it is best we keep a low profile and not draw too much attention to ourselves."

"Does anyone know what those things are?" she pressed.

Gregor chimed in. "Some say they are from a country far to the south, but I've never heard of anything natural being that huge. They look artificially constructed. The local militias have attempted and failed to bring one down. So the consensus is just to avoid and leave them alone."

"It doesn't seem like that'll stop them from doing what they did to Palaveve." Taylor still had that vision of the mushroom cloud lucid in her mind.

"All the more reason to get you back to my employer soon," Trevor said, his tone indicating the conversation was over.

A sudden chill enveloped Taylor as Ahya instinctively wrapped herself around Taylor's shoulders. She looked around and wondered where she was going to sleep. The fact that there were only two spreads was making it abundantly clear that this might end up being a miserable night.

Trevor noticed her anxious look and smiled, shaking his head. "Come on, Taylor." He beckoned her over to his sleeping bag. Her look was a mixture of horror and embarrassment as he indicated his roll. "Oh, I didn't mean for you to share it with me. I meant, just take it. I'll take first watch and when it's Gregor's time, we'll just swap out with his bag."

"Aw, come on! Really?" Gregor whined. "You know I hate having anyone else in my bag!"

"You'll survive." Trevor rolled his eyes, then turned back to Taylor. "So, did you want to take my bag or not?"

Emphatically sweeping past him, she immediately slipped into the insulated fabric. "Yes!" She wiggled down deep until her toes touched the base, Ahya struggling to stuff most of her bulk in alongside Taylor.

"Well, don't let me try to convince you." He rested a paw on his hip, clearly having expected more resistance. He shrugged, picked up his gun, and slung the strap around his shoulder before taking up his position opposite Taylor, his eyes lingering on her prone form. "You know this night watch is just as much making sure you don't escape as it is for our protection, right?"

"I'm aware." She returned his stare.

They sat in silence for a time, the fire crackling between them. The sun's lingering rays had turned to darkness, Gregor's snoring could be softly heard. Taylor snorted as she shook her head at him. He could fall asleep amazingly fast.

Aside from Gregor, it was deathly quiet in their small, arched shelter. Usually there was some wildlife sounds even in the dead of night when Taylor was in Palaveve. Out here, there was nothing. It was unnerving, making her ears flick this way and that at the slightest sound.

At length, she spoke quietly. "Do you enjoy what you do?"

It took Trevor a moment to realize she was talking to him. "Bounty hunting? Not always, no." He let his gun hang down in front of his chest as he set his stump of an elbow on his knee, flexing the metal fingers, letting the clack of their gears accentuate the silence. "Some days I wonder why I chose to get into this profession, but then I remember times are tough and the world isn't what it used to be anymore."

"Was it ever better?" Taylor ruminated.

"It actually was…" He cracked a smile. "I was young once."

She blinked a moment before catching onto his joke. "Yeah, you're pretty old."

He curled his lip, but realized it quickly. His expression falling, he said, "Ha ha, but if I'm honest with myself, I wish I could turn back time and do things differently."

Taylor rose up, resting on her forearm as she listened. "Like what things?"

He eyed his sleeping companion. "I used to be a big city cop before." Taylor's brow rose at this revelation, but she remained silent. "I was proud to serve my city and defend its citizens. Then the corruption began to seep through the cracks, and what was so unyielding became malleable and fluid."

At a tilt of Taylor's head, he expounded. "The seed of crime in the gutters of the city had risen all the way to the top tiers of leadership. It was all one big joke." He shook his head. "I find myself freer than ever before doing this job. I don't have any law to answer to and I can enjoy my freedom, but even this job isn't safe from corruption either. It's just one vicious circle of lies. So I have to chart my path in-between them as best I can."

Taylor could understand his feelings. She was never one for government or law; all they wanted to do was capture her, torture her, or kill her. She didn't have any fond memories of any leader figures. The only one that resonated with her even today was her mother, Murana, as foggy of a memory of her as it was.

"I'm sorry, Trevor." She meant it.

He bristled a bit for getting too heated. "Don't worry about it. It is my burden to bear. You should get some sleep. I'll be watching over us."

She went to say something more, but the furnace that was Ahya was convincing her to fall back into her tail's embrace and just relish in the warmth. She couldn't remember the last time she had been in such a warm cover. Within a few short minutes, she was fast asleep to the crackle of fire.

"Taylor." A squeaky voice chirped in her ear. She murmured and tried to roll over onto her sleeping back, her face melting into the fluffy fur of her tail. "Taylor!" the small voice hissed.

"Go away…" She attempted to take the top of the bag and pull it over her head.

"Taylor! It's me, Pine!" The skunk tried to nuzzle into the opening between her and the fabric to nip at her neck.

The name sparked her awake. She flipped over and checked on Trevor and Gregor. Their transition of the guard had already occurred. Trevor was sleeping while Gregor was doing a poor job of keeping watch. He was dozing off sitting beside the fire, his chest leaning on his gun as it was standing up butt down on the ground.

Shifting onto her stomach, she rose to eye level to the two critters sitting expectantly in front of her. Ahya was either completely oblivious to their presence or just didn't care enough to be happy at their reunion. She put a finger to her muzzle to show them to be quiet.

"How did you two get here? We must be miles away from Palaveve by now! I thought you two had died in the explosion." Tears began to form at the edges of her eyes and she reached out to hug them.

Without much prompting, Pine and Mitchell flew into her arms, creating an awkward mess of cuddles, fur, and limbs. Ahya grew irritated at the disturbance, clapping her teeth a few times to express her displeasure of Taylor moving so suddenly and filling out the sleeping bag to almost cramped proportions.

She had to keep shushing them. They couldn't stop giggling. "You two need to be quiet or you're going to get in trouble with those two." She held both firm and forced them to look at Trevor and Gregor.

"Who are these wolves?" Mitchell asked.

"Are they bad people?" Pine apprehensively cuddled closer to Taylor's breast.

"I'm not sure," she expressed truthfully.

She really wasn't. On one hand, she didn't actually trust Gregor at all. He seemed more focused on the job at hand and didn't make any attempt to get to know her any better. In fact, he seemed perfectly happy ignoring her and letting Trevor do all the talking. Trevor, on the other paw, was something of an enigma to Taylor. He was courteous to her, but there was a distance and focus on ensuring she knew where her place was in this. He also had a lack of empathy for others and didn't care for those he had injured or killed.

"They won't hurt me. That much I do know." She assured them. "However, they don't know who you are and I'm afraid if they figure out how important you two are to me, they might use that as leverage against me and then things could get ugly."

Mitchell nodded knowingly. "I understand, Taylor. You want us out of sight, following you at a distance?"

She bit her lower lip, undecided. "I think that would be best. It's just a relief to know you are nearby and alive."

"But we just got here and we're starving and thirsty!" Pine whimpered, his tiny paws clawing at her necklace strap.

Taylor noticed how dusty they were and the mess they were making in her sleeping bag. "Oh my gosh, I'm so sorry! You two must have been trailing us this entire time with nothing! How did you survive?"

"It wasn't easy," Mitchell admitted, slowly crawling out of the bag.

"Do they have anything we could take?" Pine suggested, the thought of food in his belly getting the better of his timid nature.

"Unless you two like meat jerky, I'm not sure if they have any more fruits left in their bags. I do know they have some canteens of water strapped to their bikes." She gazed over the campfire at the dark shapes parked up against the rock face.

"That actually sounds good!" they both agreed in unison.

"Of course. I should have known better." She shook her head in exasperation. "Alright, get out of my bag. Let me help you procure some sustenance." She shared a grin with Mitchell.

"Just like old times?" he offered.

"Old times?" She chuckled. "You barely went out with me when I stole food, and when I was better at it, you two sat on your laurels and let me do all the work."

"Details." Mitchell waved a paw, hiding his mirth.

"You cheeky little...hey!" She was tugged back by Ahya, who was using all her weight to stay warm within the sleeping bag, causing an awkward situation where Taylor wanted to walk forward but couldn't.

"What's wrong with her?" Pine peeked around Taylor's legs to look at the obstinate tail.

"She's being difficult!" Taylor put both her paws on her tail and yanked hard, causing Ahya to bare her fangs.

If she had vocal chords, she could have been growling. As it was, it was a silent display of menace that was just the right amount of creepy because it had no sound accompanying it. Impervious to Ahya's threats, Taylor stood her ground. She was confident that her tail would not harm her. It became very clear growing up that Ahya harming the very body she was attached to was a bad idea, especially since everything Taylor felt could be felt by Ahya, including pain.

"Are you quite done?" She stared down the faceless mouth.

At length, the tail licked its lips in a pouting fashion and conceded defeat, allowing to be waved behind as Taylor went about her business. She could express her irritation all she wanted, but Taylor was the master of this ship and she was going to sail it where she wanted tonight.

"Now follow me and be quiet." She motioned them to stay close to her heels.

Gregor hadn't moved much from his unusual sleeping position since the appearance of Pine and Mitchell. Carefully tiptoeing around the edge of the fire, she sneaked over to one of the knapsacks placed precariously close to Trevor. She knew that there might be some food left in there.

Squatting next to it, she opened the top flap, not accounting for the metal buckle that usually kept it locked closed. It clapped loudly against the backside of the pack and elicited a snort from Trevor only a few feet away. Staying completely still, she watched as he rolled over to face her, eyes still closed. He wiggled a bit more to get comfortable again. It was a long tense minute to see if he'd wake and see her.

With the small scare passing, Taylor rummaged through the bag and only found a few scraps of unfinished jerky that seemed to have been cooked well before tonight. She grimaced at the sight of such a paltry amount. Immediately feeling guilty that she ate the last two pieces of fruit, she plucked out the meat and turned to her friends, holding them out.

"I'm sorry there isn't much left." Her heart went to them and their crestfallen faces.

"It's okay, Taylor. We can't expect a buffet when we're on the road and they don't know we're tagging along," Mitchell said, trying to appear cheerful.

She nodded, unsure if they blamed her for enjoying the food from earlier, even if they had no way of knowing what she ate. With a paw, she motioned for them to follow her to the bikes. The two of them happily tore into the small strips, trying their best to tear off pieces of over-dried meat to chew.

Using her natural night vision to spy the canteens tied to the bikes, she unhooked one and twirled open the top. She handed it first to Pine, who seemed to be making grabby paws for it. He immediately overturned it and began gulping profusely, water splashing everywhere, making a complete mess.

"Would you try and be careful? I swear, you can't ever drink properly!" Taylor decided to hold the container for him, ensuring he got the perfect flow into his mouth. Even then, he had some dribbling out the sides of his mouth. "Now, your turn." She moved the canteen to

Mitchell and assisted him too. "Seriously? Not you too!" She groaned, watching the water spill with him as well.

After drinking his fill, Mitchell wiped the droplets from his mouth. "We've been traveling hard this past day! Sorry if our manners are not up to snuff!" He was very polite about it.

Studying the two dark splotches in the dirt, she shook her head before getting a healthy dose herself. She took great care not to spill any. She had been meaning to put it back when Pine reached out for it again.

"You are insatiable!" She laughed softly, lowering it back down for him.

He mistimed the grab and it slipped from Taylor's hands, rattling on the ground harshly. She cursed, trying to pick it up quickly before it made too much noise and it lost all its water. The sound was enough to startle Gregor awake, his eyelids sleepily opening as he looked around for the source of the disturbance. He locked on to her and stood up swiftly, gun aimed at her.

"Hey! What are you doing?" He roared, getting Trevor to bound up from his sleeping bag.

"Run," she whispered to Pine and Mitchell.

They immediately scattered into the darkness, hopefully unseen by either captor. She prayed the light of the fire between them interfered with the night vision she knew they had as well. Gregor advanced on her, Trevor shifting out and joining his comrade.

"Taylor, I thought we talked about this." He readied his gun, prepared to shoot her back to sleep. "I will drag you all the way back to my employer if I have to."

She raised both paws in supplication, making the canteen very visible in one. "I was just thirsty and wanting a drink."

Trevor looked down at the mess around her feet. "Freaking hell." He swiped the water from her, causing Ahya to snap. She held her tail back from doing anything rash; now would not be a good time to lash out. "This was supposed to last us until we got to the next watering hole." He secured the cap back on.

"Aren't we close to that forest down the road?" Taylor looked down the path, the haze of night making the outline of the woods a bit blurry and muddled.

"Not with fresh water," Gregor snapped. "Lots of pond scum and junk. We'd have to purify the water first, and we have no more iodine tablets!"

Trevor put a paw on Gregor's quivering gun arm, forcing him to slowly lower it. "That and it is still several days ride from here. We need to conserve what's left of the water. We can purify what we need in the forest, even if it isn't ideal." He sidestepped around Taylor, tying the canteen back onto his bike. Facing her, he pointed back to her bedding. "Next time, you could ask instead of wasting what precious little we have."

As much as she despised the situation she was in, Taylor understood the importance of water out here in the desolate wilderness. She lowered her head to avoid meeting his eyes. She was only nineteen, but she had gone through far more in life than the average teenager, and hated being treated like a young kid. This authoritative tone sounded too much like how a father would speak to a child. A random thought suddenly sprung to her mind: did Trevor ever have kids?

"Yes, Dad," she said with scathing sarcasm, causing a snort from Gregor.

What happened next was wholly unexpected. She had little time to react, Ahya giving a small jerk as the only warning of Trevor's intentions. The wolf seized her tail under the mouth by his metal arm, gripping the mouth shut and causing Taylor to yelp in shock. Unbuckling one of the belts off his pants, he slapped it around the circumference of the expanding Ahya in one fluid motion. Releasing the maw for a fraction of a second, he looped the belt end into the buckle and pulled it tight.

"What are you doing?! Stop touching my tail!" Taylor was beside herself. The feeling of foreign hands on Ahya was extremely violating and nerve-wracking.

Ignoring her pleas, he locked the belt down to the tightest setting, causing Ahya to writhe this way and that. Clapping his hands together for a job well done, Trevor smiled. "That'll keep Ms. Bitey here from getting into trouble."

"Ms. Bitey?" Taylor was incensed. She made a motion to undo the belt this instant.

Without a pause, he pulled his gun out and pointed it smoothly at her face. "Shall we lose another day of your life now, Taylor?" She bared her teeth, but said nothing to his threat. "Good. If I see, for even a moment, that this belt is loose or comes off of her, you will be taking a long nap and having it put back on. Are we clear on the conditions of this arrangement?"

"Yes…Trevor." She bit back her tongue so hard. She wanted to egg him on, but knew he meant what he said. To think, she had said something remotely positive about him to Pine and Mitchell. He just proved that he couldn't be trusted all the same.

With the gun trained on her back, she shuffled back into the sleeping bag. Keeping a wary eye on her, Trevor did the same. Gregor, now more alert, resumed his position by the fire. They each kept an eye on the other until sleep overtook Trevor. With all the commotion in the last few minutes, Gregor was quite awake and seemed intent on actually doing his job as watch this evening.

Upset that her tail got muzzled, she turned over in the bag and hugged her. Ahya seemed miserable and pushed herself hard onto Taylor's face, wanting nothing more than to get that horrid belt off. She tried her best to sooth Ahya, petting her and scratching beneath the fur. It seemed to pacify Ahya somewhat, but she could tell it would be a restless night. She was just not used to having anything on her when they slept.

"It'll be all right, girl," she whispered. "We just need to take it slow and see if there is an opening to escape, that's all."

Taylor waited a good while, hoping that Gregor would get drowsy again. It was to her disappointment that he didn't seem willing to comply. Every movement she made, he made eye contact with her to remind her he was watching. The knowledge that she might be a captive that would move about at night had galvanized his determination to stay awake, which frustrated her.

A small skittering of rocks caught her ear. She turned her head to spot Pine poking his head from around the big rock that blocked the view of their camp from the road. She put a finger to her lips and he returned the gesture. She was relieved to see him, and knew Mitchell probably was nearby if not right next to him. Their presence around

88

would be their little secret. With this knowledge in mind, she was able to fall asleep more soundly.

5
EXPLOSION

"What do you mean she's on the way here?" Trevor put his iron paw up to his forehead, cringing hard at the words coming through the phone. "We already have Taylor in our custody, and we're bringing her to you now!"

"You've taken far too long, and too many mistakes have been made to bring her back to me. I am just ensuring her procurement from someone I trust. I have faith that you won't get in her way." The deep voice of the Arbiter was loud enough for even Taylor to pick up on with her ears.

"Can't you call her off? Or at the least just tell her to escort us?" He was beyond frustrated. "We had a deal!"

"So what's going on?" Taylor probed, leaning up against the motorcycle. She could see Trevor getting increasingly agitated in both voice and posture.

They had traveled for another full day before arriving at the edge of Falhoven Forest, pressing onward a few miles through the tree line until they broke out into a small clearing. Their vehicles were parked against a large sugar maple tree. The myriad of trees was laid out across the forest like a cavalcade of color, with mixtures of oak and pine. Somewhere in the distance, she noticed the light trickling of a brook at the edges of her hearing.

Gregor stirred, answering her without looking. "From what I understand, our employer sent an enforcer to come pick you up."

She trembled a bit. "I don't like the sound of that."

He huffed. "Neither do we. He's basically telling us we're incompetent and most likely not getting the money we were promised."

"Who do you think this enforcer is?" She scratched a sudden itch on her arm, agitated at the unknown coming to claim her.

"If I know the Arbiter, someone not very nice," he admitted.

"The Arbiter?" She cocked her head, trying to get a good read on his face.

He seized up and grew dour. "Never you mind!" He shifted his gun from his back to the front. "You just do what you're told and be quiet."

Taylor rolled her eyes and slouched back onto the bike. She filtered her fingers underneath the belt tied around Ahya's tail tip, keeping her mouth clamped shut. The fur was getting matted and sweaty from the temperature and the heat-trapping nature of the belt. If she didn't convince Trevor to remove it soon, she might end up with heat blisters or worse. She subtly used both paws to wipe through the dampness that even her panting was unable to alleviate, and moaned in relief at feeling the light breeze kiss the fur beneath the belt.

She resumed watching the agitated Trevor pace to and fro, his remaining paw of flesh and blood gripping the cellphone something fierce. At length, he finally snarled a final remark before tapping it off. He jammed the piece back into his pocket, his breathing heavy as he stared off into the distance. It took a few minutes for him to realize he was being watched. He turned and came tromping towards them, a determined look on his face.

"So, what's the plan?" Gregor stood taller, ready to move.

Trevor ignored him and went to a knee, shoving Taylor to the side as he inspected his motorcycle thoroughly. "He's got a tracking device on our bikes. She's coming for us, and no matter where we go she'll know just where exactly we'll be!"

"She's coming?" Gregor's eyes bulged, him joining the search looking at his own bike.

"Who's coming?" Taylor was starting to get irritated at being left out.

Trevor and Gregor shared a look before Trevor responded. "His daughter."

She couldn't fathom why this would be a problem. They were clearly intimidated by this Arbiter, but it seemed odd to her why this employer would send his own kin to come get her. Why couldn't he do the job himself? What exactly could this daughter of his do that would get even Trevor and Gregor spooked? These two battle-hardened bounty hunters were getting flustered at the idea of a young girl tracking them down.

"I don't understand." She leaned on the seat, looking down at Trevor. "What's a little kid like her going to do?"

"She's not a kid!" Trevor snapped, stopping his search. "She's about the same age as you!"

"Oh…" Taylor wasn't expecting that. In fact, she wasn't sure what to expect. It just seemed like the first thing she could think of when they mentioned his daughter. "Well, excuse me for misunderstanding."

"Dammit, I can't find it!" Trevor cursed, already on his back and looking beneath the bike.

"Maybe we should continue on and reach the nearest town as fast as we can to get new rides?" Gregor offered.

Trevor glared at him, but finally acknowledged defeat. Getting back onto his feet, he swung a leg over the motorcycle. "You're probably right. The next village is about a day's travel past this forest. Depending on how quick she is at tracking us, we may be able to make it there before she intercepts us." He patted the back part of his seat. "Taylor, arms around me now."

"Can I please get this belt off Ahya now?" Taylor asked.

"No." He faced forward in the seat, waiting for her to join him. His paw was casually resting on his side hip, just above the gun. A subtle reminder of what he would do if she resisted.

Shoulders slumping, she patted Ahya morosely, then got on the bike and held on tight. He wasted no time kicking the engine into gear and blasting down the row of trees. Gregor was close on their heels, weaving back and forth between each trunk. They soared off small hills, crunching the dirt hard on landing. No longer were they following the safe flatness of the road, preferring to take the straight line that would get them through the forest the quickest.

Taylor leaned forward towards Trevor's ear and yelled into the wind, hoping to be heard over the engines. "I just had a thought. If you're being replaced by this…daughter enforcer of his, why are you still bringing me back to him?"

"Because we had a deal," he said resolutely.

"And it's clear to me that he's probably not going to honor it. He's already sent someone else to do the job." She was probably being a bit too smug for her own good, taunting him like this.

"Are you trying to convince me to let you go? It's not going to work." He barked a laugh.

"Then why do you still want to bring me in?"

"You wouldn't understand," he growled back.

Seeing as she wasn't going to get anything further in that line of questioning, she tried a different tack. "Let's say you deliver me anyway. You think he's going to just pay you after having dropped you and sent his daughter to do the job? What then? Where will you be?" She continued to grill, even Ahya pressed forward, leaning in on his other shoulder.

He looked back at Ahya, irritated. "You're unbalancing the bike, can you just sit normal?"

She did as requested. "You didn't answer my question."

"I shouldn't have to. You are my bounty," he finished, firmly settling the matter with his tone.

Taylor didn't get to snark back before a loud boom echoed through the forest. A plume of earth and moss flew into the air mere feet in front of their motorcycle. Trevor swerved hard to the left, nearly crashing into an oak tree. The bike wobbled as he tried to maintain its momentum. Several more pillars of dirt exploded around them, each hailing down plants and debris onto their heads. The two hunters immediately went into evasive maneuvers.

"Who the hell is shooting at us?" Gregor shouted, narrowly missing another eruption to his right.

Ahya looked off to their left, as if sensing something there. The delicate shift in weight of the occupants on his motorcycle caused Trevor to follow Ahya's gaze to a small pinpoint of a silhouette on the ridge overlooking the leaf-blanketed hill leading down to them. It was actually several dark shapes taking position atop a fallen log at the top.

Trevor pointed up towards their attackers. "Up there, I spy three bogies."

"Are they with the enforcer?" Taylor's heart began beating faster.

He shook his head, dodging another blast directly in front of them, then hit the ground hard after a sudden drop-off caused by a log that was hiding a ledge. "No, that'd be too fast; he sent her out only a few days ago. I don't think anyone could make that distance this fast!"

The next shot hit the front wheel dead on, causing a miniature implosion of the air pressure. The front end flipped forward in on itself, tipping both Trevor and Taylor off. They tumbled forward, Ahya's weight helping Taylor to counterbalance and secure a safe landing from the bike. The vehicle continued its trajectory and soared over their heads and exploded into a nearby tree, causing it to tip and sag at the sudden destruction of its core trunk.

Gregor squealed his around, joining back up with Trevor who was immediately on his feet, gun ablaze with fire. Both were dismounted and securing positions of cover behind trees. They each loaded explosive rounds into their barrels and launched them back at their unseen assailants. Bits of bark and wood splintered through the air at the constant onslaught.

Taylor rolled behind the tree which was hit, and frantically looked between the two warring parties. She had no clue who the three attackers were at the top of the hill, but she knew that being anywhere near Trevor and Gregor was not going to end well for her either. Seeing the opportunity present itself, she quickly unbuckled the belt from her tail and tossed it aside. Ahya immediately opened wide, tongue unfurling as if getting a good stretch in.

Seeing no better time than now, she scrambled to her hind paws and began sprinting away from the battle. She didn't really much care which direction she was going, just so long as it was away from those two. She had wandered alone with no direction before, this would be no different. She just hoped Pine and Mitchell would be able to find her.

Her ears moved instinctively as she ran. She could hear the sound of rustling footsteps on her left and right closing in on her position. Whoever these people were, they had noticed her escape and had sent a second contingent with intent to cut her off. At the rate of closure, the sounds getting louder quickly, she knew she would have to make a stand sooner rather than later. The steps coming down the hill behind her seemed to be approaching at a faster rate. Her cloak was only slowing her down, so she unclasped it and let it fall.

She scanned ahead, spotting a low-hanging branch, and made a leap for it. Catching it with only a minor slip of a paw, she used her forward motion to let it swing her upside down. As if in unison, Ahya reached even higher to a taller branch, maw opening wide to crunch down hard on the firm bark. Releasing her grip, she let the movement and Ahya's pulling to reach the second branch above.

She was just getting arranged and stable, looking ever higher to continue the climb, when two mammals screeched to a halt below. Chancing a look down she saw a snow leopard in brown fatigues with various instruments of melee weaponry. Beside her was a tiny otter of similar garb, but with an unusually large minigun strapped to his back. It seemed comically large for his small build.

The two of them began talking in a foreign language to each other, each urgently pointing to her position. The otter sighed and unslung his weapon and tossed it toward the snow leopard, who struggled to catch it with its massive weight. The otter leaped onto the trunk and began scampering up the base at an alarming rate, his eyes focused on his goal of Taylor.

Unnerved at the frightening pace the little guy was setting, Taylor felt a boost of adrenaline as her flight or fight response kicked into high gear. She jumped to the next one above, letting Ahya secure the next highest branch, working her way up the tree trunk. It wasn't long before she was in the canopy with few options left but to switch trees.

She glanced around at the mix of maple and oak trees around her. The majority didn't have strong enough branches in their upper boughs to support her weight if she made the leap. She crouched close to the trunk at the base of the branch she was on, readying herself to fight off the otter rising beneath her. He was mere feet away when she noticed that he had a dagger perched between his teeth, his limbs full with the job of climbing.

The last few feet, he made a lunge for her position. She slipped off the opposite side of the branch, using Ahya to grab it hard and using the arcing swing to do a full revolution underneath and back up the other side. The otter was alerted to her maneuver too late, turning around a few seconds after peering over the edge to see where she had gone. She nailed him hard with her bulk, causing him to tumble off and down several branches, hitting one hard in the ribs and dropping the knife to the forest floor below.

Taylor was scared for her life. She knew that she would never be good enough for hand-to-hand combat against the otter; she was better at evading and using her attacker's movements against them than outright fighting tooth and claw. Ahya could always scoop him up and eat him. Taylor knew she had wanted to a few times already, but that would taste disgustingly awful and weigh her down so much she'd fall right out of the tree. So that was no option.

The otter winced in pain and massaged his side. He recovered abnormally fast and scurried up the trunk once more. Taylor knew he probably wouldn't fall for the same trick twice, so she decided to meet him in the middle. She hopped down and aimed for his position to tear him off the tree and drop him, hoping Ahya would catch her fall while she sent the otter falling to his death—or at the very least a serious injury.

Catching her out of the corner of his eye, he bounded off the bark and collided with her in mid-air. The impact of their velocities dropped them both like a lodestone. The otter was ferocious, immediately scratching and obtaining purchase on her clothes with his tiny paws. Taylor was wildly trying to claw his arms and legs off of her, but he was tenacious.

The first branch hit her right thigh, causing her to cry out. They both pivoted fully around, falling upside down, and Ahya surged out to bite a branch. The sudden stop and jerking tear of her pants brought tears to her eyes. It felt like her very tail was being torn out by the abrupt secession of falling. Taylor made a futile punch to the otter's face, which he deftly avoided. He bit deep into her shoulder blade and she began crying for real.

She was panting heavily, and Ahya's grip was hanging on by a thread. With little choice left, Ahya let go and let them both plummet. It was only a dozen or so feet left to the forest floor, but it was going to hurt. Whipping her tail around to get enough gyration to flip them over, she crashed otter-first into the ground. A tiny squeak burst from the otter, and then silence.

The snow leopard was upon her immediately. Taylor was yanked off the otter and subdued with a knee to the back and a lock on her arms. Ahya made a motion to gobble the cat from head to toe, and had already enveloped the upper half down to the leopard's breast when she suddenly stopped. Taylor could feel a piercing tingle inside of her tail's maw. The cat calmly held a knife of her own, ready to plunge it deep into the inner walls of Ahya.

"Stand your tail down now or I will slice it to ribbons from the inside out," she calmly ordered with a thick accent.

"Why? You're going to kill me anyway!" Taylor shouted into the dirt, doing her best to struggle against the superior grip of the cat.

"If you truly believe that, then why didn't I just shoot you down from the tree?" she pointed out, sounding as if she was asking herself the same question. "I had plenty of opportunities to take you out."

Taylor's eyes shifted over to the dropped minigun feet from her. Why did she send the otter up to come get her if they just wanted to kill her? If they didn't want to murder her where she lay, then what did they want her for? She quivered violently. What if they were the ones that experimented on her before, and not whoever Trevor and Gregor was taking her to? Why couldn't she remember what had happened?

The very thought got her blood pumping. Taylor began to thrash under the snow leopard, Ahya slithering her tongue down around her captor. She could sense the pressure being applied from inside, the knife point slicing flesh and plunging further in as her tail began to apply the corrosive acid down the length of her tongue.

The gasping pain of the snow leopard was audible when the saliva began burning through her tactical vest and eating at her flesh. "Stop your tail right now!" Her accent was getting thicker, making it hard to understand.

Taylor shook her head hard, tiny sparks coming out of her fingertips. "No! Either you die or I will! I will not be taken back to be experimented on again!" Ahya's mouth continued to close tighter.

"What…are you talking…about?" The leopard was struggling to breath with the maw closing in, acid melting away her fur and skin.

The final slice of metal, plunged deep into the inside of Ahya, set Taylor off. Her eyes dilated and flashes of lightning danced around her pupils, zigzagging down her spine and out her paws. Her entire body felt aglow with the swelling energy within her. She didn't know what was going on, only that she needed to get this snow leopard off of her and escape.

Taylor howled to the skies, loud enough for anyone to hear for miles around. Ahya released the leopard and fell off to the side, hitting the ground as if lifeless. The entire forest grew quiet before an explosion of electrical energy burst forth from Taylor, pitching the leopard yards into the air. The leopard flailed wildly before smacking into a nearby tree, crumpling into a bloodied heap at its base.

The entire air stank of sulfur, the acrid odor causing Taylor to scrunch her nose in displeasure. Her head was muffled, as if waking up from a heavy dream yet still unable to communicate with her body that her mind was awake. She sluggishly got up to her paws and knees, looking at her fingers with awe.

"Did… Did I do that?"

She rose up on wobbly legs, first one hind paw and then the other. She had been drunk before in her life, and this felt very much like what she had experienced. Her mind was all fuzzy, and it threw off her balance horribly when she turned her head to the sounds of approaching feet. The sounds of gunfire bombardment had already abated. Either Trevor or Gregor had won and were coming for her, or they were either dead or captured and she would have to make a stand.

Even trying to take a few steps blurred her eyesight, and she wasn't sure if she was seeing flames around her or if it was just illusions. The sheer exertion of moving was too much for Taylor. Her clouded vision could spy three shapes coming toward her, slowing down only when they noticed the two fallen bodies nearby. They began to spread out, each aiming what looked like some dangerous object in her direction.

Ahya was limp at her feet, but Taylor put her up dukes weakly. "You're not Trevor…" she managed to breathe out before falling face-first into the leaves, darkness once again consuming her.

A tiny beeping awoke her senses. Taylor felt like the entire weight of the world was pressing down on her body; the immense heaviness of her limbs was intolerable. She could barely move a muscle. Whatever she had done out in the woods had left her powerless and vulnerable.

Her eyes fluttering open, she gazed around the room she was in. She was in a gurney hiked several feet above the cement flooring. She had two magnetic bands that bound her wrists to the metal bar padlocks on either side of her bed. Trying to move her arms even an inch caused the strong physical attraction of the magnets to pull together and overpower her. After a few attempts, she let the hum of the gauntlets win.

"She's awake!" a buoyant peep from her left rang out.

She turned her head to see two familiar figures on a separate gurney alongside her own. "Pine! Mitchell!" She was overjoyed at seeing her friends.

They were nestled next to Ahya, who apparently deserved a bed as well. She looked miserable though. They had several straps winding around the length of the bed, each one hooked over her tail to keep it immobile and harmless. Within seconds, Pine and Mitchell soared off that bed and onto hers, each curling up lovingly between her arms. She did her best to hug them with her arms spread apart by the magnetic cuffs.

Her mood wilted when she realized where they were. "How'd you get here? Did you get captured too? Did they harm you?" She was getting angry, and would be wrathful if they had been.

Pine shook his head. "Your scent was easy to track. We snuck in here after we discovered the destroyed bikes and picked it up from there."

"Snuck in...where?" She looked confused.

Mitchell pointed at the slatted window behind her to the right. "We smelled you from in here, and squeezed through to be with you here."

Taylor took another look around. There were various rolling table carts with medicinal utensils and vials, and multiple stands with cabinets filled with unknown drugs and sanitary wipes. There was even a rinsing sink and towel rack. An involuntary shudder shot through her. Why could she remember certain things but not others about that awful time? Was this where she was experimented on years ago?

"It's like a military bunker," Mitchell observed. "Medical waystation most likely."

Taylor regarded the raccoon with intrigue. How would Mitchell know anything about those things? "Well, whatever it is, I need to get out of here. Whoever those folks were who fired on us, they are no friends to Trevor and Gregor. I can't expect them to do me any good either! Can you help get these off of me?" She began moving her wrists again for emphasis.

Pine shook his head despondently. "We're not strong enough. We tried ourselves while you were still sleeping. They need to be turned off before they can be removed."

All their ears popped up. They each heard the door at the far end of the building slam and clopping hoofsteps echo down the hall, headed in their direction. Ahya squirmed against her restraints, as did Taylor, but it served no use. They were laid bare for whoever was going to walk through that door. Pine and Mitchell hopped up onto her arms, one on each side, cuddling close to comfort her. Their eyes rapt on the door as the hoofsteps stopped.

Despite the earlier bang of the outer door, the inner one to her room was gently opened. In stepped a tall elk, the entrance small enough he had to duck his head so his antlers wouldn't smack the roof of the doorframe. He was wearing fatigue pants like the other two of his group she had encountered. However, unlike them, he was sporting an obnoxious button-up shirt with green palm trees against an orange backdrop. To complete the look, he had a set of black, rectangular-shaped glasses perched on his snout.

Noticing her quizzical stare, he smiled at her with his hazel eyes. "I usually wear this to put my patients at ease. I find that the silliness of it helps get them to open up and trust me."

"I'm not sure it is working," Mitchell scoffed, still wary.

Shutting the door behind him, the elk pulled over a rolling chair with a hind hoof and plopped down on it with practiced ease. He brought the nearest roller and himself right alongside her gurney. The swiftness of his actions quite alarmed her, causing her to recoil a bit in the bed.

He raised both fore hooves up. "It's all right. I'm not going to harm you." He chuckled, taking an empty vial plugging it into a needle receptacle. "I should honestly ask if you will be harming any of us now."

Seeing him ready the needle, Pine hissed, his tail flaring straight up. He would have been bent on releasing noxious spew if his body produced any. "What are you going to do with that needle?"

The elk firmly gripped Taylor's bicep and put an alcohol swab on the inner crux of her arm, ensuring that it was disinfected. He looked her directly in the eye. "Relax! I'm only drawing blood to be sure that everything is normal with you internally. That's all." Without waiting for permission, he expertly jabbed the needle into an artery and blood began pumping into the vial. "Heavens me, I forgot to introduce myself!" He beamed again as he looked back up at her eyes. "My name is Fey Darner. You could say I'm both the leader and medical physician out here."

Taylor winced when the needle went in, but was now transfixed by the red liquid pooling into the empty container. "Why do you need my blood?"

Fey laughed, eyes twinkling. "Didn't I just say what I was taking it for?"

"No, not entirely." Her whole body was tense. "Soon, you'll be coming back for more and poke and prod me with sharp instruments for no reason!" Her chest was beginning to heave.

Having finished the draw, he removed the needle and put a non-furstick bandage on the tiny prick wound. "Sweet sassafras, my dear. What in blazes do you think we do here? Why would I possibly want to do those awful things to you?"

"Then tell us why she's here!" Pine suddenly blurted.

102

"Why did you fire on her when she was just passing through?" Mitchell chimed in.

"This is exactly why I ran away in the first place! Too many people wanted to lock me away, to study me and hurt me! Waking up too many times handcuffed to beds and at the mercy of whoever wanted to torture me next!" Tiny sparks began whizzing off her fingertips again, spiraling out into the air before dissipating.

This caused Fey's nostrils to flare and him to push back hard, his chair rolling to the far edge of the room. "Now you just need to calm down. I have absolutely no idea what was done to you in the past, but by the sounds of it, it is awful. I'm sorry for what happened to you. Truly I am. However, at this very moment, I have two of my colleagues in critical condition because of you and your friends." He pointed a hoof directly at her.

Just that small burst of frenetic excitement seemed to drain the color from her face and she slumped down into the bed. "Probably just me." This got his attention. "I'm a danger to everyone I meet. They either end up injured, dead, or eaten. That's another reason I run away from everyone. It's safer if I'm alone...but at least I have Pine and Mitchell here to keep me company. They've never let me down."

The two small critters beamed and began to nuzzle their cheeks against hers, both enjoying the warmth of the other. They soon drew apart and returned to looking back at the elk, whom seemed quite flummoxed. He took his glasses off and cleaned them with his shirt before returning them back to his snout.

"Erm... So you're saying you alone were at fault for taking down both my troops and not your friends?" he clarified, an unreadable expression on his face.

"Well, yeah..." She thought back to the last thing she could remember. "I fell out of a tree with an otter and my tail almost ate a snow leopard, but to be fair, I was defending myself. They came at me in a not-friendly way."

Fey nodded. "That corroborates with the injuries they sustained. Thankfully, they will get better with time and rest. You are certainly a very dangerous wolf... Dear me, I don't even think I got your name."

"Taylor Renee," she answered flatly. "Was it you who shot us down from on that hill?"

"No sense hiding it. Yes, I was one of the ones who did." He left it at that, crossing his arms, content to not say more.

"Why? We were no danger to anybody. You could've just let us pass through the forest and we'd be on our way," she reasoned, hoping for a way out of this mess through logic.

"Why?" he repeated her. "My men and I are tasked with a mission from the High Council of Zabökar to search for extraordinary mammals such as yourself, bring them in for asylum, and to secure a place of refuge for them. I guess that would be the best way to put it at this juncture."

"I don't understand," Mitchell butted in. "How did you know Taylor was special in the first place?"

"Do you not know whom you were traveling with?" Taylor didn't respond, so Fey sighed and continued. "Your friends are not what they seem. They are working for a person named the Arbiter; his insignia was on both the motorcycles they were riding. The shell of the tortoise on their wheels, did you not see it?"

It was Taylor's turn to look bewildered. "Shells? They looked like just fanciful designs of the wheel hubcaps. I didn't recognize it at all. And why would you even assume that someone special like me was even traveling with them?"

Staying silent a moment to judge her response, Fey explained, "We identified you by several factors, not the least of which is your uncanny red fur. The Arbiter deals specifically in the realm of paranormal operations, and has contributed to the rise of multiple cases of mammals with special conditions such as yours. We know not how he is capable of doing these things, but it is not for the good of Zabökar. That is for certain."

"You're saying…I'm a product of whatever he's doing?" Taylor was afraid of the answer.

Was her entire life a lie? Just how exactly was she born? A sudden terrifying thought came to her: what if her mother she recalled so much in her memories was just a caretaker hired to keep watch over her until she grew of age for whatever the Arbiter had planned for her? What about her brothers? Was anything rational anymore? In that one existential moment, she was faced with the question of the point of her life.

"That's exactly what I'm saying," Fey confirmed for her, unaware of the inner turmoil raging inside of her this moment. "He's taken innocent pups and kits from their families and changed them into unholy beasts for his army." He saw the hurt look on Taylor's face, his eye darting over to the inert tail strapped to the other gurney. "My apologies, I did not mean for that to sound so insulting. He is gathering them for some vain crusade of his that the High Council is very much fearful of."

She quickly got over the slight, since she was used to such affronts. "And what about you? Aren't you gathering us all up to do the same thing? Why should this High Council of yours even care about what happens to us?"

Fey adjusted his glasses a bit. "All valid questions. You are right in asking them. Does the High Council care about what happens to mammals like you? Hard to say. I am not privy to such conversations behind closed doors, but here is what I do know: the leadership in Zabökar does not divulge their reasoning with those they send to enforce their decisions."

"I suppose not." Mitchell sat back on his haunches, relaxing by leaning into Taylor.

"The more important question that we should be asking is, are you going to continue to be a danger to us? Shall we lock you up with the other two?" Fey's tone was firm.

"Why haven't you done that already?" Pine asked.

"Don't you think I'm part of the Arbiter's men?" Taylor finished.

Fey stared at Taylor for a few moments. "Dear, if it was clear beyond a doubt that you were one of his men, you would have been incarcerated with them. Thankfully for you, your tail gave you away, as did the entire situation we found you in. First, you being separated from the other two clearly meant you were escaping. Second," He held up two hooves. "There were multiple brush fires surrounding the place where we found you. Fires we could not put out easily."

"I'm sorry… I didn't mean to do that." Taylor glanced away, a bit ashamed for causing yet more trouble. If she wasn't hurting other people, she was now hurting the very environment. "Guess it makes sense you'd be afraid I'd kill you too."

He scooted back towards her on the chair, the immediate threat of another explosion having passed. "You're fine…for now. I don't expect I'll be dying that way, but for precautions, you do understand why I will have to leave you in these cuffs for the night?" He gestured to the magnetic binds. She nodded glumly as he continued. "Good. With two people incapacitated by your paws, we are going to convene later on how best to deal with you. We are tasked with a mission to secure mammals like you, but not at the cost of our own lives if we can help it."

"So, you're going to kill me then?" Taylor tensed, both Pine and Mitchell rising back up to hear the answer.

"What? No, I never said that!" he snapped. Immediately regaining composure, he took a deep breath and put a hoof on the gurney handlebar. "We're just going to discuss whether it is safe or not to let you loose and have you come willingly with us to Zabökar."

Taylor did her best to display her wrists and looking over to her tail. "I understand. I'm just tired of this. Of waking up being strapped to some table or bed and being experimented on for no reason. I never asked for any of this! I couldn't help being born this way!"

This did catch Fey's attention. "You…were born this way?"

Taylor affirmed with a nod. "I was born and raised this way. I can't remember a time when I didn't have Ahya as my companion stuck to my butt." She had to chuckle at a long-forgotten memory of her tail eating her fifth birthday cake when she wasn't looking. "I remember my mother having a hard time trying to give me a normal life."

He patted the bar once before getting up from his seat. "Well, at the very least you are safe now. I will see to it that someone comes in later to bring you some food before nightfall. We will speak again on the morrow." He picked up the used needle and vial before walking towards the door. He held it ajar for a brief moment before regarding her. "It was nice to meet you, Taylor. I'm sorry it wasn't on better terms."

He moved to shut the door when she called out, "Can you ask them not to bring me any meat? I can't stand the taste!" Her stomach was growling, but she feared that they'd bring her something that might suit her species' needs, and that was not what she wanted.

He smiled at her request. "Of course. I'll let them know when they come to bring it to you." With that, he closed the door with a click and his hoofsteps disappeared down the hallway. They couldn't even detect the outer door shutting this time.

"He seems nicer than Trevor at least," Mitchell admitted, a collective exhale of relief from all of them.

"But Taylor is still tied up as a prisoner! Possibly even worse!" Pine threw up his paws, walking around to be by her stomach, angrily glaring at Mitchell. "At least Trevor and Gregor allowed her to roam free without tying her down to a bed."

"They didn't give her that much freedom though," Mitchell reminded. "They kept threatening her with a gun."

"Guys, please don't fight," Taylor intervened, raising a knee to provide a physical barrier between the two critters. "We're alive and that's all that matters." She took a few breaths, trying to remain under control. Things were not going to end up like before. They were not. "I thought for sure they were going to hurt me after they saw what I had done to their friends. I'm just happy they didn't."

"That could change though." Pine was all doom and gloom.

Mitchell was fed up with the attitude. "Let's try to stay positive for once. We could have all died back in Palaveve with that monster. It was only because of your scent, Taylor, that we were able to track you down and find you after we had left town."

"You're right…" Pine relented. He flopped down and curled up next to Taylor. "Still, I'm very hungry and I wonder what they're going to bring us to eat."

"I'm very thirsty too," Mitchell added.

"That's all three of us." Taylor laid her head back on the bed and looked up at the nondescript ceiling.

She could still smell the scent of the forest through the slats. Bird song was carried on the breeze. It sounded nice, almost peaceful out there. Rotating her head to gaze out the window, she could see swaying branches and the rustling of the wind through the leaves. The light was waning, and it wouldn't be long before it was dark in her room. She wondered if they'd bring a light for the evening, or if her bedtime was the sunset. Hopefully they'd bring the food before then.

After a time, she turned to Ahya. The poor thing hadn't moved an inch from the time she woke up. Taylor could feel that she was depressed, understanding that pain all too well. She was depressed that all those awful memories from years ago were coming true all over again. Why did she have to be so special to be born as something that would cause headache for others? What if what Fey said was true, and the one responsible was the Arbiter? Was he the cause of all her problems? She knew she needed to talk to Trevor again about this the next chance she got.

"Hey, girl. How you feeling?" she called out to Ahya. No response. "Pine, Mitchell, can you hop on over there and give her some rubs? I'd do it myself, but…"

"It's okay, Taylor. We got you covered." Mitchell smiled.

Both him and Pine leaped over the bars and landed on the other gurney. They started scratching and petting her fervently. However, it seemed it was all ignored. Ahya was probably just as hungry as she was, and most likely not going to get any of the food she would be receiving tonight either. She almost had half a heart to have allowed her to eat that snow leopard.

Taylor's eyes widened at the thought of having almost eaten her. The knife. She remembered being stabbed on the inside of Ahya with it. Was it still inside? She couldn't feel it anymore. She willed Ahya to lethargically move her tongue around the inside of her mouth. She couldn't feel any obstruction there. They must have removed it. In fact, she couldn't feel any residual pain from it at all. Ahya's potent saliva most likely repaired the wound while she was out.

That momentary crisis over, she called out to her two friends. "Don't worry about her, just come on over and keep me warm. This blanket they gave me is a bit thin!"

"Yes, Taylor!" They chimed in unison, bouncing over and curling up between her arms, one on each side.

Her thoughts began to wander as she waited for whoever was going to bring them food. They considered her a danger to everyone. They found her with flames all around her. She looked at her fingertips,

108

covered with her paw pads and claws. What exactly did she do out there? She couldn't recall how she did it. It had never happened before, at least as far as she could remember. Just what was she even capable of?

6
MIKHAIL

"Get up." a gruff voice commanded.

Taylor was jolted awake by the loud clamor of silverware on a plate. She was shaken even more by the size of a large, older tiger sitting just a foot away from her bed. Beside him was the rolling medical tray with a plate of steaming hot food and some fruit. The look on the tiger's face was unreadable, and he seemed to be waiting for her to get her bearings before addressing her again.

"Get up." he repeated in the same tone.

"All right, all right! Stop being pushy. I'm up!" Taylor fumed, doing her best to sit up in a bed that was already tilted up high. "What do you want?"

"I'm here to feed you and let you out of your cuffs," he responded matter-of-factly.

Scrutinizing him a bit more carefully now, he was an aged tiger with many wisps of grey fur bleeding through the once-vibrant orange and black—memories of a younger time. What was immediately noticeable were his brilliant emerald eyes, marred by four claw marks from the bridge of his nose to the bottom of his left jawbone. The lack of fur growth there was a blemish on an otherwise imposing face.

His answer shook the remainder of her drowsiness away, the rumble in her belly coming back in full force. "Is it dinner time already?" She looked confused at the brighter rays of light streaming in through the open slats of the window.

The tiger barked a curt laugh as he shook his head. "Of course not! It is morning. Terrati did not want to disturb you when you fell asleep, so he didn't bother delivering the food." He seemed a bit upset at this fact. "He's probably scared out of his wits to be near that tail," he mumbled as an afterthought.

He turned to the plate of food, his muscles flexing in the motion underneath his black tank top. From what Taylor could tell, he was wearing fatigue pants like all the rest she had seen of this group. Were they a separate section of some military faction within whatever army they were a part of for Zabökar? Was this the only type of clothes they were able to procure for themselves? She felt it would be a bit rude if she tried asking.

He held up the plate for her to see what they had prepared for breakfast. It was a mix of assorted greens and some fresh apple slices. However, there was one item on the plate that made her groan: a warm scramble of eggs. She had no idea where they had gotten such food out here in the woods, but she had not seen fowl since leaving the city of her birth. Most were in such high positions of wealth that they never interacted much with commoners.

"I said no meat." Taylor pointed at the eggs.

It took a second for the tiger to realize she was pointing at them. "This isn't meat. These are eggs. It's good protein, and an excellent substitute for meat. It is proven to curb instinctual cravings in predators like you and me. We are mandated by law to get either these or protein supplements."

"I'm not like other predators. I've curbed my cravings just fine, thank you!" She turned her head away from him. She didn't mean to be this obstinate, but the remembrance of Grunier on her tongue was more than enough to not have her touch meat again.

The tiger was unimpressed at her rebellion. He glanced over at her tail and then back to her. "Reports of a wolf with a monster for a tail eating people in a trade town of Palaveve tells me you are in dire violation of the common law, and should be put to death for your crimes." This indictment brought a pit of terror to Taylor's stomach, but the tiger shrugged and rattled on. "Thankfully for you, the High Council's mission to secure mammals like yourself overrides such things. You should be thankful and eat your food. I will not be asking again."

"I rather lost the taste for such things thanks to Ahya eating others," she admitted truthfully. She used to enjoy things like eggs, but having living people inside your tail being devoured by your own body put a damper on those instinctual cravings. "Can't you just scoop those off? You say I ate them, and I can have the rest of what's on there?" she requested hopefully.

"Little girl," he said, exasperated, "you don't really have a choice in the matter. You're nothing but skin and bones. Gods know how you've been surviving all this time. Besides, the rest of the gang would feel much safer if you and your tail were fed before we released you."

"The name is Taylor." She rejoined feeling slighted at being called a little girl.

"Mikhail, pleased to meet you," he said indifferently, scooping up a huge helping of scrambled eggs. "This is quite the delicacy out here; you should be grateful we agreed to spare some for you. It'll put some fat on those bones."

"Now wait a minute, I just said—" she began.

With the swiftness of a trained veteran, he set the plate down and smacked her stomach with the back of his free paw. This caused Taylor to cough out hard at the shock of the impact. With her mouth open, he shoved in the spoon, closing her lower jaw with a finger. Slipping the empty spoon out, he gripped her mouth tight and glared at her with deadly resolve.

"Now chew that all and swallow." Mikhail ordered. It was clear he was not going to be moving from this position until she did what she was told.

It had been a long time since she had eggs, and she had forgotten what it was like. On one paw, she was revolted at having something from another animal in her mouth again. On the other, the delectable taste was bringing back memories of a better time when her mother used to cook these for her on a lazy weekend morning. Yielding to his strong grip, she acquiesced and chewed her food before swallowing it with reluctance.

Mikhail finally cracked a small glimmer of a grin. "There, that wasn't so hard, was it?" He retracted his paw to go fetch another spoonful. "Now you just need to finish the rest of it."

As he withdrew, Taylor worked her jaw, feeling a nice pop after being handled so roughly by him. She noticed the unusual stripe markings on his forearms, where each black stripe was a sharpened oval in a sequential pattern that traveled down the outside of each arm. She also spotted several missing claws from either paw. Claws grew back for most predators, and cats were no exception. Something bad must have happened to Mikhail to have them be permanently missing.

Mikhail spooned another mouthful before raising it towards her. "Are you going to behave? Or am I going to have to be tough on you each time?" Taylor looked at his other paw, already getting ready to grip her mouth again. She quickly shook her head. "There's a good girl," He crooned.

She flattened her ears. Glowering at him the entire time, she begrudgingly ate each bite he offered her without complaint. It felt very humiliating having to be fed like this as an adult. Sure, she was still a teenager by common standards, but she wasn't that young to be treated like a child. She wasn't sure if Mikhail was enjoying this or not, because he began a low melodic hum in his throat as he continued to feed her. His eyes grew distant as if not seeing her in front of him.

In that way they finished the entire plate, fruit and all. Setting it down, he grabbed a napkin and began dabbing her muzzle. She vehemently wobbled her head, attempting to avoid the napkin. "I'm not a child." She began to lick her lips of any remaining food crumbs.

He sat back with an amused look on his face. "Of course not. Nobody said you were."

"Yet you're treating me like one," she steamed.

First, she was shackled and poked by some elk with a needle, and now she was being fed like an infant by a tiger. She felt powerless to do anything and she hated it. She just wanted to escape and run far away from here.

He didn't seem fazed by her attitude. "How else was I going to feed you before demagnetizing your cuffs?"

"You could have just let me use my own paws," Taylor suggested, like it was the most obvious solution in the world.

"After what they said you're probably capable of? I don't think so." If there was a hint of mirth in his voice, his expression did not show it. "It is far safer to calm the beast of hunger first before addressing anything else."

Satisfied that his answer was enough, Mikhail pushed the tray away until it settled against a wall. He pulled out a key from his fatigues pocket and slipped it into a hole on the underside of each magnetic lock.

114

They immediately dropped her wrists to the bed with a shudder. He cracked open each and sat back to observe Taylor massaging her matted fur and arms. It was an immense relief to be fully freed from her bindings.

"And my tail?" she asked, eyeing Ahya who seemed agitated and wiggling beneath the many straps. Taylor was free to get out of her gurney bed, but she wouldn't be able to get away from the other one with her tail still bound to it.

"One thing at a time," Mikhail reminded. He got up and held out a paw to assist Taylor out of the bed and onto her hind paws. "Are you strong enough to stand?"

"I think so." She affirmed it with a nod.

"Good. Now let's get one thing straight here." He stared down at her, his size immediately becoming evident. He stood at least a good foot or two taller than her and was quite muscular and fit, his back impeccably straight. "You will be released outside under my care. You will keep that tail of yours under control at all times. If it goes and bites or eats someone, you will be shot. If you try to escape, you will be tranquilized and brought back. Is that understood?"

"Aren't those the same thing?" She was not sure why he made a distinction.

"No. I meant what I said when you would be shot." He folded his arms. "Shot as in dead. Just because we have a mission to bring you in by the High Council does not mean that it'll be at the cost of our own lives. We've suffered casualties as it is, and you are not worth more than our lives. You will be put down if you present a danger to us."

"And tranquilized because I'm still wanted by your High Council." She filled in the remaining blank.

"Now you're catching on," he spoke flatly.

"So why did they assign you to me? Am I to follow you everywhere?" Taylor was bemused as to why none of the others was tasked to being her personal watcher. She thought for sure that Fey would be the one to do it.

"Yes, you are not to be let out of my sight. And I actually volunteered." He walked around the second gurney and began unbuckling the straps, tossing each one over the side irreverently.

"Volunteered? But why would you do that?" Someone actually wanted to watch over her? Most people were terrified of her tail and considered both her and it freaks. If anyone got near her voluntarily, it was to experiment on her or do tests. She hated that.

Mikhail ignored her question and continued to undo the final strap. He swiftly backed up as Ahya reared up fast and opened wide, her entire maw, teeth, tongue and all visible. Her saliva was flecking off everywhere as she whipped her tongue back and forth, her bulk getting larger by the second as if preparing to eat Mikhail whole. Arms refolded, the tiger just stared back at the intimidating tail mouth and stood firm, unyielding.

"Ahya, down!" Taylor shouted. It took a few seconds of fighting against her own tail's willpower before it finally relented and shrunk down to a normal size, dropping back behind her. Its fanged opening disappeared into the fur as if nothing strange was ever there at all.

"Fascinating," Mikhail said dryly. "If you're done showing off, I will show you around the compound."

Taylor seemed stunned she was being blamed for what Ahya did just now. "That wasn't me! She was fighting me and not listening to me! She wanted to attack you!"

Mikhail raised a brow, not buying it. "You've given it a name and you don't have full control over it? It's your tail, attached to your body, which you have control over. Even in the times where I may be absentminded, I am still acutely aware of where my tail is at all times. I find it hard to believe you don't."

Taylor huffed. Even she knew how ridiculous it sounded, at how contrived it seemed to others that she just so "happened" to be unable to control her tail sometimes. "I know how it sounds, but nobody wants to believe me that she has a mind of her own."

He regarded the unassuming tail waving leisurely behind her legs. If he had not just witnessed its impressive display of malice, you could hardly tell it was anything unique other than the vivid red fur at its tip.

He sighed before motioning her to follow. "Time will tell if you are speaking the truth. For now, just follow me and don't stray or wander off. Everyone is watching you and is trained to put you down in one of the two ways I mentioned."

Taylor shivered at this casual threat. She surveyed the room and realized Pine and Mitchell were missing. "Have you seen my friends?"

Mikhail turned to see her looking around. "They are being taken care of right now, do not worry yourself with them. We did not harm them, if that's what you are wondering."

A wave of relief washed over her. As long as they were safe and hopefully fed like her, she felt a lot better. "Can we go see them? I want to talk to them."

Mikhail frowned. "We'll see." He pivoted and opened the door, stepping aside to allow her to step out first. After a few seconds of awkward silence, he cleared his throat and made a sweeping motion of his arm to indicate she was to go ahead of him.

"Oh, sorry!" She sheepishly walked past him, not wanting to meet his eyes.

Taylor knew it wasn't going to be easy to get an opportunity to escape from Mikhail. The tiger had rapidly closed the door behind them and was directly behind her. If he had been any closer, she figured she'd be able to feel his breath down the back of her neck. He didn't say anything, just kept close pace behind, expecting her to continue forward towards the end of the hallway and outside.

The light from the morning sun blazed in as she pushed the metal door outward, causing her to squint as she stepped out into the fresh air. She paused a moment to get her bearings. They were still deep in the colorful woods of oak and maple. She even spotted a weeping willow bordering a river off to her left.

There were multiple makeshift tents that had tarps of camouflage made to look like leaves, similar in color to those found nearby. Each one was pinned to the ground by several stakes, and the overall design of them looked like they could be dismantled in a hurry should the need arise. Spinning around to look at the solid structure behind her, she noted it was the only permanent building in the entire campsite. Everything else was temporary.

"Over there." Mikhail rapped her arm to get her attention before pointing off to her right, to a lowered depression where a small crew was gathered around a campfire.

"Right." She frowned at the smack, but didn't address it. She needed to feel out this new situation she was in and take stock of her options.

Fey Darner, now wearing a new palm shirt of a tacky blue, was already at the circle of folding chairs. He was working on a plate of greens and a healthy dose of beans. He smiled and nodded towards an empty chair opposite him near the fire. Sensing that it would be rude to deny the offer of a seat, Taylor hurriedly padded over and took a seat in a folding chair that sunk further than she had expected upon first glance at it.

Folding Ahya back over the armrest to have her rest in her lap, Taylor looked around the pit and spotted the snow leopard staring at her. She was sitting with her back tilted forward, but she was doing her best to keep it straight—either from not wanting to look weak in front of Taylor, or maybe to hasten the healing of her wounds. She had several bandages that wrapped around her abdomen and looped up and over her shoulders that matched the places Ahya's tongue had touched.

Mikhail walked over and sat down next to her and regarded Taylor with an intense gaze. "This is Natalia." He motioned with his paw to the snow leopard. "I'm sure I don't have to introduce you beyond that."

Taylor flushed and didn't meet Natalia's eyes. Their last encounter with each other nearly killed them both. However, it was Natalia that first broke the ice. "Good morning, Taylor." She did her best attempt at a smile, her accent still thick. She spread her arms wide to have her get a good look at the damage done to her body. "As you can see, we did not kill each other!" She laughed heartily at that, cringing only when it brought pain to her wounds, causing her to clutch her chest.

Taylor tried her best to laugh weakly with her. "That's always a good thing." She looked away, feeling it awkward to be staring down someone who she almost had Ahya eat.

A glint of light flashed off of metal directing Taylor's attention to Fey, who had flipped up the very knife Natalia had used to stab the inside of Ahya's mouth. "We recovered this from the inside of your tail yesterday. What surprised me more was the fact that the injury received from this was not there when we checked again. You are a very unique wolf, Taylor." His compliment didn't hold much inflection.

"So people keep telling me." Taylor crossed her arms and sagged into the chair. "Frankly, I'd rather just be left alone and be free to just live out a simple life away from others."

"Is that a recent decision of yours?" Fey questioned, putting his glasses on and leaning over to pick up a manila folder with paperwork inside. He flipped through a few sheets before pulling out what were obviously a few older photographs of Taylor.

Taylor looked around at the three of them. "Where did you get these pictures?" She waved a paw at the folder Fey was flipping through. "You're not doing a good job convincing me you're not all from some shadowy organization bent on capturing and experimenting on me!"

"Relax. As I told you before…" Fey closed the folder and adjusted the papers inside neatly. "We are in direct opposition to the Arbiter. It is our business to discover, locate, and track any and all subjects he has experimented on and bring them in." This brought a look from Mikhail, but the tiger remained silent.

"Locate?" Taylor snorted. "Does he just let them loose after he's done with them?"

He moved to answer, but Natalia jumped in. "Not at all. In fact, he keeps all of them nearby and trains them for battle. The few that have escaped—or we managed to extricate—are the ones we currently track."

Fey shot a glare to silence her. "Yes, what she said is true. The Arbiter is very protective of his specimens. Which brings me to my point: you are unique among others that I've seen. I wondered how it was that he let you go for so long before attempting to bring you in. You seemed to have lived a good life in Zabökar, only recently becoming a target. I couldn't quite figure out why until you told me last night that you were born this way. We had honestly thought the Arbiter was back to making more of you."

The ensuing silence after his statement made Taylor a bit self-conscious, she shrunk a bit in the chair and brought Ahya closer to her chest. "Why are you telling me all this? If you're from this High

Council, wouldn't they pride themselves on secrecy and not want you to give out information freely like this?"

Fey tented his hooves, regarding her over his spectacles. "You would be correct. The common civilian has no need to know what goes behind closed doors with regard to this…matter. However, I decided to make a judgment call and reveal to you what you need to know about the whole situation."

"Why?" Taylor pressed. "You still haven't answered that." This tenacity brought a small chuckle from Mikhail, causing a withering look from Fey. Mikhail didn't seem perturbed.

"Because we need your cooperation." Fey put it plainly. "It is in the best interest of Zabökar that the Arbiter is stopped, and to halt the production of any more like you."

"Like me?" Taylor wrinkled her nose. "You make it sound like I was a mistake."

"He does not mean it that way," Mikhail defended. "What was done to each of you was abominable, however we are positioned to relocate and secure better lives for those affected like yourself."

"Excuse me if I'm not very trusting of anyone right now." Taylor let Ahya fall back into her lap as she sat up a bit straighter.

The idea of a better life was tempting. She had promised herself one for not just herself, but for Pine and Mitchell too. Too long had she been on the run since being kidnapped the first time. Ever since that moment, her memories were a big, jumbled mess, and she lived in fear of some sinister presence lurking in the shadows wherever she went. Still, despite the promise of these mammals before her, she couldn't exactly trust them, given all that had happened.

"First you all shoot at us on those motorcycles, then you send her and that otter after me, and now you're saying you are here to help me and provide a better life for someone who you say shouldn't exist? I'm finding this all very hard to believe." Taylor looked around the camp and the tents. "Speaking of which, where is that otter? Was that Terrati?"

"No, Terrati is currently on a resupply errand at the nearest town. He should be back shortly." Mikhail informed. "The otter, Finnley, is still recovering from his fall." He pointed back towards the medical ward they had left earlier.

"Resupply?" Taking in her surroundings, Taylor saw plenty of crates, equipment, and what looked like food rations that would last for weeks. "I don't think you are hurting for it."

"He's not going for much," Fey clarified, leaning over and tucking the folder into an unassuming brown suitcase by his chair and clicking it shut. "We're just topping off what we have in terms of fuel, food, and medical supplies. No thanks to you," he added with some severity. The brief bout of bitterness washed away to reveal a smile again on the deer's face, "We're actually set to leave on the morrow, or when Finnley recovers well enough to travel."

The news shot a bolt of adrenaline through Taylor. She would be again on the move with people she barely knew, let alone trust with her safety. "Where are we going?"

Fey gave her a curious look. "Heavens to Betsy! Have you listened to anything I said? We were sent from the High Council in Zabökar. We are heading back there with you in tow."

Trying to stall for some time to think up of some sort of plan to escape, she hesitantly offered, "Didn't you say you were stationed out here looking for others like me? Surely there might be more around? Maybe we should stay a bit longer?"

"Little girl." Mikhail leaned in, resting an elbow on his knee. "When Fey said we were tracking anomalies like you, he meant we were actively tracking via radar and technical bio scanners. We were setting to leave this position anyway until you three came barreling through these woods like nobody's business."

Taylor outwardly displayed her vexation at Mikhail's term for her, but said nothing as Fey continued Mikhail's thought. "Imagine our surprise when you landed right in our laps. We picked up your unusual metrics at the border of the desert." It seemed the deer was not overly happy about what Mikhail revealed on their tracking capabilities.

"What's so unusual about my metrics?" Taylor asked. She found it a bit miffing that she somehow gave off some unusual aura that others could pick up on.

"Anything that has some connection with the paranormal and what the Arbiter does gives off a unique signature that we've been able to identify. That's pretty much all you need to know now," Fey explained, his tolerance waning.

Picking up on Fey's cues, Mikhail stood up and abruptly walked over to Taylor until he towered over her. She looked up at him. Even Ahya opened up slightly, angling her mouth to "look" in his general direction.

"Yes? May I help you?" Taylor edged away slightly in her seat. The tiger was getting a bit too close.

"I'll show you to your quarters, where you'll be staying the duration until we come to you for meals." Mikhail lowered a paw for her to take to right herself onto her hind paws. She simply stared at it. He let a growl rumble in his throat. "I wasn't asking."

Rolling her eyes, she took the proffered paw and yelped when he pulled her up faster than she was expecting. "You sure do know how to make guests feel welcome around here." She tried to jerk her arm away from Mikhail, but he held his grip and was gently, but firmly pressing her to move.

"I never said you were a guest." Fey rectified the confusion.

She scowled at him. "You were a lot nicer yesterday. Now you're just an asshole."

"Come on, Taylor." Mikhail nearly dragged Taylor away. Using Ahya as a conduit, Taylor had her tail stick its tongue out and blow a raspberry as a parting insult.

"It was good to meet you too!" Natalia called out after her with genuine sincerity. Fey remained quiet and watched them go.

After they walked several meters away, Mikhail finally released Taylor. She yanked her arms away from him as she stomped forward. "What the hell is his problem anyway?"

The tiger pursed his lips before responding, not breaking stride and encouraging Taylor to keep walking. "Fey is under a lot of stress right now. If you hadn't noticed, you are the only one among us that is different. We've located no other unique individuals such as yourself during this mission. And if I were you, I'd watch that flippant tongue of yours. You are in no position to be mouthing off to any of us."

This admonition sobered up Taylor's ire. Her tone dropped. "Sorry. Force of habit. I've never been one for people in positions of authority."

"Indeed," Mikhail agreed cryptically. "I'll just chalk it up to teenage stubbornness. Keep moving."

Taylor chanced looking back towards the fire pit and saw Fey wearily getting up to stoke the fire with a stick. He was speaking to Natalia, but they were just out of earshot and she couldn't pick up much of their words. Something she hadn't noticed the night before was how tense he held himself. There seemed so much of him that was just bubbling under the surface, but it was hard to tell if it was just anger, sadness, or in Mikhail's assessment, stress.

"By the sounds of it, you all were sent off on a fool's errand to keep you out of the way." Taylor chuckled at the theory. Her laughter was cut short by Mikhail's stern silence. She gestured to the wilderness around them. "Oh come on! You can't expect me to believe they sent you out in the middle of nowhere for some top-secret mission, to a place so empty of anything remotely resembling what you're looking for!"

He continued to glower at her. "Teenage stubbornness," he repeated.

"Oh fine… Forget I said anything." She threw her hands up.

They continued to walk in silence. They passed another tent on their way to a smaller one. She peeped in as they swept past. She saw several cots and multiple stands of personal effects positioned next to each. She wondered why she was sleeping separately from the rest of them if they wanted to keep a close eye on her. As if in answer, Ahya did a swooping bite at a lizard dashing by along the forest floor.

"Did you do that?" Mikhail studied the odd mouth for a tail.

Taylor sighed. "I told you before, she has a mind of her own. Most times I can control her when I concentrate, but she usually takes advantage when I'm distracted or busy. She can be quite…mischievous."

"It is just very odd to me," he confessed.

Gauging his response a bit, she spoke more softly. "It's why I'm alone more often than not. I find it easier to manage Ahya with less people around."

"We're here."

Mikhail flipped up the flap on the entrance to the tent, raising the drooping camo-netting to allow her passage. He ducked in after her as she explored the living space. It was equipped to handle several occupants, but given what she heard of their success rate, it was only her right now. Each cot had some semblance of comfort with a few blankets and some rudimentary pillows that were not plush in the slightest.

Her eyes lit up when she noticed her belongings draped over one of the cots at the end of the small row of six. With an overjoyed cry, she dashed over to it and knelt down to inspect it all. Her beige cloak was frayed, but no worse for wear. Laying atop the wool fabric were her two personal belongings she brought with her from Palaveve: her pine tree necklace, and the kitsune plush Mrs. Hircus gave her before she died.

"You found them for me?" She was at a loss for words.

"We inspected the things that you left in the forest and on your person before changing you into the plain clothes you're wearing now. We needed a sterile set of clothes after addressing your wounds." He pointed at the small blossom of red on her shoulder blade where Finnley had bit her. It seemed the wound had not fully healed when they put the shirt on her.

Taylor had wondered where she had gotten the drab-white, loose-fitting pants and shirt when she awoke the previous night. She nodded at his explanation. "Thank you for getting these back for me, I appreciate it." She perused the surrounding area and found it devoid of much else. "What happened to my clothes?"

Mikhail leaned up on one of the supporting beams of the tent as he talked across the tent at her. "Natalia offered to launder your fatigue pants this morning in the river, but your shirt was a complete loss."

Taylor's ear's drooped. "Oh…" She didn't have many clothes to her name to begin with, so the fact she had even less than when she started was disheartening.

"That's also why Terrati is in town right now." Mikhail's tried to smile to assure her. "He is looking for clothes that will fit you. You may not be a guest here, but we're trying to be courteous enough of your needs."

"That is nice of you—wait!" Her eyes flashed wide. "Who dressed me last night?"

Mikhail put both paws up to placate her fear. "Relax, Taylor. There will be no one taking advantage of you while you are here. I will make sure of that. Besides, nobody else wanted to get near you, let alone carry you back to camp and get you dressed down on account of your tail." He pointed out.

"Nobody else?" Taylor was connecting the dots. Looking directly into Mikhail's eyes, she blushed hard and involuntarily tried to turn away from him.

"I'm not that type of tiger." He groaned at the implication in her expression. "I've dealt with many trauma victims in my lifetime and had to evacuate them to medical help before. Getting them prepped for surgery and such is normal for me. You were no different." Her body language wasn't changing much. Exhaling loudly, he continued. "You are under my care, and I will do what I can to see that you are safe, or to shoot you if you do something stupid like endanger either myself or anyone else."

"You almost had me sold until that last bit," Taylor commented dryly.

Mikhail shrugged his shoulders. "I'm just keeping the situation real."

"Taylor!" squeaked a voice as both Pine and Mitchell bounded into view and skittered through the legs of Mikhail.

"Pine! Mitchell!" Taylor met them halfway in the tent and got to her knees as she opened her arms for them to leap into them with gusto. They nuzzled their heads up against her neck and hugged her tight. "Glad to see they didn't lock you up too!"

Mikhail was looking confused, checking around his ankles before gazing up to see what was going on. After a few moments, he calmed himself and just observed. "Oh, right. Fey told me about your friends."

Taylor looked up, a smile on her face, feeling happy for once in the past few days. "Yeah? I hope they didn't get into too much mischief today. They can be little stinkers!"

Mikhail had an odd mixture of amusement and befuddlement. "Nothing we couldn't handle, I'm sure. I wasn't the one watching over…what were their names?"

"Pine and Mitchell," Taylor reminded, giving each another squeeze.

"Yes, that." He nodded. "However, I was not the one watching over them since I was in charge of you. You'd…have to ask one of the others to find out."

Her merriment turned to one of concern. "Wait, if you're watching over me, then who is watching over these two? Based on how you all have treated me, I'm surprised you just let these two run amok."

Mikhail thought long on how to answer. "If they're your friends like you claim, then they are with you. We know the other two wolves are with the Arbiter or at least were hired by him, so they cannot be trusted and must be watched. You are our target of interest, so we need to make sure you are delivered back to Zabökar safely. As long as they stick with you, we see no problems keeping them around." He finished with a grin.

Taylor clucked her tongue, setting both the skunk and raccoon down. "All roads lead to Zabökar it seems." At a grunt from Mikhail, she explained. "You guys want to take me there. Trevor and Gregor want to take me back there. Everyone seems to want me to return home for some reason." She had to laugh at the convenient absurdity of it.

"You used to live there?" he asked. Taylor responded affirmatively. Mikhail thought on it a bit. "One could definitely see that as being ironically coincidental. However, one could also attribute that to fate as well."

"Fate? What is that?" Pine scratched his head, hopping up onto the cot that would be Taylor's.

"It is the order of the universe, of things out of one's control that happen to you regardless of what you do to prevent or enable it," Mikhail rattled off, looking at Taylor.

Taylor scrunched her nose at the concept. "Sounds too much like the Script to me."

"Probably because it is." He relaxed a bit and followed Taylor's lead when she sat down on her cot.

Mitchell cocked his head to the side as he studied the large tiger. "You don't look the type to believe in that stuff."

"I'd be surprised if he didn't." Taylor mumbled.

Mikhail laughed at the assertion, his gruff demeanor melting. "Of course I don't. Not at first, anyway. I was a down-to-earth TALOS operative. I was very much a firm believer in carving out my own destiny and directing the flow of my life by my own actions." His eyes grew distant, as if remembering something unpleasant. "Things change however, and lives lost cannot be reclaimed. I soon discovered that it mattered little what I did, things would always turn out the way they should. This was one of the hardest lessons of my entire life."

Taylor blinked at him. "So you were a cop?"

"I was a special operative for the government," he clarified.

"Then what are you doing with these hooligans and bounty hunters?" Pine pointed out the entrance of the tent to where Fey and Natalia were sitting.

"That does seem suspicious." Taylor narrowed her eyes.

Mikhail frowned at the accusation. "I do not consider us to be part of such lowly professions. All activities performed by this group are sanctioned legally by the High Council. As for me joining them, their goals matched my own, and so I am riding with them for the time being."

"Was it because of the Script that you stopped being a cop?" Taylor leaned back on her paws, trying to get into a relaxing position on the cot. It seemed pretty futile; they just weren't that comfortable.

Mikhail scratched his chin. "Operative... But you could say that." He watched the small sparrows collecting seed just outside the tent flap for a moment, the small hush of wind gently swaying the tent with its push. Then it looked as though he realized he had been quiet a bit too long. "I made many mistakes in my life. Mistakes that cost me those I hold dear. Once I realized it was all meant to be and none of my decisions meant a damn thing, I chose to have my entire Script read to me. To know exactly how my entire life was going to go."

"Wouldn't that get boring?" Her expression turned serious. "I think it would make life completely pointless if I knew how it was going to happen. What is the point of living after something like that?" She realized she was echoing Trevor's sentiment about the Script.

"It seems like it would be a dull life if you just go through the motions of what some piece of paper says happens to you," Mitchell added.

"There are plenty of reasons." Mikhail clasps his paws together, sitting forward a bit, smiling at Taylor. "Once I realized nothing I did mattered, I felt a huge burden lift from my shoulders. It was extremely fascinating and interesting to see my life play out in exactly the way my Script predicted it would. Trying to guess the cryptic meaning behind the aged words and how it actually happened has been a curious experience."

"Have you ever tried changing your future?" Pine suggested, finding a comfortable spot on Taylor's lap and curling up.

"Like, now that you know what is coming, tried doing things to stop it from happening?" Taylor finished for him.

Mikhail shook his head. "I did several times, but it did not matter. The vague wording revealed in my Script was broad enough to fit the eventual outcome despite everything I did."

"I hate the Script," Taylor blurted. "I don't even know why it exists."

"Or even how it exists." Mitchell seemed hard in thought.

"One of the many mysteries of this life, to be sure," Mikhail agreed. He grumbled as he worked himself back to standing, a few pops coming from his kneecaps. "As much as I've enjoyed this chat, there are other things I must attend to." He pointed a finger at her. "Just because I'm not around in the immediate vicinity does not mean I'm not keeping an eye on you. Don't try anything funny and we'll get along swimmingly."

With this final warning, he flashed her his teeth before stepping out of the tent and closing it behind him. Taylor stared at his departure for a while before turning to her two companions. Pine seemed to be tired and was stretching out on her thighs. Mitchell was pacing back and forth, agitated at something.

"He seemed nicer than the others." Pine yawned.

"Mikhail is, yes." Taylor had to concede the fact, despite his initial gruffness. "I thought so too of Fey, but now I'm not so sure. He seemed conflicted on a lot of things. I don't even know who to trust less, Trevor or Fey."

"And that is what I'm worried about." Mitchell continued to wander the tent.

"What's wrong?" Taylor asked.

"Two different groups want you for something, yet neither is telling you the full truth of why." Mitchell stopped and looked her directly in the eyes. "Taking you in for safety, protection, or refuge is all nice and well, but that seems to be just some broad encompassing reason to get us to relax and let our guard down."

"You really are worked up about this, aren't you?" Taylor smiled, lightly picking Pine up from her lap and setting him beside her on the cot. "Would you two mind looking away for a moment?"

Without asking why, Mitchell did as she requested and kept talking. "Yeah, I am. We were doing fine, just you, me, and Pine, for a year. Nobody bothered us and we made a decent living. Then suddenly everyone wants a piece of you, and nobody seems to want to tell us the real reason why."

Taylor let him speak as she took off her stained shirt and examined the wound on her chest from Finnley's teeth. Having Ahya swoop around to her front, she allowed her tail's tongue to gingerly press up against the laceration and begin pulsating as saliva was generated to coat the bite. A soothing feeling of rushing relief surged through her breast as the wound began to close up and the tissue mended itself whole once more.

Having only taken a minute, she stuffed her head and arms back through the shirt openings and addressed Mitchell on his concerns. "I knew this day would come. I knew it was only a matter of time before those who had been chasing me caught up to me, and our perfect little life was disrupted once again."

"I just wish we could have had more time together," Pine mumbled.

"We are having plenty of time together now." Taylor beamed at the skunk.

"You know what I mean." He seemed exasperated.

She stepped over to ruffle his head fur, causing him to playfully bat her paw away. "To tell you the truth…" Taylor plopped down beside Pine, Mitchell finally clambering up to be along her other side. "I expected far worse people to show up to kidnap me once again. All things considered, we could be with far worse people."

"That doesn't mean we should trust them," Mitchell cautioned.

"No, I didn't say that." She poked the wary raccoon. "All I'm saying is, we are probably in the best place we could be." She stared out after where Mikhail left them. "But I promise you this: the first chance we get, we'll bust our way out of here and escape."

7
FISH

Ari busted through the tavern doors a bit harder than she had anticipated, but she was furious. Her father, the Arbiter, had entrusted her with the task of finding this Taylor, and she had already run afoul of a dead end. She had pictures of what she looked like from social media feeds from the disaster that was Palaveve, and they had a tracking device planted in the bikes they supplied those idiot bounty hunters they hired. Between these two things alone, she should have been led straight to her quarry.

Instead, all she found were the scrapped remains of their motorcycles and the evidence of an altercation, complete with spent bomb shells and scraps of torn or bloodied fur strewn about the scene. She was so livid she tore apart the remainder of the bikes and burned a few trees around to the ground. She attempted to follow any footsteps made in the dirt, but whoever had taken Taylor knew what they were doing and hid their tracks well.

With little course of direction and not wanting to report back a failure to her father just yet, she traveled to the nearest town. From what she gathered it was a fairly industrialized town, which was an unusual occurrence this far out from one of the major cities like Zabökar. Pinning the town's name as Howlgrav on the map, she had set a course for the place, kicking her bike into gear and roaring in like a demon from the netherworld.

Irritated and wanting nothing but a drink, she had parked and locked her bike outside a tavern with the maglocks that were so common these days. She barreled through the double doors, garnering the attention of every occupant inside. Some shriveled in fear, while others stood, revolted at her appearance. Not a single soul in that establishment stood unfazed.

This was expected, but she still scoffed at the locals. She was a mix of a tortoise and a crocodile, two species seldom seen this far north in a land of nothing but mammals, if they were seen at all. Those few who were still north of the wall resided in secluded lands south of Zabökar. Walking past the staring patrons, she purposefully left her tail to drag along the floor, creating the only sound in the quiet room.

The bartender cleared his throat as he directed the rest of the customers to resume their business. The din slowly grew to normal volume levels, but there were still many a curious stare in Ari's direction. She sidled up to the bar and pulled a stool out, letting it hover a bit before sitting on it, forcing it to rest on the floor and start ticking away her time on tab.

"Can I help you?" the imposing barkeep asked, setting aside the current mug he was cleaning.

He was a grizzled brown bear with a crooked nose that had definitely seen a fight or two. His buttoned plaid shirt was busting at the seams, the center puckering around each button due to his massive bulk. His look was not unkind, but he was clearly not comfortable with having a customer of Ari's stature in his place of business.

"Give me a Tallup, on the rocks," she ordered, relaxing and putting both her arms on the bar. The two elands on either side of her shuffled their chairs away a few feet. She didn't deign to recognize their reaction.

The bear nodded at her request, seemingly appeased by her sensible customer act, and went about making it for her. Ari continued to face forward, but allowed her cybernetic red iris to rove about the room.

As far as backwater town bars went, it wasn't too awful; it was evident that the owners of this place took great pride in its cleanliness and décor. Several neon lights were illuminating the dark corners of the bar, advertising their brand-name liquors or drinks. There were even a couple posters for local musicians and bands that would be playing live at this venue, although the stage looked like it might need some attention given the dust on the floor there and empty microphone stands.

"Here you go, ma'am." The bear slid her amber drink down the bar. She caught it easily. "Did you want to keep the tab open?" She nodded in the affirmative and he responded in kind.

He was going to turn to another customer who had stepped up to the bar, but she waved him down to come back over. She took out a photograph of Taylor—crudely taken by a bystander in Palaveve as she was being dragged in a net behind Trevor—and flipped it to the barkeep. "Have you seen any wolf pass through here that looks like this?"

The bear ignored the honk of his slighted guest as he took the photograph from Ari and studied it. After a time, he shook his head and handed it back to her. "That's an odd one. I would remember if I had seen or heard someone come in with stories of a wolf who looked like that. I'm sorry I can't help you. Are you a bounty hunter of sorts?"

"You could say that," Ari droned, bringing the glass to her lips and taking a sip. She reveled in the hot liquid, burning her throat as it went down.

"Is there a reward for turning this person in?" The bear looked hopeful.

"For you? No," she responded flatly, taking another drink.

"Then I doubt you'll find many people here that will want to help you." He bristled.

She finally looked at him with both her one real eye and her cybernetic one. The effect was instant as even the big bear shivered from her glare. Her gaze wandered down to the nametag affixed to his chest. "Lawrence, is it? How about you tend to your customers and let me enjoy my drink."

"You came to me, little girl." Lawrence was indignant at her dismissal of his offer. "I'd watch that attitude of yours. Not many people seem to like what you are, from what I can tell. You may not have a pleasant experience if you step out of your lane."

Ari simply stared straight ahead, her eyes now on the plethora of liquor bottles lining the back counter shelves, her reflection peeking through between them in the mirror behind. Seeing he was going to get no more response out of her, Lawrence grumbled his displeasure and returned to the customer who was impatiently waiting for his attention.

Ari finished the rest of her drink and ordered another Tallup. Nursing it like she did the first, she went over everything she knew about Taylor in her mind. She pulled out a few sheets of paper from her corduroy pants with information given to her by her father. Her objective was a teenage female wolf with an unusual tail. Was once a prominent teenage celebrity in the underground circuit in Zabökar before going missing almost two years ago.

She poured over the words some more, curious as to why her father would be interested in this wolf when he had plenty of other successful subjects to draw upon for his ambitions. She sneered at the visage of Taylor, of the pretty redhead that graced the photographs. Even her heterochromatic eyes looked dazzling with what little she could see from the awkwardly taken pictures. Some people just shouldn't be on social media if they couldn't be bothered to take perfect photographs.

Ari stuffed the documents back into her maroon vest, then finished off her drink and paid her tab. Without further words to the proprietor, she got off the stool and it hovered back into position to reset its timer. Out of the corner of her eye, she noticed Lawrence making an odd gesture to two wolverines off in the corner of the room. She wouldn't have noticed them had she not caught the exchange. Now she was on heightened alert, but did not let that show when she exited the building.

Heading outside, she looked at her sleek, black motorcycle parked at the entrance. She could hop on and head out, but she was curious to see how this would play out with the wolverines. Shrugging off her method of transportation, she nonchalantly paced down the sidewalk, the buzz finally kicking in from the booze earlier.

She reveled in the reactions of the local populace as they steered a wide berth from her, some even crossing the street just to pass her by. She must have looked quite the scene, surrounded by nothing but mammals. Predators and prey alike all looked similar in their fashion by the varied patterns of their fur. Many would be self-conscious from all this negative attention, but not Ari. This only aided her in pinpointing quickly who were threats and who were not.

As expected, she glanced back and saw the two wolverines in trenchcoats exit the bar and keep a fair distance behind her, never speeding up except to keep pace. Eager now for the fight, she ducked into a nearby alley and simply awaited her would-be attackers. Right on cue, they rounded the corner and stood abreast to completely block her exit out of the dead-end alley.

"Boss says your kind isn't allowed here." The left one cackled, his voice raspy.

"You shouldn't be poking your nose around and insulting the boss like you did." The right one chortled.

They both flashed their claws and bared their fangs. Wolverines were notorious for being melee fighters, tearing their opponents to ribbons within seconds. Using her red iris to identify their rough weights and sizes, she gathered that they were of similar builds, and she probably wouldn't be able to lift either one of them on her strength alone. Traditional methods of combat were probably not an option for her—not as if she'd use them anyway.

"Boss this, boss that. Seems like neither of you have a mind of your own," she ridiculed, taking pleasure in the reaction.

"Listen here, you little shit!" the left one snarled, clacking his teeth. "We can do this the easy way or the hard way. We can either rough you up some, have some fun with you before booting you to the curb, or we can just kill you."

The right one looked at his partner a bit off. "Some fun? Uh, I don't think I would even know how to given what she is. Where would you even start?" He laughed at her, being swiftly joined by his companion.

"You're right, let's just rough up long-snout and show her the law around here." The first one snickered, advancing on her.

Ari calmly let them insult her appearance. She was used to it. Her crocodile snout was an oddity among mammals who had muzzles far shorter than her. Her leathery skin was a far cry from the soft, lush fur that blanketed the majority of people around these parts. She even wasn't insulted on being called fat or pudgy because of her half-baked shell that was not functional like a real one, and did not suit her overall appearance or body shape.

She reacted without emotion to the wolverine on the right first. As he lunged for her, she ducked under his arms and shifted to his side, her tail swinging around and slapping into his partner with a loud smack. He cried out in pain as her sharpened dorsal fins punctured through his clothes and embedded into his flesh.

"What the hell are you?" The wounded wolverine attempted to dig his nails into her hard hide, the claws securing only a small purchase into her skin.

136

"Your deaths." She smiled, her red iris shifting to the other.

Her tail muscle being far stronger than her arms or legs, she cartwheeled away from the other wolverine and flung his buddy with her tail, now loosed from the fins, causing him to sail across the alley. His head hit a metal dumpster with a sickening crunch as his entire body fell limp to the dirty pavement. His vacant eyes stared back at her, his life swiftly ended.

"No no no!" the remaining wolverine shouted at his dead companion. With an enraged growl, he surged forward to tackle the ugly reptile.

Ari smoothly whapped the ground with her tail, then went to a knee and placed two fingers to the ground. Instantly, the ground erupted in molten fire. The pavement cracked and broke into chunks as the superheated earth underneath bubbled up in a geyser of magma. She sent the lethal conflagration in a beeline towards her target.

The wolverine turned tail and ran, yelling out witchcraft and black magic. His lack of speed was his demise as the boiling line of magma pitched upward and impaled him from rectum to sternum. He screamed in howling agony as the liquefied rock was melting him from the inside out. Steam billowed out all his orifices as the air tried to find the path of least resistance from his body.

His eyes slowly turned to her in horror as Ari serenely walked over and stood in front of him, her hands on her hips. "My Script..." he gasped, his capacity for speech spent.

"Your Script doesn't matter," she cooed, patting him on the nose, his eyes rolling up before they slithered out into a goo down his face. "I think I'll leave your head as a reminder to your 'Boss' to not cross me."

She sliced him at the neck, catching the still-smoking head in her arms. Satisfied with her handiwork, she took the time to watch as the rest of his body melted on the pillar of heated rock. When nothing was left, she snapped her fingers and it instantly cooled, leaving nothing behind but upturned pavement and something odd for the local police to figure out on the morning.

As she passed by the entrance to the tavern, she entered head-first, tossing it onto the bar. Lawrence was beside himself as he stared at the decapitated wolverine, an unrecognizable lump of charred flesh and

137

fur. His eyes haltingly rose to meet her own as she brought out a picture and slid it across the counter.

"Have a copy," she said with more elation in her voice than necessary. "If you see someone who looks like this show up in town, do give me a ring. My cell phone number is on the back." She made to turn, but swung back around with a finger up in the air, waggling it a bit. "Oh, and don't call me 'little girl' anymore."

Without another word, she walked out to the terrified looks of everyone in attendance. She swung her legs over the bike, unhitched the maglock, and pulled out, roaring down the road. She may not have any leads on Taylor just yet, but she'd be damned if she didn't put a few seeds to lay in wait to sprout.

Terrati returned later that evening. He was a gazelle of unique fur pattern, where the traditional black fur on the sides of his throat went down his neck instead of disappearing around back his ears. He was dressed the same as the others, in a plain khaki t-shirt and fatigue pants. The moment he saw Ahya turn around and inspect him, he let out a little scream and skittered off to hide behind Mikhail, who was not pleased with his cohort's embarrassing behavior.

His ears drooping with frustration, Fey rolled his eyes at Terrati and addressed Taylor. "Meet our resident spy, supply mammal, and expert sharpshooter. He was with us on the hill when we first fired on you." He looked around at the small group of Mikhail, Terrati, and Natalia. Finnley was still recovering from his fall. "I believe you have met all of us at least in some form or another. When Finnley hopefully recovers tomorrow, we will move out."

"So you keep telling me." Taylor was still sore about her treatment, not that she had much choice in the matter. The least she could do was express her displeasure, even if it irritated her captors.

Fey squinted his eyes at her, but ultimately dismissed her sass. "I've said it multiple times now, Taylor. We are not here to harm you.

Not without good reason, anyway. Do not give us any reason to do so and just stay out of trouble until it is time to head back to Zabökar." He waved to Mikhail to escort her somewhere else while he attended to the packing of the truck.

It was a large, military vehicle with camo-paint the color of beige and maple leaves, something that would blend in perfectly around this area, especially in the fall. It had four hover-wheels for precision control across any terrain. There was a big wagon-like drapery thrown over the back and tied down to hooks in the wheel wells that protected the contents of the truck bed from the elements. Taylor was impressed at the amount of hardware they had on hand out in the wilderness.

He put a paw on Natalia nearby as he leaned in, speaking softly enough Taylor could just barely hear. "Can you watch over Taylor while I help these two weaklings?"

Both him and the snow leopard shared a smile. "Of course, Mikhail. I don't think she's going to give me any issues."

"Thank you, Natalia." He bowed his head before stepping off to do the heavy lifting.

Taylor and Ahya watched them pack up the campsite, breaking focus only when Taylor noticed Natalia coming toward her. "So where are your friends?" She looked around before coming to a stop mere feet from Ahya. "I heard all about them from Fey and Mikhail."

Taylor scanned the forest around them before shrugging. "They're probably around. This is the first time they've had this type of freedom in years. There is plenty for them to scavenge and eat around here besides the food you already got on paw. I'm not too worried about them."

A brief flash of disappointment washed over Natalia's face, but she recovered quickly enough. She lightly patted Taylor's shoulder, stopping only when the wolf stared at the paw touching her. "How about you and I go for a walk? I find it does one good to breathe in the fresh scent of the woods. It clears one's head."

Taylor was still not sure what to make of Natalia, but as far as captors went, she seemed the least worrisome. Despite their initial encounter which was pretty dangerous, they seemed to get along okay. She couldn't hold it against the snow leopard for trying to stab her tail; it

139

was trying to kill her, after all. At length, Taylor made a non-committal face and just let Natalia lead the way.

They walked in silence for a time, neither really wanting to say much to the other. Ahya seemed more interested in scrounging for things to eat, moving this way and that to "examine" things either along the ground or near the trees. Natalia would sometimes be caught staring at Ahya as they walked, causing her to immediately cast her focus elsewhere. The sound of water was getting louder, and it seemed Natalia was guiding them to the riverside.

The scattering of trees thinned out and the scenery opened up to reveal the river. It was flowing fast, but not to the point where it would sweep them up and carry them downriver if they had ground for purchase under their hind paws. Taylor saw her own fatigue pants hanging to dry along a branch yawning over the water. Natalia probably wanted to take her here to grab the remainder of what little clothes Taylor came with before they had to leave this forest.

"I'm sorry for stabbing you," Natalia finally confessed, friendly but still aloof.

Taylor looked confused, wondering why she would even be apologizing at all. "It's fine. I was about to eat you. Well, um, my tail was anyway. I don't blame you for defending yourself."

Natalia gave a nod, before taking in the river before them. "I don't usually like to harm others, but I do what I must. You seem like a nice girl, so I was pretty distraught at having to hurt you. You giving Fey attitude has endeared yourself somewhat to me."

"That's surprising." Taylor smirked, sitting herself down by the tree overlooking the water, her pants dangling above her head. "You and Finnley seemed very intense, and it seemed like you were trying to kill me."

"Things were getting wildly out of control," Natalia admitted, turning her head back to Taylor. "We needed to secure you and quickly. The entire operation was a mess straight from the start, so urgency was paramount." She clasped her paws behind her lower spine, standing up straight like a trained soldier would.

Taylor had to stifle a chuckle watching the snow leopard. "It feels like you're giving me a situation report. You can relax. I'm your prisoner. You don't have to report to me."

Natalia seemed to notice her stance and brought her paws down to her sides, flicking her tail with silent admonition of her instincts. "I'm sorry." She gazed back out over the flowing river. "You're not exactly a prisoner. You're our charge."

"One without many rights," Taylor reminded. She focused on Ahya, who suddenly seemed interested in the water, sometimes dipping low to inspect the surface.

"Right." Natalia agreed with hesitation. "Still, we are tasked with bringing you in safely."

"Safe and unspoiled?" Taylor asked.

"What?" It was Natalia's turn to be puzzled.

"That's what Trevor said." After a silent pause, she clarified. "One of the two wolves you captured with me." That brought recognition to the leopard's eyes. "They also wanted to bring me back to Zabökar, except they made a point to say unharmed. Is that the same with you?"

"I would think it be obvious," Natalia said matter-of-factly.

"No, it really isn't." They remained in silence for a time until Taylor gestured to Natalia's chest. "I'm sorry for Ahya hurting you. She was just doing what she had to do to defend me."

It took a few minutes to realize what Taylor was pointing to, but she laughed and lifted up the bottom of her shirt to reveal bare, craggy flesh. The fur where Ahya's tongue had touched was completely gone. The acid from her saliva melted it completely away, and had almost cleared most of the upper layers of Natalia's skin, nearly reaching to her inner organs. It would be weeks before the sensitivity of those patches of skin would be safe to touch.

"I would like to say I have experienced worse, but that was one of the worst feelings I had ever felt in my life. Almost as bad as when you lose loved ones. It was like being burned alive where your tail touched me."

"I don't think those two examples are really comparable."

141

Natalia put on a brave face, but winced a bit when pulling the shirt back down, the fabric brushing the tender skin something fierce. "Is that a natural talent of your tail?"

Taylor considered Ahya. "I never really thought about it that much. I guess it is. Her saliva does different things based on what she chooses to do."

"Chooses? I heard from Mikhail that she has a mind of her own, but I wasn't sure to believe him." She faced Taylor more directly now, her attention now fully on the tail.

"She does at times." Taylor petted her tail a few times, Ahya completely intent on the water, ignoring the affection. "I can control her mostly, but like right now, this is all her. I have no idea what she is thinking or doing." She smiled at her tail, watching it "kiss" the water a few times, curious as to what she was seeing, if anything at all.

"What's it like living with something like that?" Natalia seemed genuinely enthralled with the concept of having a mouth inside of her tail.

Taylor's smile faded. "Hard." She gave herself a few beats to collect her thoughts. "I've always had to apologize for what she does. I remember having a normal life at one point. I have my mother to thank for that."

"What was her name?"

"Murana." Taylor smiled softly. "From what I can remember, she did a lot for me to not feel alone."

"You must have had a strong mother," Natalia commented. "Is she still alive?"

"I don't know…" Taylor truly didn't. "I don't remember. I don't think she is…but I hope so."

"I don't understand. You can't remember?"

Taylor broke her vigil over Ahya and looked at Natalia. "I remember her contracting some sort of terminal cancer, and that I ran away from home. I think it was a year later…maybe two—it is a bit fuzzy—that I was kidnapped. I don't know who they were. I don't know what they wanted. All I know is that since then, my memory has been spotty for that small time period and there are things that I should remember, but they're just…gone. I do remember most of it though."

"That sounds awful. So you have no idea what happened to her?" Natalia placed a paw to her breast, completely absorbed in the story. "Not even through social networks? Surely she tried to find you through there?"

Taylor shook her head, watching Ahya again. "I never used those, and I don't think she does...um, did either. I haven't been back home since. I've been on the run, in constant fear of being taken again for just being what I am."

Natalia folded her arms, something dawning on her. "Now I think I see why you were violent and resisting. You don't trust anyone right now. Especially since both parties you've encountered want to take you back to Zabökar. You think either of us are the same ones that took you from before."

Taylor snorted at the assertion. "Yeah, hard to trust many people these days, especially when they use forceful tactics and threats to make sure you comply."

Suddenly, Ahya swooped down into the water with a splash. She rose up with several fish pierced between her teeth. Within a few seconds, they were swallowed quickly and digested. Taylor already licked her lips, the taste of fresh fish upon her tongue. The bead of fullness slowly expanded in her stomach.

"Oh, that was a good one, Ahya! Catch another!" Taylor seemed ecstatic, now shifting to her knees and looking out over the river herself.

Natalia tilted her head. "You like fish? I thought you hated meat."

Taylor's head swiveled to her. "What? Did Mikhail tell you that? Geez, news travels fast around here."

Natalia simpered. "Well, when there are so few of us and you are the main topic these days, we get to hear everything that's happening with you."

"Great..." Taylor rolled her eyes, resuming her watch on the water.

Ahya scooped up a few more fish before gobbling them down enthusiastically. Taylor hummed her pleasure at the flavors assaulting her mouth. It had been ages since either of them had fish. She felt like a little kid again, looking all silly on her hands and knees leaning over the water expectantly.

Sensing the eyes of Natalia boring holes into her, Taylor turned her head. "Yes? Look, it has been so long. I'm just happy to have something other than fresh fruits, vegetables, and baked goods."

"But it is meat," Natalia reiterated.

Taylor had to sit back down against the tree to address the question in the air. "It's mammal meat I can't stand. Ever since I ate my first person, I've never been the same. I've hated the flavor ever since. Every time I try to make myself eat a bite, I am reminded of the disgusting flavors of those that Ahya has eaten. I get queasy just thinking about it."

"You can taste everything she eats?" Natalia was more intrigued than ever.

"Yeah, unfortunately." Taylor sighed.

"But you're a wolf…a carnivore. You should be used to the taste of meat."

"Not this carnivore." Taylor began losing interest in the conversation.

Natalia didn't continue that line of thought, her eyes overlooking the water as Ahya continued to splash and catch more fish. Taylor left her to her thoughts as she resumed her watch over her tail. After a time, Natalia nodded silently as if confirming something to herself.

"May I touch her?" she asked suddenly.

Taylor jerked involuntarily at the request. She gawked at the snow leopard, wondering if she heard right. "Um…I…no? I mean, no one has ever asked me that."

"Oh, I'm sorry." Natalia looked at the ground ashamed. "That actually was quite rude of me. I almost forgot that it was a part of your body. It is your tail after all, and those can be…sensitive topics for someone who isn't your partner."

Taylor blushed and glanced away, suddenly interested in the clouds through the leaves. "I just never really thought about anyone else touching her or being interested in that. I don't really have any opinion of people touching each other's tails. It's just not something that's come up in my life, that's all."

144

After a moment, Natalia persisted. "But may I?"

"Why? I don't understand why you'd want to." Taylor was feeling a bit self-conscious.

Natalia scratched the side of her left arm a few moments. "I've just not met anything like your tail in all my life. I'm curious to see if it just feels like a normal tail or something different."

"I guess…" Taylor willed Ahya to stop fishing and lay over her lap, the mouth closing up just enough to not appear threatening. "More surprised you're not scared of it."

"I am a little afraid of it. It did almost try to eat me." Natalia laughed nervously, joined apprehensively by Taylor.

She knelt down on both knees beside Taylor, her paws timidly hovering over the bulky end of the tail. With cautious movements, Natalia sunk her paws into the fur. She looked surprised at how deep her paws went, the entire bulk disappearing into the fluff. She finally reached the flesh underneath. Instead of smooth skin, it was all wrinkled and full of deep trenches.

Taylor shuddered at the touch and dug her claws into her pants. Natalia noticed this and immediately removed her paws. "I'm sorry, this must be uncomfortable for you."

"N-No… It's just an odd feeling. That's all." She tried to hide the shock it gave her to have someone touch her tail that way.

"It doesn't feel normal," Natalia commented.

"That certainly makes me feel better."

"Oh, I didn't mean it that way. I meant, it felt really…uneven. I'm not sure how to describe it, but it wasn't flat underneath your fur." Natalia reverted back to her language briefly, trying to find the right word.

"It stretches." Taylor was finally able to catch her breath. "Ahya can shrink or grow based on the size of what she wants to eat."

Natalia recalled the immense size Ahya was when she attempted to eat her whole. "I can certainly picture that." She shivered a bit at the memory.

Taylor looked at Natalia's shirt and imagined the ruined skin beneath that she caused. She gestured to her chest. "Maybe I could help you with that, um, I mean Ahya could."

145

Natalia went to look to what Taylor was pointing at, but both ladies jumped as Natalia's phone rang loudly. She popped it out and held it to her ear. "Ah, yes, of course. We'll be right there."

"Was that Fey?" Taylor asked with some hint of annoyance.

"No, actually it was Mikhail. Finnley has recovered well enough to travel. We're to meet them back at the truck." She looked back down at Ahya. "What were you going to ask?"

Taylor shook her head. "Nevermind."

Natalia studied her a few moments. "Well, if you want, you can catch a few more fish before we head back. Don't forget your pants when you do."

Taylor waved a paw at her. "Nah, I think I'm good." She hauled herself up and dusted off her borrowed pants. She took down the fatigues off the tree branch, considering them a moment before looking at the ones Natalia was wearing. They were slightly different colors and prints, but they were similar enough to be the same at a distance. "I could almost pass off as one of you if I were to wear this."

Watching Taylor drape the pants over her arm, Natalia confirmed her thought. "That's why we kept them for you. Fey had the idea that the more you looked like us, the less out of place you would be to unfriendly eyes."

"That's pretty smart." Figures that Fey would already be ahead of her on that idea.

They shared a smile before departing the river. Taylor was already feeling comfortable around the snow leopard. It started off pretty dicey, but she felt she could trust the big cat far more than anyone else she had met on this crazy kidnapping trip. Even Ahya wasn't as agitated around Natalia, which spoke volumes to Taylor. Even though she rarely understood her tail and the things it did, she usually trusted its judge of character.

Coming up on the campsite, Taylor noticed that all of the tents had been completely dismantled and were already packed up in the large military truck. From her vantage point she could see into the back of the bed, and noticed that Trevor and Gregor were nowhere to be found. Scanning the area, she couldn't even see where they had left them. Did they off them while she was gone and bury them quickly? The only other place they could be was where she woke up in the medical ward.

Taylor broke off to head towards the concrete building, turning back only when Natalia called out to her. "I think I forgot something inside. I won't be long, ok?"

Natalia's face didn't look so sure. The snow leopard gazed over at her companions, none of which had noticed them yet. "I don't think that's allowed."

Taylor gestured back to Mikhail and the others. "You guys overpower me five to one and I'm in a forest with no direction to go run off to. I'm just going to grab something I left back in the room you all had me in. Ok?"

Natalia looked back over to Mikhail and the others before meeting Taylor's eyes again. "Make it quick, ok? Just in and out, or I'll have to go in after you."

"Thank you!" Taylor placed her paws together in thanks before dashing inside through the heavy metal door.

No wonder Natalia allowed her to go in alone; this was literally the only entrance into the building. The other end of the hall was a dead end, with multiple doorways leading off from the central corridor. She hastily popped her head into each room, getting more disappointed with each passing entryway. Near the end at the second to last door, her breath caught in her throat as she beheld both Trevor and Gregor in the center of a bare room, all furniture removed.

Both were bound by heavy ropes with hind paws and arms behind their backs, each wolf resting on their knees. Their mouths were gagged with more rope to prevent them from calling out for help. Shocked at the harsh treatment of her former captors, she rushed in and noticed oozing cuts and bruises mixed with torn fur. Even Trevor's metal arm was removed. She couldn't see where it was placed.

She knelt down beside Trevor, doing her best to undo his mouthpiece. "What did they do to you?"

She managed to get enough of the rope out of his mouth for him to respond. "They're not who you think they are! They interrogated us on the Arbiter and what we were going to do to you."

"What were you going to do to me?" Taylor asked without thinking.

"We already told you!" Trevor snarled. Gregor moaned against his own restraints. Trevor grimaced at his outburst. "I'm sorry, Taylor. I didn't mean to snap at you like that, but they are planning to leave with you and leave us here to die."

"As much as I feel you deserve this type of punishment—" This brought a scowl from both wolves, but she finished her thought. "—for Palaveve, I still don't like the idea of you dying over it."

"Can you help us out of these ropes?" Trevor struggled against his, having a harder time of it than Gregor since his lack of a full arm forced Fey and the others to link the ropes to his hind paws behind his back.

Taylor studied the intricate knots and despaired. "I don't even know the first thing about untying this!"

Trevor grumbled, but remained hopeful. "Is there anything else in this building you can find that is sharp?"

She got back up to stand and slowly backed away. "I don't know. They're all outside, and it won't be long before they notice I've been gone for too long."

Trevor's eyes bulged. "They know you're in here?"

"Well, one of them does. I don't think any of the others do yet," Taylor guessed.

"Then whoever does probably doesn't know we're in here! Otherwise they wouldn't have let you come in. You don't have a lot of time, please help us!" Trevor seemed genuinely worried.

Gregor finally got enough of his mouth free from his gag to chip in. "I know we haven't been the best of wolves to you, but I don't believe you have it in you to let us die from starvation and thirst here like your new 'friends' out there."

His final quip caused her expression to sour. "You almost convinced me."

"Gregor!" Trevor snarled at him.

"Ahya, break only a single rope on each." Taylor said dispassionately.

"What are you—" Gregor began.

148

Trevor understood what she was doing and called out quickly, "Do it on the underside of our wrists so it is less visible!"

Taylor nodded acknowledgement. Ahya loomed over them, her size increasing as her maw opened wide with threatening purpose. The tongue lashed out to smack each of them in the muzzle at their attitudes, then Ahya pounced down behind each of them and snapped her jaws, her teeth strong enough to cut the fibers of the thick rope. She only loosened their restraints by a single knot, but it would be enough, given time, for them to eventually free themselves.

"That's it?" Gregor began to whine.

"Shut it!" Trevor seemed embarrassed on his friend's behalf. He bowed his head to Taylor. "Thank you. That was probably more than we deserved."

"It was," she said coldly. "The way I see it, if I release you now, either one side or the other will win, and I'll still be in custody with someone. This is not a good situation for me to run off in—even I can see that. I'm only doing this in the hopes you'll come after me like I know your boss will want you to and provide enough of a diversion for me to make a far better escape."

Trevor cracked a grin. "So sure that you'll be able to give us the slip a second time?"

"Here's hoping." She smiled. There was some yelling and a commotion from down the hall. They could all hear the lone entrance door being torn open. "Looks like Natalia told them I was in here."

Trevor did his best to turn his neck to indicate his back pocket. "Well if you are so intent on going through with that plan, make it easier on us and get a small tab in my pants here."

Taylor allowed Ahya to snake her tongue down into his pocket, causing Trevor to shiver involuntarily. She pulled out a small, square sheet of metal with adhesive on one side, then looked at him curiously. "What is the point of this?" she asked.

He turned to her with a determined look. "Try to affix that to one of their vehicle's hover-wheels. It'll go off in a few hours and at least delay them enough for us to catch up with you and provide that 'oh so convenient' escape you wanted." He gave her a wink.

149

"Guess I'll see you around then." Taylor waved stepping out of the door and nearly ran headlong into Mikhail, his immense bulk dominating her view.

"What are you doing?" he growled, his eyes not on her but the two wolves beyond.

"I just wanted to be sure you didn't kill them." Taylor explained.

His gaze shifted down to her. "What would it matter to you? Didn't think you'd be so kind-hearted to those who had kidnapped you."

"So you're saying I should be rude to you too then, since you all have basically done the same?" she sassed.

"Don't you get smart with me." Mikhail snarled to the side where Natalia was standing. "Take her to the truck and do not let her wander off again. I do not want Fey questioning your position in the group."

Natalia's ears drooped as she made a motion to lead Taylor out of the room by the arm. "I'm sorry, Mikhail. I wasn't really thinking. I didn't think she could really go anywhere from this building."

His expression softened. "It is alright. You weren't told where we had moved these two; just don't say anything to Fey about this mishap. I'll try to explain it and smooth things over. Right now, I'm going to go in and check their restraints."

This consolation broke Natalia's mood and she smiled at him. "Be careful. We'll be waiting out in the truck."

With a firm grip on her arm, Natalia led Taylor out of the medical facility. Not wanting to meet her eyes, Taylor apologized. "I'm sorry for lying to you."

The snow leopard didn't look at her. "It's fine. I let my guard down and I paid for it."

Taylor winced at the accusation that she'd abused Natalia's trust and attempt at friendship. They walked out into the sunlight, all eyes on them as she was guided to the truck. Fey had just opened the back flap and was indicating that she was to be loaded up in the back. Finnley and Terrati were already up there, buckled into their seats. The gazelle did not look pleased that she would be accompanying him on this trip.

It was quite a huge step up onto the truck bed from the ground. She would need either assistance or would need to use the large wheel as leverage to get up into it. Taking the opportunity to accidently trip when using a wheel as a stepstool, she braced herself with a paw on it. She used the adhesive on the metal tab Trevor gave her. It stuck easily to the inside tread of the wheel.

Finnley bemoaned her ineptitude of getting up into the truck. "Get on with it, princess! Get your ass up here and sit down. It should be easier for you since you're bigger than I am!"

"Charming, isn't he?" Taylor mumbled to herself as she lurched the rest of the way into the backend, her front sprawling forward onto the metal deck. Picking herself back up and settling down into one of the bare seats, she turned to Fey who was watching her with some amusement. "So, what now?"

"Now? We ride." He let the flap of the tarp covering drop.

8
BATHROOM

A huge bump jarred Taylor awake. The entire hooded cabin bed of the truck was bouncing uncontrollably, like being inside of a spinning drum rolling down a steep hill, but without the rotation. She must have dozed off while staring aimlessly out the small view between the tarp at the road behind them.

Trying to move, Taylor found that her wrists were magnetically locked again, but this time to a second pair bound around her ankles. This put her in an awkward position, crudely buckled into her uncomfortable metal seat that folded out from the truck siding, and leaning forward at a bad angle.

She raised her head as best she could to look around the interior, and saw that Mikhail, Terrati, and Finnley were still in the back riding with her. Fey was most likely driving and Natalia up there with him— probably admonished for letting her go unsupervised, depending on what Mikhail said to Fey.

Mikhail was in the seat across from her while Terrati chose to sit as far away as possible at the other end. Finnley was being very intrusive by sitting directly next to her, his beady otter eyes watching her every move.

"I don't like you," he stated plainly, his disdain evident in his face.

"That makes two of us." Taylor groaned, the aches of her body from being asleep in that distorted position coming in full force now that she was fully cognizant.

"Good. You should hate yourself." Finnley was brutal.

"Finnley!" Mikhail scolded. "Lay off of her."

"Humph!" He folded his arms and lounged back in his chair. Taylor noticed he was the only one not buckled in. "My lower back still throbs because of her, and this bumpy ass ride is doing me no favors!"

His comment forced Taylor to examine his diminutive body. Finnley had a full back brace that was tied snugly in front. His muscles were mushrooming over the edges of the brace, demonstrating just how constricting it was for him. If it was looser, any wrong movement could tweak his back in an awful way. Dealing with this injury was probably not coloring his opinion of Taylor in a positive light.

"Then maybe you shouldn't have come at me like you were trying to kill me with that stupid knife of yours!" Taylor was fuming. He was blaming her for his actions that caused this whole mess!

"If you had just come along quietly, then there would have been no need for us to come at you aggressively!" Finnley fired back.

She did her best to lean over into him. "Excuse me for thinking you were trying to murder me when all of you decided to fire upon us with explosive freaking shells! Of course I was trying to get away from you! I was running for my life!"

"If you weren't such a freak, we wouldn't have any need to bother with your sorry ass!" Finnley roared, standing up in his chair despite the bouncing.

"Finnley!" Mikhail roared. Terrati just shriveled in the corner where he sat.

"That does it, you stupid otter!" Taylor was wrathful.

She willed Ahya to rise up and swallow the insufferable otter whole. She didn't even care if it tasted awful. The prick was getting on her last nerves and she just wanted him gone. He had the gall to call her a freak and even had bit her shoulder once.

A restrictive tugging brought her attention to the state of her tail. She swiveled her head to look on her side opposite Finnley and saw that they had drawn Ahya out across several of the metal chairs, cross-hatching the seat buckles between them to entangle the tail in a mess of tight nylon. Taylor raged against the belts, but with her arms unable to assist, she could do nothing but thrash Ahya against them.

Taylor did her best to glare at Mikhail, raising her shackles as high as she could. "Really? I thought I wasn't to be treated like this anymore?"

"After explaining what had happened back in Falhoven to Fey, he decided it best to restrain you for our safety, and to prevent you from running off at the earliest opportunity," Mikhail informed without much regret.

Taylor stared at Ahya incredulously. "And you let them do this to us?"

"To be fair," Mikhail interceded on her tail's behalf, "the moment you fell asleep, we shot you up with a sleeping drug which, as we've discovered, affects your tail as well. That made it quite easy to secure you."

Finnley chortled loudly, finding great amusement in Taylor's anger. "Serves you right, you freaky wolf. I'm so glad that I'm getting paid to do this stupid job." With that, he flopped back down into the seat, his mirth dying the moment the jolt from his sitting jerked something fierce in his back. "Freaking crap!" He grimaced in agony.

It was Taylor's turn to chuckle. "I don't think I could have planned that any better."

Mikhail cleared his throat, giving them both a stern glare. "It's like I'm babysitting children."

"Well, technically she is one, isn't she?" Terrati spoke from the corner.

"I'm an adult, actually," Taylor clarified.

"Teenager," Finnley corrected her.

Taylor made a motion to smack Finnley with her head, but he slithered to the next seat over just in time. "I will headbutt you!" she threatened.

Mikhail stood and reached over to grab Finnley in his large paws, forcing the otter to sit beside his imposing bulk. "I will separate you two if I must. Can we at least try to have a nice journey to Zabökar?"

"Kind of hard to do that when you're chained like a criminal," Taylor snarked, glowering at the big tiger.

His expression never wavered at her ire. "You knew the boundaries laid down when you were with us, yet you still broke them and left the care of the one appointed to watch over you to go where you weren't supposed to."

"And how was I supposed to know that medical building was off limits? Nobody specifically told me I couldn't go back after you made me leave!" She was indignant.

"Finding you in the very room with those two wolves already makes your motives suspect." Mikhail folded his arms, confident in his reasoning. "As insulting as it is to you, we were paid to bring in people like yourself. The job description did not state that we needed to be gentle if the subject was not cooperative. It only stated you needed to be alive. So yes, you are the job, Taylor, whether you like it or not, and this makes you our prisoner if you wish to think of it that way."

Frustrated that she couldn't do anything to get out of her binds, she puffed some red hair out of her face with a breath. She examined the rest of the truck. "Where are Pine and Mitchell? Did you forget about them?"

Terrati and Finnley both gave Mikhail an odd look, each waiting on him to answer. Seeing that all eyes were on him, he relaxed in his chair as he gestured to the front of the truck, covered by the tarp so they couldn't see the front cabin. "They're both up in the driver's compartment with Fey and Natalia. They're fine."

This satisfied Taylor. She loosened her muscles, having grown taut from the tense altercation with Finnley. She allowed herself to droop again so the pressure on her wrists and neck weren't so painful; the magnetic locks were unusually strong this time around. Ahya looked despondent. She had never been constrained this much in all her life. Her tongue was flopped out and depressingly licking the side of one of the flipped open chairs.

"This sucks," Taylor commented to an unfeeling audience.

A loud bang and sudden lurch caused all of them to fall sideways towards the front of the truck. Some loud cursing could be heard from Fey through the fabric and glass as two car doors opened and banged shut. Mikhail was the first out the back, the canopy tarp flipped open to show Taylor that they were on a pleasant road of dirt and grass. Just at the edge of her vision through the opening sat some buildings.

"What happened?" Mikhail called out to the front. He was leaning out the back, his legs perched on the edge while he hung on the side with a paw.

Fey was already on the ground, inspecting one of the front tires. "We had a hover-engine blowout." He gestured to the large depression that encompassed the entire width of the road and beyond. "We must have dipped too low on the autoleveling and overloaded the gears. Gauging by the hole in the back wheel here, the failure of the tire engine blew out the entire siding. Hard to say what the ultimate root cause was now."

Taylor smirked as she heard the news. Whether by chance or by Trevor's design, they were now stranded. Now she just needed to wait for the right moment to make good on her escape.

Mikhail gazed down the road, squinting his eyes to accentuate his vision. "I don't see any behemoths nearby." He looked back down at the enormous footprint left in its wake. "This is a bit too close for comfort."

Fey waved off the observation. "This is an old vehicle. It was probably just its time to die on us, behemoth pothole or not."

"Do you think you can fix it?" Natalia was rounding the front of the truck, coming to see how bad the damage was.

Fey shook his head. "Unfortunately, no. The rubber is ripped clean through, and there is no patching that." He indicated the torn hole of the flat tire. He turned to look at Mikhail. "Was that our final spare?"

"I'm afraid so," Mikhail confirmed. "Besides, we'd need a new hover module installed into the wheel."

"Great... Come out here. We need to talk and decide what we're going to do." Fey used the truck to get back onto his hooves, dusting off his fatigues.

Mikhail did as was ordered, and hopped down and disappeared from view. Their voices were hushed enough that even Taylor's excellent hearing could barely make much out of what they were talking about. It took her some moments to notice that both Finnley and Terrati were staring at her. Finnley had his usual expression of contempt for her, but Terrati just looked plain frightened.

She addressed the gazelle calmly. "Hey...Terrati." This seemed to spook him, but he gathered his wits and focused on her. "You don't really seem to be the bounty-hunting type to me. Why are you here with these guys?"

"We're not bounty hunters," Finnley rebuked.

Taylor ignored the surly otter and continued to coax something out of Terrati. "Well, whatever you call yourselves, you seem to be a bit too...I guess you could say timid to be someone who throws their lot in with people like him." She didn't look at Finnley, but it was clear she meant him.

Terrati turned to see if Finnley would stop him from answering her, but the otter was rapt on keeping a keen eye on the wolf. After a few false attempts at speaking, he finally got the courage to speak above a whisper. "You're right. I'm not really cut out for this job." This got the otter's attention. "I was hired specifically for my skills at sniping, not that I'm really good at it."

Finnley pointed directly at Terrati's face. "You are the fucking best! Don't sell yourself short. You saved my life several times already."

Taylor's eyes grew wide at this startling display of support from the otter. She had half expected him to prevent the gazelle from speaking any further to her. Instead he was complimenting Terrati on his aptitude with a rifle.

Noticing her surprise, Finnley grinned and chucked a thumb in Terrati's direction. "If this guy wanted to, he could pop your head off from miles away and you wouldn't even know you were dead until your body hit the dirt!" He cackled at the thought of Taylor's head being blown to smithereens. Taylor just growled and bared her teeth, causing the otter to waggle his hands in mock fright.

"For the record, I hate you too." Taylor did not break eye contact with the otter.

"Good. At least I know where I stand." He smirked, folding his arms again.

A small voice peeped over the side of the truck. "Taylor? Are you okay?"

Upon spotting the albino skunk, her anger dissipated and she beamed brightly. "Pine! Where is Mitchell?" She scanned beyond him, hoping to see the raccoon's head pop up alongside him, but nothing else surfaced.

Pine struggled to lift himself onto the high truck bed, but he managed with an adorable flop, gasping for breath. "He…is still in…the driver's seat. He fell asleep."

Taylor had to roll her eyes at that explanation. It would be just like Mitchell to sleep through just about anything. "That little stinker!" She laughed. "Tell me, have they been treating you right?" She tried her best to lift her shackles, but the magnetic hum increased the harder she tried, so she just let them drop. "As you can see, I've been better."

Pine's brow furrowed, paws on hips. He pointed an accusing finger at both Finnley and Terrati. "You all should be ashamed of yourselves! She's not some criminal! Why do you have to lock her up this way?"

The otter gave the answer some serious thought before responding to Taylor. "Because you can't be trusted not to run away." Finnley's demeanor took on a curious tone, his former antagonistic manner gone. "Let's say, for example, that you were sent to go get something from the market and you acquired it fair and square. Now let's say that this item you bought ran away from you or was stolen. Wouldn't you want to get it back by any means necessary and make sure it never got away from you again?"

Terrati sarcastically clopped his hooves. "Bravo. That was a terrible analogy."

Indeed, both Taylor and Pine were giving him incredulous looks. "So now she's nothing but property that you buy at the market?"

"Good to know where I rank in this world." Taylor shook her head at the otter.

Finnley shrugged, carefully sitting himself back down. "Hey, I just call it like I see it. If you don't like the answer, then don't bother asking the question."

"Can I spray him?" Pine asked Taylor for permission hopefully, leaping up to be near Ahya.

Her expression melted with love at his request. "How I wish you could. Remember, you don't have anything to spray with."

His shoulders sagged. "Yeah, I know... My gland is faulty. I really wish I could, because he deserves it!"

Fey slapped the side of the truck to get their attention, causing Terrati to jump. "If you're all done chatting it up, we need to make a quick pitstop at Howlgrav to see if we can secure a new tire and motor, or at the least find something big enough to patch what we already got and use the engine proper."

"Who is going to watch over Taylor?" Finnley demanded. He didn't seem to trust the wolf one bit.

159

Fey's face was firm, but his voice softened when talking to him. "I think you just volunteered yourself, hun." He caught his slip when Ahya gave him an odd "look".

The otter was about to protest when Taylor piped up. "Hey, can I come with you? I really need to pee!"

"Can't you do it out by the road?" Fey said without emotion. "We're all animals here anyway."

"Fey!" Natalia swooped in from the side and smacked his arm harshly. "Can you let the girl get some privacy to do her business?"

The elk turned to face her and gauged the looks of the rest of his crew. He sighed, pinching the bridge of his snout before addressing Taylor again. "Hell's bells... Fine, but I'm assigning both Mikhail and Terrati to be your escort. They will walk you into Howlgrav to find a latrine while Natalia, Finnley, and I find a replacement for this tire."

"Me?" Terrati was flabbergasted. "Why should I go with the tailmaw?"

"Tailmaw?" Taylor looked at him funny.

"Is that what we're calling those now?" Fey was amused.

"Those? You mean there are more?" Pine was instantly alert.

"There are more people with tails like mine?" Taylor was confused.

"I didn't say that," Fey responded, his eyes on Ahya.

"Can Pine and Mitchell come with me too? They've not been to many other cities outside of Palaveve. They will probably want to see this one!" Taylor hoped she didn't sound too excited.

Fey studied her for a long pause before waving a hoof. "Very well, just keep them close to your person. But I know you'll do that anyhow."

"Mitchell!" Taylor yelled, surprising all of them at the suddenness of it.

She could hear a small snort and faint grumbling emanating from the front driver's cabin. She smiled as she heard the small scampering of tiny paws climb out the window, up to the roof of the curved tarp covering, and down the length of the back end of the trunk. All eyes were on Taylor as she followed the sounds of her tiny friend. Mitchell poked his head upside-down, looking at her from above.

"Hello, Taylor!" He still seemed groggy. "What are we doing? What's going on?"

Taylor gave meaningful glares at Fey and Finnley before refocusing back on Mitchell. "These kind mammals were just about to free me from these things and take us into town where we can get a bite to eat and hit the bathroom."

"I didn't say that," Fey reminded.

Relief washed over Mitchell's face as he swung down and hit the truck bed lightly. "Thank goodness, I'm starving! When are we leaving?"

"Hopefully, right now." Taylor stared at Fey.

The deer had a curious expression on his face, but he patted Mikhail on the arm. "She is your charge now. Maybe you'll be a better caretaker than Natalia was." The snow leopard cringed at the public outing of her failure. She said nothing, however, and took it in stride.

"I said it wasn't entirely her fault," Mikhail whispered to the elk.

"Doesn't matter. It still happened," Fey rebutted. He gave a rallying signal with his hoof. "Finnley, Natalia, come with me." He waved a goodbye to those left behind and they walked off in the direction of Howlgrav.

"Please don't try anything stupid again, Taylor." Mikhail was resolute, but there was a hint of sincerity that he didn't want to have to knock her out again and restrain her.

"Okay…" Taylor simply nodded, watching the tiger undo her cuffs, unlocking them with a special key and deactivating them.

After unslinging them from her wrists and ankles, he set them aside and worked on releasing the seatbelts keeping the poor tail in place. "Am I going to have any trouble with Ahya too?" There was a hint of uncertainty in his voice. Taylor wasn't sure if he fully believed her that she wasn't always in full control of Ahya.

"I make no promises." She did her best to look innocent.

Mitchell joined Pine alongside Ahya as they observed each buckle being undone and the tail flexing and moving to take advantage of the new freedom it was getting. Terrati was edging away from them the more Ahya moved and rose up.

"I wonder what we're going to eat?" Mitchell was licking his lips.

"Maybe a surly otter," Pine joked. He also did not like Finnley.

"Yeah, otter sounds really good right about now." Taylor snarked along with Pine.

"You do that and you're going to get a very stern lesson." Mikhail was face-to-maw with Ahya. She opened wide, teeth glistening in the light, her tongue slinking out and appearing frightening. He didn't even balk, meeting her head on and not backing down. "I bet your tail wants to kill me, doesn't she?"

Taylor squirmed a bit at Mikhail's unflinching stance. He was unlike many other mammals when they discovered her tail. He was unafraid. "She doesn't like that you put us both to sleep and tied us down," she answered at last.

"I can understand that. I did what I had to." Without giving the malevolent tail a second thought, he got up and grunted at Terrati. "Get off your butt and help me with her."

"Y-Yes!" He was beside himself with terror. He rushed past Taylor and Ahya, hopping down off the truck with graceful ease. He trotted a good distance away before turning and watching Mikhail get her out. "I'm ready!" He wrung his hooves together.

Mikhail shook his head at the gazelle before raising his own paw to assist Taylor down the steep full-body drop from the back of the truck. Pine and Mitchell found their own ways down, using the wheel wells to reach the ground. They joined back together again around Taylor's feet, each climbing up the plain clothes Fey had supplied her until they were hanging off each of her shoulders.

"Is that the city?" Taylor pointed toward Howlgrav off in the distance, the figures of Fey and the others getting so small they couldn't make anything out but his antlers clearly.

"Town, more specifically," Mikhail corrected. "A city would be far bigger than this."

"This is not a very reputable town." Terrati fell in line behind them, hanging out on the opposite side of Mikhail to keep a healthy distance from Taylor. "Being in the middle of nowhere with very few officially documented trade routes traveling through it, there is not a lot

162

of effective law enforcement here. That, and it's also the kind you don't want to get on the wrong side of."

"I'm sure we will be fine, Terrati." Mikhail smiled and put a comforting paw on the ever-terrified gazelle. "We're both trained in how to take out common thugs and punks."

"Well, yeah…" He acknowledged the point. "Still, I would rather not put my life in danger if I can help it. You know that."

"Oh, I'm well aware." Mikhail smirked.

"So what sorts of food do they have there? Anything like fried apple cakes?" Taylor asked hopefully. Pine was looking like he was reminiscing about those delectable treats Taylor would bring back to them in Palaveve.

"I don't think so." Terrati looked doubtful, glancing over at Taylor. "Given this region of the world, you're probably going to find more things like noodles and rice common. Baked goods and stuff that isn't fried in a wok is probably going to be pretty scarce here."

"I've had something like that before." Taylor remembered a time when her mother would come in late some nights and be bringing small boxes of take-out that were just bursting with fresh, licensed meats and fried rice. "I'm looking forward to this. I haven't had a decent meal in months."

"Does the one that I fed you not count?" Mikhail snickered, enjoying the annoyed reaction from Taylor. "Besides, I don't think our goal here in town is to find someplace to eat. It was to find you a place to go to the bathroom, or have you forgotten already?"

Pine looked affronted. "You're just going to let her starve?"

"So it is okay for all of you to get full meals, but when it comes to people whom you consider to be prisoners, it's fine to treat them like trash?" Mitchell chimed in. Both looked like little gargoyle defenders perched on Taylor. "Are we prisoners just like her, just without the cuffs?"

"They both have a point." Taylor said defiantly.

"It's complicated…" Mikhail put a paw to his forehead. "Fine, depending on how long it takes them to find a tire replacement, we probably will have time to find some quiet place to enjoy a good meal, but then we need to return back to the truck immediately after that."

163

"That sounds better." Pine looks satisfied.

"She is an odd one…" Terrati whispered up at Mikhail—though too loud for Taylor not to hear—doing his best to keep pace.

He looked back down at him. "She is indeed."

"What makes you think they'll find what you're looking for in the town?" Taylor ignored the comment and glanced back at the large truck parked impromptu in the middle of the road at the edge of the tall grass. "I wouldn't think a place like this would have this type of hardware."

"You'd be surprised." Terrati perked up as he began his explanation. "Howlgrav is actually a very unique hub for the black market. Military-grade parts and components eventually find their way here through hired couriers, and are bought by private sellers for who knows what purpose. So finding a tire module that would fit or even match the one we blew out might be easier than you think, depending on who we talk to."

"I thought you said this wasn't a hub for trade routes," Taylor interjected.

"Ah!" Terrati lifted a hoof. "This isn't a hub for nationally known and approved trade routes."

"And the truck?" She glanced back at it. "With all this black market stuff you're spouting, aren't you worried someone would steal your stuff?"

"Not really. We actually took an unmarked back road that barely sees even a caravan or two on the worst of days." Terrati chuckled.

"You seem to know a lot about this place." Mitchell seemed suspicious.

"Well, they did say he came here to get some supplies earlier," Taylor recalled.

"Yep." Mikhail nodded. "Despite his skittish nature, Terrati is actually quite the adept spy and master negotiator, in addition to being one of our best marksmen."

"I'm not all that great." Terrati looked away, but it was evident that he was enjoying the attention.

"What else are you good at?" Taylor asked, sensing an avenue of conversation that might get the timid gazelle to open up.

164

"He's good at math." Mikhail answered for him.

"Only because you refuse to learn the finer points of it!" Terrati criticized playfully.

"I don't need to learn anything further about it. I've got you." Mikhail flashed his teeth.

"Bah!" Terrati waved a hoof, not wanting to hear any more of that nonsense.

They walked in silence for a time, the town getting larger in their sight. They had been several miles out when they broke down, so it was a fairly lengthy walk. The skyline wasn't exactly impressive, but Howlgrav had its fair share of tall buildings. There were a few that looked like slanted spires rising up from the center of town, the setting sun glinting off their sheet glass sides, forcing them all to raise their paws to shield their eyes from the glare.

Terrati moved closer to Taylor, excited about something. "That there is the seat of government for the city."

"Town," Mikhail corrected again.

Ignoring him, Terrati continued. "Although it is actually a puppet state, already bought out by lobbyists and other private sectors. The only real thing they are responsible for these days is paying the local crime lords money so they don't erupt in gang wars and tear the city apart from all the conflicting mob families... Not that it deters them much."

"It doesn't sound much different than Zabökar in my mind," Mikhail snorted.

Terrati had to think on that a moment. "True, but at least the government actually has power there, and the High Council has enough clout to keep law enforcement on the books and not have corruption within its ranks."

"You don't know the half of it," Mikhail muttered, but let the matter drop.

"And you want to take me back there? It sounds pretty awful." Taylor wasn't so sure about returning home anymore, even in the company of these less-than-savory mammals. How they described her former home didn't seem to be what she could remember from her youth. Was it really so different? Or did she just have rose-tinted glasses of the past?

165

"That is where the High Council is, and those that hired us. So we take you back there. It doesn't matter the state of the city." Mikhail seemed to be reminding himself of his purpose as well.

"In the end, I'm nothing more than a paycheck to everyone." Taylor was no longer interested in Howlgrav or much else for that matter. She continued walking, but stared at the ground.

"What are you talking about?" Terrati finally realized how close he was getting to Ahya when she bumped his shoulder, and he skittered back to his place next to Mikhail.

Mitchell answered for her. "Nobody has ever bothered to come after Taylor for anything other than either a payday, some wicked experiment, or other terrible purpose. Nobody wants to be just friends with her."

Taylor looked over at him glumly. "How would you feel if the only people interested in you at all were only concerned with what you could earn them?"

"When you put it that way, it does sound like we're terrible people." Terrati coughed and chose not to meet Taylor's eyes.

Mikhail's expression cooled, his face expressing genuine sympathy for the wolf. He motioned off with a paw ahead of them. "We're nearly here. Keep your wits about you and…" He looked back to check on Ahya, whose mouth was wide open and gaping. "Could you please make sure she doesn't do that?"

"What? Oh, right." Taylor was broken out of her thoughts by his request and willed Ahya to close her mouth and disappear into the fur. Her tail appeared normal for all intents and purposes, and the only thing odd people would see would be the unusual red fur she had.

The dirt path gave way to pavement flanked by cobblestone sidewalks. The lights from the drooping lamp posts had just flickered on as they reached the outskirts of the town. The various buildings had odd slopes to their rooftops, some stuttered at intervals with colorful designs of seafoam, burgundy, and orange. The siding of each home was intricately criss-crossed with wooden beams built into adobe-like filler in between, giving the entire town a more rustic look than Taylor would have expected.

There were still elements of higher technology as they ventured further in. Unlike Palaveve where only the police or the elite had hovering cars, it seemed every citizen had one; the traffic flowing and hectic. They stuck to the sidewalks as they began to reach the city center, the bucolic homes giving way to more modern structures with neon-blue highlights spanning the expanse of the building corners and sides. It was like a colorful wonderland she could scarcely remember seeing when she was young.

"Don't get too entranced by the pretty lights," Terrati reminded. "This isn't exactly a place for the unwary."

"I'm sure Taylor is aware." Mikhail edged a bit closer to Taylor.

His warning didn't go unheeded by her. Redirecting her attention from the snazzy advertisements blazing atop each of the food and clothing establishments, she began to notice the quality of the life here in Howlgrav. Quite a few mammals were lounging up against buildings, some smoking and looking miserable, others trudging down the sidewalk with the weight of the world on their shoulders.

A brief glance as they passed by several alleyways showed the state of the city's homeless and downtrodden. Many hovered around barrels filled with pitch to burn, providing flames and heat to comfort those with minimal protection from the elements. The trash and refuse, although cleared mostly from the primary roads, gathered like locusts in these back streets and dark corners, like a sinister rot that was eating it up from within.

With a sad look, Taylor probed, "And you said this was just like Zabökar?"

"Not exactly." Terrati followed her line of sight to these unfortunate sections of the city. "Zabökar is a bit nicer, but there are still problems that aren't addressed just like here."

"This place looks good." Mikhail stopped abruptly, looking up at a lit "open" sign for a tavern. "I'm comfortable not going any further into town than this."

They pushed open the double doors and padded in. It was a cushy place with several curtain booths along the far-left wall, and a nice stage set up for live music. There was even a band setting up for that night's entertainment. The proprietor looked them up and down as did a few of the bar's patrons, but none gave them much mind after a few moments.

Scanning the dimly lit room, Mikhail pointed out two signs in the far corner left of the stage. "There's your bathroom. Terrati will go with you to ensure you don't escape while I secure us some seats and hopefully some good food, although I don't have high hopes for this place."

"Then why did you pick it?" Taylor grilled, looking downcast. She was really hoping for some "good" food right now. Something fattening perhaps. That sounded lovely.

"Because it is low key and most importantly, cheaper than some of the other restaurants around here." He smiled without mirth. Mitchell crossed his arms and pouted.

Splitting off at the entrance, Terrati followed Taylor to the bathroom hallway and insisted he led the way when they got there. They had to round a corner, passing by an open-door view of the kitchen, rife with stains on the floor and steam obscuring everything else. Finally coming to the end of the hall, they found a lone bathroom meant for either sex. The swinging door was half off its hinges, but was still functional.

"I'll stay out here for you." Terrati backed up, allowing the wolf to pass. "Just try to make it fast?" He sounded nervous. She entered the bathroom and closed the door behind her.

Pine and Mitchell hopped off her shoulders and situated themselves on the alabaster sink counter that lined the wall adjacent the door. It was a far cry from a pristine bathroom, with uprooted tiles showing the mortared glue underneath. Lots of graffiti and obscene pictures littered the stall booths, and random phone numbers taunted her above the urinals.

"Maybe we should have just done our business outside." Pine scrunched his nose up at the scene.

"It's all we have right now." Taylor sighed, pushing in a squeaking stall door and taking a nice look at the cracked toilet seat. "At least it isn't clogged."

"That's a blessing." Mitchell laughed. "We'll wait right here for you."

"Go do what you're going to do in the other stalls." Taylor suggested.

"Will do!" Pine leapt down off the counter and headed on over to a lowered urinal meant for smaller mammals.

Shutting the door behind her, Taylor pulled her pants down and was about to sit when she noticed she needed to take some toilet paper and clean the seat before sitting. Finally on the decrepit throne, she was gratefully able to relief herself. It truly had been a long time since she had to go. Her eyes lost focus as she sat and stared at the dingy floor tiling of this place, her mind wandering.

How did she end up here? She fingered her pine tree necklace as she pondered. As much as she hated being treated like this, there was something about being able to talk to other people that made her long for more interaction. She had been alone with Pine and Mitchell for so long, fending for herself, that she nearly forgot what it was like to be a part of a group, to be around other people. Fate could have chosen worse people to be her caretakers at this point; she should just be glad they weren't people who wanted to harm her.

Fate. Why did she think of that term? Supposedly it was destiny that Mrs. Hircus died, and everyone else in Palaveve. Sheriff Watters said his end would be in a supernova of unbelievable glory. His death certainly reflected his Script. He died with the rest of Palaveve in a ball of fire caused by whatever the hell that monster was. Even Trevor and Gregor did not know, or at least told her as such. Were people truly slaves to something out of their control?

A light tapping broke her reverie. "Taylor, are you done?" Terrati called out.

"Yeah, I'll be right there." She cleaned herself, pulled her pants up, and patted Ahya on the "nose", forcing her to retract her mouth again so she could appear somewhat normal. She opened the door and headed to the sink to rinse her paws, where Pine and Mitchell had just finished drying theirs. "Sorry I took so long."

"We don't question." Mitchell smiled, heading out the door with Pine following.

Terrati kept it open for Taylor to pass. "You took an awfully long time," he reprimanded.

"Did you want to come in and help?" She was feeling bold.

"Oh… Um…no." The gazelle was tripping over himself with her implication.

"Relax." She put a paw on his arm, giving him a shudder at her touch. "I'm just joking with you. You really need to loosen up, Terrati."

"R-Right," he agreed, trying to sound confident.

They walked back out to the main eating area, where the band had already started to play some smooth rock. The infectious beat got into Taylor, and she was already humming it by the time she reached the bar. The grizzled bear bartender stared at her as she jammed past, rocking her shoulders to the tune. Mikhail noticed the reaction when he hailed her from one of the curtained booths.

Sliding into the maroon plush seating, they were greeted by several plates of tofu burgers and smothered fries. Taylor, Pine, and Mitchell were practically salivating at their meal. They were quickly interrupted when after Terrati sidled in next to them, Mikhail quickly drew the curtain closed.

"Don't want anyone to see us eating?" Taylor asked.

"Already paid for the meal. Make it quick; I don't like the way that bartender looked at you," Mikhail noted.

"He's just Lawrence," Terrati jumped in. "I've dealt with him before. He actually managed to get us some of those grenades that you love two weeks ago, Mikhail."

"Be that as it may—" His eyes turned back to Taylor. "—the moment he saw you enter this bar, to the time you left the bathroom and came here, he had his eyes on you the entire time."

"Maybe he's just surprised a wolf like her has red hair. That isn't a common sight," Mitchell reasoned, diving into the fries with gusto, trying to fight for them with Taylor.

"That's why I had my hoodie and cloak back in Palaveve." Taylor explained, trying to push back her hair behind her ears to little success.

"That's my concern. Taylor is too recognizable with her unique fur-markings." He banged the table softly with a fist. "I was an idiot. I should have taken the time to go back into the truck and get your cloak.

Now I know why you had it; it really is a great cover for your more unusual features."

"I think you might be overexaggerating the issue." Terrati peeked out from behind the curtain to get a good look at Lawrence, who was now tending the bar customers. "I don't think anyone would be looking for Taylor here."

"Trevor said there was." Mikhail was serious.

"Trevor?" Taylor muffled through a mouthful of burger. After swallowing, she continued. "When did you speak with him? I thought you all had them locked up."

"We did. I interrogated them," Mikhail explained.

"Oh…" She felt dumb, but took another bite. That would explain the injuries they had when she last saw them. Still, she didn't want to waste this precious opportunity for a good meal. Even Terrati took several bites of the fries.

Mikhail continued. "The Arbiter has apparently sent his daughter in search of Taylor. Trevor and Gregor are out of the running, as it were, from securing Taylor for him. So now we have a new threat to worry about."

"His daughter? I know he has one, but I'm not entirely familiar with her. What could she do?" Terrati had the same impression of her that Taylor did when she first heard of this.

"I don't know," Taylor said after another bite. "But I do know that they were both scared of her and what she could do."

"She's bad news, whoever she is," Pine fearfully added on, burping after having stuffed himself in so short a time.

Taylor reached over the table to pull the curtain shut a bit more before lounging back and pointing up at her tail, whose mouth was peeking through the crimson fur. "Do you mind if she takes the rest of the stuff on the table? She's feeling hungry too."

Terrati's face was a mixture of horror and fascination. "It has a stomach too? Where does it go?"

She was a bit dumbfounded at the question. Glancing over at Mikhail, it seemed both were interested in this answer. "No one really cared enough to even ask the question. I'm not entirely sure if she has one. I just know that she gets hungry like I do. As for where it goes or how, I am a bit…unsure."

"Does it just stay and get digested inside the tailmaw?" Terrati's captivation to how her tail worked seemed to be overriding any sort of fear he had of it right now.

She shrugged. "I'm not sure." Seeing as nobody had said anything against it, she let Ahya swoop down upon the table, lapping up all the food and burying it deep inside her maw, licking her furry lips as she did so. "I just know that it isn't there after she dissolves it, and suddenly I can feel myself being full from her meals and I can taste what she's eaten."

Terrati nearly yelped in fright at the swift movement and consumption of the dinner remnants. "Dear gods, that thing is fast."

"So you can taste anyone you've eaten as well." Mikhail broached the impending topic.

Pine and Mitchell stopped and stared at the tiger as Taylor grimaced at the question. "Unfortunately yes, and I hate it. I feel bloated and gross for days afterwards." She gripped her arms at the thought and trembled.

The gazelle looked her up and down. "But if she eats someone, where does it all go? How do you get rid of something like that?"

"Terrati…" Mikhail seemed to have wanted to stop him, but it was too late, as the question had already left his lips.

Taylor looked at him awkwardly. "The normal way anything does that you eat and drink… The bathroom."

Terrati flushed, turning away immediately in embarrassment. "Oh, I'm sorry, I didn't mean to…"

"Let's just forget the topic and enjoy the music for a while. We can leave in a little bit, right?" Mitchell suggested, cuddling up next to Taylor.

"Yeah, I wouldn't mind staying." Taylor settled in and wrapped her arms around Pine and Mitchell.

Mikhail pursed his lips, but relented. "Fine, but only for a few minutes. We do need to be heading back to the truck."

They reclined back into the booth cushions and moved the curtain slightly to watch the band. They had switched to a heavier set of pieces, the beat picking up the overall mood of the crowd immensely. Taylor was enthralled, and watched as the primary guitar player shredded his strings. The lead singer was belting out a mournful ballade about a lost lover and trust betrayed. It wasn't long before Taylor began singing along with the next chorus.

"I didn't know you could sing…" Terrati's eyes grew round. Even Mikhail seemed surprised.

Taylor stopped to answer. "You never asked. I was in a band once. Didn't Fey show you the pictures he has of me?"

"You never told us this!" Pine seemed offended at this huge secret being kept from him.

"I was on the run. I never had a need to get back into music. Why would the topic even come up?" She smiled and ruffled his head fur before returning to produce more dulcet tones, matching the lead singer note for note.

"She's got a good point," Mitchell mused, patting his full belly.

"You are certainly a curious creature," Mikhail admitted, watching Taylor enjoy herself. Even Ahya was weaving back and forth and getting into the groove. They had lost count of how many songs they sat through, but the crowd was raucous and wanted more.

"This really brings me back… I miss this." Taylor let loose a single tear unbidden down her cheek.

Terrati opened his pocket watch and his eyes bulged. "Good grief! We have been here over an hour! We need to start heading back."

Mikhail nodded. "Yeah, probably for the best. Taylor, make sure—"

The curtain slammed open, causing Terrati to scream in fright and nearly jump right onto Ahya. Standing next to their table was a reptile, but Taylor couldn't quite place what species she belonged to. The fact that she knew so few reptiles in the first place made it harder for her to even venture a guess. The girl's cybernetic eye settled on Taylor, its iris narrowing with purpose. The toothy grin grew wide at what she recognized to be a leering smile.

"Taylor, how very nice to finally meet you," the reptile crooned.

9
LIARS

Ari moaned as she refitted the red gem back into her cybernetic slot. The slight click and crunch of the needle-like optic threads resyncing back up to their mated pairs deep within her embedded accessory felt like knives thrusting through her forehead. Sometimes she hated this "gift" her father had given her. Having to clean it out after weeks of use and exposure to the dust molecules in the air was an excruciating chore.

Collapsing onto her bed, she began to weep as the insufferable pain slowly ebbed away from her inner skull. She manipulated the eye to browse about the room, letting it recalibrate to her brain waves so that she could control it. The software operating system began to boot up and started scanning objects, listing their functions, uses, and manufacturers if such information was available.

She remembered when she was first fitted with this damned piece of fabricated metal and plastic; the amount of information that flooded into her brain was overwhelming. She could do nothing but break down and cry. This angered her father who chose to punish her more for it by forcing strenuous exercises and battles with it or, as he preferred to call them, training.

Ari continued to persevere for her father's sake, to be the good little girl he knew she could be. She knew a lot was resting on this mission, and that this would most likely make or break her currently stable relationship with her father. She was furious. She was desperate. She didn't want to fail again. She wanted something to be a success for once.

Her iris wandered over to the television, its databanks researching and analyzing the actors of the soap operas playing. Such stupid mammals pretending at their stupid stories. Not once did she ever see anything other than a furred person playing a part in those shows and movies. It was almost as if her kind didn't even exist. Technically speaking, she shouldn't even exist, being as manufactured as the stuff around her.

The harsh brightness of the neon light flashing on and off outside her room was dimmed fruitlessly by the sheer curtains covering the wide window, casting a baleful glow across the entire room. Resting here was abysmal. Ari had to sleep with pillows over her head to keep out the garish light. She had been in despair for several days, biding her time here without any direction on where to go. The trail had gone cold.

Ari's head shot up at the buzz of her cell phone vibrating on the nightstand. Crawling across the bed, she reached over and flipped the lock screen off. It was from Lawrence – that bartender. Flutters of excitement danced in her chest as she brought the phone to her ear. The gruff voice of the bear was unmistakable.

"I found your girl," Lawrence grunted, clearly not happy with their arrangement. "She's currently in the bathroom, but it looks like she has two friends with her and they're going to be here for a spell. One just ordered some dinner."

"Did you say two friends? What are they like?" This could pose a problem. If they were Trevor and Gregor, they were easily taken care of, but if these were two new mammals, then another faction she wasn't aware of was at play here.

"One is a small gazelle, doesn't look too menacing." The bear coughed a bit before continuing. "But the other is a mean-looking son of a bitch, a large tiger with obvious military roots."

"How can you tell?" Ari prodded.

"If you've gone through what I have, you can tell the type. Between the two of them, I think they're combat trained." It sounded like he put down the phone a bit, the ambience of the bar and band overtaking the speaker. After a few moments, he brought it back up to his mouth. "I've got to go, but she's here. Get here quick."

"Good job, Lawrence." She moved the phone away from her ear to end the call.

"What about my mon—" Lawrence was cut off as she tapped the screen.

Bouncing out of the bed, her tail slapping the floor, Ari skipped over to the bathroom, still steamy from the shower she took. She paused

176

to reflect on herself in the mirror. She was pretty, wasn't she? Scorning her pudgy middle shell, she scrutinized her snout, how it curved inward to a pointed v-shape. Her scales were a slight sheen of blue amidst all the greens and browns. She scoffed at herself. Not like there was anyone like her around that would find her attractive.

"Guess I better get dressed and meet this wolf," she said to herself, strapping on her utility vest before sliding into a black undershirt and jeans. She completed the look with an extra-large black leather-looking biker's jacket with dangling chains from the pockets.

She slammed the door on the way out and made her way through the hotel. Stepping out into the cool night air, she frightened a few oryx, causing them to bound away from her. She smirked at their reactions, as she casually strolled down the street, looking forward to the night.

Within minutes, she spied the tavern and hoped she had made it in time. If not, she was sure Lawrence would have several of his wolverines trail them for her. After all, he was now on her payroll. She took a deep breath before entering. This was it.

Nobody noticed her this time upon entry. All eyes were focused on the band and the boisterous music they were performing. She caught the eye of Lawrence who beckoned her over. Circumventing the central section of tables, she unknowingly passed by the very booth Taylor was sitting in. She stepped up to the bar and laid an elbow onto it before beaming her teeth at the bear.

"So where is she?" she demanded nicely.

"Over there." Lawrence pointed to the very booth she passed. "Good luck. Looks like you're going to need it."

"If I trounced your men easily enough, I'm sure I can handle whatever this tiger and gazelle can throw at me." She continued to grin. He just growled and bared his teeth, the hate plastered on his face. Ari gave a mock expression of empathy. "Oh, do lighten up, Lawrence. Here is some money for your troubles, but mostly for the damage that I might cause." She slipped several-thousand in bills across the counter.

"Damage? What are you…" If he was confused as to her intent, he never got his answer. Ari was already walking over with purpose to the booth.

Ari stopped just feet from the booth. She could overhear them talking. Was that even another girl singing? She took a few more deep breaths. She couldn't afford to screw this up. Her goal was to capture, not kill this Taylor, which made the job infinitely harder. She needed to think up of a way to get her away from her two friends and not cause trouble on the return trip to Zabökar.

With a flourish, she gripped the curtain and zipped it open. It took a few seconds to recognize the wolf, her red eye assisting in the matter. "Taylor, how very nice to finally meet you," she crooned.

The reptile raised a clawed finger up to stop them as all those seated were about to make a hostile move. "Ah-ha, please don't get up on my account. Do we really want to make a scene here? I just want to have a seat and chat with you all." She flashed her best crooked smile, her red iris scanning Taylor quickly. "Fascinating," she mused.

"You're the one the Arbiter sent to collect Taylor, I presume?" Mikhail's voice was laced with venom. His tail was flopping on the booth cushion with agitation.

"I guess you could say that, yes. The name is Ari. Don't bother telling me your names; I'm only here for Taylor." She used her hips to bump Terrati out of the way, shuffling into the booth awkwardly, her tail looking to make it difficult to sit comfortably since she couldn't maneuver it as deftly as her mammal counterparts. "Thank you for saving me a seat. Now, where were we?"

"Leaving," Terrati stammered. "We were leaving."

"And you only just got here!" Ari appeared shocked. "I see you didn't save me any of the food."

"It wasn't even yours." Mitchell seemed miffed.

"Well, I wasn't asking you, little guy." She smiled at the raccoon. Both Terrati and Mikhail shared an odd look.

"What do you want with me?" Taylor asked, cutting to the chase.

Ari shifted a bit more before putting her hands on the table and leaning across Terrati, making him extremely uncomfortable. "Nothing terrible, actually. I just want you to travel back with me to Zabökar. My father really wants to meet you."

"For what purpose?" Pine was suspicious too, but was a bit less bold with it. He retreated back to the safety of Taylor's neck and shoulders as he questioned the odd reptile.

Ari's red iris zeroed in on the albino skunk. "Just to talk. To offer her a deal in exchange for her assistance. Nothing more." This caused a few more curious glances.

"That is a lie and you know it," Mikhail snarled, his paw reaching below the table to his pocket to pull out his cellphone. "You are not here for Taylor's benefit."

"And you are? Shhh, quiet. The ladies are talking." She shot the tiger a withering glare. Immediately shifting to a more amicable expression, she turned back to Taylor. "He may call me a liar, but they're doing no different with you. You're probably wondering why everyone is so interested in you, Taylor, aren't you?" Taylor stared at her but made no movement. "What if I told you that I could answer that for you? The Arbiter can answer all those questions you've probably been asking yourself for years."

"What is this nonsense?" Mikhail was getting angrier now, his fingers flying fast over the phone keyboard, texting Fey and the others to find them immediately. "You can't possibly know what she's been asking herself."

"Easy." Ari leaned even closer. "Why were you born different? Why do you have powers and abilities others don't? Why do these fine folks here want you at all?"

"She does make some fine points," Mitchell admitted.

"I can't believe you're even thinking of agreeing with her!" Pine admonished.

"I'm sorry, but I really don't know you and—" Taylor began.

Ari interjected. "And do you know these two fine gentlemen better?" She mocked Terrati and Mikhail. "You've talked to me for five minutes, Taylor, and you're already taking their opinions and reactions about me like it's truth. I'm gathering quite a lot of people want to take

179

you back to the same place, am I right? So what difference does it make if you go with me rather than with them? At least I've not attempted anything harmful to you, and I'm just asking politely for you to come with me instead."

"Would Pine and Mitchell be able to come with me too?" Taylor queried.

Ari smiled at her two companions. "Of course. If they're with you, they are more than welcome to come. I would enjoy it, actually."

"Taylor, don't listen to her!" Terrati warned.

Mikhail seemed a bit calmer now that he had sent off his text, slipping the phone back into his pocket. "You're making an awful lot of assumptions here. We have not hurt Taylor in any way that—"

Ari shut him down as well with a hush, reaching across the table to grab Taylor's wrist and lift it above the level of the table. Even Ahya reacted to this sudden motion, unveiling herself with teeth bared. Ari paid the appearance of the maw no mind as she shook the wrist for all to see.

"And these markings?" Ari parted the matted fur, showing some rawness of the skin underneath. "You mean to tell me these sorts of things just naturally happen on wolves? I don't think so." She let Taylor's wrist go, allowing her to massage it after their rough handling. Sitting back more comfortably in the seat, she looked at Mikhail again. "At least I wouldn't treat her like a prisoner, which you two seem to be doing."

Taylor had to admit, Ari was making a very compelling case to simply ditch this current group of kidnappers for her company. Despite her reluctance to even go back to Zabökar, given how all current roads seemed to lead there, Ari had made the best pitch of them all. She may yet figure out a way to escape, but it would be a lot easier to evade a single person than many.

"I've heard enough." Mikhail stood up, getting ready to leave. "Come on, Taylor. I'll see to it that you are treated better. It is unfortunate we had to restrain you earlier. We were under orders to ensure your cooperation by any means necessary."

"I don't know. Sounds like a pretty violent instruction to me." Ari placed her palm over Terrati's, firmly holding it in place even after

180

he attempted to struggle to get his hoof away from her touch. She continued speaking to Mikhail. "Why don't you sit your cute butt down and we just talk this out. I'm sure we can come to a mutual arrangement where both parties win."

"Not with the High Council involved, we won't!" Terrati continued to resist.

"Get your paws off my friend," Mikhail warned, pulling out a pistol and aiming it directly at her face. The action caused several patrons to gasp and begin pointing at the rising altercation happening in the booth.

"What are you going to do, shoot me?" She sneered. "I bet I can burn through your friend's wrist before you can even pull the trigger." Terrati began to scream as smoke rose from beneath her hand, the intense glow visible as she began burning through his fur and skin.

"She's got special powers too!" Pine and Mitchell both tweaked out, leaping behind Taylor and Ahya for protection.

"That's not going to kill him. You'll still be dead either way." Mikhail stood firm, his gun still cocked.

"True…true. But then, would you really be able to live with yourself if you could have stopped your friend from losing his entire hoof? Could you face him daily and say to yourself, 'I saved his life, but at the cost of his hoof that I could have easily prevented if I just had put down my gun'?"

"That is a flimsy excuse for me not to shoot you right here, right now." Mikhail put his finger through the trigger guard, getting ready to fire. More onlookers began to notice and the band stopped playing.

"Please, Ari, just let Terrati go," Taylor pleaded, not wanting anyone to get hurt on her account.

Ari was fixated on Mikhail. "You're right, it is a flimsy excuse, but it did allow me enough time to do this!"

Mikhail looked down in shock. Ari had used their conversation to maneuver her tail underneath the table to be alongside his ankle. With a quick flick and grab, she used her tail to yank him off balance and jerk his hind paw into the air. He was twisted upside down and his head was slammed into the table, knocking him out cold. The gun went off, the bullet ricocheting off a metal pole holding the curtains up.

181

Ahya unleashed her full size and descended upon the reptile, swallowing her down to the waist. Ahya lifted her up off the booth seat, legs flailing, causing many of the bar's customers to scream in terror causing a stampede. It was pandemonium.

Before Ahya could unleash the acid component present within her saliva, Ari let go of Terrati and shoved her hands upwards deep into the squishy flesh of the mouth and started heating up her palms. The raging inferno concentrated at the tips of her fingers was enough discomfort to have both Ahya drop Ari immediately onto the table, breaking the plates, and to cause Taylor to howl in pain.

"Go, go, go!" Terrati ordered, scrambling out of the booth, nearly yanking Taylor with him.

"What about Mikhail?" Taylor halted, looking down at the comatose tiger.

Terrati followed her gaze and cursed. "Crap! We're going to have to wait for Fey and the others to help lift him or at least get him roused awake."

"Well, she won't wait for that to happen!" Pine yipped, scampering after Mitchell away from the booth.

Ari was groaning, rolling over onto her stomach to ease the transition off the table and back onto her feet. The look on her face was no longer friendly and agreeable, but was now one of rage. Ignoring the safety of anyone in the bar, she thumped her tail on the ground and brought two fingers to the ground. A single line of violent fire spiraled upward from the floor, surging forward in a direct line towards the band stage, splitting it completely in half.

"What the hell is that?" Terrati had run back for Mikhail's body and dragged it to safety, kicking a table over to provide some sort of flimsy cover between them and a reptile that could literally explode the very earth they stood on.

"There's no way we can fight against that!" Mitchell wailed, shivering alongside Pine against Taylor.

"We need to find a way to—" Taylor stopped short when she heard another thud of Ari's tail. "Freaking move!"

She pushed Terrati away from her as she rolled from behind cover to a second upturned table. Another trail of rising heat cut the table in two, pluming upwards into a column that hit the ceiling and began catching the wooden boards there on fire. The last remaining screams of the tavern's occupants were fading into the street. Taylor breathed a sigh of relief as she saw them flee. At least there wouldn't be more casualties than necessary, but how would they escape Ari?

"It doesn't have to be this way, Taylor!" Ari heaved, threading through the still-smoldering ruins of the bar. "Just come with me and this will all stop. You can't win anyway!"

Taylor peeked behind the table and saw the approaching figure, wreathed in flames. Whether she was truly engulfed in it and it just didn't affect her, or she was manipulating the fire around her body as a form of protection, was unclear. Either way it was an imposing sight, her red iris locking on to her.

"Mikhail? What's going on? Is everything okay?" Natalia burst through the double doors, followed by Fey and Finnley.

They saw Ari advancing on Terrati and Taylor's position, a limp Mikhail next to the gazelle. Simultaneously drawing their guns, all three began firing rounds at the reptile. Ari expressed her disgust at the intrusion, immediately switching targets and making a shield of magma thrust up from the ground to protect herself. The bullets melted the moment they hit the barrier, the heat rendering their efforts fruitless.

Not wasting time for her to recover, the three of them split off and flanked the barrier, their guns drawn. Taylor assumed each intended to fire upon Ari as soon as they got in view, figuring she could not ward off their bullets from multiple sides. Ari was a few steps ahead of them, however. With another hit of her tail, she shot out two rows of upturned floor, zipping off at angles on either side of her initial barrier. This effectively cut off both avenues that Fey and the others could have taken.

"Damn it!" Finnely dashed back and forth between the two pyre walls. "I can't see a way through."

"Terrati!" Fey called out. "Do you have a gun over there?"

"Not one that would help me at this moment!" He was still dragging Mikhail to another futile bit of cover.

"Then take this and shoot the hell out of her!" Fey tossed a submachine gun over the flames, its tips licking the cold metal as it soared towards Terrati who caught it effortlessly.

"I'm not sure this is going to do much good!" He dove for cover as another line of conflagration separated him from Mikhail.

"Stop making this harder on yourselves. Just give Taylor to me." Ari's voice was calm, but she was still furious.

"What about up there?" Taylor pointed at the sagging ceiling, already weak from the fires consuming it.

Terrati followed her finger to the burning boards. He nodded in understanding and aimed his bullets to cut a wide circle swath, causing the entire roof above Ari's head to cave in. She only had a split second to look up, but it was enough for her to duck and liquefy the floor beneath it. The ceiling crashed with a cacophonous roar, spitting out more contagious embers of fire that ignited more of the bar around them.

The collapsed roof had fallen with enough force to shatter part of the initial wall Ari put up, now cooled and safe to the touch. Natalia, Fey, and Finnley were immediately climbing over it to get to Mikhail. Fey grilled Terrati for a status report. "What happened? Is he okay?"

"He's fine. He just knocked his head hard on a table when she ambushed us." Terrati seemed to visibly relax with the others around. "She's after Taylor as well, and is the Arbiter's daughter. She has some sort of freaky power the likes I've never seen!"

"Yes." Finnley snorted. "We can see that."

"I have something for him." Fey brought out a small vial and began putting it under Mikhail's nostrils to awaken him. "Natalia, can you secure Taylor and make sure she's safe?"

"I'm on it." She rushed over on all fours to where Taylor lay huddled. "It's okay now. She's gone. Are you hurt?"

Taylor was biting her lower lip a bit, but managed to nod. "Just a burn inside of Ahya, that's all. She's taking care of it now as we speak, but it still stings."

The entire place felt like a furnace. "We have to get out of here! It could come down on top of us all at any moment!" Fey shouted, already assisting Mikhail up onto his hind paws.

"What about Ari?" Terrati looked over at the gaping hole, now visible where the roof caved in. It appeared Ari had liquefied the floor beneath her to provide an escape route to the sewers.

"Forget her!" Fey roared. "We need to move!"

Without another word, they all hurried out with Natalia bringing up the rear. They each looked at the hole in the floor where Ari had fallen through, expecting her to pop out at any moment. They knew she wasn't dead yet, but none were willing to risk following in after her to see where she had gone. Their immediate concern was for their safety.

They busted out into the cool night air, stumbling over to the far sidewalk opposite before bending over, panting. They all had various degrees of soot and ash in their fur, and they looked like a group of right miscreants. Turning back to look at the tavern, the neon sign was already consumed in flames. The fire had already reached the third floor of the building and was billowing out of the windows, the glass having cracked by the intense heat.

"We need to move before the police show up," Mikhail warned. They could already hear the sirens wailing not even a block away.

Not wanting to be detained further for something they had no control over, they ducked into a side street and began heading away from the sound of the roving cop cars. Finnley was leading the pack, his cellphone open to a map app that displayed the immediate area and was calling out the directions.

"Did you manage to get a spare wheel and hover motor?" Terrati called out to Fey in front of him, noticing they did not bring anything remotely resembling either.

"No!" he shouted back. "The dealer didn't have one ready for us! He needed to backorder it."

"Are you freaking kidding me?" Mikhail swore. "We can't afford to come back into this town again with that crazy girl after us!"

"I thought you weren't afraid of anyone since you already know how you're going to die?" Finnley shot back, making a quick left turn back out onto a main street.

Mikhail narrowed his eyes, boring holes into the back of the otter's head with his glare. "I'm not afraid for myself, but for those around me."

"What are we going to do? Sorry!" Terrati apologized as they nearly barreled a couple of swine over when they rounded the bend out of the alley onto the larger thoroughfare. The road was congested, nearly bumper to bumper with rush-hour traffic. "We don't have any mode of transportation out there! We're as good as sitting ducks!"

"We got no choice! We need to lie low and abandon the truck for now, but keep watch on it for scavengers until we get word our tire is ready." Fey couldn't think of any other alternatives.

"Could we just stop running?" Taylor asked, noticing Pine was getting out of breath.

This caused Natalia to stop short as the others turned around to see Taylor slowing down, kneeling down to lift up both Pine and Mitchell to be on her shoulders. "Their little legs can't keep up with the rest of us. They're tired. We need to slow down. I don't think we're being chased anymore." Taylor said.

Finnley seemed irritated with her request, but it was true. None of them could hear the sirens anymore. "Fine, but we keep moving!" he snapped, looking down at his phone and pointing to their next direction.

Now at a slower pace, they tried to act more casual despite how they all looked. Mikhail was keeping pace with Fey, looking down at him as he talked. "Plans have changed. I don't think we can wait on the tire with this…Ari out there tracking Taylor down. She is beyond our ability to fight. Maybe if we had a small division of troops we could take her out, but us five is not enough."

"And is that your expert opinion?" Fey asked. What sounded like a flippant question to Taylor's ears was actually serious, his expression grave as he listened to the tiger. "What would you suggest we do?"

"If Finnley would check his phone map, there is another, smaller town about a day southeast of here that we can trek to on foot. We may be able to find suitable vehicles there," Mikhail suggested.

"Wait… What app is he using?" Terrati was alert.

Dismissing the gazelle's concern, he zoomed out the map and flicked the image left. "Yeah, right here, not even eighty kilometers from here is a decent size town called Cheribaum."

"How did you know that town was there?" Natalia asked.

"I met my wife there," Mikhail answered plainly, which seemed to satisfy everyone.

"Alright, that sounds good." Fey nodded. "Let's head back to the truck, get anything we can carry on our backs, and abandon the truck. No point carrying anything we won't be able to use."

"Is that the FurMap app?" Terrati persisted, trying to peer over the otter's shoulder.

"Yeah, what's it to you?" Finnley was stressed like the rest of them, and quickly apologized for snapping at Terrati.

"That's not a safe app. It can be tracked by those linked in to your wifi signal," the gazelle pointed out.

Finnley gave him a smug look. "Relax, I highly doubt anyone is going to be tracking specifically this—"

All of them cringed and shied away from the road when two cars exploded into the air. Gigantic pillars of magma tossed them skyward, causing them to crash randomly into other cars on the road, igniting their engines as well. Rising from the open sewer manhole was Ari, a cooled platform of rock beneath her scaly feet, the hot molten rock pushing it higher.

"Does she ever stop?" Mitchell was beside himself with panic.

People were freaking out in their cars. Many took to the streets, deserting their vehicles and making a run for it. The street was filled with running bodies. Ari was paying them no mind as she descended down a walkway of chilled rock, creating the pathway as she approached. Cars caught in its path were set on fire immediately. One poor soul was melted on the spot when they froze like a deer in headlights at the oncoming lava footpath.

All of them stood in front of Taylor and withdrew their guns, firing with impunity at the reptile. None of the shots hit their intended target. Whapping her tail on the rock, Ari uprooted the very concrete beneath their feet at angles, causing vacant cars to soar back and forth between them, deflecting all their bullets. She kept calmly walking, keeping up the barrage of flying debris. Lethal contact seemed imminent.

"What do we do?" Natalia's calm was breaking.

"Keep firing!" Finnley roared.

"I don't think she can keep this up forever. She's going to run out of stuff to fling through the air in a few seconds!" Mikhail said confidently.

"Yeah, but then she'll be on the same ground as us and she can screw us over then!" Terrati said.

"Are we going to die?" Pine began to moan.

"We should ditch these guys and make a run for it!" Mitchell was already pulling her shirt collar.

"And have her chase us anyway?" Taylor was backing up, her rump hitting a windowpane peering into what looked like a clothing store. She didn't have anywhere else to turn to. "She'll probably just kill them all and take me instead."

"Would that be so bad?" Ari was close enough to have heard her.

The moment Ari touched down on the sidewalk, the effect was instantaneous. A haphazard dome of gooey magma gushed up from around the small group of hunters and enclosed them in a cage of stone and concrete. All that could be heard from within were their muffled shouts and pounding on the inner rock walls.

Coolly walking around her handiwork, she regarded Taylor. "As a gesture of my goodwill, I am keeping them alive. However, I suggest you make your choice quickly, because the air inside their temporary coffin is hot and they don't have much oxygen to breathe. I will ask you one last time nicely, will you come with me?"

"You'll release them if I go with you?" Taylor was incredulous.

Ari considered the dome, her breathing rapid. "Not right away, no. I'd rather we get a fair distance away, probably out of the city would be best." Taylor was about to protest, but Ari added, "Only because if I let them go now, they'd try to stop me, and we'd have more senseless fighting. I'm guessing you wouldn't be okay with that, would you?"

"And what about us?" Mitchell was adamant, surprisingly standing up to the fearsome reptile with arms folded. "I really don't like you much and I think you're lying through your teeth. Taylor is my friend and I won't let anything happen to her!"

Ari went to a knee, her red iris locking onto the raccoon. "You are free to join us to Zabökar. You don't have to like me to accompany. I would find it most fascinating if you two came along. Seeing as you three are a family unit, I'd be loath to break that apart."

"That's a bit better." Mitchell seemed somewhat appeased.

"And what about them?" Pine pointed at the still-steaming rock dome. "That seems rather small for the five of them. They probably don't have that much air left!"

Ari stood back up, still looking to be catching her breath, distracted slightly by the renewed sound of police sirens. "Best that we leave quickly then, both for their sake and the fact we don't want to be here when the police arrive. It'll just make my job...messier." She paused a moment for the effect.

Taylor knew she wasn't joking. Ari wouldn't hesitate to endanger more lives if it interfered with securing her target. Taylor just nodded and waved on. "Lead the way then."

"Not so fast." A familiar voice rose above the burning din of car fires.

Just a few dozen meters down the broken sidewalk were Trevor and Gregor, standing side-to-side with guns drawn. They looked worse than before, with their previous injuries and wounds, but they stood tall and determined. Trevor had his metal arm refastened to his torso, a round object held in its clutches. Taylor's mouth dropped as she noticed he was also wearing her cloak.

"How fortuitous for us to be meeting here." He leered at Ari. "Two can play this tracking game."

"How charming." She did not look amused. "The two failures my father hired. He did not state you needed to live, so if you value your life you would do well to stay out of my way."

"She's lying, you know," Gregor informed, looking directly at Taylor.

"Well, that was obvious!" Pine yelled out to them.

"All of you are lying to me in some fashion," Taylor pointed out. "So what difference does it make if I'm kidnapped by you or them or her? This has all been one ridiculous trip the moment we left Palaveve." She was starting to get angry. "I'm just tired of being dragged along, and would rather just be left alone!"

189

"I can see that being very aggravating." Ari's face did express some empathy, surprising due to the snout she had. "However, I can promise that once my father is finished talking with you, I'll see to it that you are given the peace you want."

Trevor finished Gregor's thought after the interruption. "She's lying about your new 'friends' in that dome. I figured out how her powers work. She can only manipulate the ground around her in a certain radius. Why do you think we're standing this far away? The moment you two leave the city, those five will die. She had no intention of keeping them alive since she wouldn't be able to release them that far out."

"Is that true?" Taylor was starting to edge away from her.

Every one of them was some sort of wretched killer, each wanting her for some gods forsaken reason that nobody had a truthful answer for. She might just be better off by herself like before. She was getting fed up of being fought over with promises of being treated better than the previous.

"Even if it was." Ari noticed her moving away and took a step towards her. "Would you really want to go back to those who treated you like nothing but a paycheck? At least I'm not doing this for the money. I'm genuinely interested in fulfilling my father's wish, and I want to take you back peaceably."

"But at the cost of many lives!" Mitchell gestured to the flaming sea of cars behind Ari.

Taylor's eyes darted back and forth between Ari and the two wolves, lips pursed. "You know what? I think it may be best if I just go solo from here."

The police were closer than ever. They could see their cruisers parked at the far edge of the traffic jam. Ari's patience was growing thin. "Taylor, we don't have any more time. Come with me now or things will get ugly!" She bared her crooked teeth.

Trevor fired an errant shot to goad the reptile. As expected, a steep wall of sidewalk and swiftly cooling lava rose up to deflect the bullet. Taking the advantage, he motioned for Gregor to start flanking by the sidewalk. Trevor adroitly climbed onto a car in the road and leapt from hood to hood in a wide arc, taking potshots at Ari, forcing her to surround herself with barriers.

"Freeze!" one horned bull officer cried out, pointing a pistol at Trevor.

"That's fair." He smirked, lowering the gun. "My part in this is over."

Indeed, he had forced Ari to trap herself in a ring of overturned concrete and earth, blocking her from any avenue of escape except down the sidewalk towards Gregor or back towards the cops.

Trevor shouted over to her. "You tired yet? You can't keep that up forever!"

Ari, running out of breath, let out a frustrated snarl and grabbed Taylor by the wrist, causing Pine and Mitchell to cry out and Ahya to snap her teeth at her, threatening to devour her.

"Oh, go ahead and try that again." She pointed up at Ahya. "I guarantee you'll be burned from the inside out before getting a chance." She shifted her eyes back to Taylor's. "If you all had just cooperated with me from the beginning, this wouldn't have to be so complicated!"

"If you all had just left me alone, we'd all be happier, wouldn't we?" Taylor fired back, sparks beginning to fly from her fingertips.

"What...are you doing?" Ari looked down in surprise at the flickering glow from Taylor's paws. Even Pine and Mitchell stared in awe at the sudden power she wielded.

Taylor tore her paw away from Ari, looking at it in confusion. "I'm not sure." The dancing sparks wavered and died.

"Grenade!" an approaching cop yelled out.

Trevor had used his metal arm to launch the spherical weapon through the air from his distant position so that it would land directly between Ari and Taylor. The warning shout was enough for Ari to witness it fall, landing squarely at her feet. The slight ticking grew faster as it rocked back and forth.

"Taylor, get back!" Ari shoved Taylor forward, causing Pine to fall off.

Ari hit the ground with her hands, sinking them into the concrete with her self-generated heat. A small dome was erected over the grenade. Suddenly the entire earth around them shook as the concussion

191

imploded the sidewalk beneath them. Ari screamed as she spread her arms wider, doing her best to keep the structure of it all intact, reforming it as best she could so they wouldn't sink to the sewers.

At length, the shaking subsided and Ari collapsed to the ground, gasping for air and weakly looking up at Taylor. "Are you okay?"

"You… You saved me." Taylor stared dumbfounded.

Ari chuckled. "Of course I did. My father tasked me to keep you safe when escorting you back to Zabökar."

"She's out of juice! Gregor, now!" Trevor ordered.

Both Taylor and Ari looked up as Gregor rounded the bend of rock, his eyes down the sights of his gun. "Say goodbye, bitch!" He laughed, getting ready to fire at Ari.

"No!" Taylor shrieked.

She put out her paw instinctively towards Gregor. The sound of a sudden flash bang went off, then nothing but dead silence as the very air seemed to be sucked inward towards her position. A moment later it detonated with force of a small bomb, expanding outward in a large circle. Glass shattered everywhere and cars were inverted as Gregor went flying through the air and busted through a second-story window several buildings down.

Although the focus of the blast was aimed at Gregor, the side lobes of the explosion coursed through Ari too. Even Trevor slipped and lost his footing on the car he was on and hit the ground hard. It cracked the dome behind her, allowing precious air to the occupants inside. The entourage of police was calling in units from all over the city to contain this highly volatile situation.

"What did you do?" Ari wobbled up to her hands and knees, attempting to creep over to her.

"I don't…" Taylor's head was getting fuzzy, darkness obscuring the edges of her vision. Her entire brain seemed to be shutting down. Ahya dropped to the ground like a dead weight. She gave Ari one last horrified look before pitching face forward onto her, completely lost to oblivion.

10

INTERROGATION

Trevor slumped up on his only good arm—his mechanical one still missing—and leaned himself against a tree, the last before Falhoven forest broke out into the tall grassy plains surrounding Howlgrav. He nursed an arm laceration, a harsh reminder of their skirmish with the High Council's hired mercenaries and their recent imprisonment.

Gregor stopped and limped back to offer his own body to lean on. "You going to make it, buddy?"

Trevor smiled at him. "I'll be fine, just exhausted. We've not really had a break since we left their camp, following nothing but their hover scorch tracks to gods know where, with no idea if we're even getting close to their current stopping point." He grimaced when he checked his thigh and rib wounds. "That and I'm sure these are going to get infected at one point."

"Yeah, mine too most likely." Gregor had to laugh at the absurdity of their situation. He regarded his own injuries with the same care. "I'm surprised we made it out alive. I thought that tiger was going to kill us for sure."

"I'm surprised that snow leopard stepped in for us during our interrogation. Who was she?" Trevor pushed off from the tree and began trudging down the path where the tread marks led.

"No idea. Definitely the most decent one of the bunch though," Gregor said.

"Just glad he didn't notice what Taylor did to our binds." Trevor breathed with relief.

"That would have been an interesting day to be sure."

They walked on in silence for a time. There were no trees around to rest on as they opened out into the vast fields. The sun was starting to set, and it wouldn't be long before they would be beset by the night's chill. The only thing they had going for them was that Howlgrav wasn't too far off. In fact, the glow of the lights could be seen in the distance reflecting off the river on its eastern side.

"Does this remind you of anything?" Gregor sniggered, not slowing down his pace.

Trevor thought a moment. "That one time in Venuzärk?" He began to share Gregor's humor. "Man, we were so screwed then too!"

"No comm radio to our name. No guns to defend ourselves with or medical kits to patch up our wounds," Gregor recalled. "Yet somehow fate gave us a boon in the form of that abandoned weapons cache!" He seemed to marvel at the coincidence of it.

"Yeah…fate," Trevor agreed.

The thought brought his mind back to their first true night with Taylor. Like her, he was not one for the Script, let alone believing in its destiny that it imposed on all people in the world. He wondered if stumbling upon that huge trove of weapons and food at that opportune time was something that was meant to be, or if it was truly a result of them making the decision to ignore the river flowing past Venuzärk and head deep into the mountain range surrounding it.

A small grunt from Gregor caught his attention and he looked up from his musings to see a dark shape parked in the middle of the road. "Looks like fate is on our side yet again, Trevor!" He was practically ecstatic at this turn of events.

Coming closer to the vehicle, he could tell it was the same truck that elk and the others were using. On further inspection, they had stopped due to a blown-out tire. "Good girl." Trevor smiled as he knelt to inspect the handiwork of the device he had entrusted to her.

"I half expected her not to follow through with it," Gregor admitted.

"I had my doubts too." Trevor rose back up. "But it seems she is just as eager to have us disrupt their plans as we are. If anything, it'd benefit her, so this should come as no surprise."

He gazed off towards Howlgrav. Taylor was most likely there with them, since it seemed they had left their only method of transportation behind, and all their tracks went off in that direction.

"You think they kept going on paw?" Gregor hopped into the back of the truck bed and began to sift through the gear packed in there.

Trevor shook his head, following Gregor's lead. "No, not in the current direction they are traveling. It would be almost a week before they hit the next town. They probably went to Howlgrav to get a replacement tire. It makes the most sense."

"Ah-ha!" Gregor giggled like a mad wolf, pulling out a small twist flashlight from a side pocket of one of the backpacks left behind on one of the seats. Using it to illuminate the darkening gloom underneath the tarp covering the back, his eyes lit up. "Hey, Trevor! I think I found your arm for you!"

"Those bastards!" Trevor swore, seeing Gregor lift his torso-mounted arm, complete with all straps and attachments. "I'm more surprised they actually kept it instead of tossing it to the side of the road like trash."

"Probably didn't want you to get ahold of it." Gregor tossed it to Trevor, watching him catch it with practiced ease. "They probably knew we'd follow them. Besides, some of these parts can go for a nice chunk of change on the black market."

"True, but they weren't expecting to break down on the side of the road." He barked a laugh. "All the better for us!" He situated the metal appendage at the nub of his left arm. After a few moments, he called out to Gregor. "Hey, can you help me get this back on? It is a bit hard to do with only one paw."

Gregor rolled his eyes in jest, but came over to do as requested. Working his way around Trevor, he meticulously clasped every strap and ensured it was snugly tightened. "So, when we get Taylor back from them, we're still taking her back to the Arbiter, right?"

Trevor's face was distant, standing still letting his friend finish putting his arm back on. "I don't think so; the last call with him wasn't promising. I don't think he will honor any deal we had before."

"But we had it all in writing. He can't just back out from that, can he?" Gregor looked hopeful, finishing up on the final strap.

"You know just as well as I do that he is not in accordance with the High Council of Zabökar. We would have no legal recourse to force him to honor his bargain since they don't consider him or his operations legal." Trevor sighed. "This was supposed to be the last mission, the one that would get us enough pay to retire."

"If you knew it was a bad deal, why did you take it for us?"

Trevor looked at his friend for a while, at long last sitting down on the foldout seats along the bed siding. "Because I made a promise to an old acquaintance of mine." He looked away from Gregor's inquisitive look. "I wouldn't have taken it normally. I knew the Arbiter was a dangerous reptile, yet once I saw who it involved, I knew immediately I could finally make good on that promise."

Gregor's face was unreadable. "What promise was that?" He sat down opposite him.

"To bring Taylor home...to Zabökar." He exhaled deeply. "I don't know if what we're doing anymore is a good thing. Maybe we should just walk away."

"And you think you can live with that? Being unable to fulfill a promise?" Gregor interrogated, his voice firm.

Trevor flexed his metal fingers, making sure he had full range of motion again in his artificial appendage. "Probably not." He cracked a grin, mostly at himself. "I'm sorry I didn't tell all of this to you before. I just wanted it to be simple and easy: we get Taylor, bring her back to Zabökar, and then get our money. Maybe even put in a good word on Taylor's behalf for the Arbiter to return her to her actual home."

"You think he'd actually do that?" Gregor seemed just as in the dark as Trevor when it came to that tortoise's intentions.

Trevor shrugged. "No idea. I'm just running on assumptions and guesses at this point. What I do know is that our lives are probably forfeit if we set foot back in Zabökar again without Taylor. We may be able to run away and live out a meager life for ourselves out in the boonies, but that isn't what I promised us. I said we would retire and damn it, that's what I want us both to do!"

With this declaration stated, Trevor got up with purpose and grabbed the flashlight off Gregor, then began searching through the gear until he found some weapons. He lifted a few guns tied down in the back and found a few grenades stashed onto a utility belt. He threw one up in the air to catch to get a feel for its weight before tossing one to Gregor.

"Let's go get ourselves a girl and her mouth of a tail." He grinned with mischievous resolve. "Now that I've picked up their scent again, I can track it flowing the strongest from Howlgrav."

"Wow, you can still pick out her smell? I flushed that the moment they left with her!" Gregor guffawed.

"And you call yourself a wolf," Trevor scoffed playfully. "No, actually, it's because of this." He walked over to the chairs to where a cloak was left crumpled on one of the seats. Being further north from the desert, there was a slight chill. He strapped it on around his shoulders to cover his bare shoulders. "Might as well take what is rightfully ours...or rather, hers. Come on, let's go!"

With renewed determination, they crouched low and sifted through the tall grass, their skills honed to the point none of the blades even wavered as they padded along. The closer they got to the town, the more they could hear sirens and what sounded like explosions. They picked up the pace, stopping only when Trevor raised up his fist.

"You think that's them?" Gregor asked.

"Not sure, but knowing Taylor, she's probably involved somehow." He couldn't suppress a smirk.

They began to rush at a dead sprint, their injuries ignored thanks to all the adrenaline coursing through their veins. Both skidded to a halt as they turned a corner to see the gridlock of a few dozen cars. Their metal bodies were being thrown in revolving arcs back and forth as Trevor recognized the five who had taken Taylor from them. They were unloading bullets into what looked like a reptile who was manipulating the very earth itself.

"Who the hell is that? Is that Ari?" Gregor looked stunned.

Trevor nodded grimly. "There isn't much information on her, but I know enough. However, if she's here, then things have just gotten a whole lot worse."

"What do you propose we do? We can't fight someone who can do those things!"

"She has limits, just like anyone else. After that amazing display right there, I'm sure she's going to be pretty tired. We need to get her to that point and maybe a bit beyond." He pointed out her encasing the five in a dome as she set foot on the sidewalk. "See that? It seemed she waited until she was within range to do that, otherwise why wait until she got closer? She probably can't do things outside a certain distance. We can use that to our advantage."

"You really think we can do this?" Gregor looked nervous, but was willing to follow Trevor.

He nodded confidently. "It's either this or we just accept being poor for the rest of our lives, fighting for the next big bounty."

"I'm in. Let's do this."

The blaring buzz of the fluorescent bulb split the darkness like an atom bomb, causing the seated suspect in the chair to wince away from the harsh light. The officer cleared his throat as he adjusted the hovering camera, its illumination casting a wicked glare on the elk. He squinted his eyes at the officer, not overly happy with his situation. He was already dressed down in an orange jumpsuit with handcuffs around his wrists and rubber sheathes on each of his antler tips to prevent them from being used as lethal weapons.

Pushing the camera up higher into the air, the uniformed peccary grunted and waddled around to the other end of the table after ensuring his subject was securely fastened in the chair. He struggled slightly to climb up onto a chair clearly not meant for his stature, but stood tall on the seat and patted his shirt blouse down with his hoofs, giving a snort of satisfaction at his appearance.

Looking confidently at the elk, he sniffled and wiped an errant booger from his nostril before flicking it and asking, "I believe you know why we are detaining you tonight, Mr…"

"Fey Darner." Fey sighed.

"Right." He nodded sagely. "My name is Officer Mendezarosa. It is my objective tonight to figure out what in blazes happened out there on Growling and 5th. Though you were not directly the cause of the destruction, you were found with multiple illegally procured weapons in your possession, which makes you and your group highly suspect as the instigators in tonight's altercation."

"Is that a fact?" Finnley smirked. "Last I checked, you all are having a devil of a time keeping them in your coffers. It shouldn't be a surprise to you anymore that almost every gangbanger in Howlgrav has military-grade weapons. You're lucky we were incapacitated at the scene, or you'd not have been able to apprehend us."

"I do not take kindly to threats and you," He pointed a hoof at the camera hovering nearby. "...are under video recording. Anything you say or do can and will be used against you. Now we don't have any firm evidence of any wrongdoing per sey, but until I get to the bottom of this massacre in my town, we are not releasing you. Is that clear?"

Mikhail just sat in silence, leaning back into his chair.

"That's fine. You can be like that. I've got all evening, and as far as I'm concerned, you are not going to get a wink of sleep tonight until I'm satisfied." The pig smiled smugly.

"I'm n-not trying to be argumentative!" Terrati stuttered, looking very sheepish and wringing his hooves. "I'm just saying it should go as to no surprise, given the black market that you and I both know exists in this town, that we would be bearing arms when you found us! That doesn't mean we caused all that destruction out there...or killed anyone!" he added as an afterthought.

"You're right. I'm not surprised." He snorted, conceding to the gazelle's point. "It is clear that militarized weapons were used tonight. What concerns me more is what exactly was used. Completely upheaved sections of road and sidewalk, unusual rock formations like a scene from a science fiction movie, and an explosive blast akin to an EMP burst. I've not seen the like around these parts which means all of you, on both sides of the fight, are not from around here."

"You could say that." Trevor grinned, slouching in the chair. His entire balance looked to be off after they'd removed his metal arm and confiscated it. "We were here on a job and things got complicated as things do. I'm sure you understand."

"Was it a legal job?" Mendezarosa cocked his brow, looking dubious. "I highly doubt a job of any official law-abiding function would purposefully endanger the lives of civilians in the streets and cause massive property damage that someone now has to pay for! To top it off, such ruckus could bring the attention down upon our heads from a behemoth not even several-hundred miles south of us! Another infraction we can nail you all for." He snorted with disgust.

"Of course it is legal. It was sanctioned by the High Council themselves," Natalia explained, lifting her paws in supplication to the extent her cuffs would let her. "If you do not believe me, then talk to our leader, Fey Darner. He has the official writ signed by the council. It should be all the proof you need of our intentions."

"Hmmm, yes…" The pig scrutinized the paper on the table between them, adjusting it so its edges lined up with the ends of the table. "This does look all official and authentic. However, I can just as easily chalk it up to a very competent forgery. Then there is the matter that you are well out of your jurisdiction and if I'm not mistaken, by common law, you needed to have checked in with us first about your mission here to log it in our books. You did not do that."

"I'm sorry. I didn't think it was appropriate given the highly classified nature of this mission." Fey was petulant, but looked to be maintaining his composure and keeping his voice level. "When the High Council of Zabökar tasks you with a secret mission, your first thought isn't to announce your presence to every single precinct you pass by. Besides, we are not police officers and do not have to report to you."

"So you are not." Mendezarosa grunted to himself, almost as if confirming something he already knew. He read the writ slowly, tapping a hoof tip to a specific part. "From multiple reports from other officers on scene and eyewitness accounts from citizens who escaped, you were in direct confrontation with another unknown party fighting over what I suspect to be this Taylor. Who is she? I've seen pictures of her on social media, but do not understand her importance."

"A no-good punk kid who had the gall to injure my damn back," Finnley scoffed, folding his arms and looking away from the camera. "Fey wasn't happy about that, but I know he doesn't say anything because he's got a job to bring her in. I think it'd be better off if we just kill her and be done with it. She's more trouble than she's worth!"

"This Taylor is pretty dangerous then? Should we be worried at her current holding cell conditions?" He felt a bit nervous. "Based on what I've been hearing, she seems to be a high-risk person to be held behind simple bars."

This did catch Mikhail's attention. He just huffed derisively at the pig. "You don't even know the half of it. Is she safe at least?"

201

Mendezarosa was surprised. This was the most he had gotten out of the tiger so far.

Recomposing himself, he looked back down at the writ. "According to this, she is a wolf of high value to your employers. What sort of wolf would require the presence of not one, not two, but three different sets of individuals to come pick her up? This sort of thing is quite unheard of around these parts, and it makes some of us mighty uneasy, or as one could put it: trigger-happy."

Terrati looked nervous. "You wouldn't believe me if I told you. She's not like any other wolf you've seen, officer…sir."

"Try me." Mendezarosa smiled. He yelped as the bulb popped and blew out, then cursed as he dropped down to the floor of the barebones interrogation room and jumped a few times before he was able to grapple the hovering camera back down to his level. "Stupid hand-me-down piece of junk." He grumbled to himself as he stomped over to the supply box in the corner.

Trevor leaned over to look past the end of the table at him. "Is something the matter? I haven't even gotten to the best part about Taylor. I think you'd find it pretty fascinating. She has a mouth in her tail. Can you imagine that?" He began to chuckle.

Mendezarosa was getting flustered at the way this was going. Shoving a new bulb into the camera, he came back to the table and released it back into the air again, the fresh light seemingly brighter than the last. After situating himself back up on his chair, he smoothed himself down and addressed the snow leopard.

"So this…thing Taylor has is a tailmaw?" He checked the paperwork to ensure he caught the term correctly. "What exactly can it do?" He was incredulous.

"That's what Terrati calls it, anyway," Natalia informed him. "It can eat people whole. She doesn't want to do these things, but sometimes the tail gets hungry and it just eats whatever it can find."

Mendezarosa seemed a bit shook at this description, but he did his best to hide it. "So she's killed before? She is a criminal then, and the entire lot of you is fighting over who gets to bring her in? Sounds like bounty-hunting to me—which is not lawful unless reported up front to our precinct, which, as I've stated, you did not."

202

"We are not bounty hunters. We are officially employed veterans by the High Council, like I stated before." Fey clarified, glaring at the self-important pig. "Bounty hunters would be the two wolves who were brought into custody with us."

"Two wolves? Clearly you can't seem to count. We only found the one wolf with the odd-looking arm." Mendezarosa did seem a bit confused. "So if he is not with you, then who is he with?"

Finnley looked completely disinterested with the conversation at this point. "What difference does it make? You small-town hicks wouldn't even know who I'd be talking about if I told you. Another rival faction, I guess. What's it matter to you? It's clear you are not asking us questions to prove our innocence, but to get more information for our conviction."

"With that attitude, your words will become prophetic," Mendezarosa snorted, wiping his nose again. He looked back down at the writ as he made a decision. "It is clear to me that this Taylor would be safer with us behind bars and separate from the rest of you until we can figure out just how dangerous she is."

Mikhail was getting cross, leaning forward and straining his metal bindings, causing the pig to back up a bit on the chair. "You didn't answer me. Is she safe?"

Mendezarosa waved a hoof dismissively. "Yes, yes, of course. She's been unconscious since we found her on the sidewalk. She's yet to rouse. When she does, we'll bring her in and question her too."

Terrati laughed nervously at that. "I don't think she'll take kindly to being in handcuffs again. You'll probably get quite the fright from what she can do. I know I did. She really is quite fascinating, but her tail is downright terrifying."

"You keep going on about this tail, but none of my officers has seen anything on what you're describing. Still, I have taken precautions and have kept everyone watching her at a safe distance." He tapped on the table a few times, trying to gather his thoughts. As if remembering something he had forgotten, he fidgeted with a start. "Ah, and this...other female, I'm not even sure what to call her. She's not a mammal."

"She's a reptile," Trevor schooled smoothly. "Not seen much these days north of the wall. I'd wager she is even more dangerous than Taylor is. If I were you, if she hasn't woken up by now, I suggest you stop wasting your time talking to me and restrain every limb and tail on her body. I would have every gun in your precinct trained on her. We are not the true threat here, she is. The sooner you realize that, the better off we'll all be."

"If you think I'm just going to let you go by warning us of this danger in my station, it's not going to work." Mendezarosa puffed out his chest at the wolf. "Now tell me your purpose here and why you are in my town. The more you resist, the worse it'll be for you."

Natalia was exasperated. "I've told you time and again. We were hired by the High Council! I swear, it's like you don't even listen! You stubborn, obnoxious pig!" Natalia began spouting a steady flow of curse words in her language at the pig.

"I've heard enough." He signaled to someone behind the one-way mirror. "Off you go to your cell. We'll come when we've decided what to do with the lot of you."

"You're making a big mistake." Fey watched the second officer, a hippo, fumble with the key to unlock him from the bolt ring in the floor. "Release us with Taylor and we'll be on our way. The longer you delay, the more danger you and your men will be in."

Mendezarosa ignored the elk's plea, instead focusing on the camera and bringing it back down to turn it off and remove the tape recording from within it. Following the hippo and elk out of the room, he looped back around and through a door into a dark room. Now on the other side of the glass, he clopped up to a cheetah standing stock still. She was staring directly through into the interrogation room, looking very pristine with her well-pressed mauve suit.

He stood beside her, his lack of size evident between them. Looking up at her, he grunted. "I don't believe them one bit. They're hiding something, yet other than the gazelle and snow leopard, I've not been able to get much out of them. Grilling each one-by-one for the past three hours was exhausting. Can I take a break?"

The cheetah was stroking her chin, her tail flicking back and forth with agitation. "No," she commanded plainly. "There is more here than meets the eye. I wish to speak to this Taylor."

The pig's demeanor soured. "The weird red-headed wolf? They all say she is dangerous, but I'm starting to get a bad feeling about that reptile they kept warning about. We should deal with her first."

She continued to stare straight ahead. "Negative. Taylor is the key to this whole mystery. I feel if we talk to her personally, then she will fill in the gaps of the lies and half-truths the rest of these fools are spouting."

The red alert lights began spiraling, casting the room in a dull undulating gloom. The alarm resounded throughout the building. Mendezarosa was startled, squealing a bit at the suddenness of it. "What's going on? Did any of them escape?"

The cheetah was quick to reach down to pick up a phone receiver and press a button. "Report. What is the situation?"

The voice on the other end was hysterical. "She's burning up the place! There's fire everywhere! We're dying here! Call code delta! Call—" The signal on the phone died abruptly.

The cheetah calmly put the receiver down, waiting a few moments before speaking. "This is my cue to leave. We will see how this plays out. Order your officers to fire at will on all except Taylor. You'll hear back from me in a few days."

"Will you put in a good word for me and my request with the council?" he asked, his groveling become apparent in his tone.

She stared at him a few moments before stalking out. "We'll see."

Ari moaned, waking up groggily only to find that she was restrained by a single handcuff to the metal part of the bunk bed they had laid her on. Above her was the bare underside of the mattress on top. Shifting onto her side, she let her vision coalesce to behold a holding cell lacking any furnishings. If there was a guard set to watch over her, they weren't at their post.

Using her free palm to focus her heat on the metal, she was easily able to melt the cuffs at the link and dislodge it from her wrist. She stood up and stretched, wondering how she got here. The last thing she remembered was Taylor causing some unknown explosion that rocked through her body like a tidal wave. It was painful, but not unduly so. She had experienced worse under her father's carefully crafted training.

Now she was starting to see why her father wanted Taylor so bad. She knew about the tail and some of its capabilities, but she was completely unaware of the secondary power that the wolf wielded. With the pulse ray her father had developed, subjects like herself only developed singular powers; not once had any of them acquired any more than that. Their recent success was only because they engineered him that way, and the end result was a bit less sustainable or controllable. So something as natural as Taylor was indeed a rarity.

Understanding the full scope of why so many factions wanted Taylor, Ari stepped up to the bars and poked her snout out enough to get a view down the hallway. She used her cybernetic eye to zoom in her vision, spotting two rams dressed in police uniforms. They were chatting about something mundane, completely paying her no mind.

She gripped the bars tightly and began to run her heat down their length and into the ground. The concrete around the base of the poles began to liquefy and form a bright line that traveled up the length of the wall and hit every bar along the ceiling. In short order there was nothing left for the caged wall to hold onto, and she let go and allowed it to clatter into the hallway, giving her ample room to step out.

"Hey!" One of the rams pointed at her. "What do you think you're doing? Get back in there!"

The second ram slapped a button on the wall. Immediately, the red lights started cycling around the prison and alarms resounded through the compound. The first ram yelled a charging cry and booked it down the corridor, his head bowed with intent to bowl her over. Yawning, she waited until he got close enough within her range before she melted the floor beneath his hooves, slamming him up into the ceiling like a pancake before solidifying the entire macabre structure.

The other ram shook as he watched his buddy's innards ooze down the column of concrete, then shrieked at the sound of the phone when it rang next to him. His eyes glazed over in terror, he shakily picked up the phone. Ari casually sauntered down the row of cells, extending out her arms to catch the walls on fire as she went.

"Report. What is the situation?" the stern voice on the other end demanded.

"She's burning up the place! There's fire everywhere! We're dying here! Call code delta! Call—" His voice gurgled on the blood frothing in his throat as she impaled him where he stood with a heated column of rock.

"Now where is Taylor? That red-headed wolf?" Ari asked. The ram just stared at her horrified, unable to speak. "It's okay, no need to use words. Just point to the cell, I can handle the rest."

His hoof trembling with effort, he pointed at the one two down on the right. His purpose finished, she intensified the heat and melted the rest of him where he was. She extinguished the flames as she came within range, then pivoted at the second cell and saw Taylor lying unconscious on a bunk bed not too dissimilar to the one Ari woke up on.

Ari melted the entire barred entry like the first and heaved it to the side with some strained effort. Padding into the cell, she knelt down next to Taylor and whispered her name, gently pulling a lock of red away from her face to get a better look at her. She was a very beautiful wolf, with rounded features and a youthful face that even Ari was jealous of.

Ari whispered Taylor's name once more, but the wolf continued to be unresponsive. Knowing that it wouldn't be long before she was flooded with more cops to deal with, she poked the tail to see if it would attempt to eat her again. Seeing it was comatose too, she snaked an arm under Taylor's body and carefully lifted her onto her shoulder, wrapping the tail around her neck to hang off her other shoulder.

"Oof, girl…" Ari muttered. "You're a bit heavy for such a petite thing!" She didn't want to admit that her upper body strength wasn't what it should be.

Looking around, Ari knew she could probably blow out the nearest wall and leave the room directly, but not knowing the layout of

207

the police station she was most likely in, she may end up in a far worse situation. Instead, she took the walking route and headed out of the first cell compound to find herself at a hallway intersection that connected several of them together. She was unclear which direction led out of here.

Ari sighed as she heard the multitude of paw and hoof steps headed her way. Rounding the corner were several dozen cops with guns. They each drew their pistols and began to fire. She cursed under her breath and brought up another wall of rock to cordon off that cell block entrance. It looked to her like that was the way out, and she just denied herself passage. Maybe she'd be making holes through walls after all.

She was halfway down a random cellblock when a voice from the side distracted her. "Hello there. I see you're having a bit of trouble, I take it?"

Ari turned to see Trevor lounging back against his bed rails on his own bunk bed, smirking at her through the darkness. "Ah yes, the failure of a bounty hunter. I'm doing just fine, thank you very much," she snarked.

"Really?" He sat up straighter and leaned forward. "From what I'm hearing, you're outnumbered out there and you're already breathing heavy from what you've done with your powers." At a look of menace, he continued. "Yes, don't think I haven't read up on you and what you can do. How about we call a truce and we work together to get Taylor out of here, and we can discuss later what we'll do to each other then, alright?"

"I'm not discussing this with you. You have no leverage here." Ari checked her breathing and leered at the one-armed wolf. A blast down the hall garnered her attention.

Trevor followed her gaze, "It seems like I do. Why else are you heading in the opposite direction of the cops? Because you know you can kill a bunch of them, but don't have enough endurance to manage them all, especially if they are bringing their entire force down upon your head."

"We can help." A timid voice sounded behind her, causing Ari to swivel around to see a gazelle hovering in the corner of his cell.

"You're from the High Council, aren't you? You and your team," Ari deduced, finally recognizing them for who they were.

"Yes, we are." Mikhail had his head pressed against his bars, his face turned towards her. "All we want at this moment is to escape with Taylor intact. I'm sure we can agree that is in the best interest for all of us."

Trevor shrugged. "I can't argue there. We can discuss what we'll do with each other regarding Taylor later, but I'd rather be free to claim my money than to be locked away with little recourse but to rot."

"Free us, and we'll help you escape Howlgrav with Taylor intact," Fey spoke up several cells down, clearly listening in this entire time.

Ari was glancing around at all of them peering out at her, Taylor still slumped over her shoulder. She snarled in disgust as another blast and some audible shouts could be heard down the hall. "Fine, but if any of you try to turn on me with this, I will burn the lot of you to ashes and me and Taylor will go out in a blaze of bullet fire. Is that understood?"

Ari hated to resort to such negotiations, but they had a point. She was powerful, but she wasn't infinite. The more help she got to escort Taylor out, the better her chances of returning to her father victorious. If any should die along the way, all the better for her. Another explosion reverberated down the cells. She hastily set Taylor down on the floor and got to work on melting through the bars, nearly exhausted as she got to the final one.

Fey regarded the winded reptile and nodded appreciatively. "I always honor my debts. Thank you for this." Ari did not respond the gesture in kind, favoring catching her breath instead. Fey and Finnley shared a look as he swept past her.

"If nobody else minds, I will carry Taylor," Mikhail offered, stooping down to pick her up. This caused a near instinctual reaction from Ari, but Taylor began to stir under his paws.

"Wha? Who? Hello?" Taylor was disoriented and fumbled attempting to get up, assisted only by the strong arm of Mikhail. Ahya was just starting to move as well, bumping clumsily against the tiger's thighs. Taylor scanned the myriad of faces all staring at her. "What's going on? Where are we?"

Trevor was first to respond, getting down to her eye level. "Taylor, I know you probably have no reason to trust any of us after what we've put you through, but hear me out." This got her full undivided attention. "We are stuck in the police station prison somewhere in the center of Howlgrav, and we need to all work together to escape. We can work out the details of what we do with you later, but right now we just need your assistance in cooperating with us and making a run for it."

"Where's Pine? Mitchell?" Taylor was scanning the faces around her.

Natalia stepped forward, urgency in her face. "Hopefully escaped. Let's go!"

Taylor nodded her head, offering her arm to be taken so she could be lifted up onto her hind paws. "I'm used to running. I can do that very well. Where to?"

"Well, first we need to get all our gear back." Finnley stepped out from behind the towering tiger. "If we don't have anything to defend ourselves with, we're as good as dead." He turned to Ari, arms folded with a contemptuous look. "Think you can get us at least to the confiscated items lock-up, and we'll handle the rest from there?"

"Of course I can. Can you survive long enough to make it worth my while?" she snapped.

"Does anyone know where it is?" Natalia pointed out.

"I do," Terrati piped in. "It's actually down this hall and to the left. We'll be there before long."

Trevor whistled. "And just how does a gazelle merc from High Council know that about a police station in the sticks?"

"I've done business here before." Terrati seemed offended.

"Can we cut the chatter? We will be overrun any moment!" Mikhail growled.

"On me!" Terrati waved a hoof, booking it down the cells.

They all rushed en masse and hit the intersection Ari had passed earlier. The cops had made a big enough hole through to be able to spot them and deliver some gunfire in their direction. Ari went to a knee and touched the floor with her fingertips. A deep rumble echoed through the ground and traveled away from them, underneath the wall she had made to impede their progress. Suddenly on the other side, two mammals were impaled from the ground to the wall with molten rock causing several onlookers to scream.

"That sounds pretty nasty in there," Finnley commented, some measure of respect in his voice.

"Better them than us," Fey reminded, continuing to follow Terrati.

"Here, right here!" the gazelle shouted, busting through a door with a glass window blocking their path to a visible side room with boxes of marked articles and weapons.

"Think you can blow us a hole through?" Fey asked of Ari.

She was breathing profusely, her expression wavering. "Not if you want me to be useful later."

"I could go for that." Trevor chuckled.

"Not helping." Fey glared at him.

"I can do this," Taylor offered, stepping forward from behind them. All eyes turned to her, shocked that she had spoken up. "What? Just because I'm not professionally trained like you all doesn't make me useless."

"Nobody said that, dear," Natalia consoled.

"Then let me help," she stubbornly insisted, walking right up to the glass.

Taylor turned back to see Fey giving her the go-ahead, while Mikhail peeked out the door to see if anyone was coming, she turned back to the task. Bringing Ahya around, she had it open its maw and slather its tongue all over the glass. The pane immediately began to melt and dissolve, as if touched by corrosive acid. Within seconds the entire plate had collapsed and fallen into distinct chunks of still-fizzling glass.

"Extraordinary…" Terrati breathed.

"No time to gawk! Let's get our shit and go!" Finnley roared, bounding over the now-open counter and yanking out the bins to find his stuff.

With the exception of Mikhail, who graciously took his affects when Natalia delivered them to him, the rest was pandemonium as they scavenged through the articles. Trevor recovered his iron arm while Taylor lighted up to her cloak, necklace, and kitsune plush. Each mammal managed to acquire their armament, tagged and catalogued for later inspection.

"Now what do we do?" Taylor asked Fey as the leader, something that did not go unnoticed by Trevor or Ari.

Fey regarded her a brief moment, sharing a glance with Finnley before turning to Terrati. "We need a mode of transportation out of here. Do they have a parking garage for their cruisers?"

"Yes." The gazelle thought hard. "It isn't too far from here, but my memory is a bit hazy."

"Well, lead the way. We'll cover you," Fey ordered, gently, but firmly nudging him back out the door. He gazed around at the rest of his men. "If anything should happen, it has been an honor to serve with all of you."

"Wow, that's ominous," Trevor pointed out. "You sound as if we've already lost!"

"Just being realistic," Fey responded, wasting no more time on the conversation.

It became a whirlwind of corridors and passages. Multitudes of cops were bursting in from various rooms and back doors. Each was put down with two shots to the chest and one to the head, the mercenaries holding true to their word for protection. One even got slammed through a wall by Trevor's iron arm. Taylor winced and muttered apologies to each one in passing. She hated that so much death was probably incited on her account. If they had just left her well enough alone in Palaveve, so many deaths could have been prevented.

"The garage should be just about here." Terrati was laughing now, almost giddy that they might actually escape this alive.

They pounded the door open only to have their faces drop at the entourage of police lined up like an execution firing squad with Officer

Mendezarosa in the center. Terrati's laugh choked in his throat as his eyes grew wide like saucers. He froze like a deer in headlights.

"Get down!" Fey roared.

The elk grabbed the gazelle by the shoulder and jerked him back into the corridor, causing him to fall on his rump hard. Fey stood in the doorway as a makeshift blockade, his entire body shaking and quivering from the hail of bullets boring holes through his soft flesh, popping out the back in spurts of red like a ghastly fireworks show. Silence followed, the elk not moving a muscle for several seconds before slumping to his knees and face-planting to the tiled floor.

They could hear pounding hooves behind them. They were trapped.

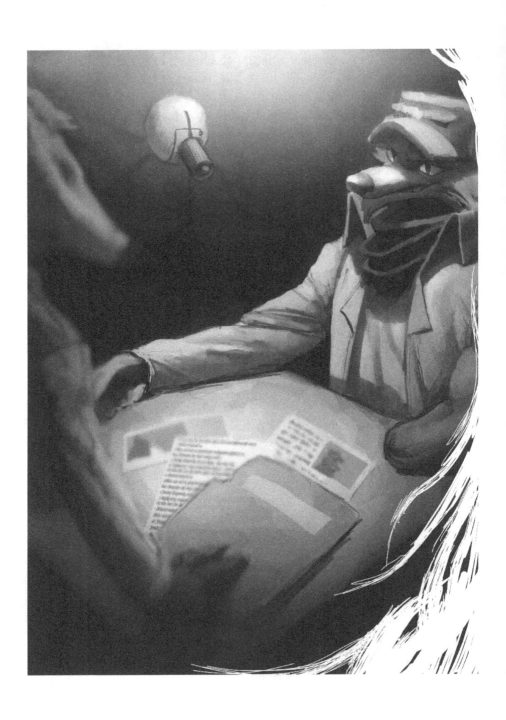

214

11
MIRACLE

"Baby! Baby! Talk to me!" Finnley screamed, tumbling over onto Fey's prone form and trying his hardest to yank him out of the line of fire.

"Get away from the door!" Mikhail roared, attempting to extend an arm to jerk the hysterical otter from the hellfire that exploded through the open frame.

"Oh gods... He died because of me!" Terrati began to whimper, trying to back up into a corner and shrivel away to nothing.

"No, he didn't! He would have done that for any of us!" Natalia looked nervously back as her ears twitched from the sound of hooves getting louder.

"You think you can get us a clear opening, Ari?" Trevor demanded, cocking his gun in preparation.

"Yeah, easily, but I'll be just about spent and I'm going to need cover once I'm finished," she reminded, peeking out the door to assess the situation. The gaggle of officers had ceased firing and were advancing on their position, well within her range

"Whatever you're going to do, you better do it fast!" Mikhail rumbled. He had his fingers on Fey's carotid artery. "He's barely got any pulse. We need to move!"

"Oh, freaking hell! Ahya, no!" Taylor shrieked. "Spit him out! Spit him out!"

All eyes twirled to see Ahya lift up a flailing pair of legs, the teeth sinking into the soft flesh of the unfortunate victim in her jaws. The tail was adamant and refused to obey Taylor's command, snapping the mammal in half at the waist. Blood gushed to the floor as the legs flopped in a twisted display, causing those behind them to yell in shock and back away. Ahya turned to them and lunged forward, spitting out the top portion at the group. The velocity of the now-inert body barreled them over. Terrati barfed on the spot.

Natalia shook. "I didn't have to see that…" She heaved, nearly unable to hold her own stomach in either.

"Ari, go now!" Mikhail yelled.

Ari slapped her own tail on the ground and poked out from beyond the doorframe. Her palms resting on the tile, she pushed two lines of intense heat beneath the ground towards the firing squad. The two lines diverged and wrapped around the group before connecting together behind their position. The entire floor underpaw was ablaze with rising flames, the ground no long solid, but a liquid mass of melting rock.

"You." Mikhail pointed at Trevor. "Cover me while I pick up Fey. Natalia, can you get Finnley and Terrati together so they don't slow us down?" He shouted at Taylor, but she was still stricken at the horror of what her tail just did. "Taylor! We go, now!"

They rushed out into the parking garage, guns blazing. Trevor was unloading rounds into the group before them, catching any who weren't burning in the temporary hell Ari had created. Mikhail had Fey's body slumped over his shoulder while Natalia was near-dragging Terrati. Finnley followed closely onto Mikhail's heels, his eyes only for the elk. Taylor was followed up by Ari who was watching the rear, doing her best to block their path back.

"That cruiser, there!" Mikhail pointed to a large van in the corner. It seemed big enough to house them all.

Their eyes met Mendezarosa, his portly figure not joining his comrades in the assault. He squealed a cry of fright and ran off, probably to summon more of his colleagues. Ignoring the cowardly swine, they clambered into the van. Mikhail gingerly laid Fey's still body in the front row of connected seats, his blood staining the plush cushions. Finnley was immediately upon the elk, tears dripping onto Fey. Trevor took gunner while Mikhail slid into the driver's seat. Taylor and the rest squashed themselves into the back as best they could.

"Forget strapping in, we're going!" Mikhail hit the engine and screeched back out of the parking spot before shifting the gear and blasting forward in a cloud of burning rubber.

The remainder of the cops had pooled out from the hallway into the garage, their attention divided between their dying comrades and the runaway cruiser. They opened fire on the car, bullets ricocheting off the bulletproof glass and siding, some missing the tire treads by millimeters. Mikhail rounded the first turn up the ramp to street level and was gone.

Trevor punched the dashboard screen with a finger, turning on the street map app. An array grid of Howlgrav's layout illuminated, the cruiser at the center of the depiction. Trevor studied it intensely. "If we head north on this road three blocks and turn right, we should have a clear shot to the city's edge."

"On it," Mikhail said with determination.

Natalia glanced back through the back window at the sirens. "Guys, we got company!"

Several police cars skidded out at insane turns from the garage exit, their lights brightening the buildings around them. They were gaining, their lightweight frames able to accelerate to top speeds within seconds. They had just reached the third city block at their next turn when the first cop car attempted a wide turn in to ram their van at an angle, forcing a spin.

"I see it!" Mikhail answered Natalia's warning.

Swerving left, away from their intended turn, he narrowly missed the first car. It sailed past their back bumper, crashing over a sidewalk and flipping sideways as its front right tire ramped up and over a fire hydrant. Two other cars went to take their place, but Mikhail was already on them and veered in a drifting motion past two cars in traffic, putting both between them and the cops, before taking the parking brake off and surging ahead down the left street.

"Woo, you can really drive!" Trevor whooped.

"I was a part of TALOS," Mikhail scoffed. "This is a lazy weekend for me." Trevor low-whistled in respect.

"Now we missed our turn!" Terrati yelled from the backseat.

"I know!" Mikhail snapped. "Can you shoot out their tires or do something useful?"

"Are you able to break up the road like you did before?" Natalia turned to Ari.

The reptile looked miserable; she was sweating and barely able to catch her breath. She shook her head weakly. "I've…never had to do this much before…in my life." She panted. "I need to rest a bit."

"Bah, she's little help." Trevor rolled his eyes. He slid down his window and leaned out, his butt perched on the door ledge. He began firing back at the vehicles trailing them, holding onto the roof tightly at Mikhail's rough turns. "Hey, keep her steady!"

Taylor was acutely aware of the chaos happening around her, but her eyes were locked onto Fey and Finnley. The otter hadn't left the elk's side the moment they entered the van. He was pawing at Fey's chest, rubbing his tiny claws through his neck fur and weeping. Watching Finnley nuzzle his face into his, something stirred inside Taylor.

She knew she owed them nothing and by all accounts, she could just disregard Finnley's pain and let the elk die. She did not know if what she had in mind would actually work or not, let alone figure out how to convince them it might. She knew Ahya was a dangerous thing—had known that since she was a little girl—yet Ahya was still capable of much love and healing too. Could it also work here?

"Get me up there with him," Taylor said suddenly, trying to nudge Natalia out of the way.

"What? No. Stay where you are, it's dangerous right now!" Natalia was confused.

"I think I can save him!" She continued to press, now actively trying to climb over the front row backing.

"What the hell does she think she's doing?" Finnley noticed her presence at last.

"I don't know!" Natalia was having trouble holding the wolf back. "Terrati, come help me!"

Ahya gnashed her teeth at the snow leopard, causing Terrati to coil back in his corner seat. "Oh, hell no! I'm not getting snapped in half by that thing! You saw what it did!"

Ari was curiously observing Taylor from beside Natalia. "Let her do what she's going to do. I want to watch."

"Let me try and heal him," Taylor stated again, already halfway over onto Fey's chair.

"Don't you touch him!" Finnley stood up on the chair, his face inches from Taylor's, his teeth bared. "Don't you fucking touch him!"

"What is going on back there?" Mikhail's attention was being drawn back to the altercation in the rearview mirror.

"Watch your driving!" Trevor snarled from outside. "We almost hit a lamppost!"

"Taylor is going rogue! We need to tranq her now!" Natalia cried to the front.

"No, you do that and I'll make sure you have a burning hole in your stomach." Ari glared at the snow leopard, her red iris locking onto her. "I want to see what she can do."

"You're crazy!" Terrati shivered uncontrollably in his seat, his hooves over his face.

Taylor stared Finnley directly in the eyes. "I need to get Fey inside Ahya if he has any hope of surviving."

"You wouldn't…" Natalia said under her breath, disbelieving of Taylor's proposition.

The otter's eyes bulged. "Absolutely not, you cracked bitch!" He lunged forward, teeth snapping and his tiny claws flashing towards her throat.

"Get them off each other!" Mikhail boomed, spinning the wheel into a hard right, their left wheels bumping up against the sidewalk curb hard.

"We're trying!" Natalia exasperated, her paws already on the otter trying to tear him off Taylor.

"You hurt Taylor and I will destroy you," Ari growled, also making a grab for Finnley.

Taylor was in full fight or flight mode, gripping the otter and digging her claws in deep. Ahya's bulk was pinned between the floor and the bottom of the backseat row, desperately trying to reach up and around to snag Finnley's tail and gobble him up. To the surprise of all, Terrati whacked Finnley upside the head, rolling him off Taylor and directly into the jaws of Ahya. The tailmaw clamped its teeth around the otter and was beginning to squeeze.

"Don't eat him!" Natalia gripped Taylor frantically. "Tell it to let go!"

Taylor, blood now pouring from her lower lip and neck, shot daggers at her. "Then you tell him to leave me alone! I'm trying to help!"

"How? By desecrating his body and eating it?" Finnley was beyond reason. He squirmed and struggled fruitlessly in Ahya's clutches.

"I don't know!" Taylor's mind was flying a million miles a minute. "You're just going to have to trust me!"

"I trust her already," Ari mused, seeming to find this unexpected series of events most entertaining.

Everyone yelped in the car as the back end of the van vaulted up, an explosion rocking their ears and shattering the back windshield, glass shards flying everywhere. The jolt shocked even Ahya who had released Finnley, allowing the otter to sail freely into the roof of the van, smacking it squarely with his back before smashing onto the carpet flooring down below.

"Holy hell, it hurts!" he cried, barely able to rock back and forth.

"Terrati, get Finnley off the floor and try to get him comfortable!" Natalia ordered.

"They got rocket launchers!" Mikhail called from the driver's seat.

"No shit!" Trevor mocked, reloading his gun with his last magazine he had snagged from the police station. "Take a right here!"

Taylor used the opportunity to scramble over into the front row. She turned to Ari and reached out her paw. "I need you to burn off his antlers before I do this."

"Burn off? Why?"

"If I'm to take him into Ahya, I'd rather not have his antlers cutting up the inside of her mouth. It'd be somewhat counterproductive. We don't have much time. He looks like he's almost dead, if he's not already." Taylor gestured with her paw to come closer.

"You're not satisfied enough with a quick snack, you want to mutilate his body and humiliate him too? You're a monster! A freak!" Finnley was frothing at the mouth, being held back only by his spine injury and the firm hooves of Terrati.

"Taylor... Don't eat him." Natalia was fraught with worry, watching Ari sidle up beside the body of Fey, his jumpsuit completely drenched in red.

"Do you trust me?" Taylor looked back at her firmly.

"I don't know." She cast a glance down at Fey's pale face. "Have you done this before? Do you know what you're doing?"

"No, I don't." Taylor answered her truthfully, causing Natalia to blanche. Turning to Ari, Taylor pointed to the base of Fey's antlers. "Can you slice them off here and here, please?"

Ari gave Taylor a probing look before doing what she was told. Her nails sliced through the rough bone like butter, splitting them cleanly off. Without much prompting, she took both racks and opened up the sliding van door.

"Whoa, what you doing?" Trevor nearly slipped from his position at the sudden appearance of Ari with the sharp bone structures in her palms.

She gave him a cursory glance. "Helping you fools out."

Ari tossed each one high in a wide arc. They landed squarely in front of two oncoming squad cars. The rocket gunner of the left car squawked a warning too late, and both cars' front wheels blew as they hit the fallen antlers. One car swerved and careened off up and over a parked vehicle, launching directly into a glass display of some unfortunate owner's shop. The other hit the antler just right, jamming the front wheel hard, pitching the backend up from the sudden inertia stop and flipping it entirely upside down.

She gave a smug look up at Trevor before retreating back inside and shutting the door. She was met with the scene of Finnley sobbing miserably, making every effort to hurl insults and blasphemous curses at Taylor. There was a wellness of tears pooling at the edges of Taylor's eyes, but she did her best to not letting her weakness show. She was still sitting beside Fey, staring at his body.

Ari reached out and massaged Taylor's shoulder a bit, bringing her out of her torpor. "If you're going to do something, do it now."

After another jerk to the side from another impromptu swerve from Mikhail, they all stared at Taylor, watching what she was about to do next. Taking an unsteady breath, she let Ahya enlarge herself until she filled the rest of the empty space in her row. Ahya lowered down to the level of the seat and began to use her tongue to slither underneath the elk's body until it reached his neck. Coiling around his chest and throat, it began to slide Fey into its maw until nothing was left but a large bulge inside the crimson tail.

Finnley broke down and went limp. "I hate you…" He sniffled.

Taylor ignored him, instead focusing on the inside of Ahya. The weight of Fey was enough that she could barely lift her tail anymore, instead letting it rest on the length of the seat. She could feel the flow of saliva increasing, flooding Ahya's inside cavity, wrapping and encasing Fey in a thick soup of sticky liquid. Its flow permeated and penetrated deep into his wounds, filling his entire system with its invasive nature.

"Please don't eat him… Please don't eat him…" Taylor begged her tail quietly, her eyes closed and concentrating hard on getting as much of her tail's saliva into Fey while hopefully staving off Ahya's tendency to turn it all into corrosive acid.

"Whew, that actually worked, Ari. I think we created a good enough blockade that they'll have to take another route to reach us now!" Trevor finally slipped back into his gunner seat and looked back at the ghoulish scene. "What in blazes is going on back here? Where's Fey?" He scanned the interior, his eyes alighting on the huge bulk inside Taylor's tail. "What the—"

"I don't know!" Natalia began to cry herself. "Taylor just said she could help him and said she needed to have Ahya eat Fey!" Mikhail looked back at her in the rearview mirror, a knowing look on his face.

Trevor looked deep in thought, then spoke softly. "I think she intends to bring him back."

"Impossible. You saw how he was shot up." Mikhail released the tension of his grip on the wheel. "I may be no medical surgeon, but I can assure you there is no recovery from that."

"Then why did you bring him along as dead weight?" Trevor shot back.

"To give him a proper burial like he deserves." Mikhail scowled at the petulant wolf.

Shaking his head at the tiger, Trevor turned back to Natalia. "I think she can do it. Taylor sustained some wounds when we were getting her out of Palaveve. She managed to heal them all by herself with Ahya. I say leave her be and let Ahya do what she can." He caught Taylor's grateful smile and returned one of his own, winking at her. Trevor loaded up his gun with a new type of round, then looked at Ari. "So, how you feeling now after all that?"

It took a few moments for Ari to realize he was speaking to her. "I'm recovering. I should be able to assist more in a little while."

"Fantastic." He smiled, aimed the gun at her neck, and fired off a tranquilizer. It sunk deep into her leathery hide.

"You...bastard." She exhaled, her face contorting into one of rage before hitting the floor of the van, her tail flapping hard against Natalia's legs.

"What are you doing?" Taylor backed up from Ari's snout as it thumped roughly against her hind paws.

"Saving us from her killing us all." Trevor glanced around the van. "You're welcome." With the lack of response, he sighed. "You saw what she is capable of. We needed to incapacitate her now so when we finally get to safety, we can deal with her in a way that will prevent her from interfering with us again."

"I may not approve of your methods." Mikhail gave Trevor a sidelong look. "But I do agree with his assessment of that reptile. She is too dangerous to be left free with us. She needs to be detained until we can decide what to do with her."

"I was actually thinking of killing her," Trevor revealed bluntly.

"No!" Taylor shouted, causing all to jolt. "I'm tired of people dying on my account! Ever since I met each of you, I've seen nothing but death because of some stupid reason to bring me to whatever damn idiot hired you!"

"You did see what she can do, right?" Trevor was baffled with Taylor's reaction. "She is more dangerous than all of us combined. She has no remorse and if given the chance, she'd kill each of us and then take you back to Zabökar."

"Like that would be a big loss!" Taylor retorted. "Not one of you bothered to ask what I wanted, and just treated me like some object that would get you a payday." Mikhail seemed hurt by this comment, but Taylor didn't care. "At least Ari had the sense to come at me peaceably and offer me the chance to come willingly without threat of restraining me or killing anyone. That's more than I can say for any of you!"

"I w-wouldn't exactly say it was p-peaceably," Terrati stuttered from the back seat.

She twisted around, reaching her arm over and slapping the back of her seat with it as she snarled at him. "At least she treated me like a real person from the start. You didn't even want to get to know me, only becoming interested when it seemed like I was some sort of fascinating subject of study!"

"You're a monster," Finnley croaked, his voice hoarse from crying.

"And you…" She had no pity for the otter. "If I didn't like eating meat and I cared a bit less, I would have let Ahya eat you just now. You more than deserve it. Don't test me, you little water-rat."

Finnley would have hurled an insult back, but Mikhail called from the front. "We're out of Howlgrav. Do we blow the truck?"

Natalia looked forlornly at the dark shadow on the road off to their right. "Might as well. Less things for them to track back to us or our employer."

"It'll also provide a fantastic distraction!" Trevor joined in.

With one hand on the steering wheel, Mikhail banked the car hard towards their truck then squealed to a stop. He hopped out and leapt up into the driver's compartment and grabbed a small device from under the wheel, then hopped down with amazing grace. He ran back and slammed the car door on entry, then tore off through the tall grass once more.

Once he got beyond several hundred meters, he clicked the button before letting it drop to the floor between his hind paws. A dull boom was heard behind them as several linked explosives on the underside of the truck detonated, sending a rising plumes of flames and smoke into the night sky.

"We were sitting on explosives this entire time?" Taylor was aghast.

"It is good to be prepared." Mikhail shrugged.

"All of you are insane." Taylor shook her head.

"At least that'll confuse them long enough so we can gain some distance." Trevor laughed, though the rest of the car was not sharing his mood. He grew serious and menacingly reminded, "You're not the only ones who have lost something. I don't know where Gregor is and as far as I know, he's dead thanks to whatever Taylor did tonight."

"So now you're blaming me?" Her short-earned respect for him supporting her was dashed at his accusation. "I was trying to stop him from killing Ari!"

"Who was trying to kill the rest of us," Mikhail recapped calmly.

"You're all trying to kill each other!" Taylor threw her hands up. "All because of me! It's freaking ridiculous and I'm tired of it! Ever since I was a little girl, I've always been different. My mother knew it. I knew it. My life changed the moment Ahya made her first kill. She was my best friend since grade school. We were like sisters, and Ahya ate her alive! How do you think that made me feel? Watching my best friend get devoured by my own body right before my eyes?" She was heaving, wrath in her voice.

The entire car was silent. Mikhail kept driving. Natalia's eyes opened wide in understanding. Finnley was lethargic in Terrati's arms, his face vacant and mind lost to oblivion. Trevor just looked ashamed.

"I was constantly on the move, traveling from one place to the next. No longer safe. I ran away from home, leaving my mother alone— one of the worst decisions I ever made. Since then, I've known nothing but fear and pain. Too many people wanted me for this reason or that. Experiments, testing, whatever the hell it was, it hurt and I felt helpless! I've known very little but loss and sadness, and the feeling that I can't trust anyone. All you're doing is proving to me that you're no different!" She slumped back exhausted from her tirade, the tears finally coming loose and flowing freely. "And to top it off…I might have lost Pine and Mitchell too. I've no idea where they are now.

"Tonight was a costly one," Mikhail murmured, reflecting on the past few hours.

Trevor tried to lighten the mood. "Well, hopefully we can recover at least one of those losses?" He gestured to the pulsating lump inside Ahya's mouth.

Taylor glumly regarded her tail. "Maybe…"

Terrati called out to Mikhail. "Where are we headed now?"

"Cheribaum," the tiger responded. "I know a few folks there that might still help us."

"It's as good a plan as any," Natalia commented.

"Think they'll track us there?" Trevor asked cautiously.

"Perhaps, but I'm going to take the long way around through the mountains to the south before turning northeast into town. That should slow them down enough, and maybe we can snag another mode of transport before reaching there to further throw them off the trail." Mikhail grunted, casually turning onto a well-traveled dirt road riddled with potholes.

They drove on in silence, the bare side of the road giving way to planted trees at intervals, having been seeded by others decades ago. Mikhail turned the headlights off and drove in darkness as Trevor pointed out a monstrous beast of metal ahead of them on their right. It was similar to the one that had eradicated Palaveve, but it had a stouter body and longer tail. It looked no less imposing, however.

"And just what is the High Council proposing to do about that?" Trevor grilled, looking pointedly at Mikhail.

"They have their plans, I'm sure. We do not need to start a panic in Zabökar until they are ready to execute their plans," Mikhail reasoned. "The less people know before it's time to act, the less confusion and manic hysteria will occur. People tend to rile themselves up over things well in advance of their happening, and doing that on a scale of Zabökar would be disastrous."

"I thought people knew everything that was going to happen to them via the Script." Trevor gazed back out the window. "I don't see any reason people would start freaking out now about what was in their future."

"A death here and there isn't much to be concerned about, but a future of mass death that the Script predicts? I think that would be cause for alarm." Mikhail deftly avoided another pothole so as to not jerk those in the back seats.

Trevor looked at him curiously. "Not many know what lies beyond their own Script, and besides, how many citizens actually bother to have their deaths read to them? And then put two and two together

226

with others that share a similar fate, figuring out that these behemoths could be the end of them?" Mikhail didn't seem to have an answer for this. Trevor tapped the side of his door's exterior, his arm hanging out and enjoying the breeze. "So you think people will respond favorably and with perfect obedience to whatever the High Council has planned, Script notwithstanding?"

Mikhail pursed his lips before responding. "Perhaps... Perhaps not, but it would do no good to get people worked up well before the High Council is ready to execute."

Trevor chuckled to himself. "You guys have no idea what your leaders are doing. For all you know, they're just letting their own impending deaths come to them."

Mikhail flattened his ears. "And I suppose your Arbiter has the better idea of how to stop these massive beasts?"

Trevor grew quiet, looking back at Taylor and the comatose Ari, still left on the floor of the van. "At least he started doing something about it rather than staying idle in ivory towers.

"What are those things?" Taylor broached the question.

Both Trevor and Mikhail shared a look. The tiger answered first. "Probably best to describe them as war machines. They're not living creatures; that much we know. Nobody has really investigated them and come back to tell the tale. They come from the southern country of Talkar that have been walled off since the Hordos war. Maybe they're built and launched from that same country. It's hard to say."

"So, you're saying that they're around now because of some war long ago?" Taylor was a bit confused. She never did like studying history, though the name of the war sounded vaguely familiar.

"That is a bit of a leap in assumption." Trevor stepped in. "But they're definitely not friendly, that much is for sure. We did note some patterns in their behavior, like being attracted to large bodies of light or explosions. So we used that to our advantage in securing you."

"Yeah, by condemning everyone there to death." She shot him a glare. "I still haven't forgotten that one," she added upon seeing his look, folding her arms.

"Well, let's hope no more of that will happen," Mikhail said to placate. Taylor bubbled with ire.

Diverting her eyes away from Trevor to ease her rage at the past, she watched the scenery go by. After a few moments, she voiced a sobering thought. "They're going to find Zabökar eventually, aren't they?"

"Why do you say that?" Mikhail asked back.

"Because they are attracted to large bodies of light, right? And if that is the biggest city for miles around, they'd probably see it and go to it."

"Possibly." His face scrunched up with a bit of worry.

"And yet you're all taking me to a place which might be the most vulnerable to these things," she concluded.

Trevor slouched in his seat, getting more relaxed. "She has a point, you know."

The tiger, pressed on without a response past the metal beast. With nothing but moonlight illuminating their way, it was easy to slip unnoticed past the gigantic construct. Its steam-producing feet created shockwaves that shook the cruiser the closer they got. They each breathed a collective sigh of relief as they made it past, then pressed on to the foothills at the base of the mountains ahead.

Taylor was nodding off. Whatever Ahya was doing to Fey inside her maw was causing her to become exhausted and tired. She didn't want to sleep, but the unexpected toll on her body of what was happening in her tail was forcing her paw. If she had her way, she'd be alert and awake, the terror in the pit of her stomach of what might happen should Fey not survive. The thoughts of how the rest would react to her, accusing her of getting a free meal out of Fey's death, was giving her butterflies.

Natalia looked over at Finnley, now asleep in Terrati's arms, the gazelle himself snoozing against the van's interior. She whispered over to Taylor, "Can you taste him? Fey, that is."

Taylor shook with a start at being addressed. Turning back to the snow leopard, she gave a grimace. "Thankfully no. I'd imagine he's not very pleasant to taste."

"Has Ahya already started eating him?" Natalia chanced a look over the seat at the large bulge the shape of Fey's body inside Ahya.

"Technically, she already has, but she's done nothing to digest him." Taylor breathed a sigh of relief. "Only when Ahya digests someone do I finally get their flavor. It's a blessing she's cooperating. I'm thankful for that."

"She seems like she's sleeping as well." Natalia noticed how motionless Ahya was.

Taylor shrugged. "I don't think she sleeps—rather, I think she's just concentrating in her own way. I feel like she knows how important this is to me, that I'm doing this for Fey."

"Why did you do it for Fey?" Trevor was eyeing her through the rearview mirror from the front.

Taylor had no words. She thought long and hard on why she bothered to help those who weren't her friends. "I don't know. I guess to see if I could do it...if Ahya could do it."

"Then it isn't really for Fey." Trevor smirked.

She shrugged and stared out the window, watching the random tree flit past. "I've been injured before on multiple occasions, but she has always been there for me and patched up my wounds. No matter how bad it got, she was able to heal anything that happened. I figured...if I could just do this one thing, bring back Fey, then maybe I'm not a total monster as everyone thinks I am."

Mikhail's mood softened. "Nobody thinks you are a monster, Taylor, least of all me." He revved the engine a bit to start the climb as they hit the mountain foothills. "If it is one thing I'm sure of, you are just a normal teenager given some bad circumstances, and you've done the best you could with what you had."

"If anything, that girl down there is the monster." Trevor indicated Ari still knocked out on the floor.

"No more than I am," Taylor derided.

"You're different." Natalia put a paw on the seat backing, leaning forward with a smile. "I've noticed you do not like to take life, and Ari seems to relish in it. That makes you very different from her, and I've come to respect it." Taylor returned the smile weakly.

"Speaking of differences, you are able to do some extraordinary stuff too." Trevor shifted so he could face the back of the van more directly. "What was it that you did back with Gregor? Last thing I can

229

recall was a bright flash of blue, then I was watching my buddy get flung through the air before I dropped to the ground myself between two cars. That seemed to be pretty powerful, whatever you did."

Taylor studied her paws. "I don't know. I can only remember one other time that it happened." She looked over at Natalia. "When you were on top of me stabbing Ahya. That was the only other time I can recall."

She nodded at Taylor's memory. "It didn't feel good then either." She giggled.

"Are you able to do that on command?" Mikhail pressed, looking interested.

Taylor focused hard on her fingertips, but nothing happened. She shook her head. "No, I can't seem to force anything out. I don't even know what caused it."

"Maybe it's a trigger?" Mikhail suggested. "If we could just find out what causes it, then maybe we could replicate it again."

"Why are you suddenly so interested in what she can do?" Trevor cast a pointed look at the tiger. "It's almost as if you want to see just what she is capable of, like a weapon."

"That wasn't my intention!" Mikhail growled. "I was just wondering how her power worked. She can't keep relying on her tail for all the protection. She needs to learn how to defend herself."

"Since when did you become all fatherly and protective?" Trevor chortled, much to Mikhail's chagrin. "Last I checked, she accused the lot of you of wanting her only for a paycheck!"

"I'm not, and she included you in with that group too." He glowered at the wolf. "I made a promise that I would treat her better, and she was placed in my care from the start. I make good on my promises, and I will see to it she gets to Zabökar safe and unharmed."

"Please, will you both stop fighting over me?" Taylor shouted, spooking Terrati from his slumber behind her. "I've never had this many people care about what happens to me. It's honestly draining."

As if on cue, there was a muffled cry from within Ahya. This prompted Terrati to bolt up in his seat, causing Finnley to squeak a cry of protest. "Stop the van! I think Fey is alive!"

Knowing the severity of the injuries in the back, Mikhail slowed the vehicle down swiftly but carefully. He immediately got out of the driver's seat, followed quickly by Trevor. Sliding the side door open, they struggled with Natalia to move the drugged reptile off to the side and lined her up along the floor between the far back row and the middle to allow Taylor some room to release Fey from her tail.

"Can you release him now?" Finnley was straining to get up onto his hind paws in the backseat, his back hurting something fierce.

"Not unless you want to get the entire car messy," Taylor warned, feeling very awkward, like everyone was watching her getting ready to perform a live birth.

"She makes a good point." Trevor assisted Natalia and Terrati out.

"Get me out too, dammit!" Finnley cringed, looking like he was trying not to tear up. Mikhail sighed and swooped in to snatch up the tiny otter before gently setting him on the ground beside the van.

"Can you get out?" Trevor reached out a paw for Taylor to take.

Gratefully accepting the outstretched assistance, she attempted to lift her tail and get Ahya to support some of the weight, but she was a bit stubborn and proceeded to remain still. Taylor shook her head, a bit of panic in her voice. "She's not responding to me. One of you must help me lift her and get her out of the car."

"You mean you can't lift up your own tail?" Finnley was impatient to see his Fey again.

"Not with two-hundred pounds of elk inside of it!" she rebuked, nearly stumbling out when the weight of her tail on the seat caused her to slip and fall into Mikhail's arms.

"Easy does it! Natalia, give me a hand!" Trevor hopped in, sidestepped Ari's bulky tail, and lifted up Ahya on one side while Natalia got the other.

Taylor shivered. "That feels so weird with you two touching her like that."

"I think it would be weirder if I had another person inside my tail." Terrati pointed out.

The muffled sounds were getting louder, and the movement inside was becoming very apparent to everyone looking at Ahya. Natalia was getting concerned. "Shouldn't Ahya be spitting him out now? It seems like he's alive again."

"Indeed...he does." Terrati marveled at the concept, despite them all having just seen Fey shot to ribbons not even a few hours prior.

"I don't know! She's not letting him go!" Taylor began to tug on the base of her tail, having the bulk of Ahya set on the ground beside Finnley. Natalia and Trevor backed up, observing the odd situation. "Please don't do this, Ahya... You're not helping my case here." She hissed at her tail.

"If it eats him after all this time, I will not stop at trying to kill you," Finnley seethed, having enough willpower to push through the pain and flip out a switchblade, waving it menacingly at her.

"Would you please stop trying to threaten her? You are one ornery little otter!" Trevor clicked the safety off his gun and aimed it at him.

"You do that and I'll make sure it is the last thing you do." Mikhail stepped a few paces closer, his size bearing down on the wolf.

"Everyone just calm down!" Natalia shouted.

"Thank gods!" Taylor exhaled.

Like a pouting child, Ahya final rose up a few inches and gave what could be considered a disappointed look before finally opening her maw and unfurling her tongue around Fey. He slithered out of her mouth, completely drenched in sticky saliva. He moaned and quivered on the dirt. The cold wind hit his body, the temperature exacerbated by the saliva on his fur evaporating. Ahya gave his tail one last lick before retreating the tongue back into its mouth and closing up completely. Taylor collapsed onto the ground and began to cry with joy at what she had accomplished.

Finnley crawled over to Fey, pressing his tiny body up against the bewildered elk. "Oh, baby! You're back! You're alive!" The otter finally broke down and just wept in Fey's arms.

"What... What happened?" Fey was looking around curiously.

"Your wounds... They're gone!" Terrati was awestruck.

"My...wounds?" Fey raised a hoof and felt his body, traveling up to his head where he felt his antlers were missing. But even those injuries were sealed over by the restorative powers of Ahya's saliva. Not a single bullet wound was visible, no scars left behind.

"It's a gods damned miracle," Trevor huffed with satisfaction, looking pleased.

Mikhail looked at Taylor in silence, her small form breathing heavy and looking vulnerable. Natalia was also staring at the young wolf in wonder. "You brought him back from the dead. That is impossible."

Taylor met her gaze and smiled. "I wasn't sure if that was going to work, but I guess it did?"

"This changes everything." Mikhail broke the jubilant atmosphere.

Fey looked up at him from petting his otter, realization dawning on his face too. "The High Council does not know of this. They were not aware of what she's capable of."

"Nor, do I think, does the Arbiter." Mikhail glanced over at Trevor.

"I realized that the moment I saw her heal an injury on her tail." Trevor folded his arms, looking smug at having known first. "She is the first of her kind that is not solely destructive in nature."

"Dear gods, do you know what this means?" Terrati gasped. "If we could get a hold of this liquid inside her tail, we could possibly advance modern medicine by decades! She is a living phenomenon!"

"And here I am feeling like I'm nothing but an object again." Taylor sighed, now standing and gazing around at the rest of them. Even Ahya had a look of reproach for this conversation. "I am not something to be experimented on and used as a lab rat! I've had plenty of that already in my life. Instead of being happy for the fact I just saved Fey, you are instead talking about future uses for me. Nice to know I'm still a nonperson to you all."

Everyone looked guilty and did not want to meet her eyes. In one single moment, a teenager had brought them all down, questioning their own moral fiber. It was Finnley who spoke up first. He disengaged himself from Fey's loving embrace and did his best to rise and face Taylor formally, wincing as his back did him no favors in this endeavor.

"I'm sorry," he admitted with sincerity. "I'm sorry for how I treated you. Thank you for bringing Fey back to me." He bowed his head before going back to Fey, letting him cradle his smaller form.

Taylor stood there awkwardly. "You're…welcome." She didn't know what else to say.

"Maybe there is some hope after all," Mikhail muttered quietly, deep in thought.

Fey looked up at Mikhail meaningfully, understanding what he was insinuating. "Where are we going?" he asked, still trembling from the cold.

"To someplace warmer." Mikhail reached down to help Fey up while assisting everyone else back into the van.

What had taken modern medicine centuries to remotely come close to doing, Taylor had accomplished within the span of several hours. Nobody spoke further the rest of the trip, each lost in the gravity of what they had witnessed.

235

12
UNIQUE

The morning breeze felt nice on Taylor's fur. She gazed out the open window, flanked by hand-stenciled shutter doors. In her paws was a warm cup of java that still steamed in the cold mountain air. It was hard to believe that mere hours ago, she was locked in a jail cell in some mad delirium of a dream. Being chased by cops and having to heal an elk from sure death seemed like a second life compared to the pristine peace that she felt in Cheribaum.

They had rolled into town in the early hours of the morning, nary a soul awake to witness their coming. The houses were perched in perfect layered rows down the mountainside, each layer visible from the one above it. Mikhail had driven halfway up the village and parked the ungainly van along the side of the house, visibly hidden from the road downhill, then had knocked on the door to the home at a quarter past one.

The tenant of the home was an elderly tiger, living alone after having both husband and child gone from her life. She was not altogether happy at seeing their motley crew seeking shelter in nothing more than prison garb, yet she reluctantly allowed them refuge due to her previous relationship with Mikhail. His marriage to their daughter did have some benefits, as he had alluded to earlier.

Between all the clothes left behind from her husband and daughter, the old tigress was able to secure new outfits for each person with the exception of Finnley, who was a bit too small to fit any of it. Not that he minded; he was happy enough to be back with Fey again that he didn't care what sort of cred his prison garb gave off.

Taylor, being the youngest of the group, was liked immediately by the tigress, whose name she had come to discover was Klera. To the tigress it was like having a child in the house again, and Klera did everything she could to dote on Taylor. Ahya was good and did not reveal herself yet to Mikhail's mother-in-law, which helped ease their transition into their temporary home.

236

Separating the group into males and females, because Klera would not allow any other arrangement under her roof, Taylor was stuck with Natalia and Ari in the smaller guest room. The larger one was reserved for the bigger group of males to spread out or squeeze into, as the case may be. Ari had still not awoken from her drugged sleep, but Fey and the others made sure her palms, feet, and tail were securely bound together. Natalia was tasked with watching over the two while they slept.

Taylor looked back over at the snow leopard, who was curled up in a semblance of a ball, which had provided a sort of makeshift barrier between Taylor and Ari during the night. She smiled at the cat, knowing that she meant well. It felt weird. For once in her life, she felt like people actually somewhat cared about her. True, it was nowhere near the level her mother, Pine, and Mitchell did, but the feeling was still nice regardless.

Taking another sip of her vanilla-flavored coffee, she stared out over the misty expanse. The brisk morning air caused low fog to manifest between the homes dotting the steep landscape, giving off an illusion of the rooftops floating atop the clouds. The sky above was dreary, and the feeling in the wind was that a storm might be brewing, but for now at least it was calm.

It was a quaint village, nestled into the side of the mountains southeast of Howlgrav. Every house had high, steepled roofs with ceramic plates comprising their builds, the ends of each ramped up in a vertical fashion. The siding of every structure was built from reinforced metal and wood, but filled in with hardened drywall that had seen centuries of age. This town had a history, and it felt like it. Taylor marveled at how different it was from the technological trappings of Howlgrav, not even a day's drive away.

"You know this is only fleeting," a voice emanated behind her.

Taylor swirled to look at Ari, her position unchanged, but her eye now open and red iris fixated on her, its gyros whirling. "What are you talking about?" Taylor felt it was safe to lead with that question.

"I could easily get myself out of these binds and kill the lot of them while sleeping and there is nothing that anyone could do about it." She chuckled, her crooked teeth clacking.

"You know that I would stop you." Taylor lowered her cup, looking resolute.

"Exactly." Ari smirked. "I know you'd try at least. That is why I'm choosing not to do it. As I told you before, I'd very much like your cooperation in joining me back to Zabökar. It would do no good if I had you fighting me every step of the way. I'm being compliant as a show of good faith that I mean you no harm, Taylor."

"And if your father had told you to come after my head? What then?" Taylor probed, walking along the edge of the room to get a closer look at Ari.

"Then that would be a different matter altogether." Her eyes tracked Taylor. "I take my job seriously and I honor what my father has tasked me to do. He wants you alive and me to keep you safe. I will lay down my life in seeing that done."

"You seem to really love him then," Taylor commented, stopping just feet from Ari's head.

She blinked, trying to assess the question and what Taylor was getting at. At length, Ari sighed. "You could say that, I guess." She finally looked away. "We have…a complicated relationship."

"You don't really sound so sure."

Ari seemed irritated. "He loves me in his own way."

"Did he do that to you?" Taylor pointed out the cybernetic device grafted into her skull.

"Yeah. It was to replace the one I had lost as a result of failure." Ari finally met Taylor's eyes again. "He said he felt pity for me and that it would make me look pretty."

"It doesn't," Taylor said bluntly.

"I know." The red iris wandered, as if not knowing what to focus on. "Still, it helps me more than it hinders, so I took it gratefully."

"How exactly does it work?" Taylor sat down cross-legged, cup placed in her lap.

Ari snorted. "You actually want to know?"

"Why not? We're not going anywhere. You're obviously not going anywhere." Taylor was indeed curious.

The look on Ari's face was one of confusion. "Uh, well… It actually helps me identify points of interest or targets of information to help me." Taylor figured she must have looked confused, so Ari continued. "It taps into the wifi signals in the air to deliver me information about anything I'm looking at. For example, I'm looking at you and I'm pulling up all the information that we have on file for you, which includes your latest social snapshots taken at Palaveve."

Taylor seemed visibly shaken at that harsh reminder of her doomed home of residence for the past year. "I didn't know there was that much stuff on me."

"Probably not as much as you're thinking. There is a lot if you know where to look though." Ari confirmed. "I know your mother's name was Murana, and she was a police officer in Zabökar."

Taylor shook again at the mention of her mother's name. "Stop, please stop."

"What, why? You asked," Ari reminded, shifting to get a better look at her.

"I know." Taylor looked down at her coffee, now no longer steaming. "I am just…trying to forget that part of my life."

"Why? Were you not happy with your mother?" Ari found this reaction with Taylor interesting.

"It's not that. I was quite happy. More like, I am upset with how I handled things with her. I never did get to say goodbye." Taylor began to tear up.

"You are luckier than I." Ari seemed introspective herself. "At least you actually got to meet your mother. I was born after she was long gone."

"Were you born with your powers? The ones where you are able to burn people alive?" Taylor attempted another sip, but she was no longer enjoying her drink.

Ari had to laugh. "I don't actually burn people. Rather, I am able to heat up any ground or material around me to a point where it can either melt or burst into flames. I can then shape and use it against those who are against me. Not exactly the same concept." She continued to chuckle at the misconception. "But to answer your question, I was not born with it. My father gave me these powers when I was young."

"Gave you?" Taylor cocked her head to the side. "How the heck does someone give another something like that?"

"Not directly." Ari seemed cautious, like she was trying to figure out how much she should say. "More like I agreed to participate in an experiment that ended up with me gaining the powers I have now."

"Was it painful?" Taylor set the cup down, no longer wanting lukewarm coffee.

"I guess you could say it was. Made me sick for weeks on end until I recovered." Ari shrugged while on her side. "What about you? When did my father capture you and give you your powers? Probably was a surprise when you found out that your tail now had a mouth!"

"Ahya?" Taylor looked over at her tail, still sporting uncharacteristically red fur, but otherwise normal. Ahya was absently poking around the coffee mug, sticking her tongue in to see if it agreed with her tastes. "I've always had her. She's been a part of me since I was born."

Ari was still. She stared at Taylor, trying to process the information. "You were born that way?" Taylor nodded. "What about that explosion you did in front of me? Was that learned or given to you?"

"I don't know what that was; that is only a recent thing that's been happening with me." Taylor studied her fingers. "I do know that I can heal myself and others with Ahya's saliva. Just this morning I was able to bring Fey back from dying with her." She patted the lapping tail fondly.

"You actually succeeded?" Ari seemed dumbfounded.

"To be honest, I was quite surprised too. I didn't even know she could even do that. I only had a hunch she could, and it was worth a try." She shrugged.

"And I missed all of it!" Ari fumed.

"It was actually kind of weird, having everyone stare at me while it was happening." Taylor felt a bit self-conscious just remembering the moment.

"Taylor, dear. Are you okay in there?" A soft voice called out from beyond the bedroom door, a low rapping indicating Klera's arrival.

"Yeah, I'm here." Taylor glanced over at Ari, but it seemed the reptile was asleep—or at least feigning like she was. "Come on in."

Natalia began to rouse as Klera entered the room, stretching out her back with her tail curling at the act. She stood and looked at Taylor. "Morning. I'm so sorry I fell asleep! I should have been up watching Ari all night!" She seemed a bit miffed at herself. "Did you sleep well?"

"I did, thank you." Taylor rose and handed the cup back to Klera, drained empty by the now-dormant Ahya. "I'm starving, actually. Do you have anything to eat?"

"As a matter of fact, we just got done!" Klera's muzzle broke out into a wrinkly grin. "Mikhail helped me fry some pancakes and potatoes. We even have some eggs for the carnivores in our company if you'd like some?"

Taylor put a paw to her mouth as she shook her head. "No, thank you, but the rest sounds delicious!" She beamed at the tigress and turned to Natalia, seeing as she hadn't made a move. "Are you coming with us?"

The snow leopard returned the smile. "No, I am going to stay here and keep watch on this one just to be safe." She indicated the sleeping Ari by her hind paws.

Knowing the truth of Ari's state of wakefulness, Taylor haltingly said, "Right. Want one of us to bring something back?"

"I'll bring back plates for the two of you," Klera interjected. "That odd girl down there may not be very nice, but she doesn't deserve to starve." She bowed before leading Taylor down the narrow corridor lined with doorways leading off to other rooms probably just like hers.

Climbing down the creaking spiral staircase into the living room, Taylor could see the tiny kitchen off to her right. Haze was still present in the air from smoke generated by Mikhail's cooking. He waved at her from beside the stovetop as he gestured to the smaller adjacent room that also opened out into another portion of the living den.

Inside that was a maple table expanded with leaves to accommodate a larger group of guests. Fey and Finnley were sitting very close at one end, with Terrati and Trevor taking up seats towards the other end. There were open spaces at the end opposite Fey and on the other side of the table from the gazelle and wolf. Appearing polite, Taylor took the one nearest Fey, taking great care not to intrude on the personal space of Finnley.

Placed before them was a generous spread of food separated by plates and embroidered napkins. Klera looked to spare no expense at being the best hostess. She swept up Taylor's napkin and from behind draped it over Taylor's legs as she sat down on the armless chair. Klera gave a small pat and squeeze on the shoulder to Taylor before heading into the kitchen to help her son-in-law finish up the remaining breakfast.

Fey spoke up first, his hooves clasped before his snout. "I just want to say thank you for saving my life. I would be remiss if I didn't acknowledge the debt I owe to you for that."

Taylor felt self-conscious, but knew he meant well. "It's no problem. I just saw that I could have done something about it, and I took the opportunity." It was weird saying the words, but she felt she had to respond to him somehow.

"Nonsense!" Terrati leaned forward. "You were the only one who had the ability to. Don't try and shortchange yourself. What you did last night was nothing short of miraculous."

Taylor flushed even more; she simply was not used to this much praise for what came natural to her own body, as abnormal as it was. "It's nothing...really." She picked at a string of red hair, pulling it back behind her ear in agitation. "I knew you all were trying your best to get me out of there and I wanted to do my part to help."

"Except you didn't have to," Fey stated plainly, his eyes steeled. "After everything we've done to you, at how we treated you, at how I've treated you, there was no reason you should have gone out of your way to save my life."

"You're right." She met his stare head on. "I didn't have to save any of you. However, I do not like people dying on my account. I've seen too much death because of me just existing. You were the one person I could save right there and then. If anything, I hoped it would help my cause in being treated nicer."

Trevor chuckled. "I'd say that worked. None of us are putting you in cuffs right now, and you're more than welcome to move about the house or village." He put up a single finger. "Provided you have an escort with you at all times."

"Is that something you all decided upon together?" she retorted, still upset at Trevor's blasé faire attitude towards everything.

242

"It was the only thing we were able to agree upon." Terrati informed, looking solemn.

"I should have died last night." Fey dropped his hooves quietly to the table. "I'm honestly surprised I am alive right now."

"I think we all are. I know I am." Finnley had not stopped hugging Fey, sitting on his lap and just being near the elk. He looked up into Fey's eyes. "I should have gone out first, scouted the path ahead. I'm smaller and faster and I could have avoided their fire."

"But Terrati was the only one who knew where to go. It was quicker for him to lead the way then relay it to you as we went," Fey reasoned.

"Here you go, gentlemammals," Klera crooned, setting down piping hot plates of pancakes, eggs, and potatoes. "Eat up! I'll be right back. I'm going to be delivering some food to the other ladies upstairs." She hummed to herself as she slowly worked her way up the staircase, plate in each paw.

Taylor crinkled her snout at the scrambled yellow on her plate. "I think I'll just take the pancakes and potatoes."

Mikhail had already sat down right beside her. He raised a paw menacingly. "Are we going to have to go through this once more? You show my mother respect and eat her food. She didn't have to make those eggs for us, but she's trying to be respectful of the predators in this room."

Not wanting to be smacked in the stomach again by his bulky paws, she scrambled to snatch up a fork to scoop some onto it. "Fine, fine! I'll eat, but…is it okay if Ahya has those instead? I just don't like their texture."

Mikhail squinted at her before lowering his paw. He checked the stairs to ensure Klera was still gone. "Fine, but do it quick. The less she knows of your special traits, the safer it is for her."

Without further prompting, Ahya finally revealed her toothy maw and pounced on Taylor's plate, its tongue slathering all over the food and snatching it up into its large cavity before closing tight and disappearing under the table. Taylor immediately began to taste the food upon her tongue as the seed of fullness began to grow in her belly.

"Gods, I keep forgetting how fast that thing can be!" Terrati had nearly fallen out of his chair in fright.

"Seriously, Ahya?" Taylor pouted, glaring at her tail. "You couldn't have saved me anything to eat?" She slouched in her chair and folded her arms. "Ugh, and I was looking forward to tasting those pancakes."

"I was told by Natalia that you can taste whatever she eats." Fey waved a hoof to the underside of the table. "What's the difference?"

"It's not the same." Taylor lightly booted her own tail with her hind paw. Ahya responded with a playful nip on the claw. "There is a huge difference between eating something with your own mouth than with your tail."

"I'm not exactly sure anyone would be able to relate to that." Fey began to eat his own meal, fresh fruit in place of the eggs the predators had.

"No, I guess not." Taylor looked put out.

They all ate in silence for a time. Klera had come back downstairs empty-handed, her task delivering the meals successful. She sat down at the other end of the table after having served Taylor seconds and began to daintily spoon in her own breakfast. She appeared to be older than Mikhail by a good twenty years—quite apparent in the way she held herself and walked. Despite this she seemed in good spirits, and appeared very happy that she had guests in her home again. She must have been lonely for a long time.

"So when are we going to address the elephant in the room?" Trevor rapped his fingers on the table, his meal long having been finished.

"There's none here. They wouldn't be able to fit." Klera seemed confounded.

"It's a figure of speech, Mom." Mikhail put a paw over hers calmly.

"You mean Taylor?" Fey regarded the bounty hunter shrewdly. "That is the question of the hour, to be sure."

"Do I actually get a say in this, or are you all going to decide on what my future is going to be?" Taylor dropped her fork with a purposeful clatter.

"It's kind of hard to factor in what you want, Taylor, when all of us have employers who we report to that kind of own our hides." Terrati raised his hooves up at her scowl. "What? I'm just stating the truth."

"He is right though." Trevor scratched his chin. "My boss pretty much signed my death warrant by sending Ari. She confirmed that it mattered little if I returned in a basket. You coming back with me to Zabökar basically means a stay of execution."

"Likewise, the High Council will not accept failure." Fey rubbed his temple. "I don't believe they will kill us like the Arbiter will to you, but our future careers and livelihoods will most likely become very unpleasant if we return without her."

"And it's not like we can just kill her and bring her back, since they specifically wanted her back alive." Finnley turned and faced forward on Fey's lap.

"Wait, me specifically?" Taylor wasn't sure if he had phrased that right.

"Kill Taylor?" Klera was jostled from her potatoes. "Why would anyone want to harm a darling girl like her? She's precious and I won't stand for it!" She began to rise in her seat.

"It's fine, Mom." Mikhail had to talk her back down. "Nobody is saying we're going to do that. We're just discussing conflicts of interest regarding our jobs. How about Terrati helps you clean up in the kitchen while we discuss further how best to take care of Taylor."

"But I didn't offer…" the gazelle began, but was silenced by a scathing look from Mikhail. "I'd be happy to assist you, ma'am." He bowed his head compliantly.

Klera eyed them all warily. "If I hear anything about harming a single hair on that pretty girl's head, I'll tan your rears. I don't care how old I am!" She waggled a finger at them.

"I don't doubt it!" Mikhail had to laugh.

Terrati begrudgingly clomped into the kitchen. They could hear him wail over the fact that Klera lacked a proper dishwasher. Taylor had to suppress her mirth as Klera began to teach him how to clean up dishes the old-fashioned way, toting how it was good for stress levels and helped soothe the nerves.

"If anything, I say we should kill Ari up there," Trevor repeated from before.

"That has the unfortunate consequence of upsetting your employer." Fey cracked a grin. "How mad do you think he'd be if you returned with Taylor, but his daughter did not? I think it'd be in your best interest if both came back with you if you value your life as much as you say you do."

Trevor's brow furrowed. "You're right. Trading Taylor for my life would pale in comparison to losing his daughter's. I'd be dead either way." He cracked a grin at a sudden thought. "I could always blame you and say you guys killed her."

"Doubtful. Given her abilities, I don't think the Arbiter would believe that story of yours," Fey reasoned, which caused Trevor's ears to fold peevishly. "Which is why it'd be far better if Taylor came with us, since having you both fail wouldn't be as damning than one or the other, and it would prevent any loss of life," he concluded triumphantly.

"Oh no…" Trevor pounded the table and growled at the elk. "You aren't just convincing me in giving her up just like that. I owe it to my buddy, Gregor, to fulfill the promise we made to each other."

"Again, do I count at all?" Taylor slapped her own paw on the table. "Do I get to choose who I get to go with?"

"No!" Both Fey and Trevor barked, causing Taylor to look affronted.

"What's it matter to you, anyway?" Finnley waved a dismissing paw at her. "You've been nothing but eager to escape us this entire time. Now you want to have a say in who you want to go with? Since when did you change your mind?"

"This morning, actually." Taylor bared her teeth at the annoying otter. "I thought we were past this bickering. I saved your boyfriend's life."

"Boyfriend?" Fey looked embarrassed.

"Well? How else would I describe how you two have been acting?" Her eyes drilled holes into them.

"She's got you there." Mikhail hid the smile behind his paws as he leaned onto the table with his elbows.

Finnley looked awkward, but didn't deny it. "Well, yeah, guess he is that. Still doesn't mean I like you, only that I appreciate and respect what you did for us."

"Oh great, fat load of good it did. I'm still being terrorized by the water-rat!" Taylor fumed, flopping back against her chair.

Finnley snarled and appeared to be climbing up onto the oak table to get at her when Fey held him back by the chest. "Your back, hun. Please don't injure it again." The otter groaned before settling back down into his lap. "Forgive him, he is rather protective of me as I am of him. I'll admit, I was not the nicest of people to you when I discovered you had dropped him right out of a tree when you two first met."

"That makes two of us," Taylor huffed. "I changed my mind this morning because I realized that even if I had been successful in running away, I wouldn't have gotten far. I've been on the run for several years now and I was still found, regardless of where I went. It would either be you or someone worse who'd find me again. Since none of you want to kill me or do some awful experiments on me, you're probably my best choice to stick with right now. At the very least I have you all as my protection against the really bad people who are after me."

"That is an interesting way of putting it." Trevor laughed, scratching his chest. "Your captors are now your bodyguards. I like the way you think."

"That still doesn't solve the overall problem about who she goes back to Zabökar with." Mikhail shared a look with Fey. "We need to tread carefully, or we will be at each other's throats again over her. We may be at a truce for now, but it cannot last for long."

"What about Ari?" Taylor glanced up towards the spiraling staircase, trying to weed out what Finnley had said earlier about them looking for her specifically. "Didn't you say that the High Council had sent you out with the direction to find any mammal with special abilities? It was just luck that I stumbled your way. How about just take her back to your High Council? They won't know the difference. One mammal with powers is as good as another."

"That's a very astute observation to make, Taylor," Fey admitted. "However, the Arbiter would know, and tensions that are already at a breaking point now would erupt into an all-out conflict within the bounds of the city. The High Council would discover it is his daughter and most likely exacerbate the issue by holding her ransom. That and…we were sent specifically to find you."

"So you lied to me earlier." Taylor dared him to deny it, her suspicions confirmed.

"Yes and no." Fey went to fiddle with his antlers, only to be reminded they were gone, settling instead to petting Finnley. "By the time you came across us, we were looking for any anomalies on our biometric scanners. We had lost your trail months ago, and were instead camped at the farthest and last known area you were picked up at."

"I don't understand," she said. Ahya began to rise back up from under the table, joining in on Taylor's confusion.

"What I said earlier was correct." Fey inclined close to her. "We are tasked to track and locate any specimens that the Arbiter has experimented on and bring them in to the High Council. However, our team specifically was tasked to find you." He put a hoof up to stop Taylor's question. "We didn't know it was you exactly. We were just told to find a high-value asset that had recently gone missing in the direction of Falhoven from the Arbiter's collection of mammals he had gathered and changed. I only received detailed information about you after we had captured you and I reached back to my contact in Zabökar."

"Gregor and I just happened to go a little further," Trevor filled in the gap. "We knew the rough direction where you had gone, but not the specific location where you were. We kept our eyes and ears out for any hint of where you might be. Social media and your killing incidents in Palaveve are what led us straight to you."

"Wait, so you're telling me that I'm the only one either of you were tracking this entire time? Why the hell am I so special?" Taylor began to get angry now. "I'm just a freak, according to Finnley and just about everyone else I've met. What good can I possibly be to anyone on your High Council or the Arbiter?"

"I think the answer should be obvious." Mikhail tried to place a comforting paw on Taylor's shoulder, removing immediately as she jerked away from it. "You are the only specimen that has seemingly more than one power manifest itself, and you are the only one that has the ability to heal wounds. Quite ghastly wounds at that."

"And you did say you were born with your tail. You were just living a normal life before being on the run?" Fey confirmed, getting a nod from Taylor. "Then I have a sneaking suspicion that you were not created directly by the Arbiter. You are somewhat of an exceptional case. Every mammal we've catalogued from his experiments has been either a teenager or child prior to them being turned. You are the only one we can't say that about."

"Why? I don't get it." She never asked to be unique. It just got more on her nerves now that there was now a legitimate reason why everyone is chasing after her.

"I'm at a loss too as to how you were born, or if anything was special regarding the nature of your birth." Fey relaxed in his chair, still bushed from last night's events. "It is probably why the Arbiter is so keen on acquiring you, and probably why the High Council is so interested in you: because the Arbiter is."

"What's up with that?" Taylor thumped her foot with irritation. "All I've been told is that your High Council and Trevor's Arbiter are against each other, yet no one has bothered to explain why that is!"

"It's based on a political disagreement between the two parties," Terrati came in, wiping his hooves with a dish rag, having caught up quickly on the conversation at hoof. "As far as I'm aware, there is a supposed war looming that the Arbiter is predicting, and he offered a radical proposition in how to combat it. The High Council denied his request and disbanded all funding on his research for it. This, of course, did not stop him, and he's been illegally working on his ambitions regardless. You and Ari are both results of those goals."

"Well, not entirely." Mikhail scooted closer to the table to let Klera into the dining room so she could reclaim her seat. "Ari might be, but Taylor is not. She was born this way. So there was no way she could have been experimented on unless she was in the womb when it happened. Was your mom working for the Arbiter in any way?"

Taylor shook her head. "No... I only know she was a police officer."

Terrati rubbed his chin. "Hmmm, then no, she would have not been an employee of his. Don't think the cops sided favorably with the Arbiter at all."

"This is getting too confusing." Taylor stood up suddenly, causing her chair to fall back with a bang. "I'm so sorry, Mrs. Faliden." She bowed profusely to Klera, bending to pick the chair back up.

"It's quite all right, dear." She brushed off the damage to her furniture. "In fact, I think it is high time you all get up out of here so I can clean my house and you enjoy Cheribaum for yourselves. It's clear that nothing will be settled right now between anyone; I've seen enough arguments to know that much."

"Yes, ma'am," several of those present at the table agreed.

"Mikhail, can I speak with you for a moment?" Fey got up and set Finnley down on the chair next to him, reaching out a hoof to stop the tiger.

"Of course." He nodded, calling out to Taylor as she was ascending the steps. "I'll be going with you, Taylor. Don't leave the house without me."

Mikhail watched Taylor reach the top of the stairs before stepping to the side with Fey and Finnley. Terrati had already shuffled along back up to their temporary quarters to get dressed for the day.

"Mikhail, I should have died last night." Fey was serious, his muzzle firm.

"We all know that." Mikhail patted the elk on the shoulder. "What Taylor accomplished was miraculous."

"You don't get it." Finnley paced back and forth along the small space of his chair. "Fey's Script had his death pegged for last night."

"You're well aware of how the Script governs our lives, do you not?" Fey continued to hold Mikhail's attention.

The tiger's jovial attitude turned grave. "Yes, I'm very much aware of what my future holds. As I've told you, my own death isn't far now. I've quite forgotten the exact date, but I know it is coming soon, *in the village of the love I had gained and lost*. It's why I picked this place for everyone to hunker down in; my Script led us here. It was ironically the only option for leagues around."

"Then you'll understand how important what I'm about to tell you is." Fey took a deep breath. "My Script reads, *You shall die in service to a friend in a hail of justice, escaping from the law with your job of red teeth.*" He let that sink in.

"You were shot by the cops in cold blood…" Mikhail began.

"By aiding his friend, Terrati, while escaping with our current job of bringing Taylor back to Zabökar," Finnley finished.

"Yet here I am, alive and well." Fey gestured to himself, antlers missing and all.

"What devilry is this?" Mikhail went slack-jawed. "Maybe you read the Script wrong and that isn't to happen until later?"

Fey shook his head. "As a precaution, I had my Script read to me before we left Zabökar in search of Taylor. The entry several sections before my last had us finally catching a break where the object of our search would be flanked by two wolves. The very two that Taylor was traveling with. I was to die last night."

"Yet Taylor saved you…" Mikhail began to stare off, his eyes not focused on any one thing. "Changing the Script is not possible." He turned back to Fey. "Nobody has ever heard of such a thing happening."

"Yet Taylor managed to save me from death, and now I'm no longer on the Script," Fey finished with finality.

"Are you sure about that?" The tiger pressed.

"Pretty sure. I'll be checking the local church today to verify," Fey informed.

Mikhail had to sit down at this revelation. He had his entire life's history laid out for him, paying to have his Script read from beginning to end. Nothing surprised him anymore, and if anything, he was pleasantly intrigued at how his Script played out in reality. Could Taylor stop his impending death too? What sort of supernatural powers did Taylor have to literally rewrite someone's Script?

"Have you checked to see if it changed at all?" Mikhail exhaled after realizing he was holding his breath in.

Fey shook his head. "No, but as I said, I'll be checking-"

"Yes, yes, the local church." Mikhail was distracted. "Please do, this is most disconcerting." Mikhail's mind was a jumble of emotions at the implications this revelation had for everyone.

"I just felt you should know as you go about escorting Taylor today." Fey gestured with his chin upstairs. "Finnley, can you see that the girls are ready, and tell Natalia to come down with Taylor?"

"Of course, hun." The otter put a loving paw on Fey's arm before sliding carefully off the chair and pattering up the spiral stairs.

"I want you to observe and document everything with Taylor." Fey looked Mikhail straight in the eyes. "I don't think anyone knows what we are dealing with here. This is unprecedented, and if my assumptions are correct, Taylor is far more dangerous than anyone above us is letting on. Keep her safe, but don't let her out of your sight. Report to me on anything unusual with her that we're not already aware of."

Mikhail just nodded numbly. "Of course, Fey. I'll keep an eye on her."

Mikhail called out to Taylor as she was ascending the steps. "I'll be going with you, Taylor. Don't leave the house without me."

Pausing briefly before taking the next step to acknowledge his command, Taylor reached the top and walked down the hall back to her room. Opening the sliding door, she spotted Natalia and Ari sitting across from each other, their finished plates between them. With her wrists and ankles still bound, Taylor was quite unclear how Ari managed to feed herself, but she wasn't going to ask any questions.

"I trust that Ari didn't give you any trouble?" Taylor surveyed the room and found that it was as pristine as she left it.

"No, surprisingly." Natalia beamed. "She is actually quite the talker. We've been reminiscing about Zabökar and our experiences growing up there."

Taylor was surprised. "Your father let you roam the streets freely? From what little I know of him, he doesn't seem to be that type of parent."

Ari studied Taylor a moment. "Not usually these days, no. There was a time when I took my own freedom and enjoyed the pleasures of the city. That was before their High Council began searching for my father in earnest. I've been stuck mostly underground since then."

"Your father's base of operations is underground?" Natalia pressed suddenly.

Ari looked irritated. "That's all you're going to get out of me, cat."

"Gods, the lot of you are always trying to one-up each other." Taylor shook her head, walking over to her bed padding and doing her best to make it look nice and folded. "I've never met so many backstabbing people in my life until now."

Natalia was crestfallen. "It's just the nature of our job, Taylor. When you're an ex-military mercenary for hire, you are always looking out for number one."

Taylor stared blankly at her sheets. "I guess I was like that once. Look where that got me now though."

"You were ex-military?" Natalia wasn't following.

Taylor realized her mistake and laughed. "Oh, no... I meant that I was always looking out for number one and focusing on my selfish, childish needs. It wasn't until I ran away from Zabökar completely and found Pine and Mitchell that I discovered the fulfillment of helping others."

"Those are your two friends, the skunk and raccoon, right?" Ari clarified, her red iris never leaving Taylor.

"You've met them?" Natalia seemed shocked.

"Of course, back at the bar in Howlgrav." Ari gave her a toothy grin. "They were pretty cute and spunky. I liked them."

"I liked them too." Taylor had a sad smile, her eyes welling up. "Now I have no idea where they are, or if I even killed them with...whatever crazy power I have."

"You can't blame yourself." Ari's voice was heartfelt. "You protected me from those two wolves. Don't think I've forgotten that. If not for you, that wolf would have shot me good."

Taylor wiped her tears away with her paw. "Guess not everything is permanent in this life. I need to learn to let go and not get too attached to anyone, because they'll all end up dead because of me."

"That's not a good way of looking at things." Natalia crawled over to massage Taylor's shoulders, and Taylor surprisingly found herself leaning into the snow leopard. "If there is one thing I know about life, it is always surprising and unexpected. You can't just apply what is happening now to all future occurrences. You need to be open to letting new friendships in and not shutting out the world."

Taylor's gaze wandered over to the kitsune plush that was sitting along the wall, a stark reminder of her last and only gift from Mrs. Hircus. "Not unexpected if the Script dictates what happens to you. Maybe people were just meant to die and you can't do anything about it."

"Or maybe you can. Maybe only you and I can change people's fates." Ari pressed forward, eagerness in her demeanor.

Taylor stared at her oddly. "What did you say?"

Finnley barged into the room loudly. "Alright ladies, Trevor and I will be watching this troublemaker here. The rest of you need to get out of the home. Klera's orders!"

"Freaking sandboxes, Finnley!" Natalia growled. "Can you at least knock? What if we were still undressed?"

Finnley shrugged. "Not like I'm interested in anything you've got to offer. Now get out of here!"

"If I didn't respect Fey so much, I'd give you a good beating." Natalia stood swiftly and towered over the petite otter.

"That makes two of us." Taylor chimed in, sharing Natalia's frustration.

"Ah hell, make that three." Ari chuckled.

"But you don't even know Fey," Finnley riposted, folding his arms.

"True, but I'd still give you a good beating just because," Ari cackled.

13
RABBITS

It seemed like a surreal dream to Taylor. She was out on the town in Cheribaum with Mikhail, Terrati, and Natalia—an odd group of mammals to be sure. Trevor had elected to stay behind to "keep an eye" on Fey, as he put it, and Finnley stayed behind to "keep an eye" on Trevor. So it was just the four of them.

Taylor had put on the cloak she had kept since Palaveve, so she did not draw as many stares from folk than she was used to due to her unusual fur color. They had already learned that lesson harshly in Howlgrav. Despite this, the hospitality of the local people was very surprising. They would just look up briefly and give them a smile before going about their current task.

"They all seem so happy," Taylor commented, watching an elderly aardvark washing her clothes in a wooden water basin.

"Is this not normal where you come from?" Natalia asked.

Taylor observed several leopard kits dash along the stone path ahead of them, kicking a small ball in some unfathomable game. "Well, no. I'm actually from Zabökar—you should already know. It wasn't like this in Palaveve either. In fact, most people kept to themselves and there was little in the way of social gathering there. What I can remember of Zabökar was pleasant. Maybe I was too young to really see the true state of the city as Mikhail and Terrati have stated it is, or my mother was just so protective of me that she sheltered me from all of its negative aspects. I don't really know."

Mikhail seemed deep in thought. "There are several places minors here are prohibited from going to, and most mammals are pretty keen on keeping it that way. I think it may also have to do with the overall community assisting in keeping children on the right path."

"At least, until they are old enough to make their own bad decisions." Terrati laughed.

"Like us?" Natalia joined in.

"That doesn't sound so bad," Taylor thought. "An entire town dedicated to keeping young innocents pure until they can make their own choices. That's pretty great, actually."

"You're simplifying it a bit too much." Mikhail flicked his tail. "But I guess we'll go with that for now. Yes, the people here do enjoy a simplicity of life that most other towns you'll most likely come across do not have."

Taylor was feeling a lot more comfortable here than she ever did in Palaveve; having to not hide as much helped tremendously in that respect. She was sad that she couldn't share this village with Pine and Mitchell, but she was determined to enjoy it on their behalf. Feeling happier than she had been in months, she began to skip down the path, giddy butterflies in her stomach. Natalia and the others had to keep up with her, the three of them smiling and reveling in Taylor's delight of the moment.

The path led them to the center of town where the narrow walkway down the steep mountainside opened up and leveled out to what looked like a circular festival square, with hanging wood chimes like decorative flags tied to the raised ends of several roofs, each crisscrossing the plaza to give off a sense of exotic wonder. Their dulcet melodies could be heard as the approaching storm's wind began to jingle the carved wooden pipes upon their ropes.

"We may want to see about finding a place to stay inside for a few hours." Terrati looked up at the darkening clouds above them.

"Can't we check the market stalls here first?" Taylor asked, pointing at several which had been set up around the interior of the plaza circling the fountain in the middle. "That was one of my favorite things to do back in Palaveve. I was always so fascinated with the things people were selling or what crafts they had made with their own paws for others to enjoy."

"You sound a little like me." Natalia smiled, nodding to Mikhail and Terrati. "I come from the country of Livarnu off to the west. The primary exports of my people were toys or craft tools that we developed with our own paws. I can understand your appreciation of that art, because it is fascinating for me too."

Taylor's eyes lit up as she regarded Natalia. "Have you ever created anything like that before?"

Natalia shook her head and raised her arms in defeat. "Sadly, I was never much good at it. Not for lack of trying, mind you."

"I think you should get back into it. I think you'd be pretty good at it." Taylor turned from her surprised look back to investigating the small toys that were displayed on the small shelving of the tarp covered unit.

They had nearly completed their circuit of the stalls, just as it was starting to sprinkle. The final vendor was selling a wide variety of cakes and pastries, including Taylor's favorite, apple tarts. The koala proprietor was looking a bit anxious about closing up soon, because the weather had begun to turn sour. He was a bit more pushy than normal.

"Um…Taylor? Your tail is showing." Terrati pointed out, seeing the rising terror in the koala's eyes.

"Ahya? Freaking hell, again?" Taylor was exasperated. Before she could do anything, the tail was already at the level of the food and lunged its tongue forward to slurp up several delectable treats into its maw and dissolve them instantly. Taylor put a paw to her mouth as she burped. "Ugh, as sweet as they are, those flavors did not go well together…"

"How about we find a place to huddle inside before it gets worse." Natalia glanced up at the sky and hurried Taylor along before her, both to avoid the weather and any further trouble with the local populace.

She looked back to see Mikhail put a few hundred bills on the counter, sliding them towards the koala, who was wide-eyed at the retreating wolf with the freakish tail. "This is for your silence and to pay for any lost revenue from those pastries." Mikhail made sure he made eye contact before releasing the money and walking away.

With the rain now starting to pour, they apologized to the random cheetah they had inadvertently bumped into as they rushed into a local diner. They shook off the droplets from their fur in the designated clearing space at the entrance, then scanned the place to find it more akin to an upscale breakfast café. It had several glass chandeliers in the center of the raised ceiling and multiple booths with plush black cushions lining the exterior wall, which was nothing but metal frame supported glass. They could see an amazing view of the square through it.

"How about we take a seat over there and just chill until the weather subsides?" Terrati picked the booth in the far corner.

Sidestepping the circular tables, each covered in long tablecloths that reached the carpeted floor, they finally came to their picked booth. It too had a cloth that covered its entirety and reached down fully to the floor. Mikhail scooted in after he gave Taylor the window seat. Natalia and Terrati sat opposite them. The glass siding curved up to the center structure so they could see the rain pattering the glass above their heads.

"This seems nice. I haven't been to a cute place like this before." Taylor looked around curiously.

The charming café had a light jazz melody that could be heard on the speakers adjacent to the long stretching bar at the other end of the dining area, where several patrons were seated on swivel chairs. The music was accentuated by the clinking of silverware and the sounds of working chefs and the dishwasher. The one odd thing she noticed was that every server and waiter was a rabbit. She noticed a few crawling out from under some of the tables before going about their business in delivering more food to the other customers waiting.

"They're all rabbits," Taylor pointed out.

"That's not really surprising," Mikhail answered, picking up the pre-placed menus on their table and perusing the drinks on sale. "You'll find them just about everywhere in customer service jobs like this."

"So what will you have to drink today?" Terrati paused a moment. "Do you drink coffee at all? I probably should have asked before choosing this place. That's kind of all they have to offer here, unless you like water?"

"I like coffee, yeah." She squinted at the text in the menu, finding it hard to read. It seemed to be in a language she wasn't familiar with. "I'm more of a coffee-with-my-creamer sort of gal."

"Less bitter, more sweet. Gotcha." Terrati clicked his hooves before roving with the list of drinks with a hoof. "Then I think you'd like the Tuxedo Rabbit. It's got two different types of chocolate in one."

"That sounds good. Get me that." She smiled, closing the useless menu.

Natalia had been eyeing her. "The menu is in the local dialect here. If you were born and raised in Zabökar, you're probably not going to understand any of it."

"And you do?" Taylor fired back amicably.

"I'm a well-traveled cat." Natalia winked. "I've been to quite a few places in my time, and I've learned to read and speak several different languages. It comes in handy often."

"Indeed it does. Here comes our waiter now." Mikhail was watching the pristinely tailored rabbit in a full suit walk their way.

He seemed to carry himself proudly, but there was a certain sadness to his eyes. The bowtie around his neck seemed a bit too tight and his pressed suit accentuated every curve of his body, which drew much attention to his butt and leggings. Taking a quick survey of the rest of the waiters, they seemed to be sporting similar attire that prominently featured their bodies, despite being very well-dressed and formal for such a café setting.

He was carrying a small stepping stool and set it down promptly before climbing to get at table-height to address the larger guests. "Morning, ladies and gentlemammals." He did a small bow to which Mikhail and Natalia responded in kind. "My name is Francis. How can I serve you today?"

"I'd like a large coffee, black." Mikhail grunted.

"Just a plain latte for me." Terrati smiled.

"Mocha here." Natalia raised a paw.

"Um…" Taylor glanced down at the menu for apparently no reason but to buy time since she already forgot what she was going to order. "I'll have the…" She looked back at Terrati for some guidance. "Tuxedo…rabbit?"

After Natalia translated for Francis, he bowed at each of their orders and then gathered up the menus. "Is there anything else I can serve you today?" he said without inflection, effortlessly switching to a language Taylor could understand.

The others seemed to know the drill and either shook their heads or smiled politely no. Francis's eyes finally fell onto Taylor, who was looking around, unsure of what was being asked. "You mean there's more than just coffee?" She blinked.

"Of course. All establishments of the Java Rabbit have special services provided to you, by none other than our talented staff." He seemed very jovial at reciting this advertisement by rote memory, but it seemed forced to Taylor.

"Is it on the menu?" She went to see if she could have one back, despite being unable to read it.

"Consider it more of a complimentary service." Terrati grinned. "Not required, but it does help with the stress of the day."

Seeing no other comments from either Natalia or Mikhail, who were just waiting on her to make a decision, she just shrugged. "Sure, that sounds fine. I like coffee and I like stress-free days. I've been a bit under pressure lately, so whatever you add with my coffee I'll be okay with." She beamed, excited at having a normal morning for once. She couldn't recall the last time she felt this carefree, even if it was amongst her current captors.

Francis kept his mood upbeat and acknowledged her request. "As you wish. Let me first get you your drinks." He politely stepped down and picked up his stool before heading back to the kitchen with their orders.

"So what now?" Taylor asked, her legs idly kicking the bottom of her booth frame.

"Now we wait until Fey decides what to do next." Mikhail studied the pattern of rain as it hit the plaza cobblestones.

"You mean you have no say in what you all do?" Taylor raised her brow at this.

"He was appointed leader by the High Council," Terrati explained. "We can always offer input, of course, but he is the ultimate say on what we do as a team. Since the burden of leadership was placed upon him, whatever actions we perform, he is responsible for. I'd rather not be the reason he got punished because he decided to take one of my hair-brained ideas that backfired."

"I guess I see your point." Taylor was thoughtful. "Still, I feel…anxious right now, like I'm just waiting for my fate to be decided." She looked at each one of them in the eyes. "I get that you're trying to be nicer to me now, trying to make sure I cooperate better, but the fact remains that I'm still a prisoner here and I'm being taken back not by my own choice, but because your bosses said so. I can't be fully comfortable around you knowing that behind all this, you still have a purpose for me that isn't in my best interest."

"I wouldn't say that," Natalia chimed in, reaching a paw across the table to massage Taylor's. "True, we are contractually obligated to obey the orders of our superiors in bringing you in, but I personally would not want to see harm come to you. Not now that I've come to know you better."

"Agreed," Mikhail rumbled in his throat. "If I discover they want more to do with you where they hurt you—or as I've heard you say, experiment on you—you can be damned sure I'm going to be very upset about it."

Taylor blushed at the sudden protectiveness. "That's very nice of you. Still, I can't shake that my life isn't my own and I am not free to make my own decisions."

"Well, you made the decision of what you'll drink today." Terrati laughed.

"Not the point!" Taylor jabbed a finger at him. The rest joined his laughter.

"Look, we get what you mean, Taylor." Mikhail shifted to better face her. "But you can't deny that you are a unique individual. You have uncanny abilities such as healing and some sort of explosive power, and you have a tailmaw…who is being very mischievous right now."

"What? Ahya!" Her tail was being curious, and had snuck under the tablecloth and was slowly rising up, dragging the rest of it with her as if she was pretending to be a ghost. Natalia and Terrati had to hold onto the fabric while Taylor got her own tail under control. "Can you please just stay still for even an hour?" She tucked Ahya back behind her as best the booth would allow.

"Can you not feel what she's doing?" Terrati was intrigued as to the nature of her tail.

"Well, yeah." Taylor smarted. "But not like I always pay attention to her all the time. I mean, of course when she is doing bad things, I'm vividly aware of what she's doing, but when she's just minding her own business and being good, I don't usually focus on her all that much."

"Kind of like our tails." Natalia commented, flicking her own above the level of the table for emphasis.

"Kinda?" Taylor now kept a paw firmly on Ahya, scratching her softly under the fur to keep her pacified. "It's not easy when your tail can have a mind of its own. Sure, I can control her most times—she is my tail, after all—but there are times that she just overpowers my ability to contain her and she just…eats someone." She shivered at the memory.

"Do you know why she does that?" Mikhail asked. He seemed genuinely worried for the answer.

Taylor shook her head. "I can't read her mind. I don't understand why she chooses to eat someone. All I know is that I can still remember their taste."

Terrati's eyes bulged. "Wait… You can remember every person she's ever eaten?"

"Every one." Taylor was solemn, looking down at the plain white cloth, ashamed. "I remember her first victim. She was my best friend. Sarah was her name." The three of them were rapt on her story, and Natalia's gaze bored into her own. "I had known her since elementary school. We were close friends all growing up and into high school. I think I was around twelve or so at the time."

Taylor's gaze wandered off to stare outside, losing focus as she stared past the raindrops on the glass. "I remember we were coming home from school that day after a rough baseball practice tryout, taking the long way around through the park, when suddenly Ahya just gobbled her up in front of other kids and their families. I don't even know what prompted it."

Tears began to form and drip down from her eyes. "I can still feel and remember her struggling and screaming inside my tail, of feeling that awful pit of fullness in my belly as she stopped moving and then was gone. Parents around me began to call the cops. They called me a murderer. All I wanted to do was bunch up into a small ball and disappear."

"What did you do?" Terrati's jaw was nearly dropping to the table, his breathing rapid.

Taylor turned back to him. "What anyone would do when they just murdered somebody: I ran. I ran all the way home back to my mother. I told her what happened and she began to cry with me. She held me tight. We had to move that night; I was no longer safe."

"Murana sounds like a strong woman," Natalia said as she tried to control her own breathing.

"That her name?" Mikhail seemed curious. "Sounds a lot like my wife." Mikhail folded his arms, his face darkening at the story, but he let her continue.

"She was very strong," Taylor agreed. "I never much paid attention to her or her job, but I guess she quickly had to drop out. She was a police officer and she had to answer for her daughter's crime."

"But it wasn't your fault!" Natalia was adamant.

Taylor shrugged. "It didn't matter. A young girl had died because of me in front of dozens of eyewitnesses. Her parents were demanding blood, and it was either ruin her career over protecting me or lose her one and only daughter to the law because of what my tail did."

"Clearly they'd be able to see you weren't at fault." Terrati thumped a hoof on the table. "Once they realized she has a mind of her own. They can't put all that blame on you."

"You're thinking with the knowledge you have now," Mikhail reminded sternly. "You're saying that because you know how Taylor's tail works. Consider it from the point of view of those who witnessed it or people who have never seen a tail such as hers. Everyone can control their tail with complete confidence when they focus on it. The story of a person who is unable to would be absurd and be laughed out of the courtroom as a mad mammal. She would not be given a fair trial."

Ahya began to peek back up from under the cloth and was trying to nudge affectionately into Taylor's chest. She roughly pushed her tail back down. "Don't even try to apologize to me now about it." Ahya looked hurt, but Taylor just ignored her. "I sometimes hate having a tail like this. I wonder how in the hell I was even born with it or why. Maybe I am just a freak."

"Well, have you ever tried thinking of cutting it off?" Terrati offered absentmindedly.

This drew glares all around as Taylor looked horrified. "Cut off...my own tail?"

Mikhail's expression nearly broke at her discomfort. "Maybe we should switch subjects…"

"Why? I'm apparently the talk of the town according to you three. That's what everyone wants to talk about when around me, and now I'm told I should try cutting off my own tail! Makes me feel 'real' good." She slouched and just pouted.

Taylor was startled as Francis's head popped up from beyond the table. He was carrying a tray with steaming cups of java. He carefully doled them out and put on his best smile as he did so. He finished with Taylor's drink last, and looked her directly in the eyes. "I apologize profusely, ma'am. I will get to you as soon as I can. We are just a bit understaffed right now and there are several other tables I must wait on first. Will it be alright if I get them their drinks and then come back to you?"

A bit confused, she just nodded. "Oh, uh…yeah, that'll be fine. Do what you need to do."

"Most gracious." His smile did seem genuine now. "I'll be back as soon as I can!"

With that, Francis bounced off the stool and carried it with him to the next table. He took another coffee to a cheetah off in the corner next to the door. Taylor caught her eye and she quickly looked away, suddenly absorbed in the hanging chandeliers near her position.

Taking a sip of her coffee, Natalia offered, "Well, I respect Murana immensely. I wasn't a cop myself. Terrati and I were former military. Mikhail here was a part of TALOS."

"What's TALOS?" Taylor turned to Mikhail.

"Tactical Aviation and Land Operations Service," he clarified. "It was an offshoot of the police force within Zabökar, like a special operations division. Not unlike the spec-ops units found within the military, but we've always claimed ourselves better." He gave a smug grin to Terrati who just rolled his eyes. "I might have known your mother depending. What was her surname?"

Taylor answered, "My surname is Wolford, but I've always just gone by Taylor Renee."

Mikhail's brow furrowed as he thought. "So, Murana Wolford… Name sounds familiar, but I don't think I ever met her. Regardless, I'm assuming she lost her job and decided to run away to protect you?"

Taylor studied her drink a few moments. "I think she lost her job, yeah. I don't remember much. It was a bit of a blur… That and I ran away."

"She was doing her best to protect you and you ran away?" Natalia was flummoxed. "Why would you do that? She loved you."

"I know!" she snapped, but immediately apologized. "I know… It's just that tensions were high. Father was dead already, and it was just me and her on the run trying to stay low. Parts of my memory of this time are a bit hazy, like they're missing somehow. It's kind of all blended together. It was a rough few years. I do know that she had some sort of cancer that was killing her, and when I found out that it was terminal, I flipped out. I ran away."

"I'm not exactly understanding why, but I can understand the frustration there." Mikhail stroked his chin before taking another sip.

"I got mad. I was tired of living day by day on scraps and hiding from the world, but I was also upset that I could do nothing to help my mom after everything she had done for me. I figured I should just end it early and just leave to try and live on my own. I didn't want to burden her anymore; I'd already ruined her life. I was going to be alone anyway soon enough." Taylor was furious with herself.

"That doesn't make sense. She was your only protection then. Sure, she might have died eventually, but you leaving like that just made you more vulnerable." Terrati seemed to be trying to wrap his head around her decisions.

"I was a dumb kid, ok? We don't always have the best judgment when we're angry." She gritted her teeth.

"Well, you still don't make the best of decisions now."

"Terrati, please, not now," Natalia interceded as Taylor gave him a seething glare.

Taylor's claws gripped her cup, scratching the porcelain. She had to relax before she ruined it further. "You are right though; I was alone and leaving was a mistake. I fell into a crowd that led me to being somewhat of a rebel. I joined a punk band and enjoyed my newfound fame as a novelty celebrity. Ahya was actually useful for once. People thought she was a technical prop, and it was so unique that everyone loved it."

"Were you happy doing what you loved and expressing yourself like that?" Natalia asked.

"I guess I was." Taylor wiped the flakes she had scratched off from the cup before taking a drink. "I was angry, I was hurt, and I raged at the machine with the rest of my band. It was a way to get out all that pain I had felt of being treated differently from the moment Ahya ate Sarah."

"But you said you were at school." Terrati was trying to make sense of the logistics. "Like…for years. So how did nobody treat you differently before then?"

"My mother was smart and tried to understand me with my tail, helping me work on coping skills and learning to manage and control her in public." Taylor reminisced fondly at those sessions. "Sure, quite a lot of kids didn't want to be my friend because of Ahya, but the few who did were the very best. They saw past what I had and saw me for me." Her face dropped as her memories turned. "Those coping skills aren't as effective anymore now that Ahya is more independent. She was getting worse until recently when you all showed up."

"You're a strong girl for what you've been through." Mikhail placed a calming paw on her shoulder. "I had a daughter once. She would be about your age now if she was still alive. She also had a fiery disposition and didn't shy from anything. Reminds me a bit of you."

Taylor wasn't sure how to take the compliment. She instead just watched Francis go about his business delivering drinks. Just beyond him, she noticed that cheetah they had bumped into from earlier still staring at them.

"So what about you?" Taylor said abruptly. "Whatever happened to your wife and daughter?"

It was Mikhail's turn to look inward. "They died in an attack launched upon my family by one of the Arbiter's specimens. My house exploded before my eyes with them inside. I could do nothing. I was enraged at having lost them, and so I wrenched that raccoon's head from his shoulders. I hated every single mammal who had been given powers and I wanted to destroy them all."

Taylor shied away a bit. Even Ahya seemed concerned. "Do you hate me?"

That question broke him out of his anger, and he cooled down immediately. "No, of course not. I eventually came to realize that it was not their fault they had been given powers that could do either great harm or good to others. The machinations of the Arbiter were the real cause of my family's death. The raccoon was an urchin burglar by trade. The Arbiter merely gave him the tools to be more destructive at it, and in turn was more responsible for my family's death than he was. He was easily disposed of, but the power given to him? Not so much."

"You don't hold it against me that I'm different?" Taylor was still unsure.

"I already said no." He laughed. "Besides, by the sounds of it, you were born with your powers. That, I think, isn't as a result of whatever the Arbiter has done."

"Which begs the question: just how were you born this way?" Terrati posed.

Before she could even think up of an answer, Francis popped up on his stool and bowed once more. "Ma'am, if it is alright now, I can assist with your service."

"Yeah…sure." Taylor smiled, trying to be polite. She had no idea what he was talking about.

With a nod, he got back down off the stool and crawled underneath the table, letting the fabric drop behind him, disappearing beneath their paws. Taylor thought that was kind of odd and didn't really pay it much mind. Natalia began to strike up another conversation completely indifferent to whatever Francis was doing, but Taylor couldn't focus on her words at all. Small paws were touching her legs and climbing up to her knees before stopping at her button and zipper.

"What… What are you doing?" Taylor lifted the cloth and tried to see what Francis was up to. "Wait, no, stop!" She began to panic as the rabbit was unzipping her pants and trying to pull it down far enough to get at her crotch.

"Isn't that what you wanted?" Mikhail seemed confused.

268

"What was it that I wanted?" She began to freak out, having Ahya pull Francis by the butt up from under the table and placing him on top.

"You asked for his services. He is trying to do that for you." Natalia shared Mikhail's bewilderment.

The rabbit being on the table brought some odd stares, causing him to let out a small squeak and scurry back under. He began to struggle with Taylor's paws as he plowed his head between her thighs. She could feel his tongue sticking out, trying to get at her. Getting more worked up now, Taylor yanked the bun back out again with Ahya.

"What are you trying to do?" She was shaking now.

The bunny stared around at the rest of the table, looking extremely worried. "Did you want an audience? I can do that too for you!" He hopped down onto her lap in full view of everyone and began to plunge his face back into her lap, his tongue reaching further than ever until it touched her.

She yelped and practically threw him off, Natalia having to catch the poor rabbit. He was quivering with fear. "Taylor, what is the matter? Why aren't you letting him do his job?"

"What job?" She was plastered back against the booth, trying to get as far away from Francis as possible, attempting in vain to zip up her pants.

"You mean...you don't know?" Terrati looked flabbergasted.

"Please, let me go." Francis struggled to get out of Natalia's firm grip and scamper back across the table to get at Taylor. "I need to serve my guest. I'll be in trouble!"

"I know you will!" She fought with him. He was stronger than she expected. "I'm just trying to figure out what Taylor is after."

"Tell him you relieve him of his duty," Mikhail ordered as more and more of the café starting to stare, the din of ambience dying down. "We're making a scene."

"Tell him what?" Taylor's mind was reeling.

"Just do it!" he roared.

"Ahhh…" Taylor hurriedly turned to Francis. "I relieve you of your duty."

269

"Yes, ma'am." He went slack in Natalia's arms. He began to whimper and just shiver in her grip. "Is there anything else I can do for you today?"

"Can you tell me just what the hell happened?" Taylor felt violated.

Natalia realized what was going on. "Oh gods... Terrati, scoot out and take over with Francis. I'm going to take Taylor to the bathroom with me, ok?"

Mikhail seemed to understand what she was getting after. "Of course, I'll stay here and ensure it gets smoothed over with management. Don't want him punished because of what Taylor did."

"What did I do?" Taylor's eyes spun from Natalia to Terrati to Mikhail and back.

"I'll explain in a moment! Just get out and follow me!" Natalia hissed, handing Francis to Terrati who seemed weird taking the rabbit.

Mikhail pointed at the gazelle. "Take the rabbit now. As long as he is seen doing his job, I can explain the rest during."

Terrati sighed and set the quivering rabbit down beside him. "I'll ask you of your services, Francis."

"You... You will?" Francis peeked out from behind his ears before perking up. "Yes, sir!" The professional rabbit immediately bounded down underneath the table, rising up beneath the cloth to undo Terrati's pants before setting to work.

Mikhail nodded at this before turning to address the large panda who appeared to be the manager. Taylor was looking back at this surreal series of events as Natalia was pulling her by the arm towards the far corner of the café where the bathrooms were located. The snow leopard nearly kicked open the door before ushering Taylor inside and checking each of the stalls to ensure they were empty before addressing the wolf.

"Taylor, did you not know what you were asking of Francis when he offered you himself?"

"Offered what?" Taylor was still hyped up on being touched that way. "If that's what they're for, then I don't know the first thing about rabbits!"

"Have you ever met a rabbit before?" Natalia was bemused.

270

"Well not personally. There was only one that I had any sort of direct contact with. He was just a hired bodyguard for our band. I've never really talked with any other rabbits." She shakily gripped the sink counter and tried to slow down her breathing.

"That's a bit of an odd profession for a rabbit." Natalia rubbed her chin in thought. "Still, you had no idea that they are law-bound to sexually please others?"

"Law-bound? What sort of insane law is that!?" Taylor threw her paw into the air in frustration. "I'm just lucky Ahya didn't choose to eat him for doing what he did!" Ahya didn't respond to this comment, instead contemplating herself in the mirror.

Natalia pinched the bridge of her snout as she tried to come up with the words to explain this concept to Taylor. "It's pretty common knowledge that rabbits, by their very nature, breed like crazy and were quite a pest for many years. Their populations would spiral out of control and then cause terrible famines for everyone. So we began to regulate their breeding. Still, their propensity for sexual lust was hard to contain, which is where the law came in to divert that energy to other mammals that wouldn't produce offspring. As it turns out, many other mammals were just as lustful and benefited from this law."

"That's horrid." Taylor's mouth was agape. "Who decided that law?"

"I don't remember who decided upon this law, but it has been in place for several-hundred years. With the promise that they are guaranteed a place of work, no matter where they apply to, rabbits in return are bound to please any mammal should it be asked of them, only having sex with their own kind to produce offspring on the sanction of the government." Natalia shrugged.

"How does that even make sense? What does anyone benefit from that?" Taylor wasn't grasping any positive implications of this law.

"Didn't they teach this in grade school?" Natalia tilted her head.

"I guess so? I mean, I remember them talking about rabbits once or twice, but I was torn out of school by my mother when Ahya ate Sarah. I don't think I ever got that lecture regarding rabbits!" Taylor snapped, finally recovering from the ordeal.

271

"Probably before you came of age to learn about such things." Natalia pondered, rubbing her chin.

Taylor picked up on the comment. "This is taught in all schools?" She shook her head in shock. "If that's true, then no wonder they kept rabbits separate from everyone else."

"Well, no matter." Natalia waved a paw, getting back to the serious topic. "From my understanding of history, predators and prey were at odds with each other, and although we've tried to maintain cities together to bring about a harmony and peace, this base nature of our biology kept us from truly having it. Zabökar—among other cities—was the closest we've come to about having a true partnership of species living together."

"What does that have anything to do with what Francis tried to do to me?" Taylor was still feeling upset.

"I'm getting to that." Natalia massaged Taylor's shoulder. "There were still a lot of killings, but those decreased over time as they introduced methods to curb the predatory hunger of carnivores. That still didn't account for the sex crimes that were rampant in the cities, from all species. With the lack of a decent workforce to fill all the jobs that most others couldn't or wouldn't do, and with rabbits being so prolific, it was decided that they be the ones to assist and appease the sex crime rate in return for never being denied for a job. Like killing two birds with one stone: solve the sex crime rate and curb the rabbit breeding problem."

"I don't get it." Taylor turned the faucet on for Ahya as she felt her tail trying to lick the sink for water. "How would that stop the crime rate? What if a rabbit wanted to run for office or ask for a very important job that many others were wanting?"

"That's the thing. They normally don't. Most rabbits are content with having simple jobs, and they've made it so they are educated enough so that they are perfect for such positions," she explained.

"That's rigging the system though," Taylor pointed out. "You can't just promise them whatever they want, but then teach them they are best at lesser roles."

Natalia thought on that a moment. "You're right, your one rabbit friend being a bodyguard was probably an oddity. The law is slanted more in our favor than theirs, but it's worked out fine so far. In fact,

272

since any mammal can just go up to a rabbit and ask them for pleasure, the sex crime rate has truly dropped dramatically in that regard."

"That just seems wrong though." Taylor shut the faucet off, having gotten her own fill of water from Ahya. "Putting that violation of others onto an entire species and regulating their birth rate like that?"

Natalia just shrugged. "It is what it is. It's been the law for centuries. You almost got Francis jailed by resisting his advances." At a look of disgust from Taylor, she explained, "By you asking him for his services, you legally bound him to you until he fulfilled his lawful duty to please you. By you resisting, you could have easily framed him for breaking the law of his kind and he could have gone to jail or worse. That's why he was so insistent on making sure you were happy with him."

"None of you cared to warn me of this?" Taylor gestured out back towards the bathroom exit irritably.

"We all thought you knew what you were asking for. You're an adult now! There was a general assumption you learned about this in school. I personally just figured you wanted him to relieve your stress, like you said." Natalia had to smirk a bit. "You may be our 'prisoner', but I'm not going to deny your needs if you have them."

"It's not funny." Taylor crossed her arms. "Mikhail seems to like to call me a little girl, so I'm surprised he didn't stop it." This got the snow leopard to chuckle. "Ugh, whatever, I'll be mindful what I say to rabbits from now on. I need to hit the toilet."

"Of course." Natalia waved toward one of the stalls. "Be my guest. I'll be just outside so you can have your privacy."

"Thanks." Taylor said flatly, picking the one at the far end, briefly looking back at Natalia.

"Oh, excuse me." Natalia stepped to the side as the female cheetah from earlier came in past her. Nodding at the newcomer, she shut the door behind her to stand resolutely outside the entrance, but not before noticing that the cheetah had touched her arm.

Taylor closed and locked her stall. Hiking down her pants, she went to sit on the toilet and moved Ahya out of the way in front of her. She scratched the underside of the maw, watching Ahya enjoy the attention. She threaded her fingers through the fur, to the crinkled skin underneath, massaging her thoroughly.

"What am I going to do with you?" Taylor whispered, hearing a stall down the way close. She didn't want to have her personal conversation overheard. "At least this bathroom is a far cry from the last one, isn't it?"

It was definitely an improvement from the one in Howlgrav. It was much brighter and well-lit, and had nice, carpeted flooring with the exception of the stall area which was tiled. The supplies within the toilet paper dispensers were fully stocked and the seat was clean and unblemished. The lack of graffiti was a welcome addition to the overall surroundings.

Taylor was able to really get lost in her thoughts here. She mulled over the events of the table in her mind, and what Natalia had told her. It seemed like a sick joke, but everyone was treating it like it wasn't. If she hadn't known Natalia better, she would have thought she was kidding about the law, but given how obdurate Francis was, it seemed like absolute truth.

An entire species regulated to being sexual release for the rest of the population seemed like such an awful prospect, though she understood the benefits from both sides. Yes, it curbed most sex crimes if all one had to do was find the nearest rabbit and conscript them for the evening. Yes, it filled in the jobs that nobody else wanted and was beneficial to making rabbits a great boon to society rather than pests that were a drain on it. And yes, it regulated the rabbit population and provided more food for everyone. However, deep down, it all seemed wrong somehow. Was this how that one nervous rabbit she bumped into in Palaveve saw her? Someone to please?

What struck Taylor more was the fact that the normally nice and considerate Natalia referred to the rabbits as pests. That word describing them seemed to click really hard with her. Most of her young teenage life, she was treated like a pest—something that was undesirable. It was a miracle at all she was accepted in the small circle she stumbled into in Zabökar, playing music for fans who did not see her for her. It was questionable if her former bandmates were even that fond of her, with the social distancing stance they gave her.

Taylor shook her head. It was wrong. Like her, there was no one to defend them but themselves, and the law saw to it that they couldn't even do that. She didn't know how, but she knew she was keen on discovering how she could change this abhorrent law. All the more reason she should stick with this crew a bit longer to reach Zabökar so she could see what she could affect there.

She didn't get to think more on that when Ahya angled upwards, suddenly interested in something. Following her lead, Taylor tilted her head up to see the same cheetah she had noticed before in the café silently clinging to the edge of the stall wall. She was lowering her upper body down, her finger's outstretched towards Taylor.

"What are you doing?" Taylor was shocked at being caught like this with her pants down.

Without a further word, the cheetah reached the rest of the way down until her fingertips just touched Taylor's forehead. Her mind went blank, and she could feel nothing but the sultry voice of the cheetah in her mind. *"Clean up and get dressed. Follow me calmly out of here."*

Taylor did as she was told, a blank look on her face. Pulling up her pants and buttoning them, she waited for the cheetah to gracefully leap down to the floor and open the stall door, enabling her to follow. She was close on her heels as they exited back out into the seating area. Deep down, Taylor could remember later seeing Natalia standing still beside the bathroom out of the corner of her eye, but her eyes were only for the cheetah as she led Taylor out into the rain.

Neither Mikhail nor Terrati looked in their direction as they stepped out, taking to the sides of the buildings away from the open-windowed view of the café. Taylor's mind was filled with nothing but the will to follow this mysterious cheetah through the tight alleys and pathways of Cheribaum.

The only one who was completely at a loss of what was going on was Ahya, who attempted to tug on Taylor's backside tenaciously. For once it was Taylor who had the stronger will, and Ahya could do nothing but be dragged along for the ride.

14
EATERS

Fey was shaking so hard he could barely breathe. The priest before him had stopped, his lips lingering on the last words of the Script. Fey had come to the church shortly after Mikhail and the others left, telling Finnley and Mrs. Faliden to hold down the fort with Ari and Trevor while he resolved a small matter that was niggling his conscience.

The rain was falling pretty thick, but he didn't quite mind the wetness. It felt soothing to him, and helped cool his fiery need to learn more about his fate. He was not a pious elk, but he knew to respect the Script and its unnatural ability to accurately dictate every event that would occur in a person's life.

He knew the moment he set out from Zabökar that he was going to die at the end of this. It was almost like a sort of peace had fallen over him once he knew. He could go into this mission with a clear head because he knew the moment of his death, and nothing would be able to kill him before then. He was untouchable until the moment of truth.

The only person he had revealed this untimely fate to was Finnley. The otter was distraught and hated everything about this mission, even to the point of transferring that anger over to the object of it: Taylor. Knowing that his loved one was to die indirectly because of Taylor spurred quite a few arguments between them, but he continued to stand by Fey to support him in his final task.

Now that Taylor had brought him back from the brink of death, beyond the scope of the Script sitting between him and the priest, Fey was petrified. The yawning abyss of the unknown was a well so deep he could not see the bottom. The yearning darkness could claim him at any moment, and he had no certainty of his fate. His hooves trembled at the thought that his life was now charting into the unfamiliar.

The priest was still staring at the last words on the Script: "*You shall die in service to a friend in a hail of justice, escaping from the law with your job of red teeth.*" He scanned back up the scroll a bit more, wondering if he was missing something, but it was clear the rough year and date matched up to the day prior. There was no more Script left to be read.

"I don't understand." He went slack-jawed.

"Can you help me, Father?" Fey pleaded, placing a hoof on the scroll to bring it down out of view onto the circular table. "I need guidance on what I should do next."

The antelope stumbled over himself, sputtering to make words come out. "I don't think there is anything to come next. You aren't supposed to exist now. You should be dead."

"Clearly there must be some explanation that can help understand this." Fey leaned in further, getting uncomfortably close to the priest. "I need to live, but I need to know if there is a way to extend my Script further."

"There isn't." He let Fey's script drop from his hooves onto the floor like it was burning him. "There is no precedent for this. This is unnatural! I need to contact the brethren."

Fey lurched over to stop the priest from picking up his cell phone. "No, Father. You do not need to do that. Just forget we had this conversation and I'll be on my way. I'll figure this out on my own."

The antelope shook his head vehemently. "I cannot! It is against my order to ignore this. The fates demand I report this and keep you here until someone arrives to pick you up."

Fey jerked the priest's arm back again. "No! Do you know what they'll do to me? They'll probably kill me."

"It is better to remove such blasphemies from our world than to allow them to exist, but that is not up for me to decide. You must accept the fate that your Script has written for you and cease this pointless endeavor." He reached for his phone again.

Fey's vision turned red as he lunged for the phone, snatching it from beneath the priest's hoof and smashing it onto the ground. The antelope brayed before rising up to leave the confessional room to seek help, but Fey was upon him quickly. He tackled the priest to the floor and head-butted his temple, narrowly missing the horns. Fey saw stars dance across his view as he struggled to maintain consciousness.

"You are damned, Fey Darner. Cursed!" the priest began to shout.

Worried that others would hear, he swore. "Forgive me, Father, for I have sinned."

Fey gripped the priest's head tight and slammed it against the ground, causing the antelope to cry out in pain. He kept slamming his head over and over again until the crunching sound stopped, leaving nothing but a pool of blood expanding out in a sea of corrupt evidence. Fey shuddered and began to weep over the priest, watching his hooves in horror as the blood dripped from their tips.

He snorted in surprise as the buzz from his own pocket indicated someone was calling him. Still dazed from the sacrilegious murder he just committed, he wiped his hooves on the priest's garment and took the cell out of his pants. Hooves still shaking, he clicked it on and held it to his ear.

"This is Darner," he responded confidently, despite not feeling it.

"Hun, this is Finn." The otter seemed anxious. "Where are you right now?"

"I'm still at the church, why?" The urgency in his otter's voice made Fey's nerves grow taut, his fight or flight response activating.

"Mikhail and the others just got back. Taylor is gone. We have no idea where she went and Natalia doesn't remember anything about what happened. She thinks she was still having coffee with all them." Finnley roared at someone in the background to keep quiet. "What do we do?"

"Just stay right there. I'll be right back. Make sure Ari is secured and don't let anyone leave, ok?" Still shaking, Fey hung up and dropped it back in his pocket.

Wobbling up to standing, he gripped the table hard and began to plot what he should do next. Taylor was of utmost concern, of course, but there was something else eating at him right now and it wasn't the loss of his prized objective. Without further hesitation, he burst out of the confessional room and strode across the foyer of the small church, hoping the nuns and other devotees didn't notice the red on his hooves and pants.

279

He looked around to ensure he wasn't being watched, then slipped into the priest's quarters and scanned the brick room. The church was made of old stock stone and mortar, giving it an air of history, but the living quarters of the priest was filled with a few trappings of the latest technology. There was a TV hung on the far wall and a few amenities like a humidifier and computer.

Next to the computer was the object of his search: the Script registry. It was a mystical device that every church had. Nobody could explain how it worked, but it was one of the last remnants of magic that people could remember. It had the ability to recall and send Scripts across the known world as requested. It was how a person could go to each church in the province and get his Script read at any time.

It only took Fey a few moments to see how the device was configured. He glanced over at the computer, tapping the keyboard to bring up the logon screen to see the full name of the priest. Inputting it into the device, he sat back and waited for it to work. Within a few minutes, the Script magically appeared in the receptacle for the now-dead priest. Frantically ripping it out of the machine, Fey unfurled it and let the rest drop to the floor.

He sifted through the obscenely long, yet boring Script, scanning the dates until he came across today. He blinked. The priest's Script went on for longer than what was depicted for this day. The final lines of this day read: *"For you shall enjoy the evening under the rain, having saved yet another soul from damnation. A soul of predatory might."*

That couldn't be the end of today's Script. First of all, he wasn't a predator. Fey ruffled down the scroll, which seemed to go on for many more years until he noticed something strange. The end of the roll of parchment was blank now.

His attention now focused, he saw that the entire scope of the priest's life from this day forward was disappearing. It was moving back in time. Watching in macabre fascination, he tracked its progress until it landed on today's date—to which it finally changed the ending line for the priest's future. *"For you shall meet a hornless one of the damned, and he shall be the curator of your fate."*

"Curator of his fate?" He watched further to see one more line added with terminal finality. *"The Authority has been notified."* He ripped the scroll in two, letting the tatters fall to the ground. "What does that even mean? What is even going on right now?"

Taylor unbound him from the Script. That much was certain. Why and how she did it was unclear. What was now clear was that because he was no longer living by the Script, neither was anyone else around him. He could effectively change people's fates. How much had Finnley's Script changed as a result of his "miraculous" return last night? How much had everyone's? And who was this Authority? This was beyond the scope of his limited experience in heavenly matters.

Recovering Taylor now became more important than ever. He didn't know how, he didn't know why, but he knew she was the key to solving all of this. What scared Fey even more about all this now was just what exactly did the High Council want Taylor for? Did they even know?

The cheetah quietly closed the motel door behind them. Taylor had obediently followed her every command and was now standing at the foot of the lone bed, eyes vacant and staring straight ahead. The only part of her still moving was the tail, which was "looking" in the cheetah's direction curiously. She was dressed in a sleek mauve suit, the very same she had worn back at the police station in Howlgrav.

She regarded the unique tail with supreme interest. "You are an odd one. I wonder what is going to happen tonight after I'm done." She purred with delight. Walking over to Taylor, she retouched her forehead and gently guided her to sit on the bed. "Stay here and be patient, darling."

She hummed to herself as she walked into the small alcove adjoining the cramped bathroom and looked at herself in the mirror. She needed to prepare for the ritual; everything needed to be just right or it would all fail. She pulled out her tracking device and set it down, its beacon locked onto Taylor's unique signature. She praised

Mendezarosa's ingenuity for acquiring it, as it had led her straight to her prey.

Stripping down to nothing, she unzipped her purse, left on the sink counter, and pulled out a few containers of powder and animal pieces. She took a miniature mortar and pestle and ground a few small bones from the jars into fine dust. Slicing open her palm with a claw, she dripped some blood into the pestle and struck a match and dropped it in. It lit on fire instantly. While it was still hot, she took some of the powder and tossed it into the mix, dousing the fire immediately.

With the preparations made, she dipped her fingers into the now-pasty concoction and started to paint her cheeks and breasts with symbols. She was methodical, making sure that every curvature was marked with potent incantations and glyphs.

Her nude body now ready, she picked up the pestle and walked over to Taylor, who was still staring straight ahead. The cheetah gave the inquisitive tail a small pet on the maw, which seemed to placate its intense interest in what she was doing.

She sifted the mixture in a circle surrounding the bed, making sure it was enclosed completely within the prepared ash. Once she hit the wall, she continued to close the circle by trailing it along the upper frame of the backboard. Satisfied with her handiwork, she drew additional symbols at intervals along the perimeter with the ash to complete the sacred area where she was going to work. She then meticulously let the remaining mixture fall to the carpet.

Setting the pestle on the set of lone drawers in the room, she ensured the curtains were closed tight and the hotel door bolted and locked. She sauntered over to the sink and picked up her cell, placing a call. "Hello, Officer Mendezarosa?" She could hear a small grunt on the other end. "This is Sabrina. The prisoners are hiding out in the town of Cheribaum. I will be finished here within the hour. You are then free to raze this town to the ground. Leave no survivors. I will clear your name of any wrongdoing with the High Council, should they inquire."

Sabrina clicked the phone off and turned back to Taylor, her feline tail flicking back and forth in excitement. She hadn't done this in a long time, and her last prey was a nerve-wracking, intensely difficult challenge that she overcame with help. That had forced her to split their power with one other then, but now Taylor was all hers; she would get everything and not have to share it with anyone. She was getting wet just thinking about it.

She wanted to savor this. She touched Taylor's forehead again. "Take off all your clothes and fold them on the nightstand there. Lay down on your back and remain still."

Taylor did as she was told, seemingly in a trance. At length, she was bare and spread-eagle on the sheets as Sabrina commanded. The lithe cat crept up alongside the young wolf, breathing in her scent from knees to neck. She took extra care to caress Taylor's body as she traveled up the delicious prey she was going to enjoy.

She had reached Taylor's snout and was studying her unique eyes. "You are a pretty thing. It is a shame I have to do this." She went in to nuzzle her face into Taylor's neck when she was interrupted by Taylor's tail, who had given her rump a big lick and nip. Sabrina was jolted from her reverie and attempted to touch the maw. She frowned. "That's odd. You don't seem to be affected by this."

The tail was going to be a problem; if she did not subdue it or at least restrain it somehow, then it would most assuredly eat her alive. While she contemplated how to best overcome this complication, she was leisurely stroking Taylor's stomach. She began to notice that the tail was languidly matching her movements, seemingly enjoying how Sabrina was treating Taylor.

"Oh? You like it when I do this to her?" A clever idea came to her mind. She wanted to test it out further. "What happens when I do this?" She began to massage and knead Taylor's breasts, and the effect was immediate. The tail dropped onto Taylor's knees, tongue lolled out in pleasure. Sabrina chuckled. "Ah, I see… You feel what she feels. How interesting."

With the plan in mind, she set out to rub Taylor's body up and down like a masseuse. The tail went further and further slack, slowly rolling back and forth on the bed. Sabrina attempted to straddle the tail, but it bucked a bit, apparently surprised she did that. Stymied but undeterred, Sabrina reached further down between Taylor's legs and slipped a few fingers in. That did it. The tail went rigid and then mellowed like a deflating pillow.

"Now I see what gets you going," Sabrina simpered.

Continuing to finger Taylor with one paw, she maneuvered the tail so that it was half stuck underneath Taylor and trapped in a position where she could easily straddle it in such a way where it couldn't open its mouth wide at all. She yelped and laughed nervously as the tail shot out its tongue and licked at her crotch before she clenched her thighs tight so it couldn't do that again.

"You're a feisty one!" she admonished the tail. "Sadly, this is where our paths must part. However, at least I'll have you go out feeling nice."

It was awkward, but she couldn't afford the tail to discover what she was about to do until it was too late. With fingers slickly moving in and out of Taylor with one paw, she used her other to push Taylor's head to the side, exposing her neck. Licking her lips at her feast, she grinned at the beauty of her freshly caught kill. Sabrina sank her teeth into Taylor's jugular, reveling as the gush of blood flowed into her mouth. The taste of Taylor's flesh was divine and it put Sabrina into a state of euphoria. All she had to do now was bite down harder and tear and it would all be over.

There was a loud bang on the door just as she completed the bite. A gruff voice boomed on the other side. "I can smell her very strong in here! Her scent is…intoxicating."

The distraction was just enough for the tail to recognize something was wrong. The pleasure had been replaced with pain, and Sabrina's momentary hesitation was enough to release the tension of her thighs on the tail. Using the opportunity to free herself, the tail used all its maw strength to jerk the cheetah's legs apart, causing her to release Taylor's throat. Sabrina was swift, and leapt off the bed before the tail could rise up and snap at her loins.

Louder banging could be heard as it appeared a larger body was being slammed up against the door. "Taylor! Taylor! If you're in there, answer us!" It was the large tiger.

Both the knifing pain and the calling of her name was enough to shatter whatever haze Taylor was in. Gurgling on her own blood as she convulsed on the bed, it splattering all over the sheets, she croaked, "Mikhail?" She could barely get the name out.

Taking a chance, the cheetah pounced on Taylor's prone form, deftly dodging the lunging bite of the tailmaw. She sunk her teeth into the wolf's head, trying to crush into the girl's skull with her powerful jaws. Taylor screamed in agony, more blood spurting from her throat.

"Shit! She's in there! Get it open, now! Forget subtlety!" Fey bellowed.

They fired a couple gun rounds into the door, getting the knob to hang loosely off its bolting. Mikhail kicked the door open, smashing it against the wall. They saw the cheetah naked atop of Taylor, biting into her brains. The young wolf was writhing and clawing at the insane female, trying in vain to get them off of her. Even Ahya was thrashing this way and that, completely in tune to whatever pain Sabrina was inflicting on Taylor.

"Kill her now!" Fey ordered.

Mikhail, Finnley, and Trevor opened fire. Sabrina was quick on her paws, but it was not enough for their hellfire. She was peppered with their bullets and collapsed to the bed, staining it red. Ahya was enraged and before anyone could stop her, swallowed the cheetah whole, instantly set to dissolving her. The mass of flesh inside the maw shriveled to nothing within seconds, Taylor's will doing little to slow the process down this time.

"Dear gods, Taylor!" Natalia shoved through her comrades and rushed to the poor girl's side. The cheetah had done some serious damage to her neck and had bitten off a good chunk of Taylor's head, revealing part of her flesh and bone on her brow just forward of the ears.

"What do we do?" Fey was panicking.

"Quick, use Ahya to heal her," Trevor suggested.

Natalia immediately set to work. She grabbed the tail and forcefully yanked it over to Taylor's face, placing the tongue on the horrific wounds she received. Ahya resisted the pull, but once the soothing balm of her own saliva hit the grisly lacerations, she instinctively knew what to do. She began to extend and wrap her tongue around Taylor's neck and covered her forehead, allowing the tongue to pulse and produce more saliva.

"Thank goodness." Natalia fell back onto her haunches, watching the tail get to work on healing. "I hope we got to her in time."

Trevor did his best to hide his innate canine attraction to the strong feminine scent wafting from Taylor's body. "What the hell was that cheetah doing to her?"

"Who cares? We just need her alive." Fey was examining the entire bedroom.

Finnley followed his gaze. "Looks like she was a power-eater."

"A what?" Even Trevor wasn't aware of the term.

"You've clearly been gone from Zabökar too long." Mikhail's face was grim. "There have been multiple disappearances from some of the Arbiter's specimens we have been tracking. We don't know where they've gone, but we never hear from them again. Some of our spies have informed us a new cult has sprung up centered around these special mammals."

"What do they want with them?" Trevor was mortified, staring at the naked form of Taylor, unnatural ash markings around the bed. "This looks like it was a sacrifice."

"It is." Mikhail confirmed the worst. "They are of the belief that if they eat those with powers, they will get them too. It is a stupid theory with no basis in fact, but this cult persists in believing that they can become like the gods this way."

"I never cared for her, but even she doesn't deserve this." Finnley admitted.

"How did this even happen?" Trevor asked.

Natalia looked miserable, crying as she watched Taylor quiver, eyes rolled up into her head. Ahya was doing her best. "I don't remember. The last thing I can recall was taking Taylor to the bathroom to talk to her. Next thing I know, Mikhail was shaking me awake outside of it."

"This stinks of something foul." Finnley paced back and forth.

"Can someone please get some clothes on her? Her musk is muddling my senses!" Trevor had to slap a paw to his nose.

"Then step outside." Fey pointed out to the balcony overlooking the motel parking lot.

"I think I will." He gasped, breathing in the fresh air as he gripped the railing. The pouring rain helped diminish her scent, but it was still quite strong.

"Can someone cover her up?" Mikhail was trying to avert his gaze from her naked body.

Natalia looked around and found her clothes neatly folded nearby. She grabbed her cloak and just threw it over her lower half quickly for a sense of modesty. "Here you go, Taylor," she whispered, patting her paw even though she knew Taylor wouldn't be aware of it.

"I think this is how they found her." Finnley was already roving the room, and had hopped up onto the sink counter next to the bathroom. He held up a tracking scanner not unlike the one they used to locate Taylor originally.

"That's impossible. This looks like genuine Harutan tech." Fey caught the device as Finnley tossed it in his direction. "This looks just like the one…"

"…that the High Council issued us," Natalia finished for him, darkness clouding her mood.

Mikhail was shaking his head as if not wanting to believe it. "You think the High Council is behind this? Do you think they're power eaters too?"

Fey was deep in thought. "I'm not sure. I don't believe so." He shared a look with Mikhail. "I don't think this is what the High Council had in mind when they sent us out to locate Taylor or any of the other specified targets."

"It wouldn't make sense anyway." Natalia was holding onto Taylor's paw, which had now stopped shaking. Her entire body was still, save for Ahya. She continued to stare at Taylor's face while she asked, "Why would they bother to send someone down here to do this to her if they had already sent us and just needed to wait for us to return with her?"

"Well, there's nothing much of value in here." Finnley was tossing out various knick-knacks, bags of powder, and other small cards that had no names on them. "She traveled light, and didn't bring anything which we can use to trace her origins from."

"If this is truly what they have in mind for all the experiments the Arbiter has created, then I want no stake in it." Mikhail growled. "I will not be a party to the murder of innocents. They would be no better than the Arbiter."

"Says the person who killed a whole bunch of them because of his wife and daughter." Finnley snorted, eliciting a growl from Mikhail.

"Let's all just calm down and think about this. Are we compromised because of this?" Fey was almost shouting at this point.

"I've no flipping clue." Finnley eased himself to the ground. "Whoever that cheetah was, she seems to be some random rogue agent. We do have her cell phone though." He had pulled it out from the folded clothes. "If we can crack into it, we might be able to see who her contacts are and any recent calls."

"This is too calculated though." Fey accepted the phone from Finnley. "We escaped Howlgrav with our lives and came here under cover of night. Short of tracking her unique signature with this," he said as he waggled the sensor, "there is no way they simply happened to stumble across Taylor in Cheribaum. This looks too prepared to be coincidence."

Mikhail was on the carpet, studying the ash circle around the bed. "This isn't the type of stuff you just normally carry around unless you plan to use it. This cheetah was on a mission."

"Yeah, a mission to eat Taylor alive and claim her powers," Natalia reminded, still focused on Taylor for any sign of recovery.

"I still think that's rubbish." Mikhail looked disgusted.

Trevor came back in, shaking off the rain from his fur, much to the vexation of everyone else. "Then how exactly did Taylor get captured in the first place right under your noses?" He stared accusingly at the tiger. Ignoring the death glare from Fey, he gestured to Natalia. "She mentioned that she doesn't remember a thing after going to the restroom with Taylor. That doesn't seem natural to me. Taylor would not have gone of her own accord if this was the end result. We all know that! That cheetah had powers."

Acknowledging his point, Mikhail turned back to the helpless form of Taylor. "I don't know her too well, but I know her enough that she wouldn't have agreed to this." Realizing the odd look in Trevor's eyes, he gestured back out the door. "Maybe we should give them some privacy while Natalia tends to Taylor."

Trevor rolled his eyes, but followed the rest out onto the terrace. Several other tenant heads were peeking out to see what had transpired just a few doors down. Fey waved them back in. "Nothing to see. Official business."

He pulled out a fabricated badge meant for just this reason. This seemed to placate the onlookers and prompt them to retreat back into their rooms. Most were of the mind that ignorance was bliss.

"Yeah, so maybe this cheetah is a product of the Arbiter too?" Trevor reasoned, doing his best now to stay away from the railing so he wouldn't be soaked by the downpour.

"You mean...your boss?" Fey smirked. "Then she's no safer in your hands than ours."

"Please stop fighting over her. Even I'm starting to see her side, and am getting tired of it," Natalia sighed from inside the room.

Mikhail crossed his arms in consternation. "If she was with the Arbiter, then what she did makes no sense. The power eaters, as far as we know, are normal citizens that banded together under their weird beliefs supposedly in opposition to what the Arbiter created. Why would one of his turn on their own kind?"

"There are too many unanswered questions." Fey bowed his head, closing his eyes to gather his swirling thoughts. "All we know is that we're not safe here either. The sooner we leave, the better. I'd like to be gone from Cheribaum by morning."

Trevor clicked his tongue, flexing his metal arm. "I doubt that's going to happen. We first still need to figure out what we're going to do with Ari and also who is finally going to claim the bounty on Taylor." He gave Fey a knowing look. "Unless you think they'd both allow us to split it fifty-fifty?"

Mikhail snorted. "Don't be preposterous. At this stage, I'm more of a mind to just escort her to Zabökar and remain as her personal bodyguard like she insinuated already."

"I wouldn't mind being that, actually," Natalia agreed from inside. "She's grown on me a bit. I'd like to see this through to the end and make sure whatever they've got planned is truly in her best interest."

"You so sure they're just going to let you do that?" Finnley crossed his arms, leaning up against Fey's leg.

"Do you have to be so pessimistic all the time?" Trevor bared his teeth at the otter.

He shrugged back. "Hey, it gets me through the day. It's called realism." Switching back to Natalia, he continued. "I strongly think that the High Council isn't going to care what we think should happen to Taylor. They tasked us with a mission to do, and we get paid. We ask no questions and we burn no bridges. What they do with her was never our business to begin with. We were hired as mercenaries, and that's what they expect we will be. There is no need to complicate things."

"And the Arbiter is the same way," Trevor admitted. "I don't believe he will harm her, since he has created all the other mammals just like her. It would not be in his best interest to try and kill her like this. Besides, I made a promise to her mother to bring her back home."

"You knew her mother?" Mikhail pivoted to Trevor. All eyes turned to him.

It was Trevor's turn to be smug. "Of course, I was a cop in Zabökar too before I went military. I was a great friend of her husband, Anthony, and through him I met her mother. When Anthony died, Taylor had run away. Her mother had several people secretly keeping tabs on Taylor, but knew if she had reached out to her daughter, she would have resisted at that time."

"Why didn't you tell us this?" Fey demanded.

"Why?" Trevor barked a snarky laugh. "Oh, I don't know, maybe being beaten up by your attack kitty here during interrogation made me a bit less inclined to reveal all I know." Mikhail growled and bared his teeth at the wolf.

"He was just doing his job, like we all are," Fey added to interrupt Trevor's immediate rebuttal. "You were a threat to our operations then and in direct opposition to our objectives with Taylor. You still are, in fact. However, we are working with you for the sole reason of her well-being."

"And exactly the reason why I don't divulge everything I know. I do believe the feeling is mutual." Trevor crossed his arms, his tail swishing agitatedly.

Fey shook his head, wanting to end the argument. "No matter. You keep your secrets and we'll keep ours. It is clear that we are never going to come to a consensus on what to do with Taylor." He pointed a hoof in Trevor's direction. "Just be aware we will be the ones taking her back. There are more of us than there are of you."

Trevor's ears flattened, his eyes narrowing. "Then you be aware that I will do what I must accordingly."

"Is that a threat?" Finnley flashed his own teeth, taking a menacing step forward.

"Guys, please just stop fighting. Taylor is recovering!" Natalia called out.

They all bundled back into the room, each staring at the scene as Ahya unfurled her tongue from Taylor's head and neck. The fur that was there was gone, having been torn from her body by the cheetah's teeth. However, the skin that had looked so horribly mangled and bloody was smooth and healed, as if she hadn't been on the verge of death minutes before. They all marveled at yet another miracle before their very eyes.

Taylor began to stir, blinking and unable to focus on anything in particular. A slight squeeze of her paw got her to shift focus to Natalia who was gazing at her serenely. The snow leopard smiled wide as she noticed recognition in Taylor's eyes. Her gaze wandered over the room, confused as to why she was there to begin with. She noticed the rest of the group at the foot of the bed staring at her.

"Where am I?" Taylor had to clear her throat once, her voice a bit hoarse.

"You are safe," Natalia replied.

Taylor looked down at her body, realizing she was naked for all except the cloak. She immediately wrapped Ahya over her and began to scoot up to the headboard, trying her best to hide her body from them. "Ah! What is going on? Where are my clothes? What did you do to me?" She was beginning to panic, yanking her arm away from Natalia. Ahya started to get defensive and opened her maw to show her sharp fangs.

"Whoa, calm down there, Taylor!" Fey raised both hooves up and motioned for everyone to back up and give Ahya space. "We just saved your life from being eaten by a cheetah."

"A what?" Taylor was still muddled, trying to process what was happening. She last remembered being in the café bathroom, now she woke up naked with everyone staring at her. "Where is she now?" She looked around the room.

"Ahya ate her," Trevor pointed out plainly, causing a withering stare from Natalia.

Taylor put a paw to her stomach. As if on cue, she burped, causing her to slightly wretch at the taste of it. That would explain why she felt so bloated and full now. "How did I get here?"

"We do not know," Mikhail responded. "We're not sure how, but we believe this cheetah had some sort of powers to make you comply. We never saw you leave the Java Rabbit."

Taylor began to shiver with both self-loathing that she ate yet another person, but also at how close to death she had come. Looking away from their staring eyes, she tentatively asked, "Is it okay if I get dressed now?"

"Of course!" Natalia bounded up from her kneeling position at the side of the bed, waving her paws at the males in the room. "Shoo, all of you. I'll help her get dressed."

Quickly shuffling them all out despite protests, she shut the door softly. She turned around and picked up Taylor's clothes and unfolded them, setting each aside for her to get into. She nodded her head at Taylor and turned around to watch the door. After a few moments of hesitation, Taylor pushed Ahya away and slithered off the bed to swiftly don her garments.

"Thank you," Taylor said after a time, her pants already on.

Natalia glanced back, but then continued staring forward. "You're welcome, hun. I'm just happy we were able to get to you in one piece. I thought... I thought you were a goner when I first saw you on this bed."

Taylor studied the now bloodied sheets where she had lain. It really did look like a bloody massacre had happened. Ahya had eaten the cheetah and saved her life. She watched the idly swaying tail as it inspected the bed and the ash trailing along the back headboard.

For so many years she had feared being the one to eat someone else, but here in this room she was the one in danger of being eaten. That reversal of thought shook Taylor to the core. Now she knew the unique fear of a prey in the presence of a predator, something altogether different than the fear she usually carried while being on the run.

She raised her paw to push back a lock of her hair behind her ear, noticing the bald spot just on the inside of her left ear. She was rubbing it when Natalia noticed her pained expression on her face. The leopard immediately turned and went to her side. "Ah, don't fret too much about that. The fur will grow back in time."

"It's just weird." Taylor was staring off in the distance, still feeling the odd spots of skin. "I did something like this when I was younger. Shaving off part of my fur and combing the other half over to appear edgy. Feels like it did back then."

Natalia could still see that Taylor was in shock. Even though the wounds were healed, the rest of the body and mind was catching up with it. She wrapped an arm around Taylor's shoulders, ignoring the bulk that was Ahya as she picked up the cloak on the bed, ushering her out the door.

"How about we just get back to Klera's home and rest?" she offered. Taylor glumly nodded her head, still trying to process everything. Natalia draped the cloak over her frame.

Trevor's ears picked up movement just beyond the door. Natalia opened it with Taylor next to her, causing the rest to suddenly bolt to the side. He was happy to be done arguing with them for the moment.

Mikhail was the first to speak. "How is she doing?"

Natalia looked up at the big tiger. "She is going to be fine. She is just in shock right now, and will take some time to recover. I think it is best we retreat back to your home here and let her recoup."

Fey brayed then followed close on her heels as Natalia expeditiously escorted Taylor to the stairs leading down to the parking lot. "We are no longer safe here. We need to leave now. Tonight." He was adamant.

"Haven't you heard a thing she has been saying to us this entire time?" Natalia snapped back, not looking at him. "It's because of sentiments like this that make her distrust us. She is not comfortable with us because we do not treat her as a person and see her only as an object of pay." Fey's face contorted into a twisted mix of rage and understanding of her point.

Trevor yelled out to them, still standing by the motel door. "What about all the stuff inside?"

Mikhail turned around and brushed past the wolf. "I'll dispose of all the evidence in here. Don't need local law enforcement causing a scene and tracking down a cheetah disappearance."

Seeing as the tiger was occupied, Trevor bounded up behind Fey. The elk looked to be fuming, but was keeping quiet for now. Trevor smirked. "Noticed you seem to be in an awful hurry to leave Cheribaum. Mind telling me what the real reason is?"

Fey shot him an irritated look that was shared with Finnley. "Not that it concerns you at all."

"I'd say it does." He tilted his head in the direction of Taylor ahead of them, one flight of stairs below. "That tells me when I need to be taking this business the Arbiter had tasked me with a bit more seriously than pretending to play house with you lot."

Fey stopped abruptly and turned to Trevor, putting a hoof up to his nose. "Me and the others are only tolerating you because you were of great assistance to us in getting Taylor out of Howlgrav. That does not make us friends or even allies. We just happen to share a common interest during this time, and heavens to Betsy am I going to let you dash off with the one objective we were hired to find."

294

Any mirth Trevor had was gone now from his face. "Noted. Except I had to kill an entire city just to get her. Good to know that I have the blood of many innocents on my paws and her hatred while you just reap the benefits of my labors and keep your conscience clean."

"Just stay out of my way." Fey glared at the wolf, daring him to attack.

At length, he snorted and stomped off down the remainder of the stairs and out into the rain, running after the rest of the group with Finnley. Not wanting to get soaked again at that very moment, Trevor just watched them go.

He needed to weigh his options here, but he ultimately had nowhere else to go but back to Taylor. She was the key to a lot of things going right in his life. He just needed to get her back to the Arbiter somehow without losing his own head in the process.

"So enamored with the girl that you didn't even smell me coming, eh?" a familiar voice emanated from above him at the top of the stairs.

Trevor spun around, his nose twitching, half expecting to see Mikhail. Instead he saw the spindly form of his long-time friend and companion at arms. He looked a bit worse for wear, having multiple lacerations criss-crossing over his entire body, no doubt from glass as he had been last seen busting through a window. There was a noticeable limp as he favored one leg over the other.

"Gregor!" Trevor exclaimed with happiness.

15
LESSON

Taylor could hear them in the next room. They were trying to be quiet, but her ears picked up enough of their conversation to make it out. She was lying down in a full tub of warm water, letting the heat soak into her bones and ease the tension of today's events. She had already cleared off most of the blood from her body and now was just resting there, listening to Fey and the others argue over what to do next. Her stomach was still nauseatingly bloated.

They had arrived back at Klera's house just past noon, soaked and dripping from the raging storm outdoors. The home's meager two bathrooms were not enough to cater to all guests in the house, but they all agreed Taylor could have the one with the tub. The rest of them were now cycling through the remaining bathroom's shower. It probably wouldn't be long before the hot water ran out, leaving the last unfortunate soul with a dismal rinse.

Coming in from the motel, it was strangely quiet in the home, setting everyone on alert. Klera appeared to be knocked out, but otherwise unharmed. It was when they went upstairs to investigate that their worst fears were realized, and Fey swore at himself for leaving just Terrati behind to watch over Ari. He was bleeding from the head and the reptile was nowhere to be seen. Ari had escaped.

What was curious was that she chose not to destroy the home or kill anyone inside it. Given how quickly she overpowered Terrati, by his account when he finally came to, it was a puzzle why she didn't use lethal force to eliminate him completely as a threat. Taylor knew the answer though: Ari knew Taylor would get this message that she meant what she said—that she would keep them alive as a good faith gesture to choose and trust her above the others.

And now she was sitting here, resting in the tub with her head placed on Ahya's closed maw. With arms on either side of her tail keeping it steady, she just used the position to relax and focus on the conversation happening just a few doors down from her current room.

They were currently discussing Trevor. The wolf had yet to return from the motel, and with the disappearance of Ari too, it set them all of them on edge.

"Did he leave anything behind that we could use to track him to see where he went?" Fey was pacing back and forth in their shared bedroom.

"Nothing at all. He didn't have much on his person to begin with," Mikhail commented, leaning up against one of the dressers.

"I'm with Fey." Terrati continued to rub his aching horns. "We should get out of here as soon as possible and head north to the next city."

"Right, in a tracked vehicle we stole from the Howlgrav police department." Finnley looked up from the laptop he was working on, the cheetah's cellphone plugged into it via a cable. "I discovered a bit late this morning—after you three went off to enjoy some coffee—that it was bugged from the moment we took it. Standard-issue tracker, probably installed on all their cars. They already know where we're at."

"So unless we get another method of transportation, it is fruitless to take the van further," Mikhail completed the thought. "They'll just be following us regardless of where we go."

"We can't afford to stay long either, method of transportation or not," Fey pressed.

"And why is that?" Natalia looked calm, but her own nerves were shot at this whole ordeal.

"We might be in some trouble with the local law enforcement here." At a curious look from everyone but Finnley, Fey expounded. "I killed the head priest here at the local church in town. If they haven't found the body yet, they soon will, and the investigation will ensue that could eventually make its way back to us."

"You what!" Natalia spat, expression aghast.

"It's not like I had intended to kill him!" Fey roared, throwing his hooves up in annoyance. "He was going to call the brethren and now something called 'The Authority' is onto me. I'm not supposed to exist anymore. My Script ended on the day I was shot in Howlgrav. Whatever Taylor did to me, I am no longer living by the Script. I'm sorry I hid that from you, Terrati and Natalia, I just had to be sure myself before I could tell anyone else."

Terrati looked from Fey to Finnley and Mikhail before giving the elk a sour look. "That's fine. I see where us two stand."

Fey rolled his eyes. "It's not like that."

"It's a miracle we are an effective team at all." Natalia pursed her lips, her eyes like slits. "We do nothing but fight amongst each other and try to see how we can look out for ourselves above all else. No wonder Taylor saw through us right away. She may be young and naïve in a lot of ways, but she has wisdom well beyond her years."

"And this is why predators make better leaders," Terrati accused. Fey did not defend himself, but the statement cut him to the heart.

Mikhail sighed and shook his head. "Don't look at me. I am done being leader. I've long had my fill and I'd rather just live my life the way I know it will be."

"Yeah, yeah, your Script and all that." Finnley dismissed the entire argument. "Guys, come look. I finally cracked open the phone!"

All but Terrati crowded in behind the tiny otter, each looking at the screen as his tiny paws clicked on the mouse and opened up the primary file folders for the phone. Immediately going to the images, he scrolled through them one by one. Each of their faces darkened as it showed the cheetah had been tailing them since Howlgrav, even getting pictures of them during their individual interrogations.

"Is she police or is she something else?" Terrati was confused. "These pictures clearly show she was there behind the glass while that pig was grilling us."

"I'm not sure." Fey leaned in, putting a hoof on Finnley's shoulder. "Can you check her contacts and phone info and see if we can determine who she is?"

Finnley made a few more mouse clicks and a roster of names and numbers came up. They all stared at the top few that were the most frequently called. "Other than this Mendezarosa character in Howlgrav, the rest of these numbers are in Zabökar."

Fey frowned. "I recognize these names. They're members on the High Council."

"Shit." Mikhail clenched his fists. "I knew she looked familiar, but I couldn't place it. It was so quick before Ahya ate her that I couldn't make sure."

"What's wrong?" Terrati feared the answer.

"Her name is Sabrina Fahpar—one of the newest council members hired within the last year." Mikhail brought out his own phone and searched her up on the internet. Finding a few pictures, he flipped it around for the rest to see. "She is…was, a member of the High Council."

"And Taylor just killed her." Fey spoke without much emotion, his mind racing trying to figure out where that would leave him and his crew.

"Why the hell would she even be here in the first place?" Terrati was upset. "Didn't they assign us to bring her in their stead? What is the point of sending her alone to get Taylor?"

"Another question to ask is not just why she was sent here, but also why did she have powers to compromise Taylor?" Natalia reminded, leaving the computer.

"We don't know that she had any." Finnley kept digging through the phone.

"But we also don't know if she did. Both Taylor and Natalia remember nothing since the Java Rabbit, and I highly doubt that lightweight cheetah could have carried Taylor that entire distance across town. Taylor went willingly, and that isn't something I think she would do," Mikhail finished with certainty.

"Remember, she was also a power-eater. So if she was gunning for Taylor specifically, she might have already gotten something from a previous kill," Natalia said.

"Trevor was probably right…" Terrati's eyes grew large.

"I hate to admit it, but that might be true." Mikhail exhaled.

Fey was putting all the puzzle pieces together. "I don't know what's going on right now. We have a member of the High Council who was after Taylor, completely separate from anything we were hired to do, was a power-eater, and was in league with the Howlgrav Police, judging by these photos."

"She had to have been aware of us, right? What we were out here to do?" Terrati was flummoxed.

"It's a safe bet that she knew exactly who we were, but chose not to bail us out. Her goal was Taylor and had nothing to do with us." Mikhail stood up as well. His ears perked up at the sound of Taylor's door down the hall closing, indicating she was done with her bath.

"Does that... Does that mean we've been replaced, just the same as Trevor was with the Arbiter's daughter?" Terrati asked.

They all stood in silence, pondering that line of thought. Fey finally broke the silence. "There can be no doubt the High Council is involved now, far beyond our simple hiring. How many were in on what Sabrina was doing is unclear. It might be just her doing this alone or it might be all of them. I don't know if we've been disavowed from our duties or not. One thing is certain: we cannot stay here any longer."

"So what are we going to do?" Finnley stared at Fey. "If we're technically fired, do we even bother with Taylor at all? Why not just leave her to her own devices? They'll pick her up one way or another, with or without us."

"We don't know that we're fired yet!" Fey bellowed, causing a cry of anger from Klera below telling them to keep it down. He lowered his voice. "Let me get with my contact in Zabökar and see if we can straighten this whole mess out." He flipped his phone out and began scrolling through the contact names.

"You sure you want to tell them one of their own died due to Taylor?" Natalia was giving him a knowing look.

He held her gaze a few moments. "I'm still debating that."

"While you're doing that, I'm going to prep Taylor to defend herself." Mikhail nodded firmly.

"Defend herself? Why? She's got a freakish tail that can bite people in half." Finnley snorted.

"Yes, and that's all she has. She's got no physical prowess in combat, as we've seen several times, and another power she can barely control. She needs to be able to fight back if anyone tries to come after her." Mikhail pointed a claw at Fey. "Regardless of whatever answer you get from our bosses, I am going to do this. I swore that I would watch over and protect her, and this is my way of doing just that. Do not try to stop me."

"And make it harder for us to contain her if we still need to bring her in?" Fey was incredulous, his hoof still hovering over the call button.

"If we've been relieved of our duty, then it wouldn't really matter anyway, would it?" Mikhail's jaw was etched in firm determination. He picked up the pistol he had acquired in Howlgrav off the bedstand.

"Mikhail...she's not your daughter. She can't replace what you've lost. You have no stake in her future." Finnley's anger was gone. He was looking sincerely at the tiger.

He froze for a moment before turning towards the door and stalking out, fur bristling. "I know she's not."

Mikhail's vision was fixated, his eyes only on the door down the hallway. He paused only enough to rap on the door to confirm entry. It took a few moments for a response.

"Who is it?" Taylor answered from within.

"Are you decent?" he asked.

"Um...decent enough?"

Without waiting for another response, he slid the door open and charged straight up to Taylor, who had just put on her fatigue pants and a black tank top. He swiftly used her surprise and familiarity with his presence to get close enough to Ahya to grapple the maw with one arm, jerking it firmly under his pit before bending a knee and sweeping Taylor off her paws over his shoulder. Ahya was immediately furious, but his grip on the tail was strong, his muscles bulging from the strain to keep it subdued.

"What are you doing? Put me down!" Taylor was shocked and began to kick, seeking to aim towards his face, but he deftly shifted her enough to keep her hind paws a healthy distance.

"Not until I'm done with you," he snarled.

Mikhail paced over with the struggling wolf to the door leading out onto the verandah. Looking down to the backyard below, he grunted before leaping off to the ground. He landed gracefully on his two paws, jolting Taylor from attempting to bite him. Satisfied that there was enough room for what he wanted to accomplish, he tossed her over his shoulder, causing her to fall hard onto her backside and slamming the air out of her lungs from the impact.

Taylor breathed in a ragged gasp as she coughed from the sudden rough handling. "What the hell is your problem?" she barked, getting onto all fours, Ahya in front of her defensively.

The rain had already soaked them to the fur, but Mikhail ignored it completely as he assessed his next move with the volatile young wolf. "You're defenseless and helpless," he accused.

"I'm what?" She gritted her teeth as lightning cracked overhead, giving off an evil glint to her canines. "I've got Ahya. She protects me!"

Slowly walking in a wide arc around her, keeping Ahya in view at all times, he explained, "Does she? All she does is eat people when the opportunity is ripe. Three times now, you have been captured or nearly killed when left to fend for yourself. You're a little girl lost in a big wolf's world. You need to get some backbone and learn how to fight, or you will die here tonight."

There was visible confusion on her face. "Stop calling me a little girl!" she shouted back.

"Then prove it. Show me you're a wolf to be feared!" he roared, thumping his chest.

"I don't want to hurt you!" Her hackles were raised and she was in prime fighting stance, yet she continued to hold back. "I don't know what you're trying to do, but this is crazy!"

"Very well. Then I will have to teach you the reality of this world." Mikhail calmly pulled out the pistol and took aim at her.

Taylor's eyes dilated at the weapon. She immediately dashed towards him on all fours, weaving to the left as he fired the first shot, another lightning bolt masking the sound. She swapped directions when she was almost on top of him. Ahya enlarged herself to envelope the tiger whole when he holstered the gun and sidestepped while

303

simultaneously ducking. In one swift motion, he gripped the base of her tail as she stumbled past his position and jerked her hard to the ground.

She yelped as she hit the grass face-first, mud getting into her nostrils and causing her to sneeze. She slapped her paws onto the ground in frustration. Rolling over onto her back and using the boost of her tail to right herself back up onto her hind paws, she tried to make a grab at Mikhail's face, claws fully extended. He merely leaned back, pivoted around on one leg before bringing the other up against her backside hard, causing her to sprawl forward back into the dirt.

"Your technique is weak and easily telegraphed. You will die easily," Mikhail patronized, as one would an unruly student.

Taylor let loose a cry of wrath, rolling several paces away from the tiger before hopping back up to standing. She tried a different tactic, letting Ahya lead in first. Her maw wide, she lunged forward with the vicious tail, snapping and biting at any part of Mikhail she could. Mikhail took a few steps back each time, carefully assessing the length and reach of the tail.

He kicked up a sizeable stick on the grass that had snapped off a nearby tree from the raging storm around them, then guesstimated where the next lunge of the tail would land. He stalled just for a moment so Ahya had a firm target to bite, then plunged the stick violently into the tailmaw sideways, keeping it from closing easily on the thick branch. Using the momentary shock of his action, he gripped the wood hard and heaved it to the ground with all his might. The tail slammed into the grass, yanking Taylor off her hind paws and back onto her rump once more.

"You fucking asshole!" Taylor raged.

She tried to back up and assist Ahya in dislodging the branch from inside her maw. The tail was thrashing, trying to crunch down and destroy the stick, but Mikhail had lodged it just past her row of teeth so that any compression would just dig it deeper into her soft inner walls, causing more damage.

"And this is why you cannot rely on Ahya alone. She is too easily subdued by those trained to be your better, and you need to be able to fight on your own merits." He smiled, which infuriated Taylor more.

"I don't rely on her!" she spat, still trying to remove the branch.

"Really?" Mikhail folded his arms. "Then why do you always lead with her in everything you do?" He ignored her glare. "You say you hate your tail sometimes, that you are terrified of her eating someone else, yet when it comes down to survival, you do not hesitate in using her as your first form of defense. You even threatened Finnley with her last night in the van!"

"You don't know me!" she growled, forcing Ahya to produce corrosive saliva to drip down the wood and soften it up. "I've lived with her all my life! I had to live in fear for what she can do…what she has done! You will never understand the type of hardship I had to go through!"

"I've known hardship like you can't imagine, little girl." His tone grew grim. He looked down on her with pity. "I've lost more than just my wife and child; I've lost teammates and dear friends. I've lost my way of life. Don't come to be thinking you know more than I. You have an entire life ahead of you, yet you choose to run from it and hide. Up until we came here to Cheribaum, that's all you've done: figure out how to run away."

"You're not the one who has had to be on the run all their life!" She glanced over at Ahya, the saliva finally putting a sizeable dent in the solidity of the branch. "All I've wanted since then is a normal life, but am I ever going to get that? No! I'm forced to look over my shoulder for the next villain coming to kidnap me and poke me with horrible things that hurt, all in the name of 'science'."

"You're confused and you don't know what you want." Mikhail waved a paw at her dismissively. "You need to figure out what it is you want and take it. You are letting the past bog down your resolve, and because of that, you and Ahya are not an effective fighting team. You hold her back, and she holds you by the fear of what she is capable of. This division cannot last forever, and you will die as a result of your inaction with her."

"What do you know?" she scoffed, finally extricating the branch from her tail with effort. She tossed it at him before rising up and attacking him tooth and claw.

Mikhail dodged left and right, easily anticipating her movements. "This is what I'm talking about." He pirouetted to the side, narrowly missing Ahya's downward lunge to swallow him. He punted her away with a vicious kick, causing Taylor to cry out. "You put your full effort into everything you do, just like a punk teenager, without any thought to what you want to accomplish with your actions. It is so simple to counter you."

Taylor let loose a howl of rage. The tiger was effortlessly batting away each strike, kick, and punch she attempted to land. He ducked and leaped over Ahya as she launched her own uncoordinated attacks. Mikhail was spec ops with decades of training, and while mocking her wasn't his intention, he figured that's how it came off as he proceeded to kick her ass without actually doing so. He finished by spanking her butt with the thick stick he picked up, causing her to stumble forward and nearly fall from the smack.

She spun around, claws out. "What do you care about me? I had agreed to go with you just this morning to Zabökar! Or did you forget? Why does any of this matter?"

"I said it already: you are at war with your own body, and that is making you weak." He swerved to the side to allow Ahya to snap at the air just below his right arm. Using the opportunity, he wrapped his arm around, putting Ahya in a headlock of sorts, pulling Taylor close to him with his other paw yanking on her tail. "You either learn to fight and accept what Ahya can do for you and work together, or you will die or worse: be experimented on for the rest of your life."

"Let go of me!" Taylor screamed, kicking her legs fruitlessly as Mikhail used his other arm to pin her to him, lifting her off the ground and squeezing.

"Which is it going to be?" He clamped harder, his muscles bulging. Taylor gasped for air.

There was genuine fear in Taylor's eyes now, staring up into his own. She was faced with a threat that was not going to give up unless she fought back. Sparks were coming out of her fingertips, the terror in her heart bubbling up like a raging storm. Mikhail looked down, noticing the flashing arcs of electricity, smiling as he did so.

Ahya couldn't open her mouth due to the sheer ferocity of the tiger's strength keeping her maw shut, but she was able to slither out her tongue and snake it up his back to the neck. She began pulsing to produce the saliva on her tongue, having it eat away at his shirt and fur at the top of his spinal column. Mikhail grunted at the knifing pain it brought, but he was not going to let go, powering through the agony.

"Learn to accept what you are and stop running. Only then can you have a chance to survive." He was deathly calm now.

"Mikhail! What the hell you doing? You're going to kill her!" Natalia was already at the corner of the house, her mouth open at the shocking scene before her. It must have looked like he was crushing the life out of Taylor, and she was weakly struggling at this point.

"No!" Taylor finally breathed.

Two bolts of lightning from her paws plowed into the ground just at Mikhail's feet, launching both into the air as plumes of dirt spewed into all directions. The sudden velocity jolted Mikhail's balance and loosened his grip enough for Taylor to bunch her knees to her chest and kick off of him in mid-air. As they both fell in unison, Ahya unfurled herself from his grip and swallowed him whole on the way down, causing both her and Taylor to fall like a rock with the added weight of the tiger inside her tail.

"Oh sweet gods!" Natalia shouted, running to Taylor's side and falling to her knees next to Ahya, the bulky form of Mikhail unmoving inside. "Spit him out!"

For a second time, Taylor had the air knocked out of her. She could barely respond back to the snow leopard. The only thing on her mind was the filling of fluid inside Ahya. She was preparing to dissolve Mikhail completely, causing another bout of nausea. Having two people eaten in such a short time period would overstuff her to the point where she would definitely throw up.

Taylor began crying, her entire chest heaving from the ordeal. "I can't, she isn't listening to me. She's going to eat him!" She fought hard against Ahya, willing her to stop this process, but the tail was obdurate.

"Why isn't he struggling?" Natalia was sticking her fingers into where she thought the mouth would be in the tail in hopes to pry it open by force. "He's not moving! Is he already dead?"

Taylor shook her head frantically. "No, he's not! I don't know what he's doing!"

"Please don't do this, Ahya." Natalia was now pleading with the tail, trying to pet and soothe it. "I don't need to lose another family member to this tail."

"Another...what?" This caught Taylor off guard. She sniffed hard, trying to wipe the tears from her eyes. "What did you say?" Even this knowledge brought pause to Ahya. Taylor could feel the rush of liquid inside her tail stop.

Natalia was sobbing herself, her claws digging into the lip of the maw, only managing to get a few fingers inside that vice-like grip of a mouth. She gazed up at Taylor, just now realizing what she had said in front of her. "My family... Mikhail is like family to me. We've known each other for years, and it was me who convinced him to come on this mission to find you."

With Ahya loaded down with the impressive mass of Mikhail still inside, Taylor had little recourse but to crawl over as close as the base of her tail would allow to Natalia. "No, you said something about losing someone else to Ahya. I don't remember ever meeting you before in my life. Who could I have possibly eaten of your family?"

The leopard took a deep breath before staring at Taylor directly. "Sarah. Your best friend was my little sister. Exchange student to Zabökar."

Taylor's entire body went cold. A sudden deep-seated chill burned in the core of her heart at this revelation. "Oh gods, I'm so sorry." She hiccupped.

Taylor's shoulders wilted as she began to cry anew. She put a paw on her tail and began to stroke it gently, easing Ahya's tense nerves. She willed her tail to release him. It took a few moments, but they could visibly see a stark difference in the body language of the tail now that the danger had passed. With sordid sloshing, Ahya regurgitated Mikhail out of her maw and onto the ground. His entire body was dripping wet, and he had acidic burns on his back that had been hastily healed from being inside the tail.

"You spared me?" Mikhail looked bewildered, staring down at his paws. "I tried to kill you, Taylor."

"You tried to teach me," she said after a long moment, looking down at her own fingers. "You're right. Ever since my body ate Sarah, I've been afraid of what I am and what Ahya could do. I relished in the ability to escape and to hide. By being far away from everyone, I couldn't hurt anyone."

Natalia began to laugh in relief. "I'm so glad nobody died tonight."

"Why didn't you kill me?" Taylor directed her question to Natalia. At a look of confusion, she clarified. "My best friend was your little sister. Ahya ate her. You had plenty of opportunities with me alone to try and kill me over this. Why didn't you?"

With the rainstorm finally abating, the downpour becoming nothing more than a sprinkle, Natalia flopped back onto her rump and smiled at Taylor. "I wanted to when I first took this job. I wanted to see the murderer of my sister with my own eyes before driving a knife into their heart." Taylor winced, as if Natalia had just done the deed with words. "But then I saw you lying unconscious in that bed the first night we met you, and I saw a little girl still frightened of the world, the same age my sister would be if she had lived."

"I'm sorry for the loss of your sister." Taylor felt miserable.

Natalia shook her head. "It's fine. After listening to you, I know you didn't mean to now. Still, I was interested in you and who you were and how Ahya worked. I wanted to understand you and see just what kind of person you were. Then I would decide if vengeance was justified or not for my sister."

"But she's never coming back! She's gone forever!" Taylor wailed.

Natalia looked away, not wanting to meet Taylor's eyes. "I know that. However, it was in her Script that she was to be eaten that day. I had a priest read it to me when I came to her funeral. I cannot fight the will of the fates in this matter, and so I should not bear ill will to you."

"Actually, I should be dead right now." Mikhail finally sat up, his arms across his kneecaps. "Is she still planning to eat me or not? Because this is starting to get unnerving."

"Huh? What?" Taylor looked over at Ahya, who was licking Mikhail's backside profusely. "Ahya, stop that!" She willed the tail to retract her tongue, but not without a look that could be construed as pouting. Satisfied that Ahya would retreat back behind her, she apologized. "Sorry about that. She has an affinity for new tastes, and unfortunately that also means other people." She grimaced.

"Were you Scripted to die right now?" Natalia cocked her head curiously.

"Yes." He stared back at her. "For the record, you never convinced me to come. I knew my final resting place was to be here at this very moment. My Script ends now. Here. Today. At *the jaws of red teeth*. Ahya was supposed to devour me and my life would be over. That is where my Script ended when I had the entirety of it read to me years ago. That is why I didn't struggle."

"Yet you forced it to happen by attacking me!" Taylor pointed out angrily. "If you hadn't come at me so hard and acted like you were going to kill me, Ahya wouldn't have had any reason to eat you! You could have prevented all of this and lived on! The Script is wrong!"

Mikhail shook his head looking sad. "No, for if I hadn't taught you this valuable lesson today, I don't think you'd last much longer." He raised a paw up when she went to protest. "Hear me out. When I saw you naked, wounded, and near-death on that bed this morning, I was afraid like I hadn't been in years. You reminded me of my daughter when she was first raped, and I had found her that very night."

"I'm so sorry…" Taylor's ire dissipated.

"It's okay. She died only a month later with her mother in that explosion, but I never forgot how helpless I felt that day when I could do nothing to protect her from the harsh realities of this world." His eyes never left the ground. "You see, I had no choice here. I was not going to sit idly by and let another innocent get exploited under my watch. If I could teach you just one thing to better your life outcome, I was going to do it, even if it meant the end of my Script."

"But you're still alive now...like Fey." Natalia motioned to Ahya. "She saved you, or rather let you live."

"Yes, Taylor made that choice to convince Ahya to release me. Nothing else would have saved me just now but Taylor." He nodded. "And like Fey, I am now living off the Script. I have no idea what the future holds for me." Mikhail shivered.

"The Script was never important to me." Taylor attempted to get up, shakily leaning over for assistance from Natalia. "I simply don't have one; I found that out when I was going to be executed in Palaveve by the local sheriff. I make my own decisions and choices without having some Script dictate my life to me."

Mikhail rose as well, shaking off the water from his fur now that it had stopped sprinkling. "All the more dangerous for you. You do not have the protection of the Script to dictate when you will die, which means your death could come at any moment, and quite possibly through the result of your choices."

"Just like your death now, and Fey's," Natalia reminded.

Mikhail grew somber. "I'll admit, I did not expect today to go as it did, but I am happy you are not mad at me for having attacked you."

Taylor shook her head, raising her paws up to pacify his worries. "I get it now. I realized it the moment I shot lightning from my paws that you were just trying to get me to understand my potential."

"At least she's a fast learner." Natalia chuckled. "Sarah was never a fast one, and it would take her months to comprehend the simplest of things. One had to wonder if she was doing it on purpose just to get you riled up!"

"Do you forgive me...for your sister?" Taylor began wringing her paws. Ahya poked out from beyond her shoulder, wondering if she would be forgiven as well.

Natalia looked at the two of them for what seemed like minutes before moving in to embrace Taylor, Ahya curling around like a blanket. "Deep down there is a part of me still mad at the loss of her, but I've come to accept her passing and I've moved on. I've learned to set aside my anger and forgive you. I know this may sound weird, but in some small way my sister is still with me today, living on inside of you after being eaten."

The hug became awkward after that statement. Taylor lightly patted the leopard on the back, unsure of what to do next. "Maybe a tiny bit weird?"

Natalia broke off and backed up hurriedly. "Ah, yeah, I'm sorry for that. Just a strange thought I had that makes me feel better about the whole situation."

Mikhail smiled at the two of them, but gestured to Taylor's paws. "Your power that you have, that was the most focused I've seen it. How did you do that without exploding out everything around us?"

She glanced down at her paws. "I don't know. I just knew what I needed to do, and it just happened." She put a paw to her forehead. "I'm not even light-headed either. I mean, I feel mentally tired now, but it doesn't feel like I'm going to pass out!"

"Well, that's good, right?" Natalia asked.

"That doesn't seem good enough." Mikhail crossed his arms. "It still seems so random and unreliable. You need to figure out what causes it to happen and focus on that. If you want to have any shot of being able to protect yourself from being overpowered by another, you'll need to master that, I feel."

"But it's so new! I've never done something like that until recently!" Taylor's breathing was beginning to quicken.

"Hey!" An irate voice from the verandah above them caused all to look up at the tiny otter perched on the wooden railing. "There is something on TV that you all should see." Without waiting for a response, he dropped down gingerly to the deck and scampered inside.

Mikhail put a paw to Taylor's shoulder. "I apologize for the way I came at you just now, but there was no other way I could figure on how to draw out the response I needed from you."

She chuckled nervously. "Yeah, um…you really had me going there. I really thought you were trying to kill me."

He winked at her. "That was the point."

"Please remind me not to get on your bad side." She flashed her pearly whites at him.

"You haven't yet." He laughed, motioning toward the front of house with his chin. "Now go on then. We'll be right behind you. If Klera asks, you slipped off the balcony and fell. I had to come get you."

"She's not going to believe that," Natalia pointed out with a smirk.

"From me? No. From her? Possibly." He smiled.

Taylor shook all the droplets off yet again. "Ugh, I'm going to have to wash up again. Thanks a lot, Mikhail!" She gave him a withering stare.

"Minor inconveniences, Taylor. You'll live." Despite Taylor rolling her eyes at him, he looked a lot more at peace.

Natalia's smile faded as Taylor rounded the corner of the house and disappeared from view. Without looking at him, she asked, "Did Fey know you were supposed to die right now?"

Mikhail nodded with a confirming grunt. "It is why he didn't stop me from leaving the room to go train her. He knew I would give my all to fulfilling my Script, and he wanted to see what would happen. If Taylor could change his Script, she could probably do the same for me."

"That was a risky gamble to take." Natalia low-whistled.

"I was going to die anyway, there was nothing at risk for me." He shrugged. "Besides, the moment I step back into that house, he's going to know I'm no longer on the Script, same as him. It'll be all the evidence he needs to make his decision."

"And what decision is that?" She finally looked up at him.

"If we're going to take Taylor back to Zabökar or not," He stated with finality.

This got her attention. "We're no longer following the High Council's orders?"

He shook his head. "Not if they are using us to get to Taylor so they can experiment on her, or kill her in efforts to take some of her power for their own." He looked down at her. "You know the threat possible from the power-eaters. I'm afraid of what could come from Taylor being in the wrong hands. She is young and too innocent to be tossed around in this game for power. The High Council may have been lying to us this whole time."

"And it all started for what? Rumors of war from the Arbiter?" Natalia sighed, finally heading back into the house, Mikhail following close behind.

"Which may end up being true if the behemoth we passed to get here is any indication." He opened the door for her before stepping in and shutting it behind them.

The rest of the group, including Klera, were huddled in the living den around the plasma TV that hung over the fireplace. Fey caught Mikhail's eye as he entered, and they sharing a knowing look. The elk then turned back to the TV as the Howlgrav anchor was reporting while riding in the back of a pickup truck. It appeared to be live television.

"What's all this?" Mikhail asked. He was promptly shushed by Klera.

"...and behind me, as you can see, is the full garrison of Precinct 1, 4 and 5's police from Howlgrav. Several hundred strong. We are now traveling with them to what is reported to be the terrorists' current hideout in the tiny town of Cheribaum. For those tuning in with us just now, the HPD was mercilessly attacked in the late hours of the night by what is reported to be a vicious gang of rogue mercenaries stated to have incited a terrorist attack."

The reporter continued to commentate, but what caught everyone's eye was the sheer amount of vehicles, firepower, and manpower that was being brought to bear against them. There were technical vehicles equipped with chainguns, and several vans were armored enough to be miniature tanks. The multitude of cars behind the reporter spanned the stretch of screen space behind her on the open plains. There were even some helicopters roving above them.

"Dear gods, they're going to raze the city of Cheribaum to the ground for us!" Natalia stood shocked.

"Can they do that? Wouldn't they get in trouble for killing off an entire town?" Taylor asked.

"It depends," Mikhail explained behind her. "If they're calling us terrorists and they just indicted the entire town as co-conspirators for sheltering us, then they have just declared the entire town and everyone in it a legal target. Frontier law and all that."

"Where exactly are they?" Fey pointed at the screen. "How far away are they?"

Terrati studied it a few seconds. "It looks like they are maybe a few miles out from the foothills west of us.

"That would put them about three hours out at best from here." Mikhail was already bounding up the spiral steps to their rooms to secure their belongings.

"What are we going to do?" Taylor asked Fey.

"We're going to try and leave the town as quickly as possible." He proceeded to attempt to follow Mikhail upstairs.

Taylor stopped his path by thrusting Ahya in front of him, her teeth grinning. "No!" She stood firm beside him, paws on her hips. "If we do that, we leave Klera here and everyone else in this town to die. It doesn't matter if they capture us or not, it looks like they're on a mission to destroy this place completely. I will not let that happen!"

"What's it matter to you?" Finnley snarked from the couch. "Aren't you used to running away?"

Taylor turned to Natalia briefly. "Not anymore. I want to stand and fight. Protect this village."

"You're a sweetie." Klera reached out to grab and stroke Taylor's arm.

"Sure, that's a brilliant idea," Finnley fired back. "Only six of us against hundreds of them! Like we're going to stand a chance."

"We have to try!" Taylor offered fruitlessly.

"With what?" Terrati tried to reason logically. "We lost Ari, who escaped, and was probably our biggest asset that we could use in this battle. And you, your power is unpredictable and unreliable. I don't think having uncontrolled bursts that make you pass out is going to be very helpful to us."

"Well, couldn't we just head out to meet them before they get here and convince them to leave the town alone if we give in?" Taylor suggested, now feeling stupid at her ideas.

"Oh, you're ready to go back into that cell again? Because that's where they'd put you if they don't kill us first," Finnley huffed before leaving the room to prepare.

315

"And they've always been especially vindictive over there in Howlgrav. There would be no guarantee that they wouldn't destroy this town anyway for harboring terrorists." Fey gently pushed Ahya out of the way and headed towards the stairs. "Excuse me, I need to prepare to leave."

"I'm sorry, Taylor. This is a hopeless case." Terrati slumped, following Fey after giving her one last heartfelt look.

Taylor was left standing in the den with just Natalia and Klera. She turned to the aging tiger. "Aren't you going to come with us when we go?"

Klera breathed deeply before declining softly. "No, my dear. I've lived a full, long life. If it isn't wandering behemoths outside town, it's this pack from Howlgrav coming to attack us. There's always something. Seeing Mikhail one last time and getting to take care of you was the best final day I could have hoped for. It was a good day for me. I will go down with this city that is my home. Do not worry for me. If it is in my Script to die, then so shall it be." She bowed her head sagely.

"Is this town Scripted to die?" Taylor wondered aloud.

Natalia continued to stare at the screen, her town morose. "I wouldn't know. You'd think the priests of the church here would be more alarmed that every single person's Script in town would end today. Maybe you changed things, Taylor."

The implication she was making was clear. Taylor had removed two people already off the Script. Who else's fate had she changed just by existing? A person with no Script. They could be incredibly dangerous if utilized for the wrong reasons.

Even with the newfound will to fight and become better than she was, Taylor still felt so helpless. With determination, she strode up to Natalia and gripped her paws into her own. "Can you please teach me how to fight? I want to know everything."

The snow leopard looked flushed at the sudden request. "We've not even three hours to learn much of anything useful."

"Whatever you can teach me will be enough." Taylor gave a half-hearted laugh. "As you said, I'm a fast learner."

16
MANIFESTATIONS

Gregor leaned back and groaned, his entire posture slouched into the booth at the Java Rabbit. Francis, the rabbit, was beneath the shroud of the tablecloth working him like a shark on the fresh scent of blood. Gregor rotated his head at a shiver that slithered through his entire body as a few audible pops could be heard from his neck, the pressure and tension now released.

"Aw man, Trevor. You have got to try this bunny. He is freaking amazing." Gregor panted, really relishing the service he was receiving at the café. His black coffee before him was still steaming, untouched as of yet.

Trevor shook his head, nursing his own hot drink. "I'll pass. I'd rather be of sound mind right now with everything that's going on."

The haze swallowing Gregor's expression lifted for a few moments as he considered Trevor's statement. "You mean Taylor? Yeah, I had a feeling she was going to be trouble. Too many people want her and we're just two mercenaries caught in the middle."

"It's not just Fey and the others that's a problem. I don't even consider Ari to be the worst of the issues we face in getting Taylor back to Zabökar; at least we can possibly reason with her since we're technically on the same side. I think that if we can get Taylor on our side, then Ari should follow suit." Trevor seemed deep in thought, his gaze lost in the swirl of his coffee.

"You really think it'll be that easy to bring that lizard to heel?" Gregor adjusted a bit to make more room for Francis. "I mean, she is still the Arbiter's daughter. She has his backing and we do not. Not anymore. She has the upper hand no matter what we do."

"I'm not so sure about that," Trevor refuted. "Twice I've noticed she could have overpowered us, yet she held great restraint when around Taylor. She was willing to work with us to escape Howlgrav, and surprisingly held here in Cheribaum with minimal restraints amicably.

She is doing the waiting game, knowing that either myself or Fey and his group will mess up and she will snatch Taylor away back to Zabökar."

Gregor chuckled, finally taking a sip of his drink. "She's very smart, I'll give her that. The one thing I did notice about Taylor in the short time I've been with her is that she is very strong-willed when it comes to survival. Ari getting on her good side to build trust is a brilliant move. Why didn't we think of that?"

Trevor snorted, downing the rest of his coffee. "Probably because she immediately turned tail and ran on us and we had to improvise. Then we destroyed her current town of residence on top of that, which I now regret. First impressions are pretty lasting it seems."

"Think there's a chance she'll still be willing to cooperate and come along with us?" Gregor shuddered as he finished with Francis.

Trevor curled his lip, but seemed to ignore the rabbit under the table. "Hard to say. Frankly, I don't think she trusts any of us, but if we can manage to gain her trust in the short time we have now, then Ari will have no choice but to spare us and convince the Arbiter to as well. Taylor is our ticket to fulfilling our contract."

"And you said she is here in town with the elk and the others?" Gregor turned to the rabbit rising from the side of the table. He handed the waiter a large bill, causing Francis's eyes to widen with surprise. "Go treat yourself to something nice tonight. You did a wonderful job."

Francis bowed sincerely; it wasn't often that his kind normally received tips. "You are most gracious, sir! Thank you so much!" He bounded away with his folded stepladder happily.

Trevor cocked an eyebrow. "And where did you procure that money?"

Gregor smirked. "Probably best not to ask, friend."

Trevor shrugged. "Fair enough." In their line of work, stealing was sometimes a necessity when it came to accomplishing the mission. It wasn't always chivalrous, but it got the job done. "But yeah, she's being watched over by Fey and his group. He's a stubborn ass, and I know they will be a problem when it comes time to take her back."

"Think we can do it?" Gregor zipped up his pants before leaning forward onto the table. "Think we can take the five of them on?"

Trevor rolled his eyes at him. "You know very well we can. You're just testing my resolve, aren't you?"

"Last time you did say you weren't sure going after Taylor was a good idea anymore," Gregor pointed out, his eyes focused on Trevor.

"I did. That thought lingers on the back of my mind. Still, we can handle Fey and them much easier than taking Ari on," Trevor admitted. "If we get Taylor on our side, we get Ari on our side. Then we can use her to trounce the rest of them before negotiating."

"Where are we going to get the hardware for this?" Gregor took another sip. "I only have my gun with a few bullets left, and a grenade taken from their truck."

"And only a pistol and rifle with maybe a few clips myself from Howlgrav," Trevor finished for him. "We've been through worse before, Gregor. We just need to monitor, track, and wait for the opportune moment."

"You still up for doing this?" Gregor kept his voice calm, but he was tense. "We're still in it to retire, right?"

Trevor gave him a sincere look and sighed. "I am, but like you said, I'm starting to really consider that bringing Taylor back to Zabökar isn't a good idea to begin with, even with the promise I made with her mother back then."

"Yeah, what was that even about? That doesn't sound like you at all." Gregor's ears flicked back to the sound of the television up along the wall with the mention of Howlgrav, but he was too focused on Trevor to pay it mind.

"Her husband, Anthony—Tony—was one of my best friends growing up." Trevor gripped his empty cup in both paws, holding it tight even if there was no reason to do so now. "I met him long before you and I trained together in bootcamp. We made a promise to each other that we'd look out after one another and our families in the force when we joined up. He married one hell of a wolfess and had several kids."

"Several?" Gregor was surprised. "I thought Taylor was the only one."

He looked out of the café window, the rain now petering off to nothing more than a drizzle as the waning sun peeked through. "Well, the only blood cub they had. She had adopted two others from what I can recall: a skunk and a raccoon. Odd assortment that was." He chortled before turning back to Gregor. "Point being, Tony was fanatical about his children, even the adopted ones. Alongside his wife, they were his world. I could see that plain as day every time I came to visit."

"What happened to him?" Gregor furrowed his brow. "You said you made a promise to the mother, not the father."

Trevor winced a bit at the memory. "I got the call late one Saturday night. Tony was just doing a routine traffic stop on one punk kid with a shotgun, hopped up on drugs. One blast to the face and his head was splattered across the pavement. It was a freak occurrence. Anyone could have been the one to have stopped that kid on the side of the road, but it was just Tony's turn that night."

"You think the Script had ordained it to happen?" Gregor mused, his expression serious.

Trevor gave him an irritated look. "I honestly hadn't bothered to check. The Script was the last thing on my mind at the time."

"Of course, I'm sorry."

Rumbling deep in his throat, Trevor continued. "Regardless, Taylor ran off about ten years later. Her mom called me up out of the blue one day just as I was getting separated from the service with you with a proposition to bring her home. I took the job out of respect for Tony, but I never did pick up the trail after it went cold in Zabökar with some band she had joined. It wasn't until the Arbiter put out the job advert on the deep web channels that I remembered her again."

"And here we are." Gregor sat back in the plush cushion of the booth. "Well that makes a lot more sense as to why you took this job. We normally don't do escort missions."

Trevor propped his snout on his paw as he gazed back out the window. "Yeah, this last one is a bit more sentimental than most jobs we've been on. The money offered was just icing on the cake."

"Which is more important to you then? The money or the promise?" Gregor leaned back, his look genuine. "I mean, I'm all for the money this'll bring and the retirement we hope to have, but if your heart is not in it, I'd rather not attempt it, since that may lead to us messing up and getting killed."

Trevor continued to face the view outside, only his eyes traveling back to Gregor. "I guess I just want to do one last good thing with my life before I go out. Turning in Taylor to the Arbiter in the hopes that he'll honor his deal and give me a chance to fulfill my promise to her mother is a fool's hope. I wish things did not turn out the way they did. I highly doubt she'll trust me going forward, unless Ari gives her a reason to."

"Then maybe we should just walk away and find another job?" Gregor leaned forward onto the table.

Trevor faced him directly. "Possibly. Unless we can at least convince Taylor to trust us at all again, there's really no point in trying to do anything good on that promise I made." He sighed as he stared back out in silence.

Gregor's ears flicked back to the television. He looked over and saw the huge swath of trucks roving across the open fields down the mountainside from Cheribaum. "Ah, shit." This drew Trevor's attention as he turned to the screen as well. "Whatever the heck you guys did at Howlgrav, they are out for blood."

"That moves up the timetable a lot sooner than I'd like," Trevor growled. "I thought we were going to have more time than this to think up a plan."

"Should we go to Ari first then?" Gregor suggested. "Maybe offer to work together again like you did before?"

Trevor shot him an uncertain look. "I don't think that would be wise just yet. Last interaction I had with her, I shot her with a tranquilizer to put her out and threw a grenade at her before that. Don't think she'd be happy to see either of us without Taylor."

Gregor grimaced. "Ugh, that sucks. Where are they now?" He finished the rest of his coffee in a shot before slamming the small cup down.

Trevor scooted out of the booth and stood up. "Not far from here. We'll observe and see what they do before we make a decision."

Several gasps from the surrounding patrons alerted them to the newcomer into the café. Ari's reptilian visage rounded the entryway. Her red iris locked onto them as she strode forward with purpose. Both wolves drew out their guns and took aim at the advancing lizard. She just smirked and continued towards them, stopping only a few paces away.

"I have a proposition for you two," she smugly began.

"And why should we trust anything you have to say?" Gregor snarled, cocking his gun.

"Shut your hole before I put my fist through it," she retorted without hesitation, stunning the larger wolf to silence, despite him still aiming a weapon at her face. "As much as I hate to admit it, I am going to need your help in the coming hours to get Taylor back from those idiots who call themselves High Council enforcers."

"What makes you think we'll be able to do what you require of us?" Trevor asked, wary.

"I've been led to understand you're both trained military and unscrupulous mercenaries to boot, yes?" Ari tapped the metal siding to her cybernetic eye with purpose. "Besides, I think you'll be more than comfortable wiping out another town, if social media is to be believed."

"I didn't find pleasure in doing that. I'm still regretting that." Trevor bared his teeth. "I just did what needed to be done."

"Agreed." Ari smiled, bowing her head. "Which is exactly why I know you'll do it again for me. You want Taylor. I want Taylor. We'll sort this mess out between ourselves later, but we need to eliminate the competition as it were. With you two, we are at least on the same team with my father. So I am asking you to do what needs to be done to get to Taylor."

"Taylor's not going to like hearing about another town being blown up," Gregor informed, taking a step back. "She tried to eat us when we blew up Palaveve."

"She doesn't have to know this time, now does she?" Ari grinned. "I have procured a motorcycle that is just outside. You will need to get back to Howlgrav immediately." She handed a small paper with an address written on it to a very tense Trevor. "This is where I was holing up in Howlgrav while searching for Taylor. You will find what you need there. Do it as good as you did it in Palaveve and you will be rewarded."

"But you'll be here with Taylor when we do this." Gregor was miffed. "There is no guarantee you'll wait for us to get back to you for Taylor."

"How can we trust you on this?" Trevor asked for the both of them.

"I guess you can't, but I'm the best chance you got at even remotely completing your job for my father. Are you in or out?" Her eyes bored into his own.

"We're in," Gregor answered for Trevor, causing a baleful glance from his buddy.

"One thing." Trevor held up a finger before Ari could speak. "Gregor, give me that grenade you have." After rifling through his pockets, he handed it to Trevor, who turned to Ari and placed it into her palm. "Give this to Taylor. She may not know how to fight much, but she should be able to use this to provide some distraction to save herself if it gets messy."

Ari eyed the grenade curiously before nodding to Trevor. "You have my word. Now go, set the bombs found in my apartment immediately to blow as soon as you're able to leave the city." She nodded before stalking out of the Java Rabbit with many scared rabbits cowering under the tables and behind larger mammals. They saw her cross the small plaza outside the café, beyond a few homes, and was gone.

"I don't like this at all." Trevor looked down at the barely-legible scribbling on the paper. "That was too convenient, showing up just as we were discussing her."

"You're probably right, but it's either this or poverty for the rest of our lives. Your words." Gregor gave him a pointed look.

Trevor slumped. "Yeah, I know. Guess we have no choice now."

Taylor hit the mat hard, breathing ragged and lungs gasping. Natalia had doffed her shirt and was in tank top alongside Taylor. She was standing a few steps beside her, having just tripped her violently with a quarterstaff.

Both of them went out to the garage after Taylor had asked Natalia to train her to fight, and gathered appropriate weapons that had been forgotten about in a corner of the structure. They laid down mats that were rolled up along the wall and set to work in the limited time they had.

"You reveal your paw long before you attempt to strike, Taylor," Natalia admonished, her tail skimming back and forth across the mat.

"Then Mikhail was right about one thing then." Taylor laughed, using her own staff to lean on as she rose up to a knee to catch her breath.

"What is that?" Natalia tilted her head.

"I am like the brash teenager he thinks I am. I pour my entire self into everything I do, and people can see it long before I realize it." She used the staff to push herself the rest of the way to standing.

"I'm glad you are taking well to the training." Natalia bowed her head. "Seeing how quickly you turned around from fighting Mikhail to admitting what he was teaching you was sound is commendable. You aren't a total hopeless case."

"Gee, thanks. I was actually half saying that so he wouldn't have reason to attack me again," Taylor snarked, getting back into her stance to try once more, her quarterstaff held up in front of her close to the chest as she was instructed.

"Come at me again, and this time try to not have Ahya lunge at me with no coordination or foreplanning. It ruins your offensive position and opens you up to attack." Natalia rushed forward and struck Taylor's staff with her own.

The loud crack of the two pieces of wood brought Taylor's ears flat on her head, but she continued to fight back. "It's not like I'm not trying! Ahya has her own thoughts about how to strike, and sometimes wants to do it all on her own."

As if on cue, Ahya swung around from the left and snapped at Natalia, causing the snow leopard to spin away to Taylor's other side. Natalia slipped the staff directly under Taylor's as she made a forward swipe at her, then whacked Taylor hard on the stomach, causing her to pitch forward and opening the opportunity to smack her down to the mat on her upper back.

"Ow…" Taylor groaned, rolling over onto her side at the throbbing pain splintering through her muscles. "You could go a bit easier on me."

"I don't see how that would help you better," Natalia reasoned with all sincerity. Posting her quarterstaff vertical, she gripped it for balance as she knelt down beside Taylor. "Learning how to fight with a weapon and defending yourself is one thing, having a tail that screws up your rhythm in battle is quite another. Learn to work together as one if you want to survive."

"Easier said than done." Taylor took Natalia's offered paw to rise back up to kneeling. "You speak like you have experience on fighting with a tail like mine."

Natalia finally broke a smile. "No, I do not. Of course I don't, but I can see what needs to happen with you to be a more effective fighter. There is only so much I can teach you here. The rest must be on you and Ahya to close that gap."

"And that gap isn't going to be closed today," Fey said from the side door leading into the garage.

They both turned to him, his hornless silhouette framed in the doorway. Natalia assisted Taylor up the rest of the way. "I was just training her to be able to help us out better when it comes time to defend her."

"I realize that." Fey's arms were folded, him leaning against the wooden siding. "Unfortunately, you need to get yourself ready to leave. We have no more time to waste. Head back into the house and gather your things. We leave within ten. I need to talk to Taylor here anyway."

Nodding her head at his direction, she beamed at Taylor before picking up her shirt and setting her own staff back to the side along the wall. "I know it wasn't a lot, but remember the basics and you should be okay for most untrained combatants."

"Thank you, Natalia." Taylor smiled. Even Ahya graced the snow leopard's paw with a small press of her tongue in appreciation as well.

Lingering on her a moment longer, Natalia made eye contact with Fey before sweeping past him out of the garage and towards the house. Fey waited until she was out of earshot before turning back to Taylor. "As discussed earlier, we will be leaving this town by ourselves. Mikhail has identified a mountain pass we can take to the east where, if we set off an explosion there, we can block the entire road. It'll be nearly impossible to traverse and would require anyone who wants to follow us to take the long way around, setting them back days."

Taylor walked over to set her staff alongside Natalia's. "Seems like you got it all figured out. So is the plan still to take me back to Zabökar? I overheard you guys talking that may not be a possibility anymore."

Fey shifted uncomfortably. He seemed to have forgotten that wolves have extraordinary hearing, and Taylor had only been a few rooms over during their earlier conversation. He cursed silently.

Shrugging off the momentary surprise, he responded, "Yes, that option was definitely on the table. However, after much discussion with the news of this small army coming from Howlgrav, we decided our best course of action would be still to go back to Zabökar. At least there we can have a better handle on the situation."

"And the doubts I heard you have on the High Council?" Taylor stared at Fey while patting Ahya, who had come to rest underneath her paw.

"We will deal with that as it comes." Fey unfolded his arms and gestured towards her. "However, we will not be taking you immediately to the council as we had originally planned. We will most likely secure you safely in the city first before meeting with our employers to arrange the logistics of what will happen next. That is both for your safety as well as ours."

"I bet Mikhail had a hand in that decision." Taylor cracked a grin. Ahya joined in kind.

Fey shared her mirth. "Indeed. It was a rational concession. My contact in Zabökar has stated our position is not compromised and we are still legitimate in the eyes of the council. However, this latest wrinkle with this council member, Sabrina, has put us all on guard. There is now an investigation at the highest level to determine what exactly her motive was, and if there was anyone else who was in on her actions."

"I personally am not confident in the results of that investigation." Taylor padded over to Fey, stopping a few feet away.

"You're not confident in a lot of things regarding us. This is no surprise."

"Most of you haven't been giving me many reasons to be so." Taylor scowled.

Fey's smile dropped, a more serious look spread. "I do want to thank you again properly away from the others for earlier." Both Taylor and Ahya looked confused. "If it weren't for you, I wouldn't be standing here today." He put a hoof to his bald head. "Granted, I lost my nice rack as a result, but I'm still alive and it'll ultimately grow back. For that I am grateful. So...thank you."

Taylor gave him a funny look, but ultimately accepted his thanks. "You're welcome. At the very least, it stopped your boyfriend from being nasty twenty-four-seven to me."

Fey busted out laughing, which caused Ahya to jerk back at the shock of it. Sustaining a weird look from Taylor, Fey managed to finally get his humor under control enough to respond. "He's always been like that. He very rarely is nice to others, and prefers to be by himself mostly. Despite this, Finnley is a wonderful otter and is quite loving once you get to know him."

Taylor gave him a hooded expression with a knowing smile. "I'm sure he was real loving. I honestly didn't know you two were a thing until he was all over you when you got shot up. In fact, it was one of the reasons I chose to try to bring you back with Ahya."

"Smothering blueberries, so it wasn't purely altruistic, eh? You had hoped to gain favor from the rest of us by saving me? That makes me feel much better," he mocked playfully.

It was Taylor's turn to cross her arms and shrug. "Hey, what can I say? I'm always looking for opportunities to lower your guard around me so I can run away."

Fey's humor faltered. "Joking aside, I hope we're past this." He pointed a hoof back out behind him. "I don't know what you did to my team, but you have half of us on your side now and wanting to see that you are treated fairly when we arrive to the High Council. That is a far cry from when we first captured you back in Falhoven."

Taylor raised her brow. "Now I'm not sure if you're joking or not."

"I assure you, I am not." Fey's jaw was steeled. "With the primary exception of Finnley, you have single-handedly split my team apart and revealed its flaws just by being yourself. You've shown me the inadequacies of my own leadership and unknowingly offered ways I can improve. Not that I want to."

"I'm not sure I understand." Taylor hadn't known Fey for very long, but he didn't seem the type to admit when he was wrong.

"When this mission is over, I think I'm going to step down from being a leader and just become a follower from now on." Relief washed across Fey's face, and his posture relaxed. "The stress of commanding a squad for the past few years has been a bit more than I can take, and this near-death experience...among other things, has brought things into perspective for me. It was high time for me to change career paths."

Taylor felt like she could understand a bit of what Fey was feeling. "I've been around death since I was little, although I don't think I realized it at the time. This...tail of mine—" She studied Ahya a few moments as it meandering through the air, having lost interest in the conversation. "—is the source of most of my problems, but also the solution to death."

Taylor put a paw to her forehead, a rising throb starting to manifest itself in her temples. "I was just as surprised as everyone else when you came out of my tail fully alive. I've not really had to change my life perspective because of death; it's just been an ever-present aspect of what I live with."

"Well we now have something in common." Fey noticed her look of pain. "Is everything all right?"

She shook it off, the ebb of it receding. "I'll be fine, just the beginnings of a headache."

Fey studied her for a moment before pointing to Ahya. "Alright then... I've been told that you don't have a Script. Because of Ahya, I too no longer have a Script. I am off the board, as they say."

Taylor's face contorted. "Of course. The Script is bogus to begin with! It's never benefitted anyone, and has done far more harm than good, forcing people to take choices when they think there is no other way."

"I don't think you understand the implication here." He put a hoof on Taylor's shoulder, causing a small reaction from Ahya who zeroed in on his touch. "You and your tail directly influenced a part of our world that so many people believe in as absolute fact. It physically changed my Script and as a result, I was…able to change someone else's."

Taylor lightly brushed his hoof off, feeling slightly uncomfortable with the touch. "Then isn't that a good thing? I don't really see the big deal."

Fey brought a hoof to his mouth to scratch it in thought, regarding Taylor at length. "No, I guess you wouldn't. You've been so far outside society in general, even back when you were in Zabökar, that you probably wouldn't understand the gravity of what you accomplished."

"You sound like I'm some miracle worker when I'm not," she huffed, pressing a bit deeper into her temple.

"Fair enough." He lifted a hoof to emphasis his point. "Just be aware that if several powerful people in our world were aware of the things you were capable of and could influence… Well, it would be a bad thing for you to fall into their paws."

"And you trust this High Council of yours to know what is best for me?" she inquired.

Fey shook his head. "As a rule, in my experience, I've learned to never trust anyone who hires you. I realize I'm just a cog in the machine and they could have easily just found someone else to do the same job. I just happened to be the most convenient at the time of hire. The High Council, like anyone, I do not trust farther than I can spit. However, since they've yet to royally screw me over, I am still willing to do work for them." He paused a moment in thought. "That and I signed a contract for my service that I am bound to honor."

"Sounds like you are trapped just like I am under people who want things from you," Taylor remarked, finding it funny. "Look, I need get inside and find some sort of pain medicine. This headache is not wanting to go away, and it is getting worse."

"Of course." Fey stepped aside and let her head on out of the garage first. "We've got a long way to go to get to the pass. I would imagine it be better without that pain bogging you down."

And just like that, the pain lifted. It was quite miraculous in the way that it happened. What had grown to be an overbearing weight on her brain was suddenly gone, like she was walking on clouds. Taylor straightened up. The evening breeze was brushing past her fur and ruffling her hair with its softly scented aroma of freshly cut roses. The colors in her perception become much more vivid and clear.

"That's strange," Taylor commented. She couldn't recall the last time she had a headache like that before, and stranger still that it mysteriously disappeared.

"What is?" Fey was keeping pace alongside, seemingly at ease being beside her and Ahya, mouth agape.

"Taylor?" A small voice peeped from the side.

She immediately froze and turned to see two small figures perched on the fence bordering the inner yard. She blinked a few times to ensure she was seeing things correctly. Pine and Mitchell were sitting side by side, staring at her with sobbing relief. They seemed cold, wet, and miserable, their fur all matted and clinging tightly to their small bodies.

"Are you guys for real?" Taylor sputtered, her balance shaky as she lurched forward towards them in shock.

"Taylor, who are you talking to?" Fey was looking past her in the direction she was stumbling towards. He made a motion to reach out and stop her, but she was accelerating and nearly running to the fence line.

"Pine! Mitchell! I thought I had killed you!" She wrapped both her arms around the critters and picked them off the pickets, embracing them deeply as they each cuddled close into her warmth. Ahya seem oblivious to the reunion and merely poked around with her mouth at nearby lizard rustling through the grass to escape the larger mammals stomping through its home.

"Taylor, there is no one here. Who are you holding?" Fey seemed concerned, his arms folded as he looked on with rising worry.

331

"You're joking, right?" She spun around and pushed each of them up into her arms so Fey could see them better. "This here is Pine and the other is Mitchell. We're a family of sorts. You've met them before already! I can't believe you've forgotten."

It was now Fey's turn to rub his temple. "Taylor, I think there is something you should know." He sighed deeply. "At the time, I didn't really want to interfere since I felt it was a coping mechanism for whatever trauma you had endured, so I informed the others to go along with whatever weird voices you made when you talked to your made-up friends."

Taylor was hurt that Fey would call her friends fake. She held them even closer. "This isn't funny. If this is your idea of a joke, it is a horrible one. I had thought this entire time that I had killed them both when I let loose that explosion in Howlgrav, and now you mean to ruin my mood and insult my friends like this."

"He was always kind of a meanie." Pine stuck his tongue out at Fey.

"I mean, we are small, but I don't think we are that easy to miss." Mitchell was thoughtful.

"That's just it!" Fey said exasperated. "You are talking to yourself right now as if they're actually real! I don't know what you've gone through to force yourself into making up two imaginary friends to cope with the stressors of being alone and afraid. I am no psychologist, but I know enough to see the signs of trauma and this is clearly one obvious symptom."

"Stop it!" Taylor shouted. This time even Ahya was snapping and getting angry at Fey alongside Taylor. "What do you know about who I am? From what I've gathered, you've never had to experience the type of crap I've been through! Even if my friends were fake—" She gave them both a squeeze. "—which they are not! Why bother ignoring it up until now? Why drop this stupid bombshell on me now?"

"Because I didn't know who or what we were dealing with when we first captured you." Fey put both his hooves up to indicate he was going to come no closer. "You had a tailmaw and some electrical EMP burst ability when we found you. I had no idea if these imaginary friends were truly fake or real or just another power you had. I felt it was better to play it safe and have all of us play along until we could better figure out what it was you were doing. Now that I am better versed in what you're capable of, I know this is not an ability, but a symptom of what I believe to be childhood trauma."

"Are you so sure that it isn't something she can do?" a voice simpered from behind him. He whirled around and brayed indignantly at the sight of Ari mere feet from him. She thumped her tail on the ground and snapped her fingers, and within moments his hind hooves sunk into superheated pockets of earth before solidifying around his ankles, causing him to cry out in pain. "Not so fast, my dear. You will not be interfering with Taylor leaving with me."

Tears were welling up in his eyes as he beat the ground with a hoof. "Stinking lizard. We should have listened to Trevor when he offered to kill you."

"Hmmm, last I recall you two were on unfavorable terms with each other. Being on opposite sides, was it? It seems he knew me better than you did. Pity you didn't take his advice. Look where it got you now?" Ari seemed to be enjoying the upper hand.

"I may not exactly like him much, but don't kill him." Taylor set down both her friends before standing up to face off against Ari.

Her sneer changed to one of grave sincerity. "I am true to my word. My goal has always been to deliver you to my father, but make no mistake that I will kill anyone who gets in my way."

"Paws up where we can see them!" Finnley rushed out at the sound of his lover's anguished cry, followed by Mikhail, Natalia, and Terrati, who each drew their own weapons.

Ari rolled her eyes at the interference. "Again with your guns. Like that did much good for you last time!"

With a cry, she crouched to the ground and clapped it loudly with her palm. Immediately, a burning spire of magma busted through the ground, creating a temporary blockade between Taylor and Ari and the rest of them.

Ari spun back to Taylor. "I could kill them easily, but they are trying my patience. You call them off or this elk is the first to go, and then matters get a lot more complicated."

"Watch out!" Mitchell pointed up high above them.

Ari looked up to see that Finnley had used the rapidly cooling earth to scale up to a point of height advantage before leaping off towards her. She roared and began to maneuver herself into position.

Before Ari could attack, Taylor swiped Finnley out of the air with Ahya, his small frame emitting a squeak of surprise. Gripping a bit too tightly, teeth digging into the otters clothes, she threw him aside onto the grass roughly. A far better landing than if he had been catapulted by Ari.

"You're welcome!" Taylor spat before pivoting to Ari who had expressed her derision at her saving the otter's life. "Behind you!"

Ari had mere seconds to see the rumbling tiger on all fours, boring down on her position. She attempted to impale him with a jagged spire of heated soil, but he bounded to the side before twirling through the air and plowing straight into her chest, knocking Ari hard onto her back. Her shell looked to absorb the impact.

"We will not make the same mistake twice." Straddling her, Mikhail flicked his claws out and brought them down to rake Ari's face.

Pine and Mitchell sputtered for a few seconds before flitting out of existence. Taylor shrieked as she hit the ground with her knees. "Stop it! All of you! Don't kill each other!" Ahya enlarged quickly and grabbed Mikhail by the tail before yanking him off of Ari, much to his displeasure. He roared at her, but stayed his anger. "Where are they? They were just here a second ago!" She was scouring the yard for any sign of her two friends.

"Where is who?" Terrati probed, looking around nervously as he and Natalia caught up with Mikhail.

"My friends! Pine and Mitchell!" Taylor was frantic now.

They all gave each other a knowing look as Natalia stepped forward to comfort Taylor. "Hun, they were never here." She tried to put a paw on Taylor's back, but she violently shoved it off.

"They were here! I saw them! I held them! Where are they?" She was angry. Sparks were sizzling out of her fingertips.

"Calm down, Taylor." Ari coughed, spitting out a globule of blood. Her fingers went to her face to feel the freshly swollen lacerations oozing crimson down her cheek. The tiger's claws even managed to scrape a few shavings of metal off her cybernetic eye panel. "He just knocked me a bit harder than I would have liked. I couldn't keep them maintained any longer. It's actually quite difficult to hack into neural brain waves like that for any length of time."

"I don't understand. Were they not real? Did I really kill them back in Howlgrav?" Taylor was beginning to choke up again.

This was some cruel irony. The two young critters who were her rock and lifeline for the past year were dangled in front of her face before being ripped away once again. They were the only thing that reminded her of her two older brothers, and had brought some solace during the long nights in Palaveve.

"Can someone please get me unstuck?" Fey was straining to kick his feet to dislodge the compacted earth around his hooves.

Finnley grumbled, whispering curses at Taylor for knocking him out of the air, but proceeded to sweep on by to assist Natalia in digging Fey out. The burns on his hooves were mostly superficial, but he would be walking with a limp for quite some time before they fully healed.

"They were never real. Just like Fey here said." Ari glanced over at the struggling elk.

"But you saw them... You even talked to them when we first met." Taylor was trying to rationalize it.

Ari tapped a claw to her red iris. "My eye can see into various different spectrums of visual fields. I could only see and hear them through this one eye alone. My other one did not pick them up at all, which is why I knew they were nothing but manifestations of your own mind, Taylor."

"Why is any of this relevant?" Terrati still had his gun trained on Ari. "Can someone explain to me while we haven't shot her yet?"

"Because if you do, then you'll have me to fight." Taylor grit her teeth, staring him down intensely. "I've told all of you several times before, I don't want anyone else to die on my account!"

Ari let loose a lilting laugh, which looked to grate on Finnley and Fey's ears, as they'd flapped back in irritation. "It's why I haven't killed any of you yet." She couldn't resist letting loose with her humor. "I need Taylor's cooperation, and that is why I have come back despite easily escaping you all."

"So, you come back to give her false hope that her friends might be alive only to reveal they were never real? How does that even help?" Mikhail's muscles bulged, ready to pounce on the reptile at any moment, but he stayed his paw on Taylor's request.

"I have come back to show her that she is far more attuned to the magic of this world than any of you realize." Ari gazed over at Natalia, who was having Fey loop an arm over her shoulder as she limped him over to Taylor. "It took me a long while studying Taylor's brain patterns to be able to isolate the waves that corresponded to her Pine and Mitchell, but I was finally able to get her to generate them on command for us just now."

Taylor put a paw up to her temple, remembering her sudden pain. "Were you in my head just now?" Ari nodded at her question.

"For us?" Finnley scoffed. "None of us saw them, whoever they are!"

"But she did. That's what mattered." Ari looked proud of herself.

"Can you bring them back?" Taylor was hopeful, but had the nagging feeling that what had happened was yet another type of violation to her body.

Ari shook her head. "That would require a bit more concentration right now than we have time for. They still have got to come from you. They're not gone; they're just inside your mind. Who knows? Maybe you may be able to make them real enough so those without the type of sight that I have can actually see them? For now, it was a good way for me to come back and state my proposition to you."

"Now we come to it." Mikhail seemed unsurprised.

Ari finally got back up to standing, wiping the blood off her face with a palm before licking it clean. "You are going to need me if you want to help defend this town long enough for Trevor and Gregor to do what I need them to buy us more time."

"Good to know Gregor is still alive," Finnley sneered, continuing to assist Fey.

"They now work for you?" Natalia asked, shock in her voice.

Ari smirked. "Of course. We do have the same employer, after all, and they can still prove their usefulness to the cause. Last I checked, all of you were planning to abandon this town to its fate and Taylor wasn't very happy about it, were you?"

"I wasn't," Taylor confirmed.

"How in the hell did you even know that?" Fey grumbled, a bewildered look plastered across his face.

Again Ari tapped her cybernetic iris. "One of the few good things my father gave me other than life. I can tap into the wifi signals, radio waves, and more, and listen into whatever I want. Your cell phones are easily cracked, allowing your microphones to pick up what I need to hear."

"It doesn't matter now," Fey argued. "We've all agreed to leave together. Even Taylor agreed to come with us."

"Well if there is a chance that we can save the people here…" Taylor looked to Mikhail. "Maybe even save Klera in the process, I really think we should take it."

Smiling at her, Mikhail bowed his head. "I'm in agreement with Taylor. I'd rather not see my mother-in-law die today if we can help it, and if both Taylor and I are off the Script and can influence others, maybe we have a shot at changing the fate of Cheribaum."

"This is a fool's plan to go up against that many trained cops," Finnley fumed. "We'd be making a huge mistake for staying."

Ari turned to Taylor, focusing on her with both eyes. "Since our mutual goal is for Taylor's cooperation, shouldn't we be doing what she wants right now?"

Taylor could see it in their eyes. Ari had maneuvered herself into a trusted position with her to where Taylor could turn all their plans upside down. In one smooth stroke, Ari had given Taylor all the power here. It was now her turn to dictate what happened next, and nobody around her but Ari looked happy about this.

Ari pressed. "So what do you want to do right now, Taylor?"

338

17
DIVERSION

Taylor was looking out the window in the passenger seat. Finnley was standing on the console between her and Mikhail. They had taken the stolen police van from behind Klera's house and drove it out down to the valley pass just near the base of the mountain. The oncoming horde of vehicles in the dwindling light could be seen a few miles off still. They had agreed to be the bait on Ari's assumption that Taylor could potentially still be important to Howlgrav police, considering how Sabrina had been working with them.

"I don't trust her." Mikhail was sitting relaxed in the driver's seat, an arm draped over the wheel of the van.

"You don't really trust many people to begin with," Finnley snarked as he adjusted his back brace. "Gods, that pressure is fierce!" He gritted his teeth at the pain no doubt raging up his spine.

"That seems to be a common thing with all you people," Taylor blurted out without even bothering to consider the dirty looks she received from both Mikhail and Finnley, continuing to look out the window to hide her smirk.

"Oh, and you think trusting this crazy daughter of the Arbiter is any better? If you recall, she tried to kill us when we first met." Finnley was bearing down on her neck, backing off slightly when Ahya shifted behind Taylor to put herself between them.

"Not all of us." Taylor turned to finally look at the cantankerous otter. "She actually wanted me alive and well." She couldn't help but smile at getting under Finnley's skin. "She's got a bit more of my trust than the rest of you."

"We actually didn't try to kill you either," Mikhail reminded, keeping his eyes on the mass of cars inbound.

"You certainly didn't treat me better," Taylor rejoined promptly. "So excuse me for wanting to help out Cheribaum from getting completely destroyed. I've met the nicest people in my life here, and I really don't want them to die."

"Oh right, Mikhail's mom and some rabbit who wanted to fondle your lady bits. Real nice people." It was Finnley's turn to look smug as Taylor glared at him. "Oh yeah, don't think I didn't hear about that hilarious fiasco!" he sniggered to himself.

"Maybe I'll have Ahya fondle your whole body permanently." With that, she unleashed Ahya to lick Finnley from bottom to top, getting him drenched in saliva.

"Oh, what the hell!" Finnley sputtered as he shook his entire body to get the mess of fluid off. Mikhail was just laughing in his seat.

"At least you taste better than the last person she ate." Taylor winked.

"Is that supposed to make me feel better, you little punk?" Finnley continued to shake his arms.

"Please, will you two knock it off? I'm tired of the fighting," Natalia languished in the backseat.

"That makes two of us." Taylor glanced back at her in the front row of seats. "Can we simmer down this attack otter any? You'd think he would be more appreciative that I saved Fey at all."

"I am!" Finnley snapped, still standing tall right next to her. "It's the only reason I don't cuff you upside the head and shank a knife through your ribs. I owe you a debt I wish I didn't have."

"Don't make it sound like you love it." Taylor continued to egg the otter on.

"I feel like I'm going to have to separate you two when this is all over." Mikhail twisted around and grabbed the otter by the scruff of the neck before leaning back further and setting him down beside Natalia. "Now just stay there and remember your job. We're all in this together at this point, and it's either them or us. Our lives are on the line. We can argue about debts and fondling each other later. Let's just focus on the now."

"Whatever. I can't believe you let Ari manipulate us into staying and defending this dump of a town." Finnley rechecked his sidearm one more time.

"Excuse me, my mother and former wife used to live here," Mikhail spoke sharply.

"She didn't manipulate anything." Taylor had Ahya stretch further towards Finnley, her tongue out in threat to lick him again. "I just wasn't comfortable on letting innocent people die because of me. If we hadn't escaped from jail, they wouldn't be after us. If we hadn't gotten into a fight with Ari, we wouldn't be in that jail. If you all hadn't kidnapped me, we'd not be anywhere near that town that is now after us!"

"I think you're overthinking things, dear." Natalia gave a reassuring pat to Ahya, who seemed to enjoy the attention. "Nobody could have predicted this would happen, but I am in agreement with you, Taylor. I wasn't comfortable either in just leaving Cheribaum to its fate."

"Is Cheribaum Scripted to fall today?" Taylor asked suddenly of Mikhail. "You had your entire Script read to you. Was there nothing in there about it?"

He jolted a bit at the question, but regarded her seriously. "Hard to say. My Script ended earlier this evening, as I said. We'd have to consult another Script or two of someone else who is currently living here to see if that is what is fated for this town. Something we do not have time for." He gestured forward. It would be minutes now before the first line of trucks would reach their position. They appeared to be slowing down now.

"They better be in position, otherwise we're all dying tonight anyway." Finnley plopped down next to Natalia and put his face against the window, eyes on the lights of the vehicles.

"You're so cheerful," Taylor mocked.

Natalia leaned forward and gave Taylor's shoulder a squeeze, prompting her to look. "How you feeling about this, Taylor?"

A look of fear briefly flittered across her eyes. "To tell you the truth, I'm a bit terrified. I've never done something like this before in my life. The most fighting I've ever done was through music and screaming into a microphone. All I've ever known is how to run. I want to run still, but I feel like if I do, I'd never forgive myself for it."

"Why is that? Who do you possibly got to answer to and disappoint if you were to run away again?" Mikhail was sincere, fleetingly taking his eyes off the cars ahead of them, the lead vehicle rolling to a stop and parking.

"My mother...for one." Taylor looked down into her lap, not wanting to meet his gaze. "I've no idea what happened to her since I ran away. I feel like she is still mad at me for that, and she'll be disappointed when I return, just like she'll be if she finds out I ran away to leave all these people here to die."

"For what it's worth, for all that you've been through these past few days, you have been very brave, and I'm sure she would be proud of you," Mikhail consoled as he kept one eye on the lead truck's door. A small swine officer stepped out. "I wouldn't mind taking you for a couple days in Zabökar to go find your mom and have that long-awaited reunion."

Taylor had to fight hard not to shed a tear at the feelings welling up in her chest. "Thanks, Mikhail. I'd really like that."

She gazed down at the small grenade she was rolling over and over in her paws. Ari had given it to her, stating it was for her protection if needed. She only just barely got instruction on how to use it, but the fact she held such destruction in the palm of her hand was daunting. Mikhail had not seemed thrilled with the "gift", but Ari had been of no mind to allow him to refuse it on her behalf.

"Look alive," Finnley barked, pointing out the front dash. "He's got a megaphone."

Mikhail rolled down both front windows so they could hear it better. It was Officer Mendezarosa standing on the hood of the lead tactical vehicle, a mounted minigun on the front end of the truck bed behind him. It seemed he was struggling to make the megaphone work, hitting it a few times with his hoof before it screeched into action, startling him.

Satisfied that it was functional, Mendezarosa cleared his throat and piped into it. "Fugitives from the law, lay down your arms and surrender yourselves peacefully. If you do not, we will have no choice but to use lethal force. You have two minutes to comply or we will start firing."

"What are they doing? They clearly have the upper hand!" Taylor gripped the handle on her door, her eyes tracking the helicopters circling overhead. "I'm surprised they're not going in guns blazing."

Natalia pointed at the media cars parked not far from the front line. "They have news coverage of this. They are not going to do something illegal in front of the public eye unless they are forced to do so by us. That way it makes them look innocent, and in perfect justification in whatever retaliation they do."

"Although I have no doubt he is serious about that time limit. He's not going to look like a fool in front of the entire world on live television." Mikhail nudged Taylor on the arm to get out of the car. "You best get on out there. We've got your back. We will not be attacking the car they'll take you to. Being with them at this juncture is the safest place for you right now, since we're all in on the plan and they're not."

"Just hope Fey and all them are in position." Finnley cocked his gun.

"If Ari is to be trusted, and since she suggested this plan to allow them to take her, then I feel she won't betray us yet until we're all out of the woods." Mikhail sounded confident. "I trust her to the point where it is time to decide who gets to take Taylor back to Zabökar. Then we'll see how long this truce lasts."

Taylor gazed around at each of them. "To be honest, I think I trust your employers less than I do either you or Ari. At least your motives are known, and I know you won't harm me. I can't say the same for who hired you or the Arbiter."

"It looks like he's about to speak again. Go on, get out!" Natalia pushed Ahya back to the front passenger seat.

"Alright, alright! I'm going." Taylor sighed, pocketing the grenade. She opened the door and slammed it shut a bit more forcefully than she would have liked. Like Ari instructed, she ensured that Ahya was visible and raised high, her mouth open and tongue completely out and swinging.

"You have been warned. We will have no choice but to—" Mendezarosa's words lodged in his throat as his eyes bulged at the sight of Taylor. He nervously looked around, seeing all the cameras filming him and the scene unfolding.

Clearing his throat, he recomposed himself before speaking again into the megaphone. "Are you intending to send a negotiator to discuss the terms of your surrender? This is highly irregular, and we do not guarantee we will honor any requests you may have. However, as acting agent of the law, I must see that you are given your due process no matter how heinous your crimes. You may step forward with paws up and we will talk." He motioned with a hoof for Taylor to come forward as he tossed the phone down to a moose who fumbled, trying to snatch it on short notice.

His attention focused on her now, Taylor lowered Ahya back down behind her. Tongue now retracted back into its maw, it looked like any other wolf tail sans the red fur. Her heart was pumping in her chest as she stepped forward slowly, watching the diminutive pig slide down the side of the hood with the assistance of another colleague. He marched forward with two imposing rhinoceroses, their sharp horns visible in the waning dusk.

It would seem almost comical to any bystander if the situation wasn't so dire—Taylor towering over Mendezarosa and his two handpicked bodyguards looming over her. It was clearly an unmatched affair. Taylor's nose detected a scent of fear coming from the peccary, but he was hiding it well from his less-than-olfactory-endowed officers. He was scared of her, and that thought brought some burgeoning confidence in her chest.

They stared at each other until it became awkward. Mendezarosa suddenly grunted, waving off his two officers. "Can you two step back a few? I'd like some privacy to discuss their surrender." This got curious looks from the two, but they deferred to his command and stepped back a few paces. Content with their distance, he turned back to Taylor with a more hushed tone. "Who are you? Why are you here? What game are you playing at?"

Taylor felt relief flood through her. He was shooting in the dark. Ari was right, he was in on whatever Sabrina was planning for her and knew what would happen. She wasn't supposed to be alive now in his eyes.

Smiling now, she went to a knee to be on his eye level which seemed to irritate him something fierce. "You thought I was going to be dead, weren't you? I hate to break it to you, but my tail ate your friend earlier today. She was mighty tasty, actually!" She actually wasn't, from what aftertaste she could discern after she had recovered from her near-death experience. However, to complete the affect, she licked her lips in a very predatory fashion.

Mendezarosa squealed a bit, but immediately tried to staunch his reaction. "You trying to threaten me?" He looked off beyond her to the lone police van with Mikhail, Finnley, and Natalia inside. "You and your friends are not in any position to bargain. I could have those helicopters above launch rockets into that van and your friends would be dead. The only reason I'm staying my hoof right now is because Mrs. Fahpar—I mean, my boss said you were important, and I'm going to find out why!"

"I thought you were the boss?" Taylor's cheek was gone. His threat sobered up her flippant demeanor, and her smile faded as she grew serious.

"Nevermind that!" he snorted. "This is how it is going to go: you're going to follow me back to my cruiser and be cuffed into the back seat."

"What about my friends?" she asked, her tone stern.

"What about them? What happens next is on them. They'll still have to surrender just like you are, but they'll be taken to another holding facility for questioning." His haughty demeanor returned again, feeling that he now had the situation back under control.

"How about we just go back to the van and tell them yourself?" Taylor suggested.

Mendezarosa waggled a hoof at her. "Ah, not so fast, little girl." This caused her ears to fold crossly. "You come back with me and I'll address them from the safety of my men."

345

"Fine," she agreed, "but in return, you promise to leave them unharmed when they turn themselves in."

"Of course." He waved for her to extend her wrists out so he could slap some metal on them. Rolling her eyes at the gesture, she complied, and he gleefully cuffed her. "Now then, come along now and be a good girl. We'll deal with your friends next," he chortled, looking happy that he was being filmed apprehending this larger predator and having her walk behind him, looking cowed and defeated.

As much as she hated being called that, she knew too many things were riding on her going along with this. She just hoped that everyone else would do what they said they'd do. She could hear the news reporters blaring out to their audiences what they were seeing, no doubt getting every bit of the story wrong as to what was actually happening. She sighed. This exposure would get more unwanted eyes on her, plastering her face across all avenues of social media yet again.

Ignoring the flashing of cameras and the red lights of their camcorders, she was gracelessly shoved into the back of his cruiser. There was a metal cage enclosing the interior of her half of the compartment, preventing any criminals from breaking the glass and either escaping or getting at the other occupants of the vehicle.

Mendezarosa climbed back up to the hood of the vehicle, then clicked his hooves to get the megaphone back. He put a hoof to his hip and belted out through the phone, "Your friend here has turned herself in for amnesty in exchange for ratting out this den of terrorists. She has implicated you and all of Cheribaum as enemies of Galaria, with ill intent to sabotage and destroy our great city of Howlgrav. Seeing as we have a key witness against your plot, we order you to lay down your weapons and come out with your paws up. You have two minutes to comply."

Not bothering to wait for a response, he hopped down unassisted this time and happily got in through the passenger-side door. Taylor rapped on the barred glass to get his attention. "Hey! That wasn't what I said!"

He replied without looking at her. "I know, but we don't negotiate with terrorists." Mendezarosa leaned over to his driver—a rather-imposing rhinoceros that was looking cramped in the small confines of his seat. "Put the order out to begin firing upon that van regardless of what they do."

"Yes, sir." The larger cop nodded, bringing the radio up to his mouth and broadcasting the order to all the other vehicles in the formation, unheard by the gaggle of reporters standing rapt by the side of their news vans.

"That's not what we agreed upon!" Taylor slapped Ahya up against the glass, letting the maw's tongue slather up the bars and turning them to jelly as the saliva corroded the metal.

"I never agreed to anything." He calmly pointed a pistol at her head. "And if I were you, I'd keep that tongue back in your tail unless you want to have a few extra holes in your head."

"Liars!" She hit the glass—which wasn't affected—hard with her fist. She reluctantly did as she was told. "You're a bunch of crooked cops!" As if on cue, another rhinoceros came in the passenger door, forcing Mendezarosa to scoot in between them.

"No, we just know when to invoke our right to defend ourselves against mass murderers like you." He snickered, baring his tusks. "You've killed a dozen or so people on your own, haven't you, little girl? I would be well within my rights to put you down if I felt you were a threat to my personal safety. The only reason you're alive now is because the higher-ups want you for something, and I bet they'll be giving me a mighty big reward for it."

"My name…is Taylor," she said with venom.

Two loud booms reverberated through the cruiser as the entire right side sank low, causing the rhinoceros to lean hard in the opposite direction to avoid sliding into Mendezarosa and crushing him. The large vehicle's wheels had blown out at a dead stop and the large frame was awkwardly tilted, giving Taylor the opportunity to sneak Ahya's tongue around the chain linking her cuffs together and melt clean through them.

"What the heck was that?" Mendezarosa shrieked, nearly sinking into his seat.

Before his buddy could answer, several large blooms of light crested over the mountain peaks to the southeast. They brightened up the sky as if it were daytime, pulsating wildly to give off a strobe-like effect, causing many to shield their eyes and one unfortunate soul to collapse to

347

the ground in a seizure. There was a dull roar that answered from off to the west. Violent jets of steam could barely be heard from their position.

"Shit, we need to get out of here now!" Mendezarosa panicked.

"Not in this car, sir. We need to transport the prisoner to another. We're dead in the water here." The rhinoceros looked back out his window to see several large lights in the darkness turning towards their position.

"Then destroy that van! All units, fire! Then order a retreat!" he screeched.

They had just crested the first foothill and were climbing the next rise. They left on Ari's insistence the moment the others departed in the van to meet the oncoming mob to be bait. Her reasoning was that if Taylor stayed with them, Ari knew the chief of police wouldn't let them leave alive, and Taylor might get injured in the process. Having them transfer custody—if only for a moment—over to them would be the safest place for Taylor. None of them wanted harm to come to her, since she was all their objective.

"I don't trust her," Terrati whispered, his eyes on the reptile walking up the mountain path ahead of them.

"You and me both," Fey agreed, his hoof securing his thigh holster, a pistol locked in deep. "Something doesn't seem to add up. She puts you out and escapes only to come back hours later with a fully hatched plan to keep this town safe from annihilation, and to eliminate Howlgrav's finest from interfering again. She's got something else up her sleeve."

"She's playing up to Taylor for sure," Terrati huffed, readjusting the sling of his sniper rifle that Ari had procured for him, among other armaments for the rest of the crew. "Just where exactly did she come across this stuff?"

Fey looked at the formidable rifle slung across the gazelle's back. "It's probably better not to ask questions and just accept the gifts."

He assisted Terrati up a large boulder. "But I feel the same as you. Somehow she has gotten under Taylor's skin, and has gained some part of trust far better than any of us could in such a short amount of time. I'm completely amazed at how she was able to accomplish that."

"I think it is simple," Terrati explained, slowing his pace down while still walking to get a bit more distance out of earshot. "She's been trained by one of the most charismatic and political threats to Zabökar in decades: the Arbiter. Showing up out of nowhere with nothing to his name but that he heralded from the southern country of Talkar, and then within a few short years he was a reigning member of the High Council? If that doesn't scream technical social skills, then I don't know what does."

"I'm not sure I understand." Fey glanced up the path to Ari. She seemed supremely confident that they were following her, not even bothering to look back.

"Think about it. I was there the moment she jumped us in the bar back in Howlgrav. She immediately noticed Taylor's wrist condition and rightly assumed a few things based on how we were positioned around her to prevent escape. She sized up the situation expertly and appealed immediately to that with Taylor and nearly succeeded, only stopped thanks to Mikhail escalating the situation." He held a branch out of the way for Fey's antlers, only to be reminded they were gone now and let the branch drop awkwardly.

"Still, I've half a mind she was awake all day today," Terrati continued. Seeing a look from Fey, he expanded. "We all checked in on her throughout the morning, but not once did she stir before or after breakfast. She was listening to us all and observing. Those walls are rather thin in Klera's home, so it wasn't hard to really eavesdrop if she wanted to. She understood what we've been up to, how we act as a team, and Taylor's opinion on us, which made it very easy for her to get Taylor's support when she showed up again.

"She's a class A manipulator, and my best guess as to why she hasn't killed any of us yet is because of getting Taylor's support, and eventually turning her against us," he finished, his eyes now on Ari's lumbering tail, its languid movements creating a dust trail path that they could easily follow even in the waning light.

"It must be pretty serious for the Arbiter to send his only daughter to come pick up Taylor," Fey mused. "There were already two goons hired to secure her, but it seems things changed back in Zabökar enough that it warranted more drastic measures. It's one thing sending mercenaries to do the work, but it is quite another to send your own daughter."

"With powers no less," Terrati added. "Knowing that the Arbiter is no longer on the High Council and banished from the city, things must have taken a turn for the worse to have his schedule pushed up like that. I wonder if he is upping reinforcements to locate the rest of his wayward experiments?"

"That is the case, actually," Fey confirmed, lowering his voice lower. "My contact back in Zabökar got back with me on the blood sample we sent from Taylor. He mentioned that many more mammals are going missing these days. Not enough for the majority to notice, but for those looking for the signs, it is alarming."

Terrati shivered. "I wonder how the heck they got loose to begin with. I mean, they were just normal citizens even before the pulse, right? They must have had normal lives before being dragged away to be experimented on to get their powers."

"I'm not sure if I should be telling you this, but in the brief I got before we were—" Fey began.

"If you two are finished talking about me, we are in position now," Ari interrupted.

She had stopped at a rocky outcropping. There was a gorgeous view of the valley below, seeing the foothills open out to lush plains that stretched off to the twinkling lights of Howlgrav not even out of sight on the horizon. Closer to them were huge swaths of lights slowing down to a lone pair in the middle of darkness. The time would soon come that they needed to do their part of the plan.

"That hike took a bit longer than I thought." Fey was breathing a bit heavy, leaning forward with his hooves on his knees. The limp Ari had given him wasn't helping matters either.

"You didn't actually have to come," Ari pointed out, flippant hand on her hip. "You could have just as easily been down there with your group."

"True." Fey grinned, not wanting to let her get the better of him. "But when you say you want to take my best sharpshooter out for a walk in the woods, that does give me slight cause for concern."

"You don't trust me yet?" She feigned surprise.

"You know the answer to that," he retorted. "I'm only here to ensure you don't screw my friend here again and kill him once his usefulness is complete." He laid a hand on his pistol to accentuate the point.

"Please, I could have easily just taken Taylor by force and killed the lot of you. I'd much rather have someone to talk to on the way back to Zabökar than a comatose body. It is a dreadfully long and boring trip, wouldn't you agree?"

"Quite the cheeky tongue in that one," Terrati joked.

"Well, she is her father's daughter," Fey joined in.

Ari squinted her eyes as she gritted her teeth, but the moment passed quickly and she was all business again. "I scouted this place out earlier, knowing that they'd sent an entire contingent after you."

"You were quite busy." Terrati whistled. "Did all this and got us some nice weapons to boot."

Ari shrugged. "What can I say? I am on a mission. I'm not going to lollygag on my duty, sipping coffee and enjoying homemade pancakes when I have an objective to secure. If it does not get me Taylor, then it is useless to me."

"At least that I can agree on." Fey nodded. "This looks like a good position. I'll be his spotter." He turned to Terrati. "What do you think? Where do you want to set up?"

Terrati looked at the far edge of the outcropping. "That's a bit too exposed." He walked on over to the other side and saw a smaller ledge jutting out from just beneath the primary ledge. "This looks to be better, and I can still see most of what matters."

"That's fine." Ari brought out a flare gun. "That'll free me up to lure in the behemoth."

Fey gave her a worried stare. "Are you sure we can distract this thing from killing us all? We only need it to disrupt and break apart their formation so we can secure Taylor again and escape."

"Don't you worry your pretty, bald head about it," she cooed, forcing Fey to drop his ears in irritation. "Trevor and Gregor will do their jobs and draw it off at the right moment."

"What makes you so sure it'll work?" Terrati asked. "We don't even know what that thing is out there."

"My brethren are sensitive to bright lights in the darkness. It'll get their attention for sure," she said absently, opening up the gun to ensure the two flare cartridges were installed properly before clicking it shut.

"Your...what?" Fey was confused about the term.

She just shook her head and waved them off. "Just focus on your role. It won't be long now, they've already stopped." She pointed out to the car lights below. "Just let me know when they have her and I'll launch these. Then you will be free to open fire."

Terrati appeared miffed as he got down on all fours, ultimately positioning himself on his stomach. Having unstrapped his rifle, he secured down the stand beneath the barrel and set himself up into a comfortable angle. He flipped the scope up and locked it into place, then squeezed one eye shut as he looked down the lens at their stolen cop van. Adjusting the dials, he finally was satisfied with the look of his view.

"You'll be needing this." Ari tossed a pair of small binoculars from her pocket to Fey, who caught it deftly. "It isn't ideal, but it should suffice." With that, she hopped up to the higher rock and knelt down to observe the events unfold.

Fey looked at the small set of binoculars. They were clearly store-bought or stolen, and didn't approach the zoom capability that he was used to as Terrati's spotter. Still, it would do the job if given accurate readings. Settling down next to the gazelle, he adjusted himself so he was right next to him. Ensuring that he wasn't impeding his friend's arm space, he looked down the binoculars at the view below.

"I don't like taking orders from a teenage girl," Terrati spat, his eyes still trained down the sights of the rifle, not even looking at Fey.

"Neither do I." Fey sighed. "However, I recognize a threat when I see one, and I am going to see how this plays out before making any

352

rash decisions. We need to respect her for the danger she poses and treat her as such."

"I just don't like being caught off guard." Terrati finally looked up from his scope.

"I know that better than anyone." Fey didn't meet his gaze. "I was so proud that I had made squad leader and was excited to be given my own team to lead. It wasn't until this mission I realized how unprepared I was for the task. There have been many times that I realized I had been caught off guard and been at a loss for what to do in the moment. A true leader needs to come up with solutions on the fly, but I could do nothing but stare helplessly as I feebly attempted to figure out what to do next."

Terrati smiled at him. "For what it's worth, I always thought you were a good leader. Sure, you can be a bit aloof at times, and sometimes a dick, but you at least seemed to have a level head on your shoulders."

Fey couldn't fault him for that blunt observation. "You got me there. Still, it has helped me realize that I am probably going to step down from my role as squad leader, and just follow orders instead. I feel it is a better fit for me."

Terrati put a hoof on Fey's arm. "It takes a big mammal to admit that. That makes me want to follow you even more. I do apologize for what I said earlier."

"And I apologize for leaving you in the dark," Fey responded in kind.

"Shut the chatter!" Ari snapped from above.

They rolled their eyes at each other, but acquiesced her demand. Looking back down the binoculars, Fey lightly tapped Terrati's shoulder. "Taylor's out of the vehicle and is talking to that small pig."

"Isn't he the one who questioned us?" Terrati whispered, making sure Ari didn't overhear.

"The very one, I think." Fey wasn't sure, but what other officer there had that stature?

There was a long silence. They could see Taylor squatting to be down at the same level of the peccary. At a sudden thought, Terrati probed quietly, "You said you got the blood sample results back from

Taylor? Anything unusual?" His sight was tracking Taylor walking back in cuffs to the lead squad car.

Not leaving his view of Taylor, he answered back, "Well, it is confirmed that she has most definitely been afflicted with the pulse just like the rest of the experiments, but she claims she's had all her abilities since birth, which makes no sense. There was also one other thing that seemed odd." He searched for the words to best describe it. "She has two strains of DNA within her blood."

"Two strains? What does that mean?" Terrati's focus on the car was hindering his attention to the conversation.

"I'm not entirely sure yet." Fey adjusted the limited zoom on his binoculars. "She's safely in the car now. You are cleared hot to blow out the tires."

"Gladly." Terrati slowed his breathing down and put his hoof finger into the guard, its surface lightly touching the trigger as he slowly pulled back. Aiming for the front tire, he measured his breathing and waited for it to go out before firing.

A loud crack resounded, but it missed the tire by several meters. "One click up." Fey looked on, his eyes intent on the vapor trail.

Applying the directed change to the gun, Terrati got back into position and let out another breath. The second shot hit. He swapped the rifle over to the back tire and fired again. The third shot hit. The entire cruiser started sagging to one side. That was the cue for Ari to act. She pointed the flare gun into the air and launched both canisters high. It began to pulse brightly, lighting up the night sky.

"Shall I keep shooting?" Terrati queried, his focus intense.

"Yes, take down as many of the others as you can," Ari called from above. "The more that can be crushed by the beast, the less we have to deal with."

"Savage," Fey commented. "Do as she says. Knock out those that pose the biggest threats to their escape."

Popping out the rounds he had expended, he re-cocked the rifle and took aim at several of the tactical vehicles that could either outpace or keep up with their only method of transportation. Several cars went down as it seemed the entire place had gone up in pandemonium. A group of cars had already detached and were zooming back towards

Howlgrav. The rest that hadn't been shot flat-tired were rushing forward with miniguns and other armaments blazing.

"Are Mikhail and the others safe?" Fey asked, concerned. He swung his view to the sitting van, but they had already skidded out from their position.

Terrati was tracking them already. "No, it seems they are making a beeline back to the foothills. There is some good, wooded coverage there they can use to evade their pursuers."

"Yeah, but that is leading them back to Cheribaum. Wouldn't the behemoth be attracted to that and hit the town?" Fey reasoned.

"I'm sure Mikhail has considered that. We have to trust he knows what he is doing." Terrati switched back to the chasing vehicles and shot out several more, causing them to swerve and one to even upend and explode.

"I think that is enough." Fey put a hoof on Terrati's. "We need to get down there now and pick up Taylor while the rest are on the wild goose chase. That creature should ignore the vehicle she's in."

"Oh, most likely," Ari susurrated before leaping down and stabbing each in the back with two small needles directly into their necks. They each cried out as the full weight of her body was pressed onto them, her heady breath wafting in their noses as she whispered into their ears between them. "They don't have directions to strike small targets just yet; they only are tasked to go after larger, more lucrative targets. Unless they do something to draw attention to Cheribaum, I have full confidence no harm will come to it."

"How do you know all of this? Are you saying you know what the behemoths are? Are you working for them?" Fey attempted to struggle, but whatever toxin was in those needles had hit his bloodstream faster than he had expected. His entire body was going limp, and the weight of the large reptile on top of them was making it hard to breathe.

Ari seemed to consider his question a moment, enjoying their gasping wheezes beneath her. "I know of them, yes. I wouldn't say I'm working with them—rather I'm against them just the same as every other mammal on this planet should be. However, that would be a question for my father to answer, and he's not entertaining guests like you at his doorstep."

"You're going to kill us then?" Terrati was trying to act brave, but Fey could see the fear in his eyes.

Ari licked his ear with her serpentine tongue, causing it to flick and him to shiver at the touch. "If only it were that simple. As much as I would like to kill you both right here, I made a promise to Taylor to not harm anyone in exchange for her cooperation. I'm on the cusp of earning that trust completely. That trust you fools squandered."

She dug her claws into each of their backs, causing both to grunt in pain. "Although leaving you alive poses its own problems, I can't afford your deaths to get back to her somehow and ruin my credibility. So the next best thing is to leave you here to rot. Maybe your friends will find you, maybe not. But at least I let you live, and that is all that matters to Taylor."

"We will track you down and get her back." Fey struggled to get the last few words out, the toxin causing even his vocal chords to shut down and his mind to feel drowsy.

"Ah yes, back to your High Council that even you yourselves do not trust anymore. Let me know how that works out for you. Until then." She got up and savagely kicked the perched sniper rifle off the ledge, listening to the sound of it shattering below. "You have my sympathies for working under such esteemed liars. Toodles." She stuck her tongue out and leapt down to the darkness below, then was gone.

"Can we warn them?" Terrati seemed to fare better, being far less sleepy than Fey, but he wasn't far off.

Fey had to shake his head hard to maintain alertness. His neck was going stiff. He struggled to move an arm down to his pocket. "My phone… In here. Call…them."

Terrati stretched as far as his flaccid arm would allow, his hoof barely kissing the top of Fey's pants pocket. Then unconsciousness hit him like a load of bricks. He conked out hard alongside the elk. "Taylor…" he exhaled. He passed out, his head thumping lightly on the rock.

18
BEHEMOTH

The entire field lit up like a warzone. Mikhail ignited the engine and kicked it into reverse before peeling out the van, narrowly missing a launched grenade hurling past their front hood. Their backend now safely behind a lone tree on the battlefield, he shifted gears and tore off in the direction of the woods ahead of them. A good majority of the cruisers who were not hit by the initial wave of sniper fire from Terrati gave chase.

"I'm starting to think this was a stupid plan, and it was Ari's clever way of killing us all off so she could have Taylor to herself," Finnley snarked, poking his head out the passenger side window from the seat Taylor had vacated. He aimed his gun back to the mob of cars and began firing with impunity.

"Certainly possible. Our deaths wouldn't matter much to her." Mikhail agreed.

There was a thunderous clang of pounding metal, and Natalia vaulted over the back seats to look up at the horizon where the night sky just began to twinkle with stars. Looming amidst them was a moving, dark shape outlined by their flickering lights. It stood taller than the highest building in Howlgrav, and set in the middle of its head were two glowing eyes that seemed to be moving in small, vibrating spurts as it tracked the multitude of cars fanning out in multiple directions. It wouldn't be long before it reached attacking distance.

"Shouldn't we go back for Taylor now?" Natalia asked, worry in her voice. There was no guarantee that the beast wouldn't inadvertently step on the car Taylor was in.

"Ari was confident that our diversion would distract both the Howlgrav police and that thing, so the further away we can drive them off from Taylor's position, the better chance she has at survival." Mikhail swerved hard to the left, locking the brake and drifting between two trees before unlocking it and revving forward. "Let the others do the rescuing as planned! Let's not change it up now!"

Finnley held on tight as Mikhail curved another set of trees. The cars tailing scattered, each attempting to find their own route through without smashing into the trees, or one another. He could just barely see the beast slowing down on the great field where the battle started. "We need to direct its attention this way!" he shouted, still half hanging out the window.

"I've got it!" Natalia called back.

She shifted through the back end of the truck where they had inventoried several explosive grenades from earlier. Taking what she could carry in one paw, she twirled around in the seat and unlatched the sliding door, allowing the wind to whip about the interior cabin. She leaned out and pulled the pin off one, aiming its trajectory to the nearest car on their right. It exploded right underneath it, causing it to launch into the air before smashing back down onto the truck that passed right under from behind them.

A loud screech echoed through the air as massive blasts of steam pierced the sky. The beast was shifting direction to look at the muffled explosions peeking through the foliage of the trees. It had its head tilted, taking a tentative step forward, rumbling the ground around its impact.

Mikhail could see that it wasn't fully distracted. "Damn it! We have to get back out in the open. We are not enough of a target for it!"

"That'll open us up like sitting ducks!" Finnley roared back, looking inside to glare at the tiger.

"Do you see any other choice? It's either that or chance getting Taylor squished!" Mikhail jabbed a finger at the otter. "And don't you even start! You owe her one for saving Fey."

Finnley grumbled, ducking inside briefly as several bullets hit the side of the window frame where he was resting. "Fine, let's risk our necks so she doesn't have to die. Consider us even then." He rolled his eyes, getting back onto his perch to pepper some more rounds into a few of the lead cars, causing one to veer hard into a tree and explode as he nailed the driver in the head.

Natalia looked up at him from her position at the open side door. "You going to tell Taylor that?" Finnley didn't bother to look at her, and only grunted in contempt.

"About to make the turn. How's your back?" Mikhail called from the driver's seat.

"Fucking hurts. Just do what you got to do." Finnley grit his teeth but kept firing.

Each holding on tight to the car, Mikhail made the hard turn back out onto the open plains, the tall grass doing little to conceal their position as they barreled through it. Their path was visible to anyone with half a brain to follow, and Natalia used the advantage of those errant few who followed directly behind them. She lobbed a few more grenades out the side, causing more visible explosions to light up the night.

"That got its attention!" Mikhail's demeanor was stoic, but inside he was a bit nervous, driving headlong at the towering monstrosity.

Its massive bulk turned to better face them. Its multitude of moving parts were shifting and clanging loudly as its reptilian face began to morph and slide back to reveal a set of three long barrels. More steam pulsed out of its head, seemingly from the parts that resembled a mouth. It screeched again as the triple barrels began to slowly spin. They gained speed as their tips began to glow white hot, and a hum shuddered the air.

"Oh shit!" Finnley hopped back into the driver seat and buckled his seat belt. "It's an automatic! Natalia, get your ass in now!"

Natalia didn't bother wasting time closing the door. She dived onto the front row of seats and barely got an arm through a belt loop when Mikhail jerked the wheel hard, nearly skidding the entire van on two wheels. Not a second later, the beast launched a volley of energy pulses. Each blast ripped through the cars following them, sending plumes of fire, dirt, and metal up into the air as they disintegrated from the intense heat of each shot.

"Well, you weren't wrong!" Natalia yelled from the back. "We did get its attention!"

"It's onto us now! Shall we go back to the woods?" Finnley suggested.

Mikhail remained silent, his hands steady but gripping the wheel tight as he lurched the car back into the behemoth's direction. Finnley was yelling at him for not turning back to the treeline, but he ignored the

360

irate otter, focusing on his current course of action. The rapid fire was dreadfully accurate, tracking their position with alarming precision. They could each feel the shockwaves from each hit behind them.

"Are you doing what I think you're doing?" Natalia could see his current course towards the legs of the mechanical creature.

Mikhail confirmed her assertion with a nod. "That thing is huge, but even it has blind spots. The closer we are to it, the less flexible its ability to hit us becomes." He pointed back with his thumb to the vehicles which were no longer following them. "It also helps get them off our tail just long enough to regroup and figure out what to do next."

"While at the same time putting us in range of its huge feet!" Finnley squeaked, pointing up at the rising clawed foot.

"I see it!" Mikhail acknowledged. "We got one persistent bugger behind us!" His eyes looking in the rearview mirror to see that one truck had escaped incineration and was doggedly pursuing them.

"It's going to crush us!" Finnley shouted, instinctively ducking in his seat even if it was futile.

"I'm concentrating." Mikhail was focused completely on the drive.

Locking the brake again, he drifted right just as the gargantuan foot pounded the ground with enough force to send shockwaves through the car. It nearly caused Mikhail to lose control of the steering, shuddering the wheels and causing him to veer off in a different direction from his initial drift. Quickly recovering, he slammed the brake down hard and gunned the gas pedal to pivot around one of the back legs, using its bulk to block the gunfire from the vehicle chasing.

"It didn't get them!" Natalia informed, her eyes riveted on the truck behind. "It looks like they have an RPG!"

"I can only go so fast!" Mikhail spun the wheel around again. "I'll try to see if I can get behind the other leg to block it!"

"I don't think you're going to have that time." Finnley's gaze was held by something up above them through the window.

Peeking his own head out briefly, Mikhail saw the underbelly of the mechanical beast shift and open. There was a central dividing panel that seemed to retract inwards before sliding and rolling up into its body.

Several panels detached from each end of where the rib cage should be, and tilted downward to show off its occupants.

"What the hell are those?" Mikhail could only guess before refocusing back on his driving, pulling them around the back heel of the other hind leg.

Neither Natalia nor Finnley had an answer for him. Several dark shapes dropped out of each tilted panel, kicking off flames like a jetpack. They efficiently landed on the car tailing and began to smash its windows and rip gaping holes in the metal roofing with their claws. The screams inside could be heard even from this distance as several of the dark shapes slipped into the car, and mangled body parts were thrown out seconds later.

The entire car wavered and then careened forward on two wheels before upending completely and crashing. By then all the dark figures had left the interior and were in a dead sprint towards their van. More shapes were dropping down from the belly of the beast, now that its primary focus was resumed back onto the cars that were heading to the tree line.

"Looks like we're left with whatever babies it spat out!" Natalia was readying her own gun, ensuring that enough bullets were already loaded with clips to spare in her pocket.

"I really don't think those are its babies." Finnley opened fire, causing several to snarl and shriek. Two of the dark shapes went down. "They can be killed though!" He laughed, this fact giving him some sadistic sort of satisfaction.

Natalia joined him out the side door and dropped two more that were chasing on foot. "They're fairly easy to kill if you go for the head."

"Yeah, they seem to be shielded around the midsection," Finnley noticed.

"That should be all of them." Natalia seemed relieved they had put down all the dark shapes before they got any closer to their van.

"Not entirely!" Mikhail pointed up. "There's a second wave that dropped." He had spotted them in his sideview mirror. They were aiming their descent straight at them, using quick puffs of their jetpacks to angle themselves.

"And we're sitting ducks now!" Finnley aimed high, but his bullets were fruitlessly wasted on thin air as his targets weaved through his hellfire. "Think we can make it back to the trees?"

Mikhail shook his head. "Not a chance. Brace for impact. You two need to keep them off this damn van."

"What about the creature?" Natalia looked through the back window. It had already lost interest in them and was opening fire on the remaining gaggle of police cars, generating more explosions and causing more screaming.

"Not our concern right now. We need to make a loop back around to pick up Taylor!" Mikhail did a hard U-turn. "We're going to be heading straight under these bastards. Get ready to fight!"

The first body hit the roof hard. Mikhail jerked the wheel right, causing the van to wildly lean left. They could hear the scraping of claws across the rooftop when a large, bulky shape swung down into view through the windows on the left. It had a body full of scales that gleamed in the moonlight. Its long, crooked snout was filled with sharp teeth, and its tail was thick and spiked. The armor around its chest was formidable and wrapped around each limb down to the knee and elbow.

"They're like Ari!" Natalia gasped, pointing her gun directly at its head and opening fire, shattering the glass and causing it to lose grip from the pain now tearing through its skull. It hit the ground hard and got promptly run over by the back wheel.

Two more hit the van and immediately began clawing into the metal exterior. One scuttled over to the open side door and swung down inside, causing Natalia to scream. Finnley swung around and fired into the backside of the reptilian intruder, but was met with a uniquely different assailant than the one they just ran over. This one had a stubbier-looking face and a sturdy shell that deflected all bullets he fired.

"That was a bit unexpected. Mikhail, help?" Finnley looked over at the engaged tiger.

Natalia yelled as she ducked a swipe from the turtle that had taken up the bulk of the back seats, its immense girth crushing the supports of the front row, causing it to slump on its bolts. Mikhail attempted to curve hard to the left to barrel him back out the open door, but the turtle was too quick for that and plopped his entire weight onto the seat.

"I'm a bit preoccupied at the moment. Finnley, get to the back now!" Mikhail roared.

The third attacker had poked his head down the driver's side window. He wasn't quite like the turtle inside, and was very different from how Ari looked. He had two folded flaps of skin on each side of his snouted head that now were raised and vibrating with violent intensity. He was breathing in deeply, getting ready to loose something horrid.

Keeping his foot on the pedal, Mikhail let go of the wheel and pulled the side lever to vault his chair back to the full reclining position and whacked the turtle on the head hard, causing a pained grunt. The frilled reptile melted a hole straight through the glass, its spew of toxic spit arcing from its mouth over Mikhail's position and onto the passenger seat where Finnley once was. He had already hopped into the back to assist Natalia.

"Get below the level of the seats now!" Mikhail commanded.

Without asking explanation, both Natalia and Finnley dove down under between the two rows of back seats. The turtle was just starting to recover from being hit on the head, but neither paid him much mind as Mikhail shifted his position to the right as he unlocked and kicked the door open hard. The long stream of corrosive spit traveled in a wide swath through the cabin, narrowly missing his head as it landed squarely on the rising turtle. It splattered all over his face and upper shell, instantly disintegrating flesh and bone. His guttural cries reverberated through the van.

"And time for you to go." Mikhail rose back up now that the lizard had expended all his bile.

Mikhail punched the creature hard in the face, then pulled the pistol from his holster and shot him several times. The attacker went limp, lost grip, and dropped to the ground below. Now free to control the vehicle again, he grasped the wheel and urged it back on course to the retreating beast that had wiped the floor with most of the Howlgrav police force.

"Well at least Ari was right in surmising that attracting that thing would solve our problems." Mikhail had to chuckle a bit.

"That doesn't solve our existing one!" Natalia reminded, referring to the flailing turtle that was in their midst. "Can you assist?"

"Finnley, come take the wheel. Forget the pedal. Just make sure we don't hit anything!" Mikhail unbuckled and squeezed to the back as best he could.

Finnley bounced off his shoulder before standing tall on the seat, peeking his head over the wheel as he guided the car. Not wasting any time, Mikhail blew two bullets into the turtle's brain before wheezing with effort at pushing his colossal frame out the side door. Natalia did her best to help, but the tiger did the brunt of the lifting. Muscles straining and bulging, he finally slipped the final assailant out of the van.

"Any others?" Finnley called from the front.

Mikhail gripped the frame and surveyed around. "Not that I can see. Let's go back and secure Taylor."

"What if more of those things come out when we go back for her?" Natalia could see that the beast wasn't far from the car that was holding Taylor.

"We'll deal with them too." Mikhail was resolute.

There were several sudden flashes of light. The group looked around, confused. They all turned to view the behemoth, yet it was carrying on its rampage. No additional weaponry was being expended from its body. Finnley went to speak when the entire van rocked with the noise of several loud booms. It was the sound of Howlgrav going up in flames.

Explosion after explosion spiraled into the sky, creating a cavalcade of light to illuminate the darkness. Ear-splitting roars resounded on the plains as the mechanical creature turned its head to observe the rising pyre. Its entire body jerked in awkward fashion. It rotated its entire bulk, and began running in a stroppy gait that it could barely manage given its size.

"What the hell was that?" Finnley turned the van so they could see more directly the raging inferno that was Howlgrav.

"Dear gods…" Natalia breathed. "Was this the distraction that Ari had planned?"

"Taylor isn't going to be happy when she finds out," Mikhail said.

"Where are they all going? Get out there! We need to secure a new transport!" Mendezarosa was squealing near incoherently, his eyes rapt on the gigantic monstrosity barreling down upon them from afar.

"Sir, you just ordered them all to open fire!" the rhino in the driver's seat pointed out.

"What? What the hell are you doing?" Mendezarosa shouted at the other rhino that had toppled out of the passenger door and began scrambling away as best his stubby legs could allow in the opposite direction of the behemoth. "You coward!"

"He might have the right idea, sir," the remaining rhino offered tentatively.

Mendezarosa glowered at him as he clambered over the large seat cushion to get at the radio between them. Picking it up and holding it directly onto his lips, he barked into it, "All men, I demand an escort vehicle. We are currently dead in the water with two flat tires. We need someone to come pick us and the prisoner up immediately!"

The radio chatter that came back was unintelligible as multiple incoming transmissions stepped over each other, causing many to cut out. Mendezarosa looked out his window to see several groupings of trucks making their way back towards Howlgrav, clearly in full retreat. He snorted as he thumped the radio receiver hard down on the chair he was standing on, causing even the large rhino to wince.

Taylor used the opportunity of his panic to continue what she had started earlier with the glass separating them. She carefully let Ahya slather her tongue all over the portion of glass directly behind the peccary while he was turned around. She just needed it to be weak enough for Ahya to bust through and grab him. Not to eat him or anything, but maybe as some sort of leverage against the bigger rhino. Any injuries Ahya sustained could be healed later if needed.

Without another word said, Ahya broke the glass, spewing shards all over the front seats as both rhino and Mendezarosa shied from her tail. In one swooping motion, Ahya opened wide and gobbled up the entire pig and tucked herself back into Taylor's compartment. This unnerved the driver so bad he could do nothing but stare at her in fright for a few seconds before shakily drawing out his weapon and attempting to twist in his chair enough to get a good aim at her.

"Ma'am, I suggest you put my boss down nice and easy." He ordered with a bit of a shake in his voice.

"Not until you unlock this back door and let me out," Taylor riposted, fighting with her tail from consuming Mendezarosa whole. She was having a devil of a time keeping the struggling pig from kicking her from the inside. It really hurt. Ahya's tongue was in a desperate wrestling match to keep him contained.

"Not a chance. You are an armed—" He motioned to the tail. "—and dangerous criminal, and I will not fall for that. You even have your handcuffs split I see."

He was definitely a sharp one. She glanced out her own window to see that the huge behemoth was bearing down on them. It had slowed to a stop and was looking around at the various cars scattering. It didn't seem particularly interested in their car specifically yet. She did notice that it wasn't entirely aware of where it was stepping, having squished the other fleeing rhino to bits under its front paw.

"Are you going to just sit here with me while waiting for that thing to step on us, or are you going to let me out and we both escape together?" she offered, scooting back on her butt to literally sit on her tail to keep Mendezarosa from flailing further. "Your boss doesn't have that much time left inside Ahya. There isn't a lot of air to breathe inside there, you know."

She couldn't fathom what the rhino was thinking but he was staring stock still, gun aimed at her head, for what seemed like a long while. Their attention got diverted to several booms and flashing lights from the trees just ahead of their cruiser. The towering beast above them seemed distracted too, but it didn't make much of a move off in that direction.

"When it is safe to move out, we will see," he replied cryptically, his eyes looking up as best he could at it.

"You'd let your boss die then?" Taylor was now questioning how good of a bargaining chip Mendezarosa really was now. It didn't seem his subordinate was all that keen on hurrying to free him.

Without even looking at her, he answered, "My answer to that will be no. He is too valuable for that to happen."

Taylor cocked an eyebrow, disappointed. She wasn't sure herself how much the swine inside Ahya could hear, if anything at all, but the rhino seemed to be carefully picking his words, in case the short police chief were to make it out alive. This was going nowhere. She considered just letting Ahya digest the peccary right then and there, but the reminder of having to taste yet another person prevented her from relinquishing control to her tail.

The entire cruiser shook, and the vibrations traveled through their bodies as the shockwaves of each thunderous paw smashed the ground. The immense behemoth was shifting its entire body towards the line of cars. Grinding metal plates moved and retreated into its head, causing Taylor's ears to twitch and flap down with irritation at its grating nature.

"It's distracted," the officer said confidently before staring down Taylor from the front. "Do not do anything funny or I will shoot you. It may not be in the head unless you eat him, but it'll be somewhere else on the body where it will hurt. Understand me?"

Taylor nodded and gave a thumbs-up as the rhino carefully backed out of the driver's seat, keeping a bead on her position. Sidestepping to the back door, he unlocked it with his hoop of keys and opened the door wide, motioning for her to step out. She lost her balance due to a combination of Ahya dragging the weight inside of her across the back seat and the pulse fire salvo launched directly above them at the oncoming mass of vehicles.

"Freaking hell." The rhino shrunk back and covered his face for fear of flying shrapnel from the multiple explosions.

"Ahya, spit!" Taylor commanded.

She swung her butt around, looping her tail at such an intense velocity that Mendezarosa came hurtling out of Ahya's open maw as it released him. He was a flying projectile, crashing squarely into his subordinate's chest, knocking both over to the ground. The rhino squeezed the trigger involuntarily and his gun went off, the bullet narrowly missing Taylor's arm. A deep welt appeared in the side of the cruiser. She skittered around to the opposite side of it and frantically looked around for an escape route.

"You filthy, little wretch!" Mendezarosa gasped mouthfuls of air, slapping his sides profusely to get any excess slobber off his ruined clothes. "You've got nowhere to run and now you've royally pissed me off! I think my superiors at the High Council will forgive me if we deliver you in less-than-pristine condition!"

He snapped his hooves to direct the rhino to circle around the car as he went the opposing direction to catch her unawares, but their attention was drawn to the chase happening just a few dozen meters away. Mikhail was driving the van between the legs of the creature, doing his best to avoid being hit by gunfire. Seeing as they would not be a problem, they retrained their focus back on Taylor.

"Not so fast, little girl!" The rhino clapped his palm on her thigh.

Taylor yelped as she was dragged out from beneath the cruiser. She had attempted to crawl underneath and give herself a bit more distance from her captors; she wasn't sure if she could have outrun the rhino on the open grass. She cried out when he slammed her up against the car siding, pinning her to it with one single arm.

Ahya attempted to stretch herself wide and envelope the top half of the brute completely, but he foresaw this and lodged his arm into the side lobe of Ahya's maw. She couldn't enlarge herself further before the rhino pounded the tail into the window, splintering it into a thousand shards and causing Taylor to cry out from the pain. Not relenting, he lowered his next blow and rammed Ahya into the metal door again and again, each time causing Taylor to jolt and quake. She weakly tried to smack his arm to release her, but he was too powerful. She began to cry.

"You give up yet?" Mendezarosa was gleefully enjoying this. "The less you struggle, the easier this will be on you."

"Fuck you," she whimpered, using the last of her strength to have Ahya bite down hard, causing the rhino to roar.

"Break her fingers. That'll teach her some respect!" The chief whapped his hoof on the rhino's leg, his eyes hungering for the reaction that was to follow.

There was blackness at the edges of her vision, her head lolling back to behold the unfolding panels of the stomach above them. A half-dozen dark shapes began to fall from the air, but she did not feel it was warranted to warn the two idiots in front of her. So engrossed were they in paying her back for the insult she had caused them, they did not realize the danger coming from the sky.

Taylor screamed as the rhino dropped the beaten tail to the ground, where it lay motionless, and took her middle finger on her right paw and snapped it back hard. An audible crack was heard as the knifing pain shanked itself through her nerves and up her arm. "That... That all you got?" she spat, the rebellious side of her not caring anymore.

"Do another." Mendezarosa was firm, but joyful at the proceedings.

Taylor howled again as her ring finger now got jerked back, another snap and surging pain caused tears to flow freely now. "Please...no more," she sobbed, finally defeated. For a brief moment, it seemed like the rhino was going to lay off. In fact, he stood stock still, an almost glazed look in his eyes.

"What the hell are you doing?" Mendezarosa raged. "Break another finger! Hell, break them all!" Spittle flew out of his mouth. The pig was ruthless.

The rhino shook his head as if dispelling some dream. Realizing where he was, he looked down at what he was doing only to break out into a grin again. He picked another finger to snap. Taylor continued to cry. How foolish she felt thinking she could face up against anyone and actually win. It was hopeless.

"Please don't fight it this time. Just let it happen," a voice called out in her mind.

"What did you say?" she meekly asked, sniffling as the snot dribbled out her nostril.

"I didn't say anything." The rhino was confused, his focus on her index finger now, getting ready to break that one too.

"Do you trust me?" the voice rang out again.

Taylor was confused. She looked up and saw that whatever was falling onto their position was mere meters away now, and they were using some sort of jets to slow their descent. Without warning, Ahya had

370

been slowly rising up beside Mendezarosa and suddenly snatched him once more in her maw. Not waiting for Taylor to give the okay, Ahya immediately began to fill her inner cavity with saliva and digested the peccary on the spot.

"Boss?" The rhino had let go of Taylor briefly at the shock of seeing his boss become nothing more than a shriveling lump inside the tailmaw.

With no resistance given to Ahya, the process was scarily efficient. Taylor could instantly feel the bloated fullness in her stomach from Mendezarosa alongside his taste upon her tongue, which she gagged on. However, there was another feeling now coursing through her limbs, a feeling she had never felt before after devouring someone: adrenaline. She felt emboldened to stand back up, and the weakness in her body seemed to ebb away from the consumption of Ahya's meal.

"What in the world?" The rhino was stunned. It was then that he noticed the descending paratroopers above them. One large figure was gunning specifically for him.

Taylor snatched the striking baton from its clip on his waist and did her best to dash away from the brutal scene. Her movement caught the rhino off guard long enough for the alligator-like fiend to land on him. His gnarled mouth opened wide and clamped shut on the rhino's snout between his two horns.

Taylor fumbled with the baton to extend it, watching with horror as the reptile continued to squeeze its jaw tighter, crushing bone and sinew. Crimson was gushing from the cop's snout as he swung his body this way and that, toppling over in a heap yelling bloody murder. Two lanky lizards hit the ground on either side of the miserable officer and eyed Taylor with vile intent.

The last lingering flops of the rhino's legs attracted her attention before they finally went still. The remaining bone cracked in the alligator's jaws just before her sight moved back to the two lizards advancing on her. Her heart pounded in her chest. Her initial reaction was flight, but she knew they'd outpace her in an instant. Each of their frilled flaps expanded to encircle their head, their edges shaking with anticipation.

She could feel the aching of her muscles and the pinpricks of glass in her tail from when the now-dead rhinoceros pummeled her against the car, but she fought against that feeling and let the newfound energy surge through her limbs. Raising Ahya up, she brought the baton before her as best she could. It was smaller than the quarterstaff she had trained with Natalia on, but it would be sufficient for her needs now.

"Oh crap!" Taylor's eyes bulged.

She dove to the ground as both lizards inhaled and each let loose a stream of acidic spit, their torrents crossing at the place she had once stood. Rolling back up onto her feet, using Ahya for balance with the quick maneuver, she made a dash for the right one. It began to turn its head to face her, its arc of spit still going strong, but she expected it. She somersaulted forward towards him, the trail of disgusting fluid sailing over her before he could adjust its trajectory.

Already breathing hard, she rolled up between them and whipped her tail around. Ahya was already in sync with what Taylor was intending. She had scrunched up to a more stout length, enlarging her overall bulk to be a battering ram at their legs. Surprised at the tactic, they each flipped over onto their backs, coughing up their insides into the air, their sprays sputtering in all directions directly overhead.

"Well, this sucks." Taylor gazed up at what she had wrought with a sinking feeling.

She scampered on all fours away from the three reptiles. She was barely able to escape the corrosive falling droplets, several landing on her tail tip. She gasped out in pain as the liquid sunk into her fur and deep through her skin. Ahya was quivering intensely as she suffered through it, and her tongue darted quickly out in an attempt to lick the wounds to heal them. Looking back on the two lizards, she could see that although they were in just as much pain, their scales and armor seemed to have warded off the worst of its effects.

"Is that all you got?" she bluffed, saying it more to bolster her own courage than to really intimidate the enemy. Though the awful sounds of the rhino's head being devoured by the alligator unnerved her, Taylor remembered she still had that grenade Ari had given her. She reached down and felt its oddly comforting shape through her pants.

Neither of the lizards said a thing as they rose up to face her. Instead of going for another round of spit, they each drew out their own weapons—which seemed to be spiked instruments with dangling chains—and stalked forward. Taylor yelped as she threw the baton up to block the first downward strike. The resounding crack of the two slamming together sent waves down her arm, her strength nearly buckling. The flinging chain wrapped around from the inertia and whapped the other side of her arm with a red welt.

They were relentless. Taylor lost all sense of space as she focused on defending herself from their debilitating blows. Ahya managed to pick one of the lizards up by the tail and crunched it clean off as she tossed the thrashing body a dozen yards. Taylor ducked another swing, letting Ahya spit the tail of his companion out at his face. Using the momentary opening, she rose up and split the lizard's jaw with the butt of the baton. Blood speckled the air as she kneed him hard in the groin. Much to her satisfaction he went down on his knees, but not before smacking her against the thigh with his weapon.

"Freaking hell!" she skirled, the spikes digging into her leg.

She keeled over her injury and fell upon the jagged weapon, sinking its metal deeper. The lizard was upon her in an instant. There seemed to be no opening to retaliate against him, the baton being the only feeble defense left. She kicked the lizard hard in the stomach, then tore into her pocket and pulled out the grenade. As she scrambled to recall how to activate it, she shocked herself when she attempted to smack the lizard with it when he got too close, lodging it between his sharp rows of teeth.

Taylor's eyes bulged. "Not what I wanted!"

She released it. Realizing the danger he was in, he panicked and spit the grenade out. It rolled underneath the police cruiser, detonating with a powerful concussive shockwave that launched it into the air. Taylor backed up nervously, unsure of where that truck was going to land.

The lizard had already determined the point of impact and ran past Taylor as the vehicle smashed back to the ground with a cacophonous roar. Ahya swung back around, teeth glimmering, as it chomped down to the waist of her fleeing attacker. In one sickening schluck, cerise coated the ground as his upper body was ripped off and his arm was dangling between the teeth of her tailmaw. Her inner saliva was already doing the work to melt him.

"Please... Please, Ahya, don't eat him. I don't want to know his taste," she begged.

Obediently, if not a bit disappointedly, Ahya let the mangled body slosh out of her mouth. Taylor had to look away to not retch. Looking around her and removing the horrid weapon from her leg, she had to suppress a chuckle. The boost of adrenaline and energy to fight back was starting to ebb, but it felt amazing to finally be able to defend herself for once. She had done all that with the help of Ahya. No longer hiding behind her tail, she had worked together with her, just like Mikhail suggested.

Reality hit like a load of bricks as the final munching of the alligator indicated he had finished his meal. The officer's head was completely gone, devoured by that which killed him. A shuffling of grass off to her left indicated that the lizard whose tail Ahya had bitten off was still alive. Whether he was able enough to continue the fight was another matter entirely. The odds were still against her, and now she had a much larger and deadlier opponent in the mix.

"You with me on this, Ahya?" Taylor had to laugh to keep from screaming in terror. The tail "looked" at her, as if knowing the odds, but grinned anyway with tongue flopping out. Taylor nodded. "This is it then..."

The hulking brute snapped his jaws, growling before rampaging towards her with claws out. The sight of it was petrifying. She attempted to sidestep him, but he swung his arm out wide and caught her across the stomach with his palm, clotheslining her over onto her back. The wind got knocked out of her as she dropped the baton. He plopped down onto her, his meaty bulk pressing down on her stomach.

Taylor cried out as she saw the yawning abyss of his jaws opening and descending rapidly towards her face. She let loose a few whines and groped for the baton on the ground at her side. She miraculously clutched it on her first attempt. Bringing it up to her face, she managed to lodge it deep into his mouth. The pressure clamping on its length was immense. She could already see it splintering at the middle, metal flecks peppering her face.

"You know, my lightning would be really good right about now!" Taylor muttered with some hysteria. She could feel the sparks from her still-functioning fingers, but she couldn't force it to come out.

Barring her wondrous lightning, Ahya reached around and snagged his thick tail, digging her teeth in hard. Ahya yanked with all her might, but only managed to budge the alligator a few inches down Taylor's body. He was still imposing his mighty bulk onto her with ease. Seeing the connection between Taylor and her tail, the alligator swatted her arms out of the way and began punching her face, all the while continuing to press down on the baton to snap it in half.

Taylor sobbed, fearing the end was near. Try as she might to keep ahold of the baton to maintain its grip inside the alligator's jaws, she could feel her resistance failing with each hit of his fists. Even Ahya's grip was slipping, her consciousness fading alongside Taylor's. The tailless lizard had finally caught up to the scuffle. He took ahold of Ahya and dragged her off of the alligator before brandishing his own weapon again and striking her over and over.

The final punch to the face caused Taylor to sag completely. Her arms dropped to the grass and her tail went limp. The mouth above her finally crushed the metal baton before her very eyes. Spitting it out to the side, he grinned at her and relished this brief moment of victory. He knew they had bested her, and it would be a fine feast. So, this is how it ends. She was to die in the middle of nowhere, unloved by anyone and unknown to the world.

With a grunt of mirth, he pinned her arms down as he angled his jaws to enclose her head completely. He began to rush forward to decapitate her when a molten spire of earth sliced through his ribs, blowing out the other side. Two more, larger pillars rose up from either side of Taylor and impaled the alligator from beneath. Blood flowed from his abdomen and mouth as he hung over Taylor, dazed.

"Get away from him, Taylor," Ari commanded.

Taylor did as she was told, weakly scooting backwards from underneath the dying reptile. Ari wasted no time and slapped the ground again with her tail. A big ball of magma busted forth from the ground in front of her. Roundhouse kicking the piece in midair, it plowed right into the gangly lizard who had been attacking Ahya. The sheer force of its velocity propelled his body through the windows of the car, ripping it to shreds by the shards of metal and intense heat of the rock.

"You will die an agonizing death for harming Taylor, you bastard." Ari's eyes squinted, holding no remorse for what she was to do next.

Clenching her fist, she brought up another column of melting soil straight though the alligator's abdomen. Panting with the exertion, she forced the entire piece up his breastbone, splitting him clean in half. The liquefied heat finally reached his head, then she intensified its fury, causing his entire skull to dissolve into its mass before dropping the entire bloody heap onto the ground with a satiating squelch.

Ari looked off at the behemoth. Seeing that its attention was focused nowhere near them, she rushed to Taylor's side. Taylor knew she looked a complete mess, drenched in blood and full of cuts and bruises. She was trembling profusely, trying hard to keep herself on an arm as she lay on her side looking at Ari.

She knelt down to Taylor. "Are you okay, Taylor? Think you can walk?" Ari's eyes were intense, looking her over critically before breathing a sigh of relief. "I'd rather not have to carry you the entire distance to my motorcycle."

"I think… I think I'll be alright." Her voice wavered. Taylor was not sure what she was right now. Her first true taste of battle had been horrifying, and her mind was still reeling from the experience. She numbly looked over to her tail and began to pet her lethargically. "You were great, Ahya. The best partner I could have hoped for here…" Ahya lifted herself slightly, tried to smile with her mouth, but limply rested back down.

"Well, if you feel like you can walk, let me help you up at least." Ari's voice was concerned.

Explosions rocked the earth as Ari turned quickly to see Howlgrav go up in flames. She had to stifle a grin, but she knew Trevor and Gregor had done their jobs as well. As expected, the beast let loose a roar and began to direct its wrathful ire onto the unfortunate town of Howlgrav. Within the hour, the pathetic town would be little but ashes and rubble.

"Go do what you do best, my brothers and sisters," Ari whispered. "One day your comeuppance will come, and it will be merciless."

Her countenance fell as she turned back to help Taylor up. What she found was a young teenager like her, broken and battered. She had passed out. Her entire body sprawled on the ground, helpless. Ari regarded her a few moments, examining the wolf with interest. The plan didn't exactly account for this to have happened, but it was at least good that Taylor was at least alive. So many things could have gone wrong, but in the end she was able to leave with her target intact.

"Looks like I'll be having to carry you then." Ari gave Taylor a glare. "Figures you'd be that obstinate and force me to do this!"

Humming to herself, she carefully scooped up Taylor into her arms, draping the tail over her shoulder to let it hang down. With firm resolve, she began the long trek through the tall grass. She hadn't told anyone where she had stashed the motorcycles, but knowing the keen sense of smell of Trevor and Gregor, she was sure they'd find her soon enough.

Eyes straight forward, she focused on keeping Taylor secure in her arms, as heavy as she was. She did not even flinch as the entire city of Howlgrav went up in a mushroom cloud of cataclysmic glory. She only stumbled once as the shockwave hit their position; she had calculated their distance and knew they were well out of reach of the blast radius.

Confident in her anonymity in the darkness, she continued to trudge on.

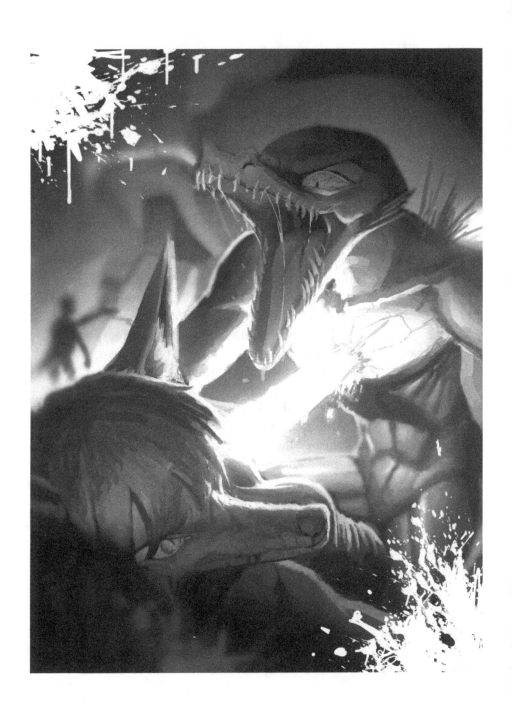

19

DECISION

Ari had just set down Taylor next to her motorcycle when she heard the click of the gun. She ensured that Taylor was on a thick patch of grass where she could lie comfortably while she situated the rest of her gear on the bike before they set off. She could hear them padding closer with cautious steps, but her focus was still on securing the additional belt loop she would need to have a passenger in tow on her ride.

"Are you going to shoot me?" Ari said without inflection.

"The thought had crossed my mind." Trevor snickered.

"Were you thinking of leaving us behind and making off with Taylor?" Gregor grilled, splitting off from Trevor and going the opposing direction to flank Ari.

"The thought had crossed my mind," she retorted, now finally turning around to face them. "I know you're not going to shoot me though." She folded her arms as she leaned up against the motorcycle, it sagging slightly under her bulk.

"You got that right." Trevor dropped the smirk. "You're my only shot at clearing my name with the Arbiter and getting us the money that was promised." He motioned to Gregor and himself. "We did our part, just like you asked. Will you fulfill your promise that you'll put in a good word in with your father?"

"I'll admit, I hadn't really given you two much thought when I first encountered you on the street in Howlgrav." She chuckled, her red iris not leaving Gregor while she stared at Trevor with the other. "I was instructed by him to actually dispose of you two as I saw fit."

This caused both of them to raise their guns more firmly and aim at her head. "And what will you do with his order?" Gregor asked calmly, but he gulped, fear in his eyes.

Ari shrugged. "I am not my father. My primary objective was to secure Taylor. As long as neither of you get in my way of that, I am free to fudge some of the facts about how I was able to bring her home." She paused a moment, focusing both eyes on Trevor. "And that includes how you two aided me in her capture and safe journey home."

Trevor relaxed a little, still not dropping his weapon entirely. "So, we are in agreement that we are traveling back together?" He looked at the second motorcycle alongside the first. "I see you prepared another just in case."

She only gave it the briefest of glances. "I had a feeling you'd agree to work with me and come along cooperatively." She gazed off to the blurry haze of smoke and flames rising into the sky where Howlgrav once stood. The behemoth was idly pushing around debris and searching for something. "You did a mighty fine job there. I trust it wasn't too strenuous?"

His ears flattened. "Not terribly."

Gregor finally put down his gun and relaxed. "With most of the police force gone out to hunt down the others, it was pretty easy to slip in and tack the bombs onto specific power plants and electrical grids for the most bang for our buck. We were lucky to even secure one of their squad cars to meet you here."

"We didn't have time or resources for much else," Trevor finished for him.

"It worked beautifully," Ari cooed, enjoying the final result. "But you'd need to ditch the car. Good thing I came prepared."

"I highly doubt Taylor would appreciate what we did though." Trevor gestured with his chin to her prone form on the ground.

"Why would you say that?" Ari's eyes were intense.

Gregor filled her in. "She literally attacked us and nearly tried to eat me. She got so furious at us having caused the destruction of Palaveve in exactly the same way Howlgrav got destroyed."

"We put explosives around the entire town in hopes to draw attention of one of these beasts to finish the job for us, to both provide cover for our escape and to eliminate any need for a chase when we absconded with Taylor." Trevor sighed. "It didn't really endear us to her at all, but it was the only option available to us when she got arrested and put in prison. Subtlety was not on the table."

"She finds out we did it again and that you were the one who planned it..." Gregor pointed at her. "How do you think she's going to feel now?"

Ari thought about it a moment, studying the still form of Taylor. Her hair was splayed out across the ground, giving her the illusion of a crimson halo. She finally spoke softly. "Does she really need to know?"

Trevor looked over to the scorched earth several miles off. "It'd be hard to explain that over there otherwise. I think we should either tell her the truth or make something up that isn't far off to settle her nerves about the whole thing."

"Explain what?" A groggy voice jolted all of them out of their conversation. Ahya was beginning to move, bumping herself up against Ari's legs and bike, trying to make sense of everything around her. Taylor put a hand to her head and winced as she attempted to sit up. "What is it you need to explain to me?"

"Yes, please do explain to her how exactly you all blew up that entire city." Mikhail stood up from the tall grass a few dozen feet from their position. Two other heads popped up alongside his, Finnley hitching a ride on Natalia's shoulder. All three had guns trained on the wolves.

That caused Taylor's eyes to shoot open. "You what? Ahhh!" She groaned as she doubled over from the pain wracking her entire body.

Ari knelt down to put a massaging palm on her shoulder. "You need to rest, Taylor. We have a long road ahead, and you don't need to get worked up right now." She shot daggers at the two wolves. "I thought you two had acute senses of smell?"

"Not when we are downwind of you, using the scent of smoke in the air to mask ourselves." Mikhail grinned at her.

"She is not going with you. Where the hell are Fey and Terrati?" Finnley snapped, his teeth flashing.

Scowling at him, she pointed up to the hills in the shadow of the mountains, the moon beyond casting darkness over them. "They were in my way, so I made sure they weren't." She continued on despite the disruptive growls from the three. "They are safe and sound, don't you fret." She smiled, her own crooked fangs glowing. "They're merely sleeping a good one off. You go up there and I assure you that you'll find them at the base of the furthest outcropping of rock on those foothills."

"How do we know they aren't just dead up there?" Natalia's accent was thick, the hackles on her upper back raised.

Ari stared at her, continuing to massage Taylor's shoulder. She reached down to pet Ahya, only after the tail finally figured out who was next to her. "That is one thing I learned from my father. If I make a promise, I intend to keep it. I promised I would spare you all for Taylor's sake. She stated she didn't want any more death to happen on her account, and that's exactly what I intend to fulfill. Your friends are alive because of that."

"And yet you lie to her face now and claim that the death of every single male, female and cub in Howlgrav wasn't your doing?" Mikhail jabbed a finger off at the burning massacre. "You purposefully used us all under the guise of preventing Cheribaum from burning to the ground, but at the cost of another town—a far larger one, meaning way more casualties!"

"You used them to do it too." Finnley accused Trevor and Gregor. "No wonder you had them gone before even approaching us. They needed to set up your little bloody diversion long before we came into the picture!"

"I don't remember hearing any of you coming up with any decent plan to save Cheribaum when I was cuffed under your roof," Ari sneered. "You were all completely content to just let the entire town burn for the sake of your objective of bringing Taylor in. I, at least, had a plan that worked, and saved the town she said she loved so much. You should be thanking me."

Taylor's mind was finally coming to grips with all the blame being tossed around. She tossed off Ari's arm and used Ahya to snap and menacingly swing around to ward off all those around her. Stumbling up to her feet, shunning all attempts at assistance, she looked around at the group surrounding her. They each had guns trained on each other and were staring at her. Ari had not moved from her kneeling position.

Taylor pointed at the lot of them. "As far as I'm concerned, I should be thanking none of you. I've known nothing but death and lies since I was so rudely kidnapped by these two here." She eyed Trevor and Gregor viciously, and they subconsciously looked away. "I had it all planned out. I was going to gather provisions and move to a better town, and start fresh on a new life with Pine and Mitchell. That was all torn away from me!"

"Hun, those two don't really exist..." Natalia began.

"That's beside the point!" Taylor roared, causing the snow leopard to shrink back. "My goal has always been to just escape and be safe from others, both from being hurt and hurting them with Ahya." She turned to Mikhail. "The one thing I did learn with you all was to stand up for myself and to fight back. Well after tonight, I feel like I've had just about enough of all your bickering over me."

"And I've apologized for that..." Mikhail looked hurt. "Now I just want the best for you."

Taylor's expression softened a little. "I appreciate it. Some of you have been kind to me since you got your head out of your asses regarding your jobs, and I'll never forget that. However, I feel like I need to decide what happens to me next."

"My father is not going to be very accepting of that." Ari began to rise.

"Shut up!" Taylor shot daggers at her, sparks beginning to flow freely from her fingers. She brought them up to look at with exasperation. "Oh, now you want to start working." With grim determination, she clenched her fists and brought them down to her sides. "Fine, you all will listen to me or so help me, I will explode again."

Finnley raised an eyebrow in begrudging respect. "You've certainly changed."

Taylor bared her teeth alongside Ahya. "Getting pummeled to a pulp and nearly dying has that effect on people. I realized something out there: if I do not stand up for myself, then I will be run over and most likely eaten by the way things are going."

Trevor lowered his gun. "By all means, Taylor, the floor is yours."

Taylor nodded at him. She was relieved that one of them understood her position and was willing to give her the leeway for it. Addressing Ari, she leaned on a motorcycle to rest her weary limbs. "You said your father was responsible for making people like you and me. You seem to have knowledge of what I am and how I came to be. I'd like to know more about what I am and why so many are interested in me, if nothing else but to explain this entire fiasco away." She waved off at the rest of them.

Ari bowed curtly. "My father and I are aware of many things. It would be my pleasure to help you find your answers."

Sensing the two wolves stepping closer, Ahya "looked" at them. Taylor made a small incline of her head towards Trevor and Gregor. "Will they be joining as well, or are they still on your hit list?"

"That is up to them, but I've no issues traveling with them if you do not." Ari shrugged.

"You're going to just ignore that they destroyed an entire city just to get at you?" Mikhail was appalled at Taylor.

Taylor crossed her arms and scrunched her nose. "No. I find it horrible that that had to happen. I knew nobody good there, but that didn't mean there weren't people worth saving. As it stands, there is nothing I can do about it now. Even if I scream and yell at you for having done it, what would it accomplish? The deed is done!"

She sighed, wiping away the beginning of tears from the corners of her eyes. "All of you have blood on your hands; nobody here is innocent. Not even me. So what difference does it make? We're all murderers in one fashion or another. What matters more to me now is who is going to give me the answers I seek, and right now that is Ari and her father. I need to know what happened to my mom and how I came to be this way. I feel she is the best chance I have at figuring that out."

"And you don't believe we'd help you find those answers?" Natalia's look was pleading.

Taylor's expression softened at the kindly snow leopard. "I'm sorry for what Ahya did to your sister, Natalia. Know that I feel awful about it even now. However, this is something I have to do on my own, and I believe Ari is the best option for me to do so. I'm done running. With Pine and Mitchell supposedly a lie of my own mind, I want to find out where the rest of my family is. My older brothers. My mother too, if she's still alive... So I'm leaving with them."

"Then I'm afraid I can't allow that." Finnley leaped over to Mikhail's shoulder for the height advantage before standing tall and aiming at the two wolves. "I may not particularly like you, Taylor, but I do listen to Fey and what he wants. If this entire disaster can be saved by bringing you in to the High Council, then that is what we will do. Fey got the confirmation from up high that our contract was still on."

"You do know what I am capable of, right?" Ari was incredulous. "I would burn you in seconds."

"Not before I pop a few bullets into any of your heads, and that is something I don't think Taylor wants to have happen at all." Finnley smirked.

Taylor was furious. This otter had to be one of the most irritating people she had ever met. Sensing a sudden burst of energy rush through her chest, she focused on it and channeled it down her arm and out her right palm. She raised her paw and observed the small, crackling ball of white-hot electricity dance above her fingers. Satisfied she could hold it for a reasonable length of time, she glowered at Finnley. All eyes were on her and the power she now wielded.

"Your job is done. You never liked having me along anyway," Taylor reminded. "What changed now?"

"Fey did." Finnley sniffed. "I'm sure by now most of you are aware, he is off the Script." He let that hang in the air for a moment. "There is no telling when he is going to die now. For all I know, if he doesn't bring you back, he most certainly will face harsh punishment. I dare not take that chance and lose him again." He steeled his jaw. "So you will be coming with us. Fey's life may depend on it."

"Don't try it," Trevor warned.

"The battle is over. You've lost and I've made my decision. I saved his life for you when I didn't have to." Taylor flinched slightly;

385

the struggle to maintain the spark was getting difficult. "Enjoy the time you have with him now, and be thankful he has a new extension to his life he wouldn't have had otherwise."

Finnley shook his head. "The Authority will be upon him. He needs the protection of the High Council or he's as good as dead anyway." He took aim with the gun. "Your choice again, Taylor."

"No," she said firmly.

"Watch out!" Natalia yelled, but it was too late.

"Gregor!" Trevor shouted.

The entire world seemed to move in slow motion as Finnley fired one round off. Ari slapped her tail on the grass and was aiming to touch the ground to strike out at the otter. Trevor ran towards Gregor, but time seemed to have slowed. Taylor reacted by instinct and let loose the charge she had been carrying. It arced and pirouetted across the distance and struck Finnley in the shoulder. It blew him clear off Mikhail and several meters away to crumple into the tall grass off in the darkness.

"Sweet gods..." Natalia rushed over to see if Finnley was alive.

"You fucking bastard!" Trevor wept, his claws digging into his buddy's chest. Gregor was gazing up at the stars unseeing, a single bullet lodged directly between his two eyes with a small trickle of blood. It was a clean hit. "I'm going to kill him!"

Trevor wiped his tears and set Gregor down. He rose up and began a mad dash towards where Finnley fell. Mikhail moved to block his way, pushing him back roughly with his bulk. The tiger calmly rebuffed the wolf. "There has been enough death for one night. Let's each take our wounded and go our separate ways."

"No! Gregor and I made a promise we would retire together! We would find a retirement beach and live out the rest of our lives in quiet! Now what the hell do I have to live for without him? Nothing!" Trevor snarled.

He went to push Mikhail out of the way, but the tiger gripped his arm and attempted to twist it. Trevor growled and whirled around with his iron arm, punching Mikhail firmly in the chest before gripping fur and skin in its metal joints. With a bellow and heave, the whirring of the arm went into high pitch as he tossed the larger predator over his shoulder, causing Mikhail to hit the ground hard.

"Stop, now!" Taylor used Ahya to enclose Trevor's upper body completely and lift him off the ground, his legs flailing in the air. "If we keep this up, then all of you will die and there will be no one left! Leave the otter. He's not worth it."

Trevor continued to struggle a few more moments in Ahya's grip, but she was too strong. He finally went slack and Taylor finally delivered him to be beside his friend, lying still on the ground. Confident that he would not put up anymore fuss, she released him and finally let out her breath. She began to wobble, causing Ari to step up to catch her before she fell. That bolt of lightning took a good chunk of her senses with it, but she didn't feel like totally passing out.

"You going to be okay?" Ari expressed some concern.

Taylor nodded. "I'll be fine. Just feeling weak. Let's go, before anything else happens."

"What about him?" Ari looked down at Gregor.

Trevor didn't look at her, his gaze intent upon his friend. "We take him with us and give him a proper burial when we can. He deserves that much."

"And I will take my friends back and recoup," Mikhail informed, slowly getting up off the ground, nursing a bruised rib. "This isn't over yet, Ari…" Mikhail sternly faced her. "You may have won this round, but we will be back. Just promise me you'll take care of her and keep her safe."

Ari seemed a bit taken aback by the sincerity in his request. After a moment, she gave him her crooked smile and a brief nod. "Of course. She is my highest priority."

Natalia had come back from recovering Finnley. She had him cradled in her arms like a swaddled babe. "He's unconscious, but he's going to be alright. Some second-degree burns that we'll have to treat, but he'll live." Looking up from him, she stared at Taylor. "Don't forget what I taught you. I hope we meet again one day, under better circumstances. Maybe I'll tell you more about my sister…"

Another tear formed at the edge of Taylor's eye. "I'd like that. I'd love to tell you all the cool and stupid things we did as cubs."

Natalia began to share her tears as she laughed. "That would be lovely, hun."

"Are we going or what?" Trevor was still down beside Gregor. "My friend just died and you all want to say goodbyes to each other."

Mikhail gave Trevor a heartfelt look. "I understand your pain, Trevor. I do. We will take our leave, but may we all meet again under better circumstances. Stay safe, Taylor. I hope you find what you're looking for with Ari. Be on your guard." He shot the reptile a distrustful glance.

Neither side wanting to release eye contact, they simply stood there facing each other. After a moment, Taylor spoke first. "Guess this is goodbye." Ahya flopped her tongue out, as if waving farewell. Without further regard for Mikhail and Natalia, she walked up to Ari. "Am I riding with you or Trevor?"

Ari looked over towards Trevor, who was already lifting his friend up over his shoulder. "I think it would be best if you ride with me for now. Give him some space."

No more words needed be said. Ari swept her leg over her motorcycle and awkwardly moved her thick tail to allow Taylor to sit behind her. Managing Ahya alongside Ari's tail was going to be a challenge on the moving vehicle, but they'd figure it out. Trevor was silent as he put his friend in front of him in the seat.

Kicking up the footrest and revving their engines, they rushed off in a haze of kicked up dirt and grass, leaving Mikhail and the others behind.

"We're disavowed." Fey slumped against the plush cushion of the back-row seating, the only one left after the turtle crushed the front row earlier. He let the cellphone drop to his side. "The High Council saw what happened here tonight and asked if we secured Taylor through it all."

"I'm sorry…" Finnley grunted, trying his best through all his various injuries now to snuggle up to Fey. "It was all my fault."

Mikhail shook his head, relaxing in the driver's seat, looking at the two in the rearview mirror. "We had already lost Taylor. Ari was too good at this; she bested us long before we knew we had lost." Mikhail chuckled, inwardly reflecting on her. "To think that even I had underestimated her. I knew she was dangerous, but only in any sort of physical capacity. I did not think she was manipulatively cunning too. I won't make that same mistake twice."

They all sat back and let the rain smack the windows of their van, causing a calming sort of ambience after a hectic night of hell. The stench of their wet fur mixed in with the blood and the acid was overwhelming. There was a hole in the passenger seat from the acidic breath that had bottomed out to reveal bare earth below. Still they kept the doors closed, preferring to seek the solace of the van.

They had come across Fey and Terrati just awakening from their stupor, both flat on their stomachs beside each other. As Ari promised, they were unhurt and little worse for wear. Both were upset that she had betrayed them all and Taylor had chosen to go with her, but it mattered little at this juncture—especially now, after being informed by the High Council that they'd been relieved of their duties. They were no longer exactly welcome in Zabökar.

"What do we do now?" Terrati asked the obvious question.

Natalia rubbed her chin, thinking hard on it. "Are we no longer a team?"

Fey glanced down at his blank phone. "For all intents and purposes, you no longer report to me anymore. Our job is finished. We can go our separate ways for all I care."

Mikhail frowned, looking put out at Fey's answer. Even Terrati seemed hurt by it. "Well I, for one, am going to go after Taylor. With nothing binding me to the High Council, I will do what I should have done since the start and protect her."

"So you're going on a daughter quest?" Finnley teased.

"No." He glared at the otter. "But if I can stop another innocent from being exploited, then my conscience will rest easier. Besides, I owe her that much since she spared me my Scripted death."

"You think the Authority will be after you too?" Fey seemed nervous.

"Who is that?" Natalia asked.

"We don't know," Finnley filled in. "It was a name Fey saw at the end of the priest's Script whom he killed. Someone called 'the Authority' was notified of Fey's actions.

Mikhail shrugged at this information. "It is hard to say. I wasn't the one who killed him. I should think you'd be far more on the radar than I would be."

"That's very comforting…" Fey felt miserable.

"And what will you do now?" Terrati pressed Natalia.

She smiled at his earnest question. "Why? Are you unsure of where you want to be? For my part, I came on this mission seeking something far different than what I got. I think it would be best if I tag along with Mikhail. I want to see Taylor again. She may be no replacement for the sister I lost, but the fact remains she was best friends with her. I owe my sister to see this journey through to the end with Taylor, and make sure she makes it Zabökar in one piece."

"What about you two?" Mikhail finally turned around and gestured to Fey and Finnley. "Are you coming with us to get Taylor out of the mess she's no doubt walking into?"

Fey shook his head. "No. I think it would be best if Finnley and I ran as far away from all this as possible. Maybe take up a menial life somewhere unknown. We'll stick with you as far as Zabökar to get some affairs in order, but we'll split from there."

Finnley looked up at Fey with affection. "After this mission, I don't really want to leave his side, so I think this is best for all of us. Also, between this shoulder now and my already bad back, I think I'm going to need a long rest before I do anything else." Fey gave him a light squeeze of comfort.

"And you, Terrati? You coming with us to Zabökar to make sure Taylor is safe? She is literally walking into a hornet's nest there." Natalia focused on the gazelle.

Terrati wrung his hooves. "I don't know. I've always had a purpose being in the field with you guys. Without that, I'm kind of lost. I don't really know where I belong right now."

Mikhail turned back to the wheel and started the engine. "Well, you'll have plenty of time to figure that out along the way. For now, I think our first order of business is to find another set of wheels. This one has seen the end of it!"

Natalia laughed. "The pressure is off of us now, so I think we can afford to take our time to stick around Cheribaum and look around for another set."

"Just what I was thinking." Mikhail returned a grin as he put the van in reverse and backed away from the ledge.

They drove down the mountain in silence, broken only by a soft whisper from Finnley as he reached out his tiny paw to Terrati's arm. "That was some fine shooting; we saw the results of it way down there. I knew you were the best sharpshooter I ever met." Finnley gave him a wink. "That's another time you've saved my life. I think the debt I owe you is getting too big that even I won't be able to pay it all back."

Terrati put a hoof over the petite paw. "It is a good thing I don't ask for anything in return. Not for a good friend."

Natalia smiled at them, doing her best to balance on the broken front row of seats. "We may have failed as a team here, but I'd like to think we came away from this retaining our friendships."

"Guess that is one thing Taylor taught us," Fey mused. "Seeing past our self-important job and pride, she saw the cracks in our façade and forced us—well, me anyway—to look at what was important. She may not have needed to deliberately say it, but I think we all felt it."

"This is why I like assassination missions better. Far less messy ethical and emotional stuff to figure out," the otter remarked.

"Finnley!" Natalia nearly whapped him with her tail.

"He is right, you know," Terrati interjected. "This was a bit more outside the norm than we are used to. We have never been tasked with escort missions before."

Natalia just sighed, facing front once more. "I just hope we can reach her before it is too late."

"She is one of a kind," Mikhail admitted. "I've never seen her like before. It is no wonder there are so many after her. The fact remains, however, that she is still a teenager. She doesn't know the consequences of her actions, and I feel like we owe it to her to make good on seeing she makes it through her decisions safely, after what we've put her through."

"I can't speak for all of us, but I do wish her well," Fey agreed, finally relaxing into the comfort of his little ball of joy snuggling him in his lap. "Although what I know of the Arbiter, I do not think there is much hope for her."

"And that is why I am worried." Mikhail furrowed his brow, focusing on the road ahead.

Taylor and her group had stopped by Klera's house briefly to pick up the remainder of Taylor's things before striking out at the mountain pass Fey had picked out earlier. It seemed the best path to Zabökar, circumventing the longer route around the mountains. The fact that it was not winter and the pass not blocked off by snow also helped their decision. Time was of the essence, and Ari did not want to chance Fey and the others tailing them, so they planned to blow the pass after having crossed through it.

"How you feeling?" Ari readjusted the cloak's hood over Taylor's head.

"I feel like shit," Taylor said sarcastically.

"Well you look it too." Ari laughed as Taylor stuck her tongue out at this jab. "And your fingers?"

Taylor brought up her right paw, fingers wrapped together in bandages and tied tight to secure them in place. Klera was extremely helpful in tending to the wounds Ahya couldn't heal. "They'll be alright," Taylor said. "They are still very sore, but the worst of the pain has subsided."

"Seems like Ahya can't mend broken bones," Ari mused with some mirth. "Regardless, they'll need to be moved around a bit in a day or two so the healing doesn't atrophy the joints and you lose all dexterity in those fingers," she coached.

"I know." Taylor let the paw drop to her side.

"I tried contacting my father, but my phone broke in the scuffle escaping Howlgrav. Trevor claims his phone was stolen by Fey and his cohorts when he was captured by them." She tapped her red iris. "I even tried emailing him, but no response back yet. I've got no other way to let him know I'm successful, which is why I want to get back to him as quickly as possible."

"Is that going to be a problem?" Taylor asked.

Ari thought about it. "I don't think so, but I'm going to keep my reservations to myself."

Accepting the response, Taylor looked over at Trevor who was standing in a shallow grave quickly filling with muddy water. The rain had not abated a single bit. "Do you think we should help him?"

Ari shook her head. "I think this is something he needs to do on his own." She looked off in the distance, the mountain pass looming ahead of them. "It won't be long before we cross over this range. I'll be honest, I'm going to be needing sleep soon, and I do not trust Trevor to handle my motorcycle with me unconscious upon it. How well can you drive one?"

"I've never driven one, just rode on one." Taylor shivered. She wished there was some cover beyond this small outcropping of rock above their heads, as it did little to block the angle at which the rain was falling, but Trevor was adamant he bury his friend here in these mountains. "I'm scared, Ari."

This seemed to pique the reptile's interest. "Why is that? In the short time I've known you, you've been pretty fearless."

Taylor coughed a laugh, her ribs still aching. "I guess so, but deep down I'm not sure if I made the right choice. I'm scared of what I'll find in Zabökar, of what your father may do to me."

Ari's expression was unreadable. "I guarantee he doesn't want to harm you, at least not at first."

"Oh, that's very encouraging!" Taylor scoffed.

"Well, my father is not a very…loving person." Ari struggled to find the words. "However, he is passionate for what he believes in. He created me and many others for the greater survival of mammals. He feels slighted he was denied his grand vision of salvation, but he did not let that stop him. So yeah, he had to turn to less than savory…methods, but his motives are true."

Taylor turned her head towards her. "You sound like you're convincing yourself of his goodness. You seem very devoted to your father's wishes."

"And why should I not be? He gave me life when I should have none." Ari gestured to herself. "Have you not seen anyone like me in your life?"

"I've not seen many reptiles in my life period, although I knew of them." Taylor regarded her entire body.

Ari looked peeved. "I meant what I am. I'm a tortoise and crocodile mixed together. My father could not biologically create me with my mother, so he engineered me after she died in hopes of recapturing some part of her after death."

"Yet you still haven't answered my question from yesterday morning," Taylor pressed. "Do you really love him as a father? You avoided the question last time."

"He is the only family I have, so it is my duty to serve his needs since he has provided me with life," Ari firmly replied.

"That's still not loving him." Taylor sniffed and turned back to Trevor. He was already scooping dirt with his own paws and pouring it over Gregor's corpse.

Ari pondered for awhile before asking, "So why didn't you bring Gregor back to life like you did Fey? I hated that I had to hear after the fact he was alive and well. I wish I could have seen it."

"Fey was still technically alive when I finally got to him. Gregor was dead the moment he hit the ground. I'm not entirely sure the scope of what Ahya can do, but I don't think I could have done anything against that." Taylor was uncertain. She had no idea the extent of what Ahya could heal. That night in the van with Fey was surprising even to her, but it was something well worth finding out.

"I guess not." Ari joined Taylor in watching Trevor finish up. "You were probably in no condition anyway, having been beaten half to death. I had seen the fight from afar, but I could not get there any sooner than I did. My intention was never to put you in harm's way last night. It was just an unfortunate consequence of the others not following my instructions and driving back out into the open grass like idiots."

"I'm a bit…uncomfortable having someone be this protective of me. It's an odd feeling, and I'm not exactly sure how to take it." Taylor gave her a sidelong glance. "The only other person in my life I can remember that was this way was my mother, and I stupidly left her when I should have stayed."

Ari laughed with a gurgle in her throat. "I'm no replacement and I do not wish to be. Would be rather awkward to have someone your age be like that to you."

"Not if you were a sibling." Taylor stared off into the distance. "I remember my two older brothers, once bigger than I was until I outgrew them. They reminded me so much of Pine and Mitchell…or maybe it's now the other way around?"

"Think you can conjure them up again?" Ari asked.

"I don't know. I haven't really tried." She raised her paws. "Like my lightning, I'm still unclear how I do it. It came to me naturally last night, but now I can't figure out how to make it happen again. And now I feel like I'm hearing voices too. It feels so frustrating to know you can do things others can't, yet in a moment of need, fail so miserably."

Ari put her clawed palm on Taylor's shoulder. "There is magic in this world people don't even remember exists. People have grown so shortsighted that they no longer recognize it when they see it. You and I are a part of it. Maybe that will be something my father and I can help teach you."

Taylor looked at Ari's palm on her. "Why are you so nice to me? We're not even friends."

"No, no we are not," Ari confirmed. "Do not mistake my kindness for wanting to be friends. I like you, Taylor, but that only goes so far. My duty is to my father and his task of bringing you in safe and whole. I will put my whole effort and life, if need be, to that mission."

"Well, at least I know I'm wanted somehow, even if it isn't in any selfless way," Taylor mocked. "Still, it is nice I won't have to look over my shoulder or worry about being backstabbed as long as I comply with what you want. In that respect, I feel a bit more comfortable in knowing what will happen next."

Ari peeked behind Taylor at the gently wavering tailmaw, content to hide under the cloak to stay dry. "Not that Ahya would allow such a thing to happen."

"You'd be surprised." Taylor smiled.

"What is she really?" Ari was indeed curious.

Taylor shrugged. "Not even I know. She's always been with me. She is my tail. She's all I've ever known. Tried living with her, tried starving her, and even tried getting rid of her. It is no use. So now I just tolerate her and hope she listens to me when I command her to do things."

Trevor patted his wet pants with his dirty paws before walking over. "It is done. He would have liked this view over Cheribaum." He addressed Taylor, clearly acknowledging he had been listening in the entire time. "If there is any place that you could find answers about your tail, it would be in Zabökar. With Gregor gone…I don't really have any other dreams to pursue." He waved off an expression of sympathy from Taylor. "All that I have left now is the promise I made to your mother, Murana, long ago."

Taylor's eyes went wide. "You knew my mother? Why didn't you just open with that!"

Trevor walked over to prepare his motorcycle for himself now that he had nobody to care for. "I didn't know her personally, but I had run into her on occasion since I was in the force with your dad for a time. Met you only once, if I might add." A semblance of a smile glimmered over his face at the memory. "Once my score is settled with the Arbiter, I will take you to where I last knew Murana to reside. If she is still there, great. Either way my role in this will be done. I'll take my money and move on." He simply stared at his empty seat, his entire demeanor indifferent.

"Will you allow that?" Taylor wondered, looking at Ari.

"As long as you hear out what my father has to say and he agrees, then I have no problems with that." Ari nodded.

"I'm sorry about your friend," Taylor offered.

"He's in a far better place than I am now." Trevor was calm, but it was very hard to read him. Taylor couldn't sense any anger or sadness in his scent.

Ari gazed up to the sky. "Looks like the rain is finally dying down. We should use this opportunity to make good time." She strode over and patted the front portion of the seat and looked knowingly at Taylor. "No better time for you to learn how to pull your own weight. I'll teach you as we go."

Taylor attempted to sit in the front, but had to move off her butt when she dug out the small kitsune plush she had been given what seemed like ages ago. She handed it back to Ari. "Can you keep this safe for me?"

Ari curled her lip at the child's toy. "Why do you even bother carrying this? It's trash."

Taylor stopped abruptly from situating herself on the bike and turned to her. "It was given to me by an old goat who also believed in the old magic that you say we're a part of. She cared for me far more than anyone else has aside from my mother. It is a memento I'd like to keep on hand to remind myself why I'm doing this."

Ari stared at the doll a few moments more before shrugging and stuffing it into her leather jacket. "Fruitless sentimentalities, but alright."

Trevor was already saddled, and watched the two gracelessly manage the small space on the seat as Taylor took front. "I'll fill you in on what I know about Zabökar. At least prepare you for what you'll be riding into."

"I'll probably have a more accurate picture for her, but sure, we'll both assist." Ari chuckled, finally getting comfortable with her tail draping straight back over the seat edge. "The throttle is that bar underneath the grip on the right bar," she pointed out.

"Er…right," Taylor said timidly.

After a few false starts, they shakily headed down the mountain pass. Taylor knew her old life was gone just as certain as she knew the life she had in Zabökar with her mother and later her band was also gone when she left it. The future was a blank book waiting to be written, one that the Script could not predict. She just hoped she made the right decision.

She wanted to know more about her powers and how she came to be. Trevor, Fey, and even Ari were all surprised that she was born with Ahya, and she had no idea why that was. What was so special about being born with something compared to having it given to you? What she looked forward to the most was hopefully seeing her mother again. Maybe even her two brothers. Were they still alive? Were they safe? She now had a new direction in life, and she was going to see it through.

"Sir, are you sure he is ready for deployment? His mental matrixes are very volatile." The nervous badger was fidgeting next to the immense tortoise, a clipboard filled with garbled notes in his shaking paws.

The Arbiter was finishing up watching a newscast on a small tablet that had been handed to him. Howlgrav was in flames and Taylor was last filmed being handed over in custody to their police. There had been no word from his daughter in over twenty-four hours. It was not looking good. He lamented his choice in allowing her to go, but she was so earnest in pleasing him. He did it because he knew it would be something his wife would have encouraged him to do: to trust their daughter.

"How little things have changed," he grunted to himself. Setting the tablet down, he shifted his bulk over to face the badger. "We need to move our plans forward sooner than later. The High Council is planning something big, and I cannot afford to sit idle on assets we have been hoarding for decades. It is time to launch the test and release him to do the mission. Proceed."

"Very well, sir," the assistant nervously said. Walking up to the viewing window down into the open room below, he brought a microphone to his lips. "Please release the subject. Execution of criminal cases #4567 and #3218 commencing." He pushed up his glasses by the brim then stepped back to watch the horror unfold.

The two tigers below were growling and ferocious. They were confused as to what was going on. A side door opened into blackness, demanding both their attention. A small, guttural growl was heard in the depths. A slithering tongue, dripping with copious saliva emerged first from the inky black, followed by a grinning maw of death. Attached to its base was a reptilian creature that resembled what best could be described as a chameleon.

It surged out of the doorway and was immediately upon the first tiger who roared. The gaping jaws above the reptile ballooned to a terrifying size before swallowing the other tiger whole, devouring him in seconds. The first tiger used the brief moment of the weight being lifted off of him to kick and scratch the underbelly of the foul creature. It seemed to enjoy this greatly, and relished in the pain it endured before skirling and bounding away. It skittered on all fours into the darkness of the room's corners.

Drip.

Before the tiger could rise back up to standing, the reptile was already on the ceiling and had descended upon its hapless prey. Gripping the head, it twisted the tiger's neck with an audible snap. The tiger's body went limp and collapsed to the floor with the chameleon on top of it. It immediately proceeded to allow its tailmaw to consume him too.

Drip.

The chameleon hunched over, breathing heavily. The lacerations in its stomach were deep from where the tiger had wounded him. The body inside the tail was slowly withering away to nothing as the reptile licked its lips and enjoyed the flavor, mixing it with its own blood it had smeared on its fingers.

Drip.

"He is ready. Bring him before me and we will establish a protocol with him so we may control him," the Arbiter ordered before getting up from his seat and lumbering out of the room.

Drip.

The blood had trickled to a slow dribble. The wounds were beginning to heal. Skin was being replaced by fresh cells as the creature began to cackle maniacally to itself all alone in the room. It looked up towards the viewing window knowing it was being watched and gave them a wide grin of gleaming teeth. It scratched its stomach as the remaining slits of red sealed over and the final droplet oozed out to the floor.

Drip.

APPENDIX A:
CHARACTER GLOSSARY

Major Characters (in order of appearance)

Taylor Renee Wolford
Age: 19 – Birthday: Jasu 8 – Species: Wolf

Protagonist of the story. Was born with a unique tail with a mouth in it that can swallow most sized mammals whole. Is being chased for the exceptional abilities she possesses, their origins mysterious but placed upon her by birth. She is seeking to flee and stay away from those who seek to do her harm or use her powers to nefarious ends.

Ahya
Age: 19 (assumed same age as Taylor) – Birthday: Jasu 8(?) – Species(?): Taylor's tail

The mute tail of Taylor's with a fanged mouth at the end of it. With a tip of crimson, Ahya is not one to be easily missed or forgotten. At times mischievous, other times loving, it is quite difficult to predict what she's thinking or will do next. Ahya is considered to be female.

Pine
Age: 12 (???) – Birthday: (???) – Species: Skunk

An albino skunk Taylor stumbled across abandoned in a dumpster when first arriving in Palaveve to hide out. He is very clingy, but loving and protective of Taylor. He would be willing to follow her to the ends of Kairñe.

Mitchell
Age: 13 (???) – Birthday: (???) – Species: Raccoon

A mangy raccoon found digging through trashcans by Taylor in the first month arriving in Palaveve to hide out. He has a bit more of a level head on his shoulders than Pine and supports Taylor as best he can.

Trevor Novak
Age: 46 – Birthday: Sempah 29 – Species: Wolf

A former cop turned military turned bounty hunter. He has been hired by the Arbiter to track Taylor down and bring her back for a large sum of money. Sporting numerous injuries from his time as both a cop and service member, he has learned a bitter sense of dark humor to go along with his missing limb. He is stern with Taylor, but has a softer side. He had ties with Taylor's family in the distant past.

Gregor Trepani
Age: 43 – Birthday: Frehous 12 – Species: Wolf

Co-bounty hunter with Trevor. He accompanies Trevor on this final mission before they both can supposedly retire to a better life. They've served time together in the military service and he has saved Trevor's life during this period which has earned him a life debt from Trevor.

Ariana "Ari"
Age: 19 – Birthday: Dulhanpah 28 – Species: Crocodile/Tortoise hybrid

The daughter of the Arbiter and a force of nature. She is both hot-headed and calculating. With powers to liquefy solid material around her and manipulate it in various ways, she is more than capable of accomplishing her assigned job of bringing Taylor in for her father. Although more jaded and acting older than she appears, she is still a teenager and is prone to making errant decisions and mistakes.

Natalia Ruyemov
Age: 31 – Birthday: Mele 2 – Species: Snow Leopard

Coming from the far western country of Livarnu, she was prior military for her country and served alongside Mikhail, whom she considers like family. She is devoted to her friends and usually ends up going where they go when they swap jobs/missions. She had a little sister, Sarah, who was sent to Zabökar on an exchange student program.

Finnley Lillibard
Age: 27 – Birthday: Agroa 17 – Species: River Otter

Joined the mercenary lifestyle on Fey Darner's insistence and has proven himself to be a valuable asset. Short-tempered and impatient, he has been known to get in fights with others. He is stronger than he looks and is able to wield weapons far larger than expected. Is in love with Fey and greatly respects Terrati for the numerous times the gazelle saved his life during this dangerous line of work.

Fey Darner
Age: 25 – Birthday: Sempah 12 – Species: Elk

The appointed leader of the band of mercenaries sent by the High Council to secure and bring back Taylor for them. In direct opposition to the Arbiter and anyone he hires to get Taylor. Fey has had extensive medical training, yet claims he is not a doctor. Is in constant doubt about his abilities as leader. Is in love with Finnley Lillibard and enjoys crazy colored tropical shirts.

Mikhail Joan
Age: 40 – Birthday: Oblepah 31 – Species: Tiger

Showing scars from missions past across his face and body, Mikhail was part of an elite force working from within a secretive subdivision of Zabökar's police force: TALOS (Tactical Aviation and Land Operations

Service). Met his wife in Cheribaum whom he had one daughter with. Served in the military with Natalia prior and considers her like family.

Terrati Cavier
Age: 29 –Birthday: Juhous 15 – Species: Gazelle

Although skittish at first impression, Terrati is a trained spy and knowledgeable about many places and underground agencies. He is also an expert sharpshooter and proclaimed master negotiator. Was former military but did not serve alongside Mikhail or Natalia. Enjoys being asked about his bevy of life experience and information, getting absorbed in the teaching.

Secondary Characters (in order of appearance)

Mrs. Hircus
Age: 73 (???) – Birthday: Jase 1 – Species: Kamori

An elderly goat that has lived out her years in Palaveve selling bread and pastries to the townsfolk in the central market. She is considered the honorary grandmother to many orphaned kits and cubs in the town. She believes whole-heartedly in the Script and believes in the old magic that was once prevalent in the world. Gives Taylor a kitsune plush as a gift.

Sherriff Watters
Age: 37 – Birthday: Mala 31 – Species: Horse

The surly Sherriff of Palaveve determined to keep order in his little section of the world. Is extremely vicious to those who do crime, preferring to unleash the entire letter of the law against them. Has made a promise to Deputy Grunier's father to watch over him and shield him from prying eyes – a promise made over a decade ago.

Deputy Grunier
Age: 26 – Birthday: Nevmelpah – Species: Wombat

A nervous and timid deputy working under Sherriff Watters, appointed as such based not on his own merit. Demonstrates some unusual powers, but is unfortunately never able to fully realize their potential.

The Arbiter
Age: 150+ (???) – Birthday: (???) – Species: Tortoise

An aged denizen from the far southern country of Talkar. Traveled north to Zabökar due to a promise made to save the mammals from their impending doom. He believes the ends justify the means and is wholly content on providing the mammals with an army to combat the rising menace of his own people, whether they like it or not. Genetically created his own daughter from both his own DNA and that of his late wife, who was a crocodile. Appeared suddenly in Zabökar thirty years before Taylor's birth and was once appointed a member of the High Council there. A mysterious figure with many secrets.

Officer Minama
Age: 26 – Birthday: Mele 9 – Species: Dik-dik

A cop under the employ of the Palaveve police department. Works under Sherriff Watters.

Lawrence
Age: 44 – Birthday: Jasu 16 – Species: Brown Bear

Bartender in Howlgrav whom Ariana conscripts into helping her after killing off some of his wolverine goons.

Officer Mendezarosa
Age: 36 – Birthday: Alahon 19 – Species: Peccary

Prideful and arrogant chief of Howlgrave Police Department. Has a secret deal with Sabrina Fahpar who heralds from the High Council of Zabökar. In exchange for Taylor, he is promised a better position and status – something he'll do just about anything to achieve.

Sabrina Fahpar
Age: 32 – Birthday: Frehous 25 – Species: Cheetah

A recent appointee to the High Council of Zabökar. She has supposedly gone rogue to seek out Taylor on her own, coordinating with and corrupting Officer Mendezarosa in the process. Is later found out to be a power eater – a secret sect of insane cultists who believe they can change the fate of the future and thus the Script by eating those with powers and gaining the powers themselves.

Klera Faliden
Age: 62 – Juhous 19 – Species: Tiger

Mikhail's mother-in-law who offers Taylor and the others a place to stay and lay low while in Cheribaum. Is an excellent cook and motherly to all.

Francis
Age: 21 – Dulhanpah 5 – Species: Rabbit

A waiter at the Java Rabbit café location in Cheribaum. Has an extreme misunderstanding with Taylor.

Unseen Characters (in order of reference)

Tavlia and Bree
Ages: UNK – Birthdays: UNK – Species: UNK

Two people murdered and eaten by Ahya during Taylor's stint in Palaveve.

Murana Wolford
Age: 52 – Birthday: Jase 20 – Species: Wolf

Taylor's mother who played a big role in her life – so much so that Taylor now wants nothing more than to travel home to make it right with her mother for having run away. Is a huge supporter of adopting young cubs/kits into her family and has done so with both a skunk and raccoon – Taylor's older brothers.

Sarah Ruymenov
Age: 11 – Birthday: Mala 28 – Species: Snow Leopard

Natalia's younger sister who died at an unfortunate young age. Was Ahya's first kill.

Anthony Wolford
Age: 38 – Birthday: Alahon 22 – Species: Wolf

Former husband to Murana Wolford. He died when Taylor was still young due to a punk kid at a routine traffic stop. Had ties to Trevor Novak through the police force.

APPENDIX B:
LOCATION HISTORY

Palaveve

A robust desert town in the county of Balkar that lies far to the west of most verdant grasslands and metropolitan areas. Was said to be the home of a beautiful forest where now only the twin oasis bodies of water sustain any source of vegetation and viable habitation. The surrounding lands were devastated by the ancient Hordos war – a war between the southern reptile empire of Talkar and the free mammals of the north. The reptiles were cast out further south and a great barrier wall erected across many provinces to keep them out. The town, once a stockpile for weapons, ammunitions and supplies during the war became a center piece of trade between the great city of Zabökar and the far-flung countries of Livarnu alongside the multitude of counties in-between. It is a fairly isolated place where the newer trappings of technology have yet to take ahold, where only the law enforcement has the funding to supply their troops with levitating cars while common citizens get smart phones and internet at most. A culture that still clings to the ways of old yet doesn't shy from embracing the future.

Falhoven Forest

A quaint stretch of woods that stretch from the far northern mountains bordering the plains where Howlgrav resides down to the first inklings of sand that spread out to give way to the vast expanse westward to Palaveve and beyond. It was once the site to a bustling underground network of supplies from mammal sympathizers during the Hordos war. Remains of those storehouses and secluded stockpiles can be seen in the neglected structures littered throughout the forest, now commonly used as resting points for travelers as they pass through the forest. Reptiles who switched allegiances and assisted the mammals here were granted amnesty after the war and given the peninsula south of Zabökar along the Grunesh. Their presence throughout the northern counties are rarely felt in recent times.

Howlgrav

An expansive city sitting squarely in the middle of the plains east of Falhoven Forest and west of the Grune mountain range that separates it from the coastal region of Zabökar. Settled by aspiring entrepreneurs who left Zabökar almost two centuries ago, it flourished quickly along the banks of the Husu River. Taking much inspiration from the grand city they departed from, Howlgrav expanded and grew, inviting multiple scientists and brainchilds into its borders. Much of the advanced technology present in Zabökar today was first invented here in Howlgrav. Despite this, there was much resentment from the High Council about the rising threat potential of a rival city to their own. Several small skirmishes between the two cities decimated its citizens in its third decade of existence. The mass howling of mourning over the graves of their loved ones from this disaster gave the town its new name, one it keeps to this very day. Ever since then, the quality of life had degenerated for its people and has become corrupt and overridden by gangs and blackmarket dealers, forcing many beneficial intellectuals to relocate – leaving it a former husk of what it once was.

Cheribaum

A charming town nestled in the northern slopes of the southern reaches of the Grunesh mountains, overlooking the plains housing Howlgrav. Founded by traveling merchants from the western country of Livarnu, it showcases classical architecture typical for its time of origin when it was first built back during the sixteenth dynasty of Szu-lar. Residents were eager to begin learning the ways of the east and welcomed visitors to their breathtaking home. Despite the foreign influence flowing through their village daily, they were a proud people who held deep rooted loyalty to their traditions and heritage – even in recent decades, after having accepted new technologies from both Howlgrav and Zabökar, they have an innate refusal to improve or change the look of their town.

Forward progress has been slow. They delight in the teaching of their young ones of their past and cultural ancestry dating back to the time they escaped from the tyrannical Szu-lar.

Zabökar

The biggest, most technological city of mammals for miles around. Named after the very country it resides in. No city has ever been so great or as well known. The exact founding of Zabökar is unclear, but many historians place its birth around thirteen centuries ago, just two centuries before the Hordos war. It was the first experimental attempt at joining mammals together, both prey and predator, under one banner to live in harmony. It continues to remain a success to this day, with multiple, smaller cities copying their example. The esteemed High Council, which has jurisdiction over several counties around it, was established shortly after the Hordos war when it was clear a more equal, yet centralized system of government was needed to combat future threats and calamities. The town's rising spires can be seen for miles and its impressive defense system is known the world over. Consisting of eight monolith statues resembling each of the original members of the High Council, connected together by magical beams of light, the city has never been assaulted or won over. It is also the birthplace of Taylor Renee Wolford.

APPENDIX C:
AUTHOR NOTES AND THOUGHTS

It has been a long road, about four years, from Taylor's inception to her first book publishing. The most obvious question I've been asked is: How did you come up with the idea of Taylor and Ahya? I can truthfully say the idea wasn't entirely mine. Tailmaws, or anthropomorphic characters with a mouth in their tail, are not a new concept in the furry community. However, they are quite niche and not as well-known as some of the other character designs out there.

My inspiration came from a friend I had met during my time in the community who had a tailmaw himself. He had taken a liking to my primary character (at the time) of Murana. I asked if I could take inspiration from his character to create a new one of my own. Seeing as having a tailmaw wasn't exactly an exclusive trait, I was given the go-ahead. Taking cues from his character (the red fur) and from mine (Murana, with all her locations of light brown fur changing to red), I created Taylor. The stripe along the back and her heterochromatic eyes were added in last to make her a bit more unique. I had no name for her until a month in where it came to me in a dream. The name for her tail, Ahya, didn't come to me until a few months afterwards and again, in a dream.

Now that I had generated a new character, what was I going to do with it? For the first half year, I can honestly say I had no clue. I never had experience with or encountered folks in that part of the fandom and so my knowledge of how one utilizes a character like Taylor was quite limited. I knew I wanted to do something with her, but it didn't exactly dawn on me what I should do until near the end of my first year since her creation.

It was during this year that I was introduced to the vore element of her design and although I am not a personal fan of the subject matter myself, the drama aspect of it intrigued me. How would one go about living with something like a tailmaw that could eat another living person alive? What sort of emotional and mental trauma could that inflict on a person who never wanted it to happen? What if it was a friend you lost to your own body? How would people react to you murdering people involuntarily with your tail? How would one's life look like with such a drastic attribute to their body? These questions formed the foundation of Taylor's character.

I still needed a cohesive story though and a journey Taylor would have to undergo from being terrified of what her tail could do to one of acceptance and the ability to manage what her tail was capable of. The biggest question in those early days was how and what logical explanations could I come up with that would explain why she was born with a tailmaw. This is where the character of the Arbiter came in and the introduction of reptiles into my story. At the time, it was a simple DNA pulse that the Arbiter created which caused this mutation, but it later grew into a more complex plot point later on.

The original pitch was a three-act structure. Taylor's series was initially planned to be a three-book series. Over the course of planning out book one, I realized that I would be leaving readers off on a cliffhanger in book three and that would leave a sour taste in many reader's mouths. So, the plan expanded out to six books during the year while I was writing book one. This ultimately ended up to my benefit as I continued to plot and explore different late narrative plot points I could foreshadow as early as book one.

However, things were still not sliding into place and many plot threads were dangling that I couldn't really string together. For the longest time, perhaps five months, all that existed of book one was just the first chapter. It wasn't until an epiphany while I was discussing the book series with a fellow friend that the element of magic entered my purview. By accepting that this existed in Taylor's world, so many things began to make sense and all the dots started to connect. I could now more easily explain how Taylor was born and how certain aspects worked, like special powers.

I was also aware of the dangers of introducing something as organic and free-flowing like magic. Too often, one could just handwave explanations away and just point to magic as the cause. I needed to ground this in a reality for this world and give it rules. The Script came into being during this process. The advent of Taylor and Ari having

413

super powers was a result of this new influx of planning. The scope of the remaining five books became a bit more solidified. The possibility of being able to add my dragon character, Llydia, was now within reach. Accepting the fantastical, yet giving it a structure helped broaden the range with which I could write and explore Taylor's story.

It took a few short months after, and a royal kick in the rear by a certain November writing challenge, to finish the entirety of book one. Over that course of time, several things cropped up that I had not planned for when I first started the writing. Ariana, for one, was never a thought when I began again on the book with chapter two. She was created on the spot during chapter three and her character formulated between then and her more official introduction in chapter seven. Her creation was one of the most delightful surprises of the entire process and served as an excellent counterpoint to all the characters I had made thus far in the story. I couldn't imagine the book without her now.

The concept of the behemoths, contrary to popular belief, were not inspired by that Zero Dawn game. My inspiration was actually from an old Final Fantasy fanfic I had written involving a behemoth enemy, but I thought to myself, what if it was mechanical instead and there were more of them and different types? This spawned all sorts of connections and ideas I could link back to the reptiles and the overall motives for the Arbiter and Ariana. Their inclusion and ultimate purpose was not fully decided upon until I was already butted up against writing the final few chapters of book one. Discovering their secret and saving it for a later reveal was one of the most satisfying bits of world building I've ever done and I can't wait to show it to you all in the future.

It has been an exhausting experience stumbling through this first book, discovering revelation upon revelation about Taylor and these characters and the world they inhabit. Much of writing this book was just as much me learning about the world I was creating as it was building an entry point for readers to dive into my novels. With one book under my belt done and the other five planned out in various stages, I am more confident than ever in knowing the direction my story will go. I hope you've enjoyed this first part and will be looking forward to the next five!

Thank you for reading my book!

AUTHOR BIOGRAPHY

Matthew Colvath was born in California, USA, where he grew up in the 'golden age' of gaming when Nintendo and Sony were having their 1980s feud and movies had a more simple and light-hearted fantastical flair to them. Movies and games captured his attention and drove him to pursue game design to tell stories and express his creativity. His interest in game design petered off, but his passion for storytelling did not.

Graduating in 2005 with a bachelor's degree in Communications from CSUS in Sacramento, Matthew faltered in direction in his life and after a year of aimless ambition decided to join the US Air Force. He was with the USAF for nearly 11 years and went through two deployments with the B-52 bombers up in Minot, North Dakota.

Through these years, he was honing his writing craft through fanfic. Being a self-taught author, he cut his teeth first on these low risk writing projects before tackling his first professional work with Legend of Ahya: Target of Interest. Now having separated from the military and picking up a career in IT (Information Technology), he currently resides in Germany with his wife and two boys where he continues to write the rest of Taylor's saga.